THE GATHERING PLACE

By
Ricardo Anaya

I

To my beloved wife -

*Your love, patience, and quiet faith keep me steady, as they have
through every storm and calm that came before.*

To my grandchildren -

*Eli and Nico, our Mages; Arielle and Archer,
Princess Elle and Prince Jetamine; and Ava and Adrienne,
Princess Strawberry and Princess Pigtails,
and to all their cousins, your laughter, wonder, and boundless
imagination have lit every page of my world
and continue to light it still.*

"Time bows to no one, yet it listens for the hearts of
children brave enough to awaken."
- Prophecy of the Gathering

CONTENTS

Foreword

In The Gathering Place, Ricardo Anaya continues the Worlds of Wonder saga first begun in The Land of Lakes and Forests. What began as a gentle tale of children discovering magic and friendship now unfolds into a story of courage, destiny, and awakening. The innocence of the first adventure endures, but here it meets purpose—the moment when laughter turns to resolve and wonder is tested by responsibility.

The children mature quickly, pressed by forces greater than themselves. They learn that courage is not the absence of fear, but the will to stand together—and that the wonder born in childhood must sometimes grow up faster than they do.

Preface

When I first wrote The Land of Lakes and Forests, it was meant only as a small gift a story for my grandchildren, a way to capture the wonder I saw in their eyes. I wanted them to remember that imagination is not something we grow out of, but something we grow into.

But stories have a life of their own. The Gathering Place began quietly, in the laughter of my grandchildren, Arielle and Archer. Their curiosity and imagination became the spark that carried me deeper into the world we first created together.

This book is not just a continuation it's a reflection. It explores courage, belonging, and the passing of light from one generation to the next. It was written for children who are learning to be brave, and for the grown-ups who still remember how.

My hope is that, in these pages, readers young and old will find a bit of themselves: the child who dreamed, the parent who guided, the grandparent who believed that stories can outlast time itself.

— Ricardo Anaya
Spring 2025

Acknowledgments

This story was born from love, family, and the grace of God, who gave me the patience to finish it. The idea to write it came from my grandchildren, Arielle and Archer, whose laughter and imagination lit the first spark.

My deepest gratitude to my wife, whose love, patience, and quiet faith keep me steady through every storm and inspired in every calm.

To my grandchildren Elijah and Nico, as Mages; Arielle and Archer as Princess Elle and Prince Jetamine; Ava and Adrienne as Princess Strawberry and Princess Pigtails and to all their cousins. Your laughter, wonder, and boundless imagination have lit every page of my world and continue to light it still.

ACT1

150 SEASONS PAST

150 Seasons Past.

The sky darkens with unnatural gloom. An old villager dabs the sweat from his brow with a worn rag, staring upward with growing dread.

"The clouds are darker than usual. I think we'll have a storm," he tells his young nephew. "Help me get this last bale of hay into the cart, and then we can go eat. My goodie has a nice lamb for dinner," he continues. The villager looks at his smiling nephew, chuckling, "I thought that would make you happy. Let's go, old girl," the villager tells his unicorn.

Tiny bells on the unicorn's harness jingle as she lifts her arthritic leg to pull the heavy cart. The wheels creak and squeak on the bumpy road leading towards the Monastery.

"We did well today, didn't we, uncle?" the nephew asks. "Oh yeah, we—"

A monstrous creature roars from the sky, plunges, and devours the old villager, the young nephew, the unicorn, the cart, and all the hay in one gulp.

The Monastery

The ancient wizard monastery lies deep in the mountains, nestled in a lush, magical valley filled with wildflowers, trees, and a diverse array of animal life. The local flora fills the air with fragrances of lavender and jasmine, earthy aromas of pine and cedar, and sweet scents of honey and citrus.

As you approach the monastery, you hear birds chirping, leaves rustling in the gentle breeze, and a brook babbling before the entrance. The path is cobblestone.

The entry to this magnificent monastery is a giant stone door carved into a mountainside. This entry is always open. The door sills are adorned with intricate carvings of magical creatures and runes that are long forgotten. Wizards, acolytes, maintenance people, and visitors walk through the doorway at all hours.

At dusk, two large torches automatically illuminate the monastery entrance through the night. More torches and candles provide a soft, ethereal light that brightens the passageways and rooms, creating a serene ambiance. Hand-woven rugs lie over polished wooden floors. Colorful tapestries depicting ancient wizards, mystical creatures, and sweethearts adorn the hallway walls. There are entrances to classrooms, filled with eager acolytes, male and female, working and studying the scrolls of magic. They study and train under the watchful eyes of the wizards.

The Chapter House is a spacious, solemn meeting room featuring chairs arranged around a semicircular table. The vaulted ceiling, carved from rock, shows the skill and craftsmanship required to build such a magnificent room in the Monastery.

A council of fourteen wizards, of all ranks, gathers in the elegant, vaulted Chapter House room, where important meetings and wizard business occur. The Dame, a powerful sorceress, chairs the meeting with the Grand Wizard, her husband. They stand side-by-side.

He asks the Dame, "How's our daughter doing?"

"She's got a strong will. Her powers are growing faster than we thought. Her glow is still faint, but she's getting stronger every day. I can tell by how bright she shines. She's more mature than her age." She continues, with a note of sadness in her voice, "I miss my parents sometimes. It still hurts. They died so young."

The Wizard replies, his voice heavy, "They're not really gone. The spirit realm is real. Our ancestors… sometimes they whisper to us. Maybe they're closer than you think."

The Dame smiles at her husband and says, "You always know what to say."

The Grand Wizard lays a bag with scrolls on the table. "Let's get this meeting started. We have many things to discuss."

An exhausted wizard then runs into the monastery meeting room, flustered, his hair tangled. He is in tattered, flowing robes, and his cloak is muddy at the bottom. His staff is broken in half; he holds only the top part. He recently lost his belt but wears an old rope to keep his robe in place.

"They're here," the old wizard gasps.

"Tell me who is coming," the powerful Grand Wizard asks. His eyes are narrow, piercing, and unblinking. "The beast is coming."

The Dame intervenes. "How do you know the beast is close?"

"I was coming back from Baggeons. Azaz, the demon worm, flew by with a swarm of screeching blackbirds. The birds attacked us. Luckily, Baggeon soldiers helped, but we were outnumbered. The villagers hid, but the village is in danger." The tired old wizard perspires profusely, breathes hard, rests his hands on the conference table, and looks at the council members. "They're already here," he shouts weakly.

The chamber echoes with the clamor of voices as the members continue talking, paying no mind to the tired old wizard standing before them. In the far corner, two figures are locked in a heated argument, their shouts cutting through the noise. No one seemed to know what sparked their fury, but the tension between them was palpable. All are oblivious to this wizard's warning of doom. All are consumed with their concerns.

The tired wizard shouts louder, "They are here!"

The room goes silent, but the two in the corner continue arguing.

He says in a calmer voice, "We need the child priestess. The beast will be here soon, and we won't survive if we fight it alone."

"Stop arguing and listen!" the Grand Wizard shouts to the two in the corner. "What happened to Azaz?" The Grand Wizard asks.

He remembers the teaching from the old one. Azaz was once a celestial guardian, turned to darkness, craving dominion over all realms, and was banished by wizards for his betrayal.

"The Baggeons' soldiers are the strongest in the area. But their numbers and my magic were not enough to subdue the monsters. We must empower the Baggeons with magic to help us battle the beasts. We also need the Child," he says, forgetting the wizard's question.

"She's not ready to do battle. Besides, she was born only eight seasons ago. She isn't strong enough yet," the Dame says.

"Yes, she is too young. And we should not allow the Baggeons to practice magic. They will be the first ones to go to the side of evil. Then, we'll have to restore order and help them rebuild their lives. We should not be involved in their affairs," the Grand Wizard replies.

One wizard from the corner asks, "Then what do we do? The Child is too young, and the villagers are not trustworthy. We are far too weak to overcome the beast. Does anyone have another plan to defeat this creature?"

The Dame takes charge. "We must protect my child. One this powerful has not been born to us in over a thousand seasons. Take her, all the young acolytes, and the old one to the hidden rooms below the basements with our most revered scrolls when the beast attacks. We need to preserve the future of—"

Panicked cries ring out, shattering the calm.

"They're here!" a wizard calls from the entrance.

Frightened and tortured screams emanate from the monastery's entrance. Piercing, ear-splitting shrills of pain and fear come from wizards and lay folk battling the monstrosities. The beasts utter piercing shrieks, screeching and cawing in a deafening chorus.

The Grand Wizard and the Dame rush to the front.

He shouts, "Push them back out of the monastery!"

The battles are long and hard-fought. The stone walls of the monastery are covered with the blackened blood of the vile creatures as the wizards crush them with their magic. Serpent creatures tangle themselves around the legs and ankles of the defending wizards, biting them and causing them to lose balance and power.

The wizards destroy hundreds of minions, but thousands more await to replenish their losses.

Most wizards lie on the ground, taking their last breaths before passing to a spiritual realm.

The Dame, the Grand Wizard, and a few of the older, more powerful wizards are all that remain when the creature's black minions flood the monastery. They combined and used the last of their power to eliminate all the remaining minions from the monastery and the surrounding area.

The heinous beast, Azaz, is the only creature strong enough to survive the combined power of its two masters. In one breath, it extinguishes the life forces of the remaining wizards, the acolytes, the Dame, and the caretakers. The evil one destroys all life in the monastery except for the Child, one wizard acolyte, and an ancient wizard elder called "The Old One."

The Child and the Acolyte are hiding in rooms below the study room in the basement. It's dark except for one candle. Large shelves filled with sacred scrolls line the walls. Several canes are placed in what appears to be an umbrella stand. Old, worn manuscripts lay on the shelves and tables scattered across the room. The walls and floor are made of stone. The silence is eerie.

Hidden beneath a study table, the Child and Acolyte watch the battle rage in the monastery through a magic mirror.

"What are we going to do? We're the only ones left, and they'll find us soon," the Acolyte whispers, his voice shaking.

"I'm not afraid. I know what to do," she says firmly, standing ready as the door creaks open, revealing the beast.He shouts, "No, you can't…"

A glow emanates from the Child's chest. It's brighter than any light. It's blinding and cleansing, filling the Monastery. "Go back to your dark realms and leave this place!"

The beast stands and walks on its hind legs. It becomes a beautiful woman who exudes kindness and love from her person. Her hair is black and hangs to her waist. With unblemished skin and long, sharp nails, she is wonderful to behold. Her hair is adorned with precious stones. She has the look of a kind, regal queen. She's wearing a white linen gown with a gold sash. Her eyes are radiant.

She senses the Child's power and lunges to strike, but the Child stands firm. With a thrust of her hand, the Child slams the beast against the wall, straining with all her might to keep it pinned. The demon's winged, wormlike appearance twists low, trying to slip beneath her spell and seize her legs, but the Child lashes out with a fierce kick, cracking its skull. Summoning all her strength, she plants both hands forward, driving the creature harder against the monastery wall.

The Child cries out, "Return to your foul realms and forget this place!" She collapses, her small frame trembling with exhaustion. "Water, please," she gasps, each breath a labored rasp.

From beneath a grand oak desk, its surface scarred by time, an old wizard rises. His movements are deliberate, weighed by age but driven by purpose. He retrieves a flask and kneels beside the Child, now cradled in the Acolyte's arms.

"I am astonished you survived," he murmurs, awe threading his voice.

The Acolyte weeps, clutching the Child as his gaze sweeps the ruins of their once-glorious monastery—crumbled stone, shattered relics, and the acrid stench of destruction. The Child takes the flask, drinks deeply, and wipes her lips with the back of her hand.

"Did we defeat the beast?" she asks, her voice steady despite her weariness.

"You banished it with a forget-it spell," the Wizard replies. "We are safe for now, but it will return stronger, with legions at its command. By then, I will have joined our ancestors in the spirit realm." His eyes glisten with tears. "I've served the council for decades and witnessed triumphs beyond count, but now our kingdom lies in ruins. Child, you and this young wizard-in-training must rebuild our world before the beast returns to ravage these lands. Invite royals from distant realms to forge new kingdoms in these mountains and valleys. Beckon common folk, farmers, artisans, and families to build thriving communities. The hidden entrance to the temple must remain sealed. The passageways from the monastery to the temple must stay concealed, though the backdoor to the monastery, near the temple, may be opened."

His voice grows solemn. "Study the scrolls diligently, Child and Acolyte, master the path of the Crone and the Mage. Some scrolls are ancient and fragile. They are preserved in sealed alabaster vessels. The Acolyte knows how to access and tend them. You'll find wisdom on philosophy, art, war, love, justice, magic, and more, hidden in the basement beneath the library stacks, behind a secret door. The Acolyte, who sweeps and dusts there, knows the way." He leans closer, his tone a warning. "Some secrets reveal themselves only when they choose. The words in those scrolls are alive. You must train children in the ways of the Wizard," he continues. "Select the finest to form a council, then scour the scrolls to find, train, and raise one worthy to bear the Grand Wizard's mantle. Child, the evil will return."

He pauses, his gaze piercing. "Your powers will unfold slowly.

Study to gain the strength to give gifts to others. When you achieve mastery, share these gifts with children—only children. An adult doesn't have enough years left to reach the true power of their gift."

"The Lost Folio unlocks the Temple," the old wizard whispers. "It's hidden somewhere in this vast monastery. Maybe it's waiting to be found."

"As a Crone, the powers you give will amplify a person's inner fortitude, accelerating their growth, maturity, and intellect. These gifts, child, can only be passed to your descendants and children. Their manifestations are unpredictable, some may command fire, others lightning, or even chaos. Certain children may inherit two gifts: one, like webbing, emerging in early childhood, and another, like lightning, awakening later in life."

The old wizard sinks into a tattered chair. Papers are stacked on the clean table, and the Monastery's shattered entrance looms as a reminder of the evil that seeks to crush them.

"Young Acolyte," he says, "you cannot reach the rank of Mage alone. Only another Mage can elevate you, but none remain. The Crone, when she attains the height of her powers, will gain the ability to raise you and others to Mage."

He raises a trembling hand, weaving a spell over the Child and Acolyte. "I grant you many seasons of life. You will grow old with time to rebuild this kingdom before the evil returns. But this spell is both a gift and a curse."

He stands, resolve hardening his features. "I will journey to the mountains to meet with the Pixie Queen. She believes our people and hers must unite for mutual survival. We need the pixies now more than ever. If all goes well, they will join you—but I am too old and weary to make a return trip. I'll stay with the pixies. You will not see me again."

He offers a final thought. "Many survived this devastation. The little folk, dwelling below ground, are clever and industrious. They can aid you in rebuilding."

The Child and Acolyte step outside, their once-verdant valley now a barren wasteland, reeking of decay.

The Acolyte, voice barely above a whisper, asks, "What do we do?"

Her knees buckle as the memory sears her: the Grand Wizard falling, her mother's scream swallowed by the beast's fire. Grief stings like acid in her chest. But then, her mother's voice, faint but steady: Stay strong, even when I am gone.

She straightens, swallows her sorrow, then looks directly at the Acolyte. "We must grow our powers," she says, her voice firm. "I will study the ways of the Crone. You, the ways of the Mage."

A heavy silence falls. The Acolyte glances toward the horizon. "And the temple?"

"It's been sealed for generations," she replies. "It stays sealed."

That night, thousands of pixies, sent by their queen, descended upon the monastery. They clear the fallen debris, sweep away the mess, and restore the rooms to their former splendor. Yet they weep, mourning the lives lost and the devastation wrought upon the once-magnificent halls.

The Monastery, once alive with the voices of wizards and acolytes, is silent. Beneath the scorched stone and sacred scrolls, a new destiny waits for seasons beyond counting.

CHAPTER TWO
THE CHILD AND THE ACOLYTE

The Child and Acolyte stand at the monastery's ruined entrance, staring into the barren wasteland. The Child clings to her lime green cloak, a cherished gift from her mother, its bright fabric faintly shimmering in the dim light. The thick, well-made cloak reaches her ankles, secured by a worn silver clasp, its hem showcasing the village artisans' skill.

The Acolyte is a thin, pimply-faced boy clutching a cracked staff, its once-bright emerald glow now reduced to a faint flicker. His simple azure cloak, stitched by village hands for wizarding apprentices, brushes the tops of his worn boots.

"All my family is gone," he whispers. His voice breaks, and then he sobs.

The Child gently lays a hand on his arm. "Then we'll build new ones," she says softly. "New lives. New families. Together.

They look at the wasteland ahead. It seems to stretch endlessly, its once-lush fields turned to ash by Azaz's sulfurous curse, which has poisoned the soil beyond repair. Burned, skeletal trees stick out under a gray haze that weakens the sun's light. No birds sing, no breeze moves, only a heavy stillness covers the abandoned land.

"There will be more battles," the Child says. "A voice told me to watch out for the deep. I don't know what that means or where the voice came from, but it sounded like my mother. I am sure we will find what she meant by the deep eventually."

The Child clutches her cloak, sensing a darkness stirring in the deep, waiting for its time.

CHAPTER THREE
ONE HUNDRED FIFTY SEASONS LATER

In a distant ocean, a massive earthquake shakes the dark, deep ocean floor in one of the world's harshest places. The seabed is in turbulence, convulsing thousands of meters deep, and where no light can penetrate. Tube worms, clams, shrimp, jellyfish, and other unidentified marine animals are among those that are distressed when their peaceful habitat is endangered.

A fissure opens into a dark, dimensionless void. The intensity weakens an ancient enchantment that seals the vile domain. What's left of the magic spell that holds the heinous realm at bay and keeps ocean water from flowing into the rift is weakened. Creatures can now penetrate the thin veil separating the ocean from the abhorrent realm.

Foul abominations that cause desolation in their wake, crawl and swim out of the vent. The crushing ocean depth does not affect these vile beings. They are initially slow and hesitant as they come through the fissure, but their numbers increase until they emerge by the thousands. Some are small, while others are huge. Most have claws and sharp fangs. Black creatures with demon faces, called Nyxfiend Vultures, more commonly known as Black Buzzards, crash through the ocean's surface and fly high into the sky. They talk to each other in horrid sounds and screech in abhorrent tongues.

Giant Unctons emerge from the opening fissure. They have scales for skin and powerful hands and arms. Sharp bones extend from where knuckles should be. The face resembles a rock, with features that convey a lack of expression.

A mighty creature, Obligoo, is evil incarnate. Its wide wingspan is leathery and purple at the base, darkening to black at the tips. The scales of this purple creature are more durable and rigid than steel. It possesses an immense mouth full of sharp, extended teeth and mighty wings, and it is heartless. The Obligoo communicates telepathically with its minions and those it seeks to seduce into darkness.

When not in battle, this diabolical creature's claws retract into its hardened paws. They emerge as razor-sharp weapons, ready to strike with lethal precision.

It's unknown when the Obligoo came to this kingdom and where it came from, but the stars and pixies whisper it has existed for eons.

But another, more deadly and diabolical creature lurks, waiting for its time to emerge.

Outside the monastery walls, something stirs beneath the deep ocean, something old, something hateful, something that has waited 150 seasons to rise again.

CHAPTER FOUR
THE RED LANDS

The Red Lands

Snow-capped mountains tower over a vibrant green valley bursting with colorful wildflowers.

Pine and birch trees fill the lowlands, while spruce, fir, and pine climb the mountains, their tops vanishing into the clouds. The dense forest stretches far to the north. Above, magical creatures soar, their strange calls echoing. Insects, animals, and birds thrive in this serene valley, where the crisp mountain air carries the scents of pine and flowers.

Colorful magic creatures fly above, making mysterious sounds. Insects, ground animals, and fowl are abundant in this green, peaceful valley. Crisp, cool mountain air, fresh with the fragrances of these trees, creates a serene and peaceful setting.

A grand castle sits by a serene blue lake, nestled among towering trees and far from the ocean. Large trees surround the castle. This grand palace is home to King Mortimer, Queen Lana, and their children, Princess Ellaria and Prince Jetamine.

The family is happy and unaware of the encroaching evil. They live their lives in what they think is the safety of their castle. But a foreboding darkness approaches.

Ellaria's friends call her Elle, and Jetaime's friends call him Jet. He likes this name because he enjoys soaring through the air, his brown hair waving in the wind. Unbeknownst to him, he will fly again soon enough.

"Hey, that's mine," Prince Jet tells his older sister. They both pull on the bucket of Legos from each other.

"I'm four seasons older than you, Jet. You can play with them when I'm done," Princess Ellaria says, grunting.

"No, I want to play with them now."

"You both are too old to fight over Legos. Ellaria, you have many toys. Jet got those Legos for Christmas," Lana says.

"Okay, Okay. You always get your way," Princess Elle replies, then crosses the room, making one-handed cartwheels, her lengthy hair and bangs hanging down.

"Thank you, Mom, I love you," Jet says as he hugs her legs.

"I love you, too, my little Jet-Man. But you should share with your sister. Besides, you and Ellaria are too old to be playing with these toys and arguing about them."

The good King Mortimer strolls into the room in his well-tailored blue tunic. It's made from thesselcloth—a soft, comfortable fabric—and decorated with intricate embroidery stitched by a villager who made it just for him. The beige sash tied at his waist adds a touch of warmth to his outfit. His gray trousers are made of a homespun fabric, simple and practical for daily wear. His black hair and beard, streaked with gray, give him a regal look.

"Yes, Jet and Elle. Listen to your mother."

Jet hears a noise of something bumping into the window in the foyer.

"A pixie is here," Jet shouts and runs.

A pixie flies through the window and loses control. "Stop, stop, nooooo."

He crashes into the wall. *Ouch, there will be a bump on my head. Ah, there's the prince,* the pixie thinks.

"Prince Jet, we need to save Princess Strawberry and Princess Pigtails. Help them, please. You can go faster than anyone else, so we thought—"

Jet interrupts the pixie and asks, "What's wrong? Where are they?"

"They're trying to escape the dreaded creatures from the abyss. We need to help them," the pixie says, breathless.

"I'll save them," Jet says as his fingers feel tingly.

"Follow me," Lethrop says and flies out the window.

Soon, Jet and the pixie are on an adventure to save his cousins.

I have to use my magical threads to go faster, Jet thinks.

Prince Jet raises his hand high, and the threads shoots out, attaching to a nearby tree. Jet pulls on the slingshot threads as it throws him into the sky. He catches up with Lethrop and passes him when he sees his cousins running toward the castle. He swings around and lands in front of Princess Strawberry and Princess Pigtails.

Princess Pigtails is the smallest and has difficulty keeping up with the others. But Jet takes her, throws her on his back, and sends threads to hold her. He shoots his threads high into the tallest trees and is soon safely at the castle.

"Pigtails, we're here," he says, astonished. Soon, the others join them.

Jet, Pixie Lethrop, Strawberries, and Pigtails are out of breath, but finally safe from the ominous, foreboding clouds and fog.

"Thank you for rescuing me," Pigtails says to Jet.

Lethrop, a slightly overweight pixie with messy hair in a pink shirt and matching pink pixie trousers that are too big for him, says, "We're safe now."

"We heard from Pixie Sill that Jet and Lethrop went to rescue you. Thank goodness you're safe. You can stay with us as long as you need," Princess Elle says.

The queen walks into the living room, hands on her hips, her long red robe trailing behind her, and an angry scowl. "What's this I hear about Jet going into the forest alone?"

"Well, a pixie told us our cousins needed to be rescued, and Jet took off before we could talk about it," Princess Elle says.

"Rescued from what?" Queen Lana asks with a smile.

"We were playing outside when we saw a black fog approaching us. My pixie told us to run away to safety. She told us to run to the Red Kingdom," Strawberry says.

"It was creatures from the abyss. We had to rescue them," Jet interjects.

I love a child's imagination. The queen thinks it must be some game and shakes her head.

"Okay, at least everyone is safe," the queen replies with a gentle smile. "Strawberry and Pigtails, welcome to the Red Kingdom. Do your parents know you're here?"

Pigtails shouts, "We were flying, Auntie Lana."

"Ahhh, you were flying. I hope you didn't hit any birds," the queen says in jest. "This isn't your lovely Land of Lakes and Forests, but you're safe with us. You girls can sleep in the guest room," Queen Lana says. "I'll send a pixie to tell your parents you're safe here. Girls, Elle, and Jet go to bed. It's getting late - good night."

"I love you, Mom," Jet says as he holds her legs.

"I love you too, my little prince," she replies.

"Elle, Jet, I want to talk with you and Mom for a while. Come sit, you two," King Mortimer says gently. "Let's talk, just you and Mom."

They sit on a long, gracefully curved bench, carved from pale ashwood and inlaid with a silver leaf that shimmers softly in the light.

"Elle and Jet, you are both young and have many seasons to grow and develop your mind, body, and some precious magical gifts you will inherit," he says. King Mortimer continues, "An Old Sorceress left a seed of power in each of you. Jet, you were still in Mom's tummy. This seed will strengthen you, and you will become more confident and mature as the seasons pass or when you are under stress. You will develop much faster than others your age. The magic will live in the shadows of your mind. This energy is called manna."

"How does the magic work? Did the witch give you a gift, too, Mom?" Jet asks.

Queen Lana nods. "She did. I could heal people—soldiers, villagers. Just by touching them."

"What are our gifts?" Elle asks.

"We don't yet know how they will manifest. It's different for everyone," Queen Lana says. "You'll mature faster than the other children, and when the time is right, your gifts will show. In time, you'll also grow stronger. Jet, you were born with the ability to shoot the sticky threads because one of our ancestors was a witch."

"She put that trait into some men in our family," the king says. "You can do a lot more than swing with it. One of your ancestors could weave a carpet out of threads and surf the wind currents at great speed."

"Why don't most adults have gifts?" Jet asks.

"The gift must be given to a child," the King replies. "It needs time; years to stir, to root, to bloom. In adults, that time is nearly gone. Their hearts have closed. Many are plagued with fear, anger, and other things. But in children, where wonder still lives, and the soul is still unfolding, the gift can truly grow."

"Will our cousins have gifts also?" Jet asks.

"Grandpa's brothers settled in the adjoining kingdoms," King Mortimer says. "They are not in the line of descendants to receive these gifts. But their children are royals like you and powerful in their own right. They received sharp minds from my ancestors."

"Was she a good witch?" Jet asks.

"We know little about your mother's family, but we have old scrolls to reference, some history about the witch, and some of her spells, if needed. She was called The Dame," the King continues.

"Will the ancestors make me strong, Dad?"

The King chuckles. "We don't know what your gift will be. You were born with the bumps on your wrists that shoot the threads material. Maybe your gift will be a part of your threads power."

"Daddy, where do pixies come from?" Jet asks.

Elle looks intently at her father. She thinks, *Yeah, where did they come from?*

"They're like us," Queen Lana explains. "They marry and have children, but they keep their personal lives private. We don't know who they marry or when a female is expecting. When it's time, she'll go to a special maternity center to give birth and stay there with her baby. When the little pixie is ready to be paired with one of our children, the child and their pixie will then grow up together."

"The adult pixies who stay with us remain by our side for life. Meanwhile, others focus on their own pixie duties," the king adds.

"What exactly are pixie duties?" Prince Jet asks.

I should have known he would ask me that question, the king thinks.

"I'm not sure, but I have heard it said they study history from the stars. They also study the language and temperament of the stars."

"The stars have tempers?"

"They sure do. That's why we have extremely hot or freezing cold days," Queen Lana says.

"But where do they come from?" Jet asks.

"We don't know their origins, and today's pixies are reluctant to talk about the past that far back. We know there was a queen of the pixies."

"I read that our ancestors fought a great battle in the monastery,"

Queen Lana says. "An old wizard, a child sorceress in training, and an acolyte wizard were all that was left of the devastation. The old wizard accepted the pixie queen's offer to join us. That's our first interaction with them. They are now a part of our daily lives."

"Kids, sit down here with Mom and me. We have something important to discuss with you," the king begins. "Elle, you're thirteen seasons, and Jet, you are nine seasons. We wanted to wait until you were older, but a voice told your mom and me that now is the right time to tell you. You will hear whispers from one of our ancestors from the spiritual realm in times of stress. She spoke to my father often when he ruled, he ruled the kingdom. She always gave him and me good advice."

"How do we know she is an ancestor?" Jet asks.

"Well, dear Prince Jet, that is a good question. I know she's an ancestor because I asked her, and she told me. She only advises me to do the right thing. She was the Dame of an ancient wizards' council. Listen to her voice but make your own decisions. She guided our family here," the King says quietly. "She whispered to my father, just like she sometimes does to me. She led our family to this beautiful valley. She often spoke in whispers to my father when he ruled. We think she and the other ancestors exist in a spirit world."

"Be careful with what you think you hear in your mind," Queen Lana says. "When you experience fear, think of good things that have happened to you. It's okay to be afraid, but don't let the fear consume you. When I feel afraid, I meditate, I realize the problem isn't big, and I feel better."

"Some evil creatures can speak with us telepathically," the king adds. "And their voices slither into our minds like snakes. They make accusations against us, tell us we're not worthy, and tell many other lies. Fortunately, these creatures are rare."

"Daddy, why did our family come to this place?" Elle asks.

"The Red Realm fulfills all our needs. It's a heavenly kingdom with tall trees, small trees, fruit trees, and many honeybees. Only a few settlers were in our realm, but many were in the distant villages. They welcomed us. The land is so fertile that we can grow abundant vegetables, fruits, and herbs. This land's striking beauty also drew us. The multicolored flower's blue, green, and red petals only grow in the Red Realm. The aroma of these red leaves is reminiscent of roses, with a hint of cinnamon and clove. The blue petals smell of lavender. The green petals smell of forest-cut basil, mint, and pine," King Mortimer replies. "The snow-capped mountains "We're lucky to live in this fresh air with the scents of leaves, pine, damp earth, flowers, and wood," Elle says.

"Your uncles and aunts established their kingdoms here also at about the same time. But you know all this, Ellaria."

Elle hugs her father. "Yes, I know. I love it here, Daddy."

"Please listen carefully. A time will come when we must fight a great evil. This evil will threaten all the known realms. I don't know when or how this will happen, but the council knows it will come in our lifetimes. They want you ready to fight and lead if necessary."

Jet twists his body, stands, and says, "How does the council know an evil is coming when they can't see it? Is this some test, Dad?"

"It's not a test, son. It's real."

Jet thinks, *I'm not old or strong enough to fight the evil coming.*

"What will we have to do?" Elle asks.

"It may not come for many seasons. We need to prepare for when the time comes. We don't know what form it will take, making preparation difficult. But the council will guide us. One of our ancestors who has already passed to the spiritual realm will speak to you. She'll instruct you on your journey of fighting evil. But for now, we are safe in our castle."

King Mortimer and Queen Lana give the kids a goodnight hug. "Okay, it's time for bed," the King says.

The royal couple sit together on a love seat. A large bay window frames a breathtaking view of a serene lake, with vivid colors of orange, pink, and indigo reflecting from the twilight sky.

The King admires the deep blue lake and says to his wife, "This lake is deep blue and home to giant red and white Coe Fish, often misspelled Koi Fish. It's said that these fish will speak to you if they are in the mood. According to some village elders, these Coe Fish can swim in both saltwater and freshwater."

"Look, butterflies are landing on the windowsill outside," Lana says to the king, her eyes getting heavy. "Butterflies represent love and hope," she continues.

"Yes, they are truly gifts from God. If you listen carefully, you can hear their wings flutter," he jokingly tells the queen as she holds his arm.

The queen lays her tired head on his shoulder and closes her eyes. "Are you ready for bed, my king?" she mumbles.

King Mortimer laughs and says, "Did the kids wear you out?"

But Lana is already asleep on King Mortimer's shoulder.

Yup, those kids have far too much energy, he thinks.

The morning air is fresh. A crisp breeze rustles the leaves in the trees. Birds sing their songs, then burst into flight in syncopated movements. Open windows in the great room allow fresh air to enter the castle.

Birds sing their songs, then burst into flight in syncopated movements. Open windows in the great room allow fresh air to enter the castle.

"Kids, we're going to visit our friends today. So be good and listen to Princess Elle when she asks you to do something," Queen Lana says. "Princess Ellaria, you are clever, wise, and kind. You'll make a successful leader in time. Please care for Jet and your little cousins while we're gone."

"If you have any problems, send us a few pixies immediately," the king says. "The guards, attendants, and your tutors will remain here if you need them. A storm appears to be approaching. Stay safe inside these walls."

The royal carriage is white with blue, gray, and pink designs painted on it. It has lanterns on the front posts. What's most interesting about this carriage is that you walk into a grand ballroom when you step inside. You can find a kitchen, dining area, washrooms, couches, and soft chairs. There are paintings on the walls and even windows.

"Why did he have to be so extravagant?" Queen Lana asks, arms crossed.

"I know, my dad had his head in the clouds sometimes," the king says. "But he had his heart in the right place. His wizards created this for him while Mom traveled to see family. I'm sure there was a lot of discussion about it in private. It took ages to replenish the magic used to create this carriage." He chuckles. "We might as well put it to use."

They leave Princess Elle, Prince Jet, and their cousins, Princess Strawberry and Princess Pigtails, with their attendants, soldiers, and many of their pixie friends to protect them.

"Look, we got Oca, Sea Beans, and pickled Fiddlehead Ferns," a slightly overweight pixie, Hector, flapping his wings hard, says to his friends.

But the food all the pixies love most is a hearty soup made early in the morning. The ingredients are fried rice, spinach, mustard (in a double portion), ketchup, pasta, oranges, and bananas. Then add goat's milk, mix it in a blender, fry it in a pan to look like a pancake, and top it with chocolate ice cream. This dish is called The Morning Soup. It's a mystery why this dish is called Morning Soup instead of the Morning Pancake.

It's winter season now, and the clouds get darker and fluffier. Fear sets in the enchanted realm as the lightning flashes and thunder booms in the sky.

The sudden flash of lightning and the booming thunder startle the unicorns. They fly to shelter with their manes and tails flailing in the wind. The herd soars and then drops to a gallop. They run to the shelter of their home in the forest, their hooves pounding the earth, their heads swinging. Their loud whinnies sound like trumpets. Wispy pixies soar overhead, frightened, and the trolls and bolls return to their homes underground. The Boll is a soft, furry creature with six feet. He'll tickle you with his smelly toes if you hold him close.

A frightening wind is blowing hard over the mountains and through the trees. It makes a loud and dreadful howling noise as the branches sway back and forth in the gale. The leaves fly off the branches and fill the air, swirling high above in the wind. Lightning flashes in the sky.

Flying, black crows soar through the air, honking, screeching, and shrieking with loud caws as the wind strengthens. Princess Ellaria, her little brother, Prince Jet, Princess Strawberry, and Princess Pigtails play in their rooms inside the castle, safe from the harsh weather outside.

"Prince Jet, please go downstairs and fill the bowls with pixie food and goat's milk for our little friends," Princess Ellaria says.

The young prince runs to the cabinet, grabs the bowls, and fills them to the top. He puts them on the counter, runs to the window, opens it, and shouts, "Come and get it."

The winter wind blows in from the open window, almost knocking Jet to the floor.

"Hey, food is here, everyone. Come on, little pixies," Jet yells against the wind. The little prince pokes his head out the window, but the gale whips his hair in all directions.

Prince Jet closes the window, turns to Princess Ellaria, shrugs, and says, "They didn't come. Maybe the wind —"

The pixies are already munching on their Fiddlehead Ferns, Oca, and Sea Beans.

A pixie lets out a noisy toot and giggles before vanishing behind a curtain of embarrassment.

***

"Let's have breakfast, and I'll tell you, Strawberry and Pigtails, about the pumpkin people."

"I had a dream last night. A monstrous shadow chased me through a dark canyon. I tried to stop it, but I needed a spell from an ancient scroll. The scroll was lost." He glances at Elle, eyes wide. "I think it's real. The scroll is lost somewhere deep in a mountain."

Just as Princess Elle is about to read to the children, a loud banging erupts at the castle's front door.

Bang, bang, bang!

"It's me," a voice shouts through the little window on the massive wooden door. "Can I come in, please?"

One pixie flies to the door and flaps her wings hard, trying to turn the knob to open the door, but it doesn't budge. A second pixie grabs onto the nob, helping the first. But again, the doorknob seems stuck. A third, then a fourth, pixie grabs hold of the knob, and with all their strength, their wings flapping hard, they finally open the massive wooden door. A fierce, bitterly cold wind blows into the castle from the outside, scattering the pixies and almost knocking Pigtails on her back.

"This poor girl is shivering," Jet says.

"Come inside. It's warm in here."

Elle takes her hand as they walk into the living room. She places a throw blanket around the shivering girl's shoulders.

The wind blows hard against the walls of the castle. The pink and gray curtains billow into the room as the gale blows.

"My name is Jenn, which is short for Jenny. My father wanted to name me Emcenedl, but my mom wouldn't have it. Oh no, she wanted nothing to do with that terrible name. She suggested Tandhuil. But Dad had a fit. My grandma intervened and suggested Jennifer."

Elle looks perplexed. "What did you say your name is? Where are you from, and why do you visit us?"

Jenn breaks down in tears. "I was collecting cherries, far from the castle, and…" She cannot finish her sentence.

"What's wrong?" Elle asks.

The pixies surround Jenn to comfort her, but she wails, blowing her nose as tears roll down her grubby cheeks.

"I was visiting my aunt, but some ghostly creatures attacked us. They came at night while I was away. My auntie held them off with a bright light and her pixies, but she's in trouble and needs help. She sent me to you since you're the closest while she continued fighting the creatures," Jenn says, sobbing.

"Ahh, Jenn. Yes, we know your aunt."

"My auntie is in the path of the creatures. A dark, gloomy cloud is approaching her castle. A dark cloud usually means rain, but I'm afraid this could be an evil presence wanting to consume us. My auntie doesn't know about the shortcut." Jenn sniffs, then sobs.

Jennifer blows her nose into a white lace handkerchief as her messy curls fall on her face.

"Where did the darkness come from?" Jet asks.

"There's a vast wasteland to the northwest of us. We think it originated in that wasteland. The Office of Magic met there a few days ago. The royals and mages who attended meditated and practiced old magical spells. That may have attracted the darkness," Jenn replies.

"Jet, Strawberry, Pigtails, and pixies, we must help her aunt,"

Princess Elle interjects.

It's safe in these walls. I don't want to go. No! I can do this. Jenn needs us, and it's the right thing to do, Elle thinks.

"Follow me," Jenn shouts and runs back into the forest.

A mighty gale whips Elle's long hair in all directions. She holds it down with her right hand and arm as she runs.

As the wind dies down, they race into a grove of fig, orange, apple, and olive trees and bushes as fast as possible.

Jenn stops, stamps her feet on the ground, and then moves the grass aside with her foot. They stand near a fig tree.

Pigtails picks up a fig.

"Hey, stop that. Those are my figs," a slow, sober voice says.

No one heard the turtle.

"It's around here somewhere." Jenn is exasperated, stomping and hopping on the grass as the wind kicks up again and almost knocks her over.

"Where are we going?" Elle asks.

They hear the sound of purring and heavy breathing as a turtle lifts its head above the grass.

Turning slowly, he points with his nose and says, "It's there. Now stop eating my figs."

Thud, thud, thud. "Yes, here it is," Jenn tells them as she stomps her foot on the ground. She opens the trapdoor to a dark and scary place.

"Thank you, Mr. Turtle."

"I don't think we should go in there," Elle says.

"It's a shortcut. You can see better if you squint your eyes like this." Jenn looks into the tunnel. But as she looks into the tunnel, her pixies fly ahead.

The pixies then fly around Jenn, conversing with one another. Their talk sounds like whispers. Jenn puts her hands to her mouth and talks with them in soft tones that ordinary people can't understand. But Princess Elle and Prince Jet understand what she's saying. They are schooled in the lifestyle, attributes, and speech of pixies, trolls, unicorns, and other magical creatures, including the Bolls.

"My pixies will show us the way," Jenn says.

The tunnel is dusty, with a clay-like floor, rocks, plant roots growing from the ceiling, and stone walls erected long ago by mages. The pixies provide a dim light from their glowing wings in the dark tunnel.

"This place is scary," Jet whispers to his sister.

They walk down a flight of rock stairs and come to a door made of sturdy oak wood with an old, rusty doorknob.

Jenn stops to let everyone catch up

"Are we going in there?" Elle asks.

Jenn whispers a magic word, and the enchanted door opens, creaking and grinding against the rock floor. A thick fog spews from inside the room.

Jet walks to Elle and takes her arm. Then Princess Strawberry, who is five seasons old, runs to Elle. Princess Pigtails, only two seasons old, isn't concerned. She enters the room, exploring, touching things, and trying to look under the furniture.

"It's okay," Jenn tells them. "It's safe. Look, Pigtails is already inside."

I hope it's safe, Jenn thinks.

CHAPTER FIVE
THE MAGNIFICENT CHAMBER

The Magical Chamber

"This place is huge!" Princess Elle whispers, her eyes wide as she turns to Jenn.

Grime-streaked windows stretched from floor to ceiling, revealing a view of meadows and endless blue skies, though the chamber lay far underground.

Between them, warped bookcases are burdened with ancient, dust-laden tomes.

A chandelier of elaborate crystal, lit with flickering candles, hangs overhead. Elle looks up, her eyes catching the soft glow.

"How do they light all those candles?" she asks.

"I don't know. They never melt, and the flames stay lit all the time," Jenn replies.

They stand on an old hand-woven rug of royal crimson and gold thread. Jars made of obsidian on bronze bases, almost as tall as Prince Jetamine, are around the walls. The jars are covered with lids that are tightly held in place with wires, a strong string, and some gummy substance resembling dried glue. The jars are colorfully decorated with elaborate hand-painted pictures of animals, flowers, the deep blue sky, and the ocean.

"Jenn, what's in those jars?" Jet asks.

"We don't know. The jars are sealed with magic older than the monastery," Jenn murmurs. "Some say they hold memories— others, curses. No one truly knows. This room is mystical. Anyone with the proper training can find the answer to any question in those books," Jenn says.

I hope those old spells still work like they're supposed to. All this gives me a headache.

"How do you know all this, Jenn?" Jet asks.

"We hosted the heads of the families once a year. They often discuss magic, the impending evil, our defenses, and many other topics."

The bookshelves are crooked but don't fall. All the books are dusty because no one reads them anymore. "There used to be a school for wizards who would come to do research and find the answers to ancient dilemmas. They haven't come for many seasons," Jenn says.

Princess Pigtails is trying to open a door that leads to the outside.

"Don't open that door," Jenn says. "The Wizards locked malicious beasts in that land. Although some of the enchantment has faded, the magic of twenty-five wizards still protects it. Don't be scared; the monsters are locked up and can't get out—unless someone lets them out." Jenn gives Pigtails a stern look.

They won't harm you. Let them out, the sugary voice, like dripping honey, whispers in her mind.

Jenn shakes her head. *I can't think this way.*

A large, beautifully adorned manuscript sits on a desk. It's made from old leather and features intricate, handmade designs in gold and silver. The book is decorated with pearls around the edge and a gold, elaborate cross in the center. One pearl is missing. The book is hundreds of seasons old and shows wear on the spine from people holding it. Brass hinges lock the manuscript shut.

Pigtails is fascinated by the ancient book. The little princess tries to lift it, but it's too heavy. In her frustration, she talks to the book. Others think it's baby talk, but it's not; it's an ancient language developed before there were people.

The book glows. A breeze swirls. Then—whoosh!—Pigtails is gone, like she stepped into a dream.

"What happened to Pigtails?" Strawberry asks, ready to cry.

A pixie whispers into Jenn's ear, "She spoke to the book in the star language. But I think she was trying to open the book to see what's inside. Instead, the words she used took her to a faraway land."

"We can call her back if we know which land she was sent to," Jenn replies.

A pixie whispers into her ear again.

"How do we know what land she was transported to?" Elle asks.

"Lethbridge, my pixie, told me there's a return spell written in a parchment on that enormous oak desk."

The old desk is cluttered with papers, books, and miscellaneous items that defy description. The desk drawers are open, with papers strewn haphazardly inside and on the floor. Jenn sorts through papers on the desk. There is dust everywhere.

"Here it is."

Jet, Elle, and Strawberry gather around Jenn as she unrolls the old, stained, and discolored parchment scroll.

"We know where she is," Jenn tells the group as she reads the document.

"Yes, and the Come Back spell is also here," Jenn tells them.

"What kind of spell?" Elle asked Jenn, concern in her voice.

"This is the 'Come Back' spell. You can reverse any spell. It only works in this room. But we'd better hurry before a creature eats little princess Pigtails," Jenn tells them.

She carefully reads the discolored scroll.

"Okay, here's what we need to do: hands on your heads, give it a tap, then jump and shout, 'Booger, booger, booger-roo!' But make sure it comes from deep in your heart—as pure love for little Pigtails."

Jet asks, "Why do we say booger-roo?" Jenn replies, "Who cares? It works."

Soon, all three jump, tapping their heads, saying, booger, booger, booger-roo, but nothing happens.

Princess Strawberry cries, "A wicked creature ate my little sister."

"Don't stop jumping. Yell louder and faster," Jenn tells them.

Soon, all three of them yell, "Booger, booger, booger-roo."

They jump so long that their legs get tired. But they don't stop.

A loud, scary wind twists like a small tornado in the room, and suddenly, Pigtails falls on the floor.

"There's Princess Pigtails," Elle shouts.

The poor little princess is crying. She runs to her big sister, Strawberry, for comfort.

Jet, Strawberry, and Pigtails rush into Ellie's arms. The pixies fly around them.

After a good cry, the group is ready to explore the chamber.

They explore the grand room and are amazed at all the clutter.

Tall bookcases with dusty books stand from the floor to the

ceiling. An old orc walks into the room.

"This is the keeper of the manuscripts, spells, and lost artifacts. He's safe as long as he isn't hungry," Jenn tells them.

I hope he isn't hungry, Jenn thinks.

The orc hobbles into the room from one of the many secret doors on the floor. "Let me get a look at these, hey. Mmmm, they look so tasty," he says as he pokes Strawberry on the shoulder.

"Hello, Mr. Orc. I'm Jenn, and they are my friends. We need help. We need to go to my aunt's castle. Can you help us get there?" Jenn asks.

A pixie flies to Jenn. "Your aunt is safe. Queen Seraphina took a squad of her best warrior unicorns to escort your aunt and defend the monastery. They'll carry her and her attendants to the monastery."

"We'll call the cousins from the six kingdoms to help us," Elle says.

"Mr. Orc, can you please help us get to Hope?" Jenn asks.

He snorts. "I suppose I can; though my bones are in agony and my heart is sick, I can still conjure many spells."

He snorts through his enormous nose with a wart on the tip. A bubble forms from one nostril and then pops, leaving a drop on his lip. He wipes it with the back of his hand and snorts.

Jet's gaze lands on a small sword, sheathed in a worn holster.

The old Orc notices Jet's attraction to the weapon. "You should take that sword, young master. You will probably need it later."

He turns to the group. "I need a clipping of hair from each of you for my collection."

"This spell will open a portal to the city. Spit on the ground and jump on your spit. Don't miss it, or you'll never get to Hope," he says, laughing, snorting, and sneezing.

After the orc ritual of cutting locks, he raises his arms into the air, twists his hands, and then sparks shoot from his fingertips. He sings an old orc-his-tra song from the bottom of his feet, and a light beam appears in the room. But a sudden earthquake causes the portal to flicker open and then close.

"Oh Nooooo. No. No. No. Not another one," the orc yells. The chandelier swings, and the crystals clink against each other. A glass bottle crashes onto the floor from the old desk.

Books and scrolls fall from the bookcases.

The orc grabs a wand from the desk and waves it at a wall. A hole forms, creating a doorway into a dark tunnel. "That way, it takes longer to reach the city, but it is the safest route. Run before it's too late," he yells over the rumbling sound of the earthquake.

The old orc hurries, hobbling back to the trapdoor he came from, and dives in, closing the door behind him.

"It's frightening, but our pixies will guide us. I'll go first," Jenn tells the group.

They run, Jenn turns her head, and locks of her hair fly inthe air. Her hair is disheveled, but it has a small white bow.

The earthquake intensifies.

Jenn turns her head. "We have to hurry. It's scary, but we need to go into that tunnel. It's the way wizards from the past used to travel. Come in. It's safe."

Jenn hesitates before stepping into the tunnel. The air around the entrance is too still. *Something waits, she thinks, though she doesn't speak it aloud. Courage is walking into the dark—even when you feel the cold breath of fear.*

Jenn pokes her head back through the door from the other side and says, "Come on. What are you waiting for? We're going through this tunnel. It's the only way. It used to be safe, but people haven't used it in centuries, so it's best if we run.

Like dripping honey, the sugary voice whispers to Jenn, *I will make you more beautiful than you can imagine. You will be the prettiest in all the land.*

Leave me alone, Jenn demands in thought.

Cobwebs hang from the head of the door, and bugs crawl up and down the door jambs. The entrance looks alive with insect bodies crawling on it. The tremors get more severe with each earthquake. As the ground rumbles, the top door beam cracks, dust falls, and insects disappear.

"Take these torches. Let's go! Hurry," Jenn says.

They enter the tunnel as the door crashes down.

"This way," Jenn shouts.

Strawberry lifts her torch high while they walk down the tunnel. She looks back and sees a fearsome, menacing shadow come off the walls and run towards them. She screams.

"Oh my gosh, I thought the shadow monster was killed long

ago. Run, run," Jenn yells. "Run to that open door. That demon prowls around like a roaring lion, seeking someone to devour," Jenn shouts as she runs and turns to look behind her. "Hurry," she yells louder.

The light from the torches illuminates the tunnel's ground and ceiling. The humans run as fast as they can, but the creature is catching up to them.

The shadow follows them as they run to the open door. The group can escape, but Pigtails falls behind with the creature at her heels.

Princess Strawberry grabs her little sister, pulling her hand hard as she and Pigtails run to safety. The vile creature focuses his glare on Princess Pigtails. He lunges at her with his jaws open wide, his long, sharp teeth glistening.

A sudden vision of a creature almost devouring Pigtails interrupts Jet's thoughts.

He feels a tingle in his fingers and sudden fear. Oh, no! Strawberry and Pigtails are in trouble again.

Save them, a kind woman's voice whispers to Jet's. Use this instead: Save them, a kind woman's voice whispers to Jet.

The beast lunges, jaws wide, drool flying like venom. Red eyes blaze. Razor teeth snap inches from Pigtails' head —then Jet dives between them.

The brave Prince Jet shoots his threads to the ceiling, swinging back to Strawberry and the fearsome Shadow Creature. Princess Pigtails is running but can't escape the shadow. He almost clamps his jaws shut with little Pigtails between his teeth when Princess Strawberry grabs her and yanks her away from the creature's snapping jaws, barely escaping.

Jet kicks the beast in the face with both feet and swings around it. The creature falls back, allowing Jet the time to get away. He then takes Strawberry and Pigtails to the front.

Jet feels more self-confident.

Jet, Strawberry, and Pigtails lunge ahead of the group toward the light that leads to the Lost Lands, away from the shadow creature. Vines, leaves, and other growth hide the exit, but the sun shines through parted branches.

"Jenn, let's pull this brush apart to go through that portal," Elle says.

The shadow creature mysteriously disappears.

"This way! That portal leads to the Lost Lands," Jenn shouts and thinks, *Wow, that was close.*

"Jenn, how do you know so much about the magic in these lands?" Elle asks.

"The royal envoys from all the realms come to our castle once a season. I used to eavesdrop as they debated magic, borders, trade routes, expansions, and hidden magical sites. They even drafted new maps for the kingdoms, though I didn't bring any."

Save yourself, the familiar sugary voice says to Jenn in thought.

CHAPTER SIX
AUNTIE GWYNNETH

Auntie Gwynneth

The Countess, Lady Gwynneth Windrider, presses on despite bleeding fingers and cracked nails. Mud-streaked sweat runs down her temples, and her once-elegant gown is torn and soiled. She breathes in shallow bursts. Her arms ache, caked with dirt as she crawls through the mulch.

She pauses, wiping the grime from her brow with the back of her hand, then braces herself on one knee and rises with a grunt. Her stomach growls. *I'm starving.*

The sun dips low on the horizon. *At least the rose bushes are planted.* She winces as she shifts her weight. *Now I can bathe and get out of these old work clothes. My knee's getting worse. I'll send a pixie to fetch the herbalist.*

With a weary sigh, she turns toward her castle, limping. It's time to wash up and make supper.

But as she reaches the stone walls of her palace, a dark fog and clouds approach from the North. Hidden in the dark fog are creatures dedicated to destroying all life in the Royal Realms. In the center is the ancient, deadly Obligoo. Ancient mages imprisoned this malicious creature in an evil realm at the bottom of the deepest ocean many generations ago to protect the locals.

But a recent earthquake weakened the spell that kept the creatures from escaping. The Obligoo was among the first to escape, with a thousand seasons of hate in his heart. It pushed its way up hard, breaking through the spell barrier. He swims through the ocean's depths and bursts out of the sea. Black clouds and fog coalesce around him as he takes flight. The Obligoo shrieks loudly, then flies south with the clouds and creatures in tow.

"Run, Run, Auntie Gwynneth," pixie Starflake shouts frantically.

Another pixie says, "Auntie Gwynneth, run to the basement."

"But Jenn is in the Outer Woodlands. It will take her all day to reach us here," Auntie Gwynneth replies.

"She's closer to the Obligoo than we are. We sent a few pixies to tell her to run to your sister's castle in the Red Lands," Starflake says.

"Starflake, I want you to pull the available pixies together. Divide them into groups and send the groups to all the realms with word of this impending danger. Send some to the monastery as well."

A magnificent white unicorn with iridescent wings and powerful muscles lands gently on the cobblestone path leading to the castle. Her mane and tail cascade in shimmering light, and her horn is a pure crystal with an ethereal glow.

It shakes its head and whinnies as if attempting conversation with Auntie Gwynneth.

"This is Queen Seraphina. She'll take you to the monastery if that's where you want to go. You must go with her and stay safe," Pixie Starflake says.

"Let's go, Your Highness," Auntie Gwynneth says.

Auntie Gwynneth and Queen Seraphina run side-by-side. Despite the pain in her leg, her hands are aching, and her arms are tired. Through force of will, she grabs the Queen's mane and pulls herself onto the back of the unicorn as it whinnies and leaps high into the sky.

CHAPTER SEVEN
THE LOST LAND

The Lost lands

Jenn takes and holds Pigtail's hand, who holds Strawberry's hand, who holds Jet's hand, with Princess Elle at the end. They pause, then cautiously step into the unknown territory. Princess Elle carefully looks from side to side for any unexpected disturbance.

"We can rest now," Jenn says, calm but watchful. "There's a fresh spring of water beside those rocks if anyone is thirsty. We can sit on the rocks, but don't lie on the flowers."

The Lost Lands are wild, lush, and overgrown with red, blue, green, yellow, and pink blossoms. Towering trees stretch into the sky, and a spring bubbles over rocks tangled in tree roots and shrubs. The air is rich with jasmine, wild roses, and something like honeysuckle. The grass is soft, green, and sweet-smelling just beyond the riverbank under a brilliant blue sky.

Dark shadows suddenly fill the sky, cast by black, vicious creatures overhead, screeching in horrid, dreadful cries.

"Quick, under the tree!" Jenn shouts, waving them toward the branches.

Soon, the threat passed.

"Elle, this place is beautiful, but corruption lurks here somewhere. I can feel it. It feels like death. We can rest, but we should hurry," Jenn says.

Jet, Pigtails, and Strawberry lay on the soft grass beside the spring. A delicate lavender scent calms them into a forbidden sleep. Their eyes are closing, welcoming slumber.

"No, no, don't fall asleep. This is dreamland. Don't lie on the flowers. It'll put you into a deep sleep, and we won't be able to wake you," Jenn yells.

She rouses the kids. "We're going into that tree hole. It will take us to the People of the Roots. Follow me. The portal is opening for us," Jenn yells to the group.

She dives into the hole in the tree headfirst. The others step into the hole slowly, fearfully, and carefully.

Something grabs Princess Elle's ankle hard as she steps into the hole, causing her to stumble. She screams in pain and fear, and falls as hundreds of insect-like creatures crawl over her body. She tries to brush them off her face and hair as she dangles by her ankle from the portal's opening to the land of the Rooters. But the bugs continue crawling on her body and in her hair.

CHAPTER EIGHT
THE QUESTS

The Quests

Two mighty young mages glide gracefully through the clouds on their white flying thornycorns in the northern sky. They're returning from helping local farmers successfully eradicate pests that threatened to destroy their crops.

Masters Eli and Nico, both mages, live and work diligently in the old monastery. They are the offspring of royals and were given gifts by an old witch when they were children. Both attended the mage school, run by an ancient mage more than one hundred and fifty seasons old. They are the only students and graduates.

"Nico, Eli," the old mage addresses them at their graduation, "Mages Eli and Nico, you are no longer wizards. I elevate you both to this rank of mage. You are not ready for this responsibility, but we will need this power to battle evil. Many years ago, an ancient sorceress gave you extraordinary gifts during your childhood. However, these powers are so potent that they could cause significant harm to the innocent if misused. To ensure their responsible use, she devised a series of quests that require honor and self-sacrifice, which have to be completed to unlock their abilities. Seek your quests and earn the full power of your gifts. Use these gifts wisely."

The old witch gave Eli the gift to create devastating weapons: swords that never dull, shields that never break, and arrows that never miss their targets.

Mage Nico was granted the ability to communicate with the animal kingdom in a universal language. She left a small hammer for Eli to keep and play with as a child, and a simple vest made of tightly woven colorful feathers for Nico. The hammer and vest grow with them as they mature.

Eli shouts into the blowing wind. "It was good that we visited those farms this morning. I hope the spell the mage gave us got rid of all the insects in their fields. I'm a little worried some pests on the undersides of the leaves may have survived." Eli turns toward Nico. "I have the scroll with the spell that makes us send thoughts to each other. I'll cast it now so we can talk clearly."

"Do you remember the old witch who granted us gifts when we were kids?" Nico asks.

Mage Nico's hair billows in the wind as his thornycorn whinnies and flies higher.

Mage Eli follows, his thornycorn riding the wind's flow patterns. He rides the shifting air currents, gliding smoothly before banking left to follow Mage Nico.

"I was too young, but I remember her faintly. I wonder if it's the old lady who lives under the library tower, the stacks."

"I thought she was a caretaker," Mage Nico replies curiously.

A gust of wind hits them hard on the side, but the thornycorns are strong and continue unfazed.

Both brothers are dressed in black leather that can only be pierced with hardened metal or the sharpest fangs from the abyss. Eli's armor comprises a shield and his helmet. He yields a simple hammer and a sharp, searing knife.

Mage Nico wears no armor except the feathered vest. He carries a short sword on his belt.

Both thornycorn's coats shimmer like moonlight on the ripples of a lake. Their horns resemble sharp, spiraling crystals, catching sunlight before reaching a deadly point. The thornycorns are tall, graceful, and proud creatures with long flowing manes and tails.

Eli's thornycorn flies closer to Mage Nico. "This village looks safe. Let's go back to the monastery and stock up. We can rest, then seek the activators for our gifts tomorrow morning."

Eli must find a pearl to activate the power of the forge hammer.

Nico must find and wear the silks, a garment made from the iridescent feathers of the Luminae Falcon. The coat will give him an added range to talk with animals and protection in battle. The silks and the pearl are mystical items that can only be found through self-sacrifice.

Eli looks sideways at his brother, his beard blowing in the wind. "Do you have an idea where these items are located?"

"Nope," Nico answers bluntly.

Nico pats his thornycorn on the side. "I know you can make it back to the monastery without stopping. Yes, thornycorns are faster and stronger than unicorns. I also know you are thirsty," Nico says to his thornycorn.

They land in a grove with many exotic tree species—elms whose leaves glow faintly at night and whisper secrets to the stars. Wizards frequently use these Elms for navigation. There are willow trees with golden honey-like sap that enhances dreams and visions.

They land on a glade of soft grass that lies down as a mage steps on it. A brook runs through the grove, pooling in some areas, creating a natural oasis. Both thornycorns relish the tasty green grass and drink from the waters.

"I don't know why she gave me the gift of Forge Master and you the gift of Talking With the Animals when we were children," Nico says. "But didn't teach us how to unleash their powers. The hammer and vest grow with us. I use the hammer to bend or break metal, but it does not affect or create enchanted weapons.

"Dad says I need a lost pearl to activate the Hammer to magically forge metal, but he didn't tell me where to find it," Eli remarks.

Mage Nico replies, "The witch who gave us these powers told Dad we were, and are, still too young for these abilities, but we need them to battle the evil ones. She said our powers would manifest when we hit sixteen seasons. Maybe finding the pearl and the silks will teach us more about our weapons."

"Maybe. I think I read every scroll in the monastery several times. No mention of a mystical pearl or the silks."

Nico looks at him in disbelief. "You couldn't have read every scroll. There are many thousands of scrolls and manuscripts covering thousands of seasons on thousands upon thousands of subjects. The library stacks go deep underground with even more scrolls and manuscripts to be restored."

Eli continues, "I saw the old lady restoring some old parchments, but she ignored me when I tried to talk to her. Maybe a clue to the activators is described in one of the older scrolls." Eli directs his thornycorn over a grove of trees. "Sometimes, I reminisce about the days we attended the wizard school in Karlek. It was fun but exhausting. The trials we went through to earn acceptance into the mage school at the monastery were tough."

Nico nods with a smile. "I was lucky. You were two seasons older, so I benefited from your screw-ups." Nico continues, "The Master said we needed to be elevated to Mage for a time to have the power to fight the evil that will invade our lands one day. Afterward, we must give up our mage powers. It's a mystery to me how a mage gives up his or her powers."

"He said we would have to die to ourselves before being promoted, and I thought that was a serious requirement to becoming a permanent mage. We haven't died but still got promoted." Nico laughs.

Eli chuckles. "The witch didn't mean physical death. She meant letting go of our egos. We should practice self-sacrifice, uphold high moral standards, and be merciful."

"Mercy is self-sacrifice?" Nico asks.

"Sure, you put aside your grievances and pride when you show mercy." Eli continues, "We learned some valuable lessons, and the gifts she gave us are impressive. You can speak with the animal kingdom. I can forge mighty armor. All we need is the knowledge of how to use these gifts. I hope we can remain mages after the war. We worked hard to learn the craft. I know we're not old or experienced enough, but we will grow up fast in the coming days. Don't you think, brother?"

Mage Nico's thoughts turn to the days they attended the school for mages at the monastery. *We had to show the old mage we were dedicated and disciplined to accomplishing our missions. It's too bad most of the others in wizard school were not ready for the mage school.*

Nico's thornycorn glides on the air currents. His long, flowing hair billows in the wind. It captures the essence of freedom, movement, and grace in flight.

Their thornycorns resemble unicorns but are much stronger, travel farther, and, with their hardened skin, they can endure more attacks from the enemy than unicorns. Their horns contain a magical power.

"Dad told us we may have to find the Lost Folio. It can tell us where to find our activators," Eli tells Nico, interrupting his thoughts.

"Yes, yes, I know, big brother. I was there when he told us, remember?" Nico replies sarcastically.

"Okay, Nico, I won't argue with…"

Suddenly, hundreds of foul black birds hit them from behind with razor-sharp claws and feather tips like sharpened steel. The powerful mages and their thornycorns lose control as thousands of claws and beaks from the creatures tear at their bodies.

"A Dark Sorcerer is directing these creatures. We need to kill it," Nico shouts.

He sends a flock of Owls to distract the Sorcerer, but they are no threat to him.

Mage Eli swings his thornycorn around, draws his knife, and slices through the bodies of the beasts like a razor through paper. His shield is silver with gold trim and a deep crimson thornycorn etched on the surface. It is more durable than any metal known to exist. The shield and his helmet protect him. But there is little to protect his steed.

Mage Nico calls down birds from the sky to help, but there are too few. The powerful black Nyxfiend buzzards crush the noble birds.

He takes a scroll, points, and casts a spell that brings shards of ice from the sky to pierce the bodies of the sinister fowl attacking them.

They grow weary, fighting so many vile creatures as their magic fades. They flee on their thornycorns, but the evil buzzards bite the legs and sides of the gracious flying beasts. In pain, they whinny, losing momentum in flight. The ignoble Dark Sorcerer casts a spell that causes the thornycorns to freeze and fall as the buzzards continue tearing their flesh. The powerful thornycorns shake their heads, whiny, as they leap back into the sky, their hooves barely touching the earth.

Mage Nico sees a flock of ravens approach them. He calls to them to save them from the fall, but they are no match for the buzzards. The ravens and Nico plow into the buzzards, forcing them to scatter, but the buzzards return in vengeance. Nico sends the surviving Ravens to help with Eli's rescue.

A small hill overlooks a tiny village. On top of the hill, a deadly ursine stands, holds its arms out, and roars at the children running from their church to the village. Master Eli and his thornycorn fall from the attack of the evil buzzards but can navigate their fall to crash into the dangerous creature, distracting it from attacking the children.

Mage Eli and the ursine battle on the sides of the hills. Eli's hammer and sword are relentless in his strikes against the ursine, but the great beast continues attacking. Eli and his thornycorn crash onto the ground hard as the ursine lunges at them with its jaws wide open. He and his steed look up in terror to see the massive ursine plunging atop them.

Eli's thornycorn turns and points its horn at the falling ursine. It impales the creature, but the thornycorn does not survive. It gave its life to protect its rider and the fleeing children.

The buzzards leave to join the beastly creature that leads them.

"Help, I'm trapped under this massive creature," Eli shouts.

Nico chuckles. "Looks like you're all tied up." They finally roll the dead, heavy ursine off Eli and the thornycorn, grunting as they push until it rolls to its side.

"Nico, look, my thornycorns' horn turned into a pearl." Eli's voice trembles as he holds up the luminous gem.

He's admiring the great gem when a voice speaks to him in his mind. *This pearl will give you one wish. Use it wisely, the voice says, then it is gone.*

A village elder and his wife approach Eli and Nico, crying, "Thank you for saving the children from that beast. We also need help from a plague that afflicts us. We are dying from this scourge. Many have already succumbed to this disease."

Eli looks at Nico. "We need to help these people."
He stares at the pearl with sorrow etched into his expression.

I can't use this for myself when these people suffer so much. But I will never have the power to forge magical weapons with my hammer if I use it to help the villagers. No. I can't use it when so many people are suffering now.

"Pearl, take this disease from the people in this village. Give them good health and long life," Eli says.

The pearl glows, then disappears. The plague is gone.

They mount Nico's steed to return to the monastery when a flock of the terrible buzzards attacks them in the air again. Both mages fight with all their might, but there are too many creatures. Eli and Nico dive to escape, but the creatures see the villagers, turn, and rush to take them. Mage Nico sees the flock and flies his thornycorn with Eli into the center of the flock.

"Eli, we must fight until the end," he says.

"Yes, I know. But these people need our help."

Nico casts another spell, bringing down sharp shards of ice on the buzzards, killing many.

"We can't overpower them," Eli shouts.

Nyxfiend Vultures, also known as Black Buzzards, screech and cry in raspy tones as they launch their vicious attack. The people on the ground are village farmers who have no weapons. They are terrified; some run towards the village while others rush towards the mountains in the north.

Mage Eli yells at them, "Grab your sickles and fight! You have hunting weapons; use those to fight with." But nobody can hear him.

Mage Nico calls for help from a small flock of large, majestic birds nearby, using his thoughts to speak their language. These few impressive fowl battle the larger blackbirds until stronger and larger majestic birds arrive. But they are scattered quickly as the blackbirds plow through them.

The blackbirds screech again as they turn and approach a trading post on the ground below. The people are screaming and running. Mage Nico looks around, but there are no more animals available to call for help.

Nico's thornycorn carries both mages towards the buzzards.

Eli shouts, "Look," then points to the villagers below.

Nico tells his thornycorn to take them to the middle of the blackbird's horde. The two mages and the thornycorn know they will not survive, but they may distract the buzzards enough for some people to find shelter.

The thornycorn flies into the flock with its majestic wings

extended as far as possible. He lowers his head, making his horn a dangerous weapon to anyone before him. This daring thornycorn crashes into the blackbirds with its horn pointed forward. He flails his head from side to side, killing and maiming many of the despicable creatures. He kills some and injures others. But there are thousands of blackbirds.

I'm out of spells. I have only my blade. Mage Nico tightens his grip on the knife, arm outstretched. Across from him, Eli mirrors the motion, his gaze steady. Together, they charge forward on Mage Nico's thornycorn, galloping headlong into doom, risking everything to save a handful of villagers.

From the skies, hundreds of Black Buzzards descend like a storm. Claws rake skin. Beaks pierce armor. Blood spills. Death closes in on both Mages and the thornycorn

Then—blinding light.

A brilliant flash erupts from Nico's vest, searing through the chaos. The air ignites with radiance. The blackbirds screech, reeling mid-air, their eyes scorched by the sudden blaze.

The blackbirds are suddenly gone. Perplexed, Mage Nico asks Eli and his thornycorn, "What happened?"

Eli replies, "I don't know, but it saved our lives."

Nico's mount shakes his head, stating that he does not know the source of the light.

A kind voice speaks to Mages Eli and Nico. *Well done. You completed your quests for power and weapons. Eli, you sacrificed your pearl to save the villagers from a devastating plague. Nico and Eli, you gave your lives to protect innocent villagers.* The voice pauses, then says, *No greater love does a man have than he who would give his life for a friend. You found the true power of your gifts and the power of magic. This power is love.*

Mage Eli, your hammer is empowered to create devastating weapons.

Nico, this vest is named The Silks. It will enhance your powers, protect you, and allow you to shoot light from your fingers. Use it wisely, young mage.

"Who are you?" Nico asks. There is no response.

ACT 02

CHAPTER NINE
CITY OF HOPE

City of Hope - only one entrance leads to Hope

Prince Jetamine, Princesses Strawberry and Pigtails, and Jenn fall into a large cavern. They land hard on the stone floor. Jet, Jenn, Princess, children, and Princess Pigtails fall into a large cavern. They land hard on the stone floor. Jet groans, pain in his shoulder as he rolls onto his back. Beside him, Jenn coughs and sits up, blinking dust from her lashes. Princess Pigtails mutters something not princess-like, while Princess Strawberry sits up wide-eyed but unharmed.

Jet's eyes drift to the cavern walls—jagged and ancient, like the bones of some forgotten beast. This place… it feels alive.

The walls are roughhewn, their uneven shapes a testament to time and water. There are two tunnels, large enough for a party of six to walk through easily. A faint breeze flows through the underground passages, bringing the scent of moisture and earth. It brushes against their skin.

The chamber glows with a dim, otherworldly light cast by veins of a strange mineral embedded in the rock. Torches are wedged into natural crevices lining the cavern's walls, providing flickering light for the party.

Jet looks around and behind. "Where's Elle?" Elle drops into the room and lands on her buttocks.

"Ouch. Don't worry, my foot got caught in a tree root. Then, my imagination took over. But I am fine now," she states, embarrassed.

A shudder runs through Elle as she remembers imaginary bugs crawling over her body and in her hair. She brushes the dirt and twigs off her green skirt.

Cousins Abby, Tori, and Naariah approach, their lanterns glowing softly, casting warm lights that pierce the gloom of the ancient tunnels. Two dignified rooters accompany the cousins.

Elle walks to the front of the group, her confidence solidifying with every step. I wonder what we'll find in this cavern.

"Allow me to introduce you to Rooter Elders Kael and Aric from Hope," Elle says.

"Thank you for meeting us here, cousins and elders Aric and Kael," Elle says warmly.

Lady Crystal stares at Jenn. I don't want to misjudge her, but I sense something dark is inside her.

Jenn shifts her stance, her eyes flicker away from Lady Crystal. Why is she staring at me?

Elder Aric looks Elle in the eyes. "We should hurry. But we have something important we must discuss with you first. Princess Ellaria, your father, King Mortimer, sent word to us through his pixies and a royal emissary that we are to raise an army of the combined forces of these realms. He said you should be the one to lead this army, Princess Elle."

"What? What did you say? My father wants me to lead an army?" Elle exclaims in horror. "Where is my father now? What's this about a combined army?"

Prince Jet looks at Elder Aric, stunned. *She's too young. Too untested. How could our father ask such a thing?*

All wait for the elder's response.

"Your parents and the other royals were summoned to the monastery. They are to meditate non-stop in shifts for stronger magical powers for all our people. The council summoned all the royal offspring for a meeting here at the City of Hope today.

Our pixies and the emissary carried a proclamation from King Mortimer. It states the Royals want Princess Elle to lead the combined armies. A voice told King Mortimer and Queen Lana to issue a proclamation assigning Elle as the leader of the combined forces," Aric says. "We think it was the voice of an ancient ancestor to the Queen."

Elder Aric pauses, then says, "Princess Elle, they want to offer you the position of commander of the armies. You are the only one with knowledge of the realms and their people. Our pixies have been going back and forth with messages, sorting out who will lead us. We all agreed it must be someone known to all the tribes and the landscape and be of royal blood. The tribal leaders trust you."

Elle looks intently at Aric. "Why offer it only to me, one of the offspring? This has to be a mistake."

Aric, stroking his beard, stops walking and turns to look at Elle. "An old witch gave the royal offspring gifts of power to fight evil when they were children. You and your abilities will grow and mature with the passing of seasons and the strain of adversity. We trust that the power will also grant you leadership qualities that will develop in you as we approach the looming conflict."

"Elle, all the tribal elders agree to send people and follow you into battle," Tori says.

Elle pauses. Her eyebrows are furrowed, her eyes are narrow, and her arms are crossed.

She huffs, turns to Tori, and snaps, "Really? Are you playing some game with me? I'm not old or wise enough to lead an army."

Jet steps forward, his voice firm. His eyes are wide, with something halfway between fear and admiration. A voice whispers to Jet. *Follow her.*

"You can do it, Elle. We believe in you."

Elle catches her breath and looks lovingly at her younger brother. This is not the boy who used to follow me through the stables. He's becoming a man, and he believes in me.

Jenn walks arm in arm with Elle. "None of us is prepared to lead an army like ours. But you have skills and knowledge that no one else possesses. No one understands the tribes, their people, and territories as well as you. You are descended from warrior kings. We'll be here to help you when you need."

"No, I can't do it. I won't do it. I'm only thirteen seasons old. We need an adult," Elle snaps. She stops walking, crosses her arms, faces the group, and glares at them.

A familiar voice whispers, you have the power. Let this power guide you.

Elle shakes her head but remembers her father's words. You will hear whispers from one of our ancestors from the spirit realm in times of stress. She spoke with my father often when he ruled, and she always gave him and mom good advice.

"How do we know she is an ancestor?"

"Well, dear Prince Jet, that is a good question. I know she's an ancestor because I asked her, and she told me. She only advises me to do the right thing. She was the Dame of an ancient wizards' council."

Elle swallows hard. I don't know if I can… but I'll try for the kingdom's sake.

Elder Kael presses his finger to his lips. "Shh, bats are harmless but spook easily. Please step where I step. We don't want to walk on bat droppings."

The ceiling is a sprawling expanse cloaked in shadows.

Hundreds of bats cling to the rocky overhang. They tiptoe through the bat cave in silence.

Jet points to a glow in the distance and whispers, "Elder Kael, what is that light?"

Elder Kael puts his finger to his lips. "Shhh, I'll tell you later."

They are all amazed as they walk into an enormous cave filled with giant crystals, some reaching up to ten meters. But what amazes them most are the many tiny bioluminescent larval glowworms. Crystalline surfaces scatter and reflect light from the glowworms and the torches in different directions. The effect is an illumination shimmering off the walls of the cave. The walls look alive in this light, and stalactites glow like crystal chandeliers. The stillness in the massive chamber gives the air a faint scent of earth and damp stone.

They walk, admiring the crystals and the glowworm's magical radiance.

Elder Aric is far ahead. He returns to the group.

"We don't have time for this. You can sight-see another time."

The journey is arduous, but they do not complain. "Cousin, why do they call you Moonchild?" Prince Jet asks.

"Before I was born, my mother had a dream that she would one day hold a moonbeam in her hand. The next day, I was born."

Jenn feels trapped. These walls seem to close in, and I get the shivers just walking through this chamber. The shadows flicker and stretch along the stone, twisting into beastly shapes. *Oh God, please let us be safe.*

Lady Crystal walks silently behind Jenn, her gaze narrowing as she notices Jenn trembling, for no clear reason. *Something's wrong with her. I can feel it.*

"When we heard the darkness was nearing, we knew you'd come," Mistress Tori says, her voice calm but firm. "We sent our fastest pixies to find you. Auntie Gwynneth's pixies have been a great help—bringing us daily reports on the invasion."

"So, you're aware of what we're facing up top. It's getting worse," Elle replies.

"We need to prepare for war," Jenn says, displaying confidence on the outside, but her inner self is frightened.

A sugary voice whispers to Jenn. *You cannot win this war. Come to me. I will protect you and your family. You will be powerful and the most beautiful of all.* Jenn ignores the voice in her mind.

"Okay—I'm not making any promises, but I will think about it and give you my answer this evening," Elle says.

How am I supposed to lead numerous armies against these creatures? Sometimes, I can't even guide my brother, but that's not saying much. There are not many people who can do so other than my parents. My brother is pretty stubborn at times. Elle shakes her head and chuckles.

A tingle begins in Elle's hand. Tiny sparks sputter from her fingertips. It stops just as quickly as it begins. Jet is the only one who notices the sparks.

The Prince proudly takes his sister's hand. He looks up at her and smiles. Elle's heart breaks. Her eyes well up with tears of love for her little brother.

Jenn pauses and glances over her shoulder. Her voice echoes softly through the cavern. "Follow us to Hope."

"The root people changed the city's name when we helped them defeat the Nasties," Naariah says. "They had hoped and prayed that someone could lead them to victory and eliminate those creatures that plagued them for generations. We could help in a small way,"

Elle takes Strawberry and Pigtail's hands. "I'll tell you about the root people and our cousins while we walk. The root people are proud. Despite being short and squat, they are strong and nimble. They map hundreds of miles of tunnels and suddenly disappeared," Elle interjects.

"The Council finally settled on The Root Folk for the regular people and The Rooters for the warriors," Elder Kael says. "But the Root Folk liked the name Rooter so much that they all called themselves Rooters. We couldn't tell a warrior from a baker when we called for one. Fortunately, Lady Grace, in her wisdom, directed that all Rooters and root people be called Rooters. All our people will be warriors, and all warriors will serve when needed, except for the children and the infirm."

Elder Aric interjects, "Chair Grace has lived a long life. She has amassed considerable wisdom over the seasons."

"Is this the only large city?" Jet asks.

"We founded several cities, but this is the largest and our capital. The closest is a mining town called A Joyful Place, where workers and their families live. They harvest the minerals we need."

"Princess Tori, Princess Abby, and Princess Naariah led the Rooters in battles to rid their land of the infestation of the nasties," Jenn says. "Those creatures are short and smelly, with razor-sharp teeth and scales. They crawl on four legs with their noses to the ground and two big eyeballs. These creatures bite people to a pulp."

"Don't worry, Princesses Strawberry and Pigtails. Our cousins defeated the nasties and saved the root people," Elle says.

"How did they defeat them?" Jet asks.

"It was a long war," Princess Naariah says. "The poor root people were almost driven from their homes. Their beautiful cities lay in ruins, and their crops were destroyed. They lost many Rooters in those heated battles."

"Our Chair lady went to the Mage Council at the Monastery to plead for their help to fight the invasion of the nasties," Kael says. "But only one elder Mage was there when she arrived. The elder, also the headmaster of the mage school at the monastery, agreed to send the ladies: Tori, Abby, and Naariah. He chose these three ladies because of a prophecy on an ancient scroll that read, 'During a time of great tribulation, three young ladies of royal blood will descend into the earth's bowels to do battle against evil.' I don't know how he selected you three ladies, but I'm glad you're here."

Naariah asks, "Where are the other mages and wizards? They can help us fight this evil."

They can help us fight this evil."

"We tried to contact him many times to thank him and ask for more help from the council, but we couldn't find him," Kael replies. "The Rooters' army proved no match for the nasties. They would slither around the feet of the soldiers, causing them to fall and then attack en masse. It was not pleasant. Many good Rooters passed into the Spiritual Realm in those days."

"We said yes, we will help, but we didn't know how we could help," Naariah says. "The leader of the Rooters told us of a mineral that burns through the shell of the Nasties. This mineral is Barkedite. They make spears and arrows with tips of this mineral, which kills them almost instantly."

Lady Tori says, "They now run from Barkedite when they see it. But the Rooters had small amounts of that rare mineral.

We helped them locate more."

"They did the rest. These Rooters are resourceful," Abby Moonchild says.

"They named the Barkedite after the Rooter, who discovered it," Naariah interjects.

"Her real name is Barkdameanolibagarotorybaudsmuones," Elder Aric says. "But only her mother, grandmother, and great grandmother could pronounce it. We call her Bark. She tried to light a firecracker on this blue stone, but the fuse fizzled. She tried it again. And again, the fuse fizzled. She tried it a third time but failed again. By this time, Bark was frustrated and angry with the rock because she had wasted three firecrackers. She grabbed the blue stone and hurled it at the wall, shouting, 'You piece of garbage. I lost three good firecrackers because of you.' The rock shattered into hundreds of pieces, some large, some small, and what appears to be fine dust."

"One of our scientists saw what happened and collected samples of this strange blue substance," Elder Kael says. "He and his team discovered the devastating properties of Barkedite on the Nasties. That may be why, even with small amounts, this and other caverns weren't completely overwhelmed in the past." Elder Kael points to a root dangling from the low ceiling. "See that unusual purple root that hangs down from the ceiling?"

The sugary voice whispers to Jenn. *I can make you beautiful and powerful. You will see it in time.* She ignores the whispers.

Kael continues, "The root will make you strong and wise for two minutes if you take a small bite. But this only lasts a short time. Each bite will give you about two minutes of strength and intellect. You can take two or three bites, which won't harm you. That will give you six minutes of strength and smarts, but you must wait for half a day before retaking it."

"If you take four bites, the ground will shake, the stalactites will fall from the ceiling, and hundreds of bats will fill the air," Jenn tells them, snickering.

Elle looks sternly at Jenn. "You're scaring the kids." Annoyed with Jenn, Jet shakes his head and says,

"We're not scared."

"Yes, you're brave, but take only three bites. Let's go this way," Tori says.

The group follows her, with Elle holding Abby's hands, who holds Jet's hand, who holds Strawberry's hand, who holds Pigtail's hand. Pigtail is watching the pixies, oblivious to their conversations. Naariah is watching Pigtail, so she doesn't run off somewhere.

Elle walks ahead of the group, her mind on her memories with her dad, King Mortimer.

I can't do this. It's too much responsibility. I'll be responsible for the little ones. That's serious. What if I do something wrong and the kids are hurt? I can't be their leader. I'm only thirteen seasons old. I'm sure an elder or one of the royals can lead them. I will tell them tomorrow that I can't be their commander.

Tears well up, and a knot tightens in her throat.

Wait! I have an idea for the kids. I'll have my pixies go to King

Eldrin for help with them. He will keep them safe, Elle thinks.

A voice whispers to Elle, *You must lead the army.*

Elder Aric tells the group, "Naariah and Tori devised a plan to use the purple roots more effectively. They assigned teams that would take turns eating the roots in three bites. When it wears off, the next team will eat the root. The purple roots gave us the intellect to find the mineral the Nasties detest."

A tall Rooter awaits them. He stands five feet tall, stout, with enormous feet and long toes. His skin is almost the same color as the rocks. His long earlobes are decorated with diamonds, rubies, jade, and other precious stones.

The dignified Rooter approaches. "Hi, I'm Lord Ennis from Hope. Please follow me. We have a long way to go."

Princess Elle cuts in, her voice firm, "I agree to lead the army."

Lord Ennis breaks into a smile. "I'm glad you accepted. You'll make an excellent commander."

Elle shakes her head and says emphatically, "Please do not call me general."

Around them, the group murmurs with relief and excitement, clearly pleased by Elle's decision to take command.

Elder Kael continues and points to small patches of barkedite. "We found small barkedite deposits along the walls of the tunnels. We know of large sources of barkedite in the death chambers. The heat and poisonous gases make it impossible to mine the minerals. We know barkedite exists inside the death chambers because we could see large deposits along the walls with the long eyes your cousin gave us."

"What are long eyes?" Jet asks, puzzled.

"It's a device your cousin gave us, and we call it long eyes. When you look into these incredible eyepieces, distant things appear close."

Lord Ennis interjects, "We discovered a way to mine barkedite without risking our lives with the help of your cousins. When we locate a rich vein, we tunnel to the rear of the deposit. The barkedite deposit shields us from the heat and toxic air while we gather the minerals. This way, we could harvest what we need without working inside the death chamber."

"We now have vital tunnels and caverns lined with this mineral, and the Rooters have shields made with barkedite ingrained," Abby Moonchild says.

They walk for an entire day until they reach an awe-inspiring underground cavern with crystal growth. A river runs through the cavern with a sloop tied to a rock. Nature's artistry is in full display.

Waterfalls tumble gracefully into the cavern, creating a soothing symphony of cascading water that echoes through the chamber.

A crystal-clear river snakes its way through the cavern, its surface glinting with reflections of the soft light above. It curves, forming a dog-leg bend that guides its flow safely away from the waterfalls.

Elder Kael unties a weathered boat from its landing, with intricate and colorful floral designs hand-carved into its sides and bow. "This boat will take us to Hope."

The small wooden boat, with humans, Rooters, and pixies flying overhead, drifts quietly on the river. A lamp hangs from the bow, while a mineral in the tunnel's walls emits a faint luminescence.

The boat ride is quiet and eerie as it exits the cavern of waterfalls.

The calm waters beckon as the boat glides toward Hope, carrying the party. Tiny silver fish dart beneath the surface, while the river softly laps against the shore.

The atmosphere is calm and humid, rich with the earthy scent of damp stone and moss. Time feels suspended, and the wonders of the natural world inspire a sense of peace.

The sounds are cascading waters from small waterfalls, the gentle creak as the boat shifts on the river, and the whispers of awe-inspired passengers.

"This boat will take us to Hope. It's not far, but we must hurry," Lord Ennis says.

"Where does that other river branch lead?" Jet asks.

"This other branch goes to an underground passageway leading to Karlek," Ennis says and chuckles. "Lots of honeymooners go to Karlek. When we defeated the nasties, we restarted building the underwater city."

"Hope is our center for commerce, education, and medicine. We now have schools, hospitals, homes, and temples in our city," Elder Aric says.

Naariah interjects, "Yes, it's growing so fast. Rooters from all over come to live and work in Hope. It's exciting to watch the many talented Rooters come together to work and study. You would think with so many new Rooters, there would be crime and other problems. But the Rooter culture is peaceful. They honor love, family, faith, and hard work. It's inspiring to watch these Rooters build a large, peaceful, and thriving community in so short a time."

They arrive to find a delegation of small people.

"The High Rooters Council is here to meet us," Tori says.

An elegant lady with waves of golden hair falling over her shoulders and face, long, delicate fingers, rings, and an opal necklace with matching earrings awaits their arrival. She's wearing simple, linen clothing with a lovely shawl.

"This is Chair, Grace. She's the leader of the root people and works closely with us to keep them safe," Abby Moonchild says.

"Welcome to the City of Hope. I'm the leader of our people. We're glad to have you with us during these times of trouble."

"Hi, Chair Grace, I'm Elle. It's nice to finally meet you. I heard of the many improvements you made to Hope."

"Thank you. I'm sorry to greet you with the bad news. Many of the kingdoms have fallen to the darkness. The realms that have fallen are desecrated. The vegetation is withering, there are no birds, the bees are dying, and animal life is sparse. Ghastly creatures and spirits roam the lands, unstoppable in those desecrated realms."

"We got word from your father that you are to lead our combined forces," Grace says.

"Yes, I accepted. We all must do our part in this effort," Elle replies. I'm going to make a fool of myself and get people hurt. How can I get out of this nightmare?

"If we are victorious in the war, we can bring back the green plants and flowers in the desolated realms," Grace says. "We discovered a broken old wand from the ruins of an ancient wizard's storehouse. The wizards of that area practiced green magic in those days. The wand's power will cause the flowers, trees, and grass to explode with vibrant color and growth. But it only works above ground."

"These ancient people existed at the time of the grand wizards. They suddenly disappeared and left many important artifacts," Grace continues. "We are aware of the encroaching darkness and the dreaded Obligoo. Our pixies keep us well informed. We know its current locations, and it's worse than we all thought. The darkness has spread throughout most of the realms. Castles lay in ruins from the heated battles. I am told the devastation is horrific in its wake. The ground is parched and cracked, trees are burnt, and the air reeks of smoke and ash. No birds or ground animals exist in the devastation. The realms' staff and soldiers hide in caves while the darkness consumes their land. They were no match for the invading forces of Nasties."

Grace takes the hands of Princess Ava and Pigtails as they walk through the winding tunnels leading to The City of Hope.

The surface is uneven, rough to the touch, pocked with small hollows where water once trickled. "I'll tell you a little about the city and the people you're defending."

They reach an enormous cavern in which a beautiful, modern city has been built. The underground city of Hope rises like a marvel of craftsmanship. Crystalline rock arches overhead, reflecting the city's ambient light in shimmering waves. Towering spires pierce the cavernous heights, their frames crafted from the densest heartwood and reinforced with dark, veined stone. The tallest structures gleam with panels of polished glass, each piece shaped and fire-hardened by the skilled glasswrights from a village famed across the kingdom for its exquisite glasswork.

"This is Hope," Chair Grace says. She turns and points to water cascading down a cliff into a pool. "If you find time, I recommend you swim in the crystal clear water of our Pavati springs. The freshwater comes from deep underground. It's comfortably warm. We also have healing sulfur water springs you can soak in to relax."

Elle looks nervously at Grace and says, slowly. "I don't think we…"

Chair Grace continues, "Tonight, we'll have Poligtia for dinner. They're small white fish you can eat raw, fried, or steamed. We'll have raw and fried, seasoned with our local herbs. We also have a variety of salads and veggies from our farms on the surface. Our foods are healthy and nutritious."

"Do you have underground farms?" Jenn asks.

"Yes, we do," Grace says. "We grow yams, carrots, onions, radishes, and many more varieties of root vegetables underground, but close enough to an opening in the ceiling to provide sunlight for the plants. Above ground, we grow wheat, corn, and sunflowers in a secluded valley next to a cave that leads into our society. We also grow several varieties of Lentils. We have Brown, Green, Red, and others."

Kael jumps off the boat to tie it to shore. The cavern is enormous, vast enough to swallow a cathedral. Centuries of underground rivers carved the walls.

The walls are rough and uneven, marked with small hollows where water once trickled. The stair steps to a conference room are all carved from solid granite, each bearing the stone's natural strength.

The stairs and conference room are a striking fusion of nature and Rooter ingenuity, carved into a solid rock from deep underground. Rough stone walls with their natural textures lend rugged authenticity to the rooms. Magical crystals are embedded into the walls, casting a warm, diffuse glow that softens the otherwise austere atmosphere.

Grace continues talking about Hope as they walk. "We'll have dinner in the conference room."

The top of the conference table has been polished to a sleek, smooth finish. The conference walls are lined with windows, offering a clear view of the City of Hope, the river below, and the bustling lives of its residents in homes, businesses, schools, and churches in this vast underground city.

Jenn looks around, her eyes wide open. "You made a lot of progress in building your great city since I was last here with my auntie." Surprised, Jenn says excitedly, "Look, Elle, Pink Dolphins." Jenn points to sleek and gentle creatures swimming in the river. "Children and attendants are playing with them."

"The Pink Dolphins swim from and to the ocean. They can live in both fresh and salt water," Elle replies.

The grandeur of the large, impressive underground city mesmerizes the group. Craftspeople work with a variety of materials, including wood, metal, pottery, and jewelry. Hope boasts a diverse range of markets, offering everything from food to clothing.

Boats enter the cavern with people and Rooters from other realms to trade food and goods. The city is thriving with activity and prosperity. Small Rooter children and their teachers can be seen walking hand in hand into caves on school trips to study the cave art left by ancient people, who may have been the predecessors of the present-day Rooters.

"We need to contact all the tribal leaders to join us in the war as fast as possible," Elle says.

A pixie flies frantically to Grace, leans close, and whispers into her ear.

Chair Grace says in shock, "No, wait!"

CHAPTER TEN
THE CRONE

The Crone

"Wait! I just got a message from my pixie. We have an unexpected…" Chair Grace says, then hesitates, interrupted by the tapping sound echoing off the hallway walls.

Slow, loud, sharp raps from each tap of her cane echo down the hallway to the conference room. An old woman with wispy gray hair hobbles into the conference room with the help of her weathered cane. Her spectacles sit almost on the tip of her nose. She wobbles, then goes to the head of the table.

Two tall, muscular, powerful mages walk behind her, appearing to be her protectors, but, as we all know, no one is more powerful than the Crone!

Mage Nico extends his hand in an offer to help her sit, but the Crone whacks his fingers with her cane.

"Ouch! That hurt!"

"I don't need help to sit down, young mage," she retorts.

The sturdy, unadorned chair is made from weathered oak. The seat is padded with woolen cushions, which are worn and faded from years of use.

Chair Grace says in a flowery voice, "Welcome, venerable one. Your presence brings—"

The Crone interrupts Chair Grace with a raspy voice, "Yes, yes. Now get me something to eat and drink."

The room breaks into a flurry of activity as pixies fly to and from the kitchen with plates of delicious, nutritious food, some sweet and some savory. They bring various nectars in crystal glasses to drink and sky cakes made from ancient pixie recipes. These delicacies are a pixie's dessert specialty handed down for generations. They make this dish on special occasions for Rooters and Humans.

Groups of pixies fly into the room, carrying numerous dishes and nectar to the table before the Crone. People and Rooters whisper with each other, all waiting to hear what she will say next.

She looks at the six plates filled with gourmet foods and the delicious nectar on the beautiful table before her. She stands, slowly collects a lettuce leaf, puts it in an empty bowl, adds a few spoons of lentils, hobbles to a free place on the table, and then sits with her bowl.

The room is in complete silence and shock.

The Crone takes a long drink of water and sets her glass down with a loud thunk. The sudden noise in the quiet room makes a few members jump.

"You can remove all the rest of that stuff," the Crone says gruffly.

Naariah lifts her finger. "We received word the mage council would visit, and they want the children of the six families here, ancient one. We thought some…"

The Crone faces her and glares.

Naariah hesitantly continues, her voice barely a whisper, "Ahh, never mind."

The Crone locks eyes with her, her voice low and steady. "Ancient one? You thought what? My lady. Did you expect old men in robes with long beards? Collect the children, including the older ones."

Chair Grace interjects, "They're happily playing with Rooter toys in the back rooms. Do you want to go see them, gracious Crone?"

"Call me Crone," she rasped dismissively. "Not gracious, venerable, ancient, or anything like that. Now, bring the children here."

"Yes, my Grace. I mean, yes, my Crone. I mean. Yes, Crone. Oh dear," Chair Grace says, her eyes beginning to water.

The Crone is not looking at Chair Grace but senses her hurt feelings. She looks to the ground, then turns her head towards Grace while still looking down, and asks, "Please send someone to bring the children to me."

"Pixies, pixies," Chair Grace yells, "please bring Princess Strawberry, and Princess Pigtails along with squires Bear, Robert, Bodhi, David, and Daniel into the conference room."

Another group of pixies brings candy-topped pizza, miniature burgers stacked like a pyramid, and Chocolate-covered pretzels with ketchup in the center.

The veggies come on a separate platter. There are two broccoli-like veggies, baby asparagus and potmatoes, a hybrid veggie made from potatoes and tomatoes. There is sour candied cabbage cubes coated with chocolate marmalade icing. The chocolate is meant to mask the pungent smell and taste of the veggie, but none of the kids are fooled. All avoid the SCCCCCTT, Sour Candied Cabbage Cubed Chocolate Covered Tasty Treat, pronounced, SksssssT as one long Hiss.

The pixies bring four lettuce leaves cut into eight pieces for each child, and one leftover in case a child has an epiphany that veggies are healthy for them.

No one touches the veggies.

Pixies bring a platter with ruby-red grapes and jugs of sweet grape juice.

Lord Ennis fondly reminisces about his childhood days with the cart of grapes. He looks at the group, thinking. *Rooter children would wash their feet and stomp the grapes to make their grape juice a specialty.*

It's pretty tasty when you add the bitter melon juice, some mild chili peppers, and a dash of ketchup to the grape juice. It tastes like watermelon with ketchup. I don't care for ketchup or watermelon, but they are delicious when mixed with squashed asparagus. We stomped the grapes in that old wooden cart with a hole at the end. We all loved stomping on those delicious, clustered berries.

His mind wanders as he continues remembering those past days. Stomping the grapes with our friends was a lot of fun.

He smiles as his thoughts go to the time he, as a child, was stomping the grapes in the cart. I was alone, stomping on the slippery cart, and fell under the grapes and juice on my back. I was in shock; my eyes were stinging from the juice, and I was blinking rapidly. Red grape juice ran down from the top of my head to my face and all over my body. The others were laughing hysterically at me.

He thinks *fondly of those lazy, peaceful days. I was covered in red juice from head to toe.*

The Crone eyes Lord Ennis with a scowl. Her forehead creases deeper than those wrinkles caused by age alone would bring.

She then turns to the crowd.

"We face a great evil and must stand together to defend our loved ones, homes, and the land we hold dear," the Crone says in a raspy voice. "I'm sure you've heard the rumors already. The creatures bring a desolation we haven't seen in over one hundred and fifty seasons."

The room grows eerily silent.

One angry Rooter shouts, "It won't be easy, but we have no choice!"

Another Rooter cries, "How can we fight those creatures from that hellish realm?"

The Crone continues, "Evil creatures escaped the ocean's abyss and crushing depths. I won't lie to you; we are all in danger. I will send the children to a place of refuge. But I can't guarantee they'll always be safe."

The worried crowd murmurs angrily, their voices rise, and some break down sobbing. Rooters cluster into groups, arguing, some shouting. Some walk to friends and talk louder, trying to speak above the loud and frightened conversations.

Lord Jonathan asks, "Crone, who will protect our children if the evil reaches them?"

"It's not if, Lord Jonathan. It's when."

The crowd grows silent. Acolyte, Mia, and Lady Chloe stand together, their hands clasped tightly. They seek comfort in each other's grip as the moment's weight settles over them.

"King Eldrin and I decided the safest place for the children is the Monastery. There are secret rooms and chambers with food supplies and water. I've been preparing this sanctuary for many seasons, anticipating the return of these creatures."

Jenn asks, "What happens if…"

The Crone turns to Jenn, eyebrows furrowed, her eyes pierce Jenn's gaze. She cowers in fear of the Crone.

"It can't read your mind, foolish child. It can only hear when you speak to it through your thoughts," the Crone says with authority. The Crone points her cane toward Jenn and shouts in a fiercely authoritative voice, "Be gone, evil one."

The Crones' magic throws Jenn to the floor. She shakes but feels a burden has been lifted from her chest.

Oh my God, she knows, Jenn thinks.

Lady Crystal eyebrows furrow, *I knew there was something wrong with Jenn.*

Princess Elle looks intently at Jenn. *Crystal was right. There is something about her that's not right.*

The crowd is silent.

A concerned Rooter shouts, "How do you expect us to battle with this evil? Some are farmers who have never held a weapon."

"I am the Crone, the last and only voice on the Mage Council. Some of you met one mage. No others exist. This mage and I were children over one hundred fifty seasons ago when we fought the evil creatures. He was a young acolyte, and I was a mere child. We enticed people from distant lands to come and rebuild our kingdoms over the past one-hundred-fifty seasons."

She continues, "The losses and devastation we endured were beyond comprehension. Entire villages were obliterated, their homes and histories erased. The Council of Wizards, once a bastion of wisdom and power, was shattered, its members annihilated in the chaos. What remains now is a shadow of what we once were. Ultimately, what was left of the wizard's council gave their lives to save the realm. They combined all their energy into one massive spell, causing the creatures to disintegrate. All disappeared but the powerful Azaz. The creature was severely wounded from their spell, but still deadly.

"I was terrified, but able to summon every ounce of my magic to bind and hold Azaz against the wall. The creature became a woman and spoke kindly, but I knew it was a ruse. The beast broke free of my magic and dove at my legs, but the force of my exile spell drove it back to the depths of its evil realm. We then enjoyed many seasons of peace, knowing we would fight this evil again one day."

The group remains silent; their eyes fixed on the Crone.

The Crone takes Strawberry and Pigtails' hands and sits on the fur-covered bench again. "Princesses, you two will grow up to be mighty warriors. I'll imbue you with magic now and with a gift so that when you're old enough to use these powers for good, you'll be ready. The magic will give you strength, good health, and intellect immediately, and it will grow as you age. The gift will come later in your life and will give you a power."

"Young acolytes David and Daniel, you will enter training in the priesthood. When you are ready, I will send you to run the Monastery.

"Acolytes Bear, Robert, and Bodhi, you will serve as squires. Your goal is to become mages and form the Mage Council. But first, you must endure the rigors of training—beginning as knights, then wizards, and finally, true mages. This path demands many seasons of hard work and sacrifice. The life of a mage requires you to lead a righteous life; you must have faith in your God, show compassion, and remain humble. Take responsibility for your actions, serve humbly, and stand firm in righteousness, even through the toughest trials. Above all, you must diligently study the scrolls," the Crone instructs.

"I'll send you to the Monastery, children. You will be with your parents. Once you're settled, I'll come and join you to begin your studies. Call the oldest of each family here. Send the others to another room."

In a sudden burst of activity, various pixies fly across the conference room, then scurry to the other rooms while others clear the table, bring drinks, and await orders.

The heads of the six families join them. Pixies lead the children back into the room with Rooter toys.

"Lord Jonathan from the Steppes, I elevate you to the rank of wizard, but with the temporary power of mage and the title of marquis. You will lead your tribe and the nomadic people of the Steppes into battle." The crone inclines her head. "Ladies Mia and Chloe, you must stand with Lord Jonathan and fight at his side. He'll need your strength in the battles to come.

Lady London, you will lead the people from Karlek. You have the gift of healing.

Mistress Tori, you will lead your delegation and fight alongside Lord Ennis and the Rooter army. I give you the gift of chaos."

The group murmurs with each pronouncement.

The Crone continues, "Lords Jean Pierre and James Dean, you will lead the people of the Enchanted Isles into battle. Your mother, Queen Saundra, will help prepare you. Wait for her instructions.

Crystal, I give you the gift of peace. You will feel inner contentment and be able to share that feeling with those around you. In times of stress, you will remain calm and make the right decisions.

Ladies, Alexis, Crystal, Kaylee, Cynthia, and Amberlyn, I have a special assignment for you. You must go to the Monastery and reopen the Temple from its hidden entrance. The entrance is on the other side of the mountain, nestled within a lush and forgotten valley."

"The temple door remains sealed but can be opened by a spell or repeated forceful attacks from the enemy. The Old Mage knows the spell needed. Behind that curtain is pure good magic. You cannot control the magic behind the curtain, but asking for help from it in this fight is possible. You are to protect the royals if they are attacked. A squad of Rooters and the Egglets is already there but will need help."

"Crone," Elle says. "These are the leaders of the six tribes in our realms. The royals and their parents have gone to meditate in the monastery."

"Yes. We need them meditating there to bring us more effective magic from the heavens and the earth."

The old Crone chuckles when she notices Jet's face. "Ah, Prince Jetamine. I see you use the threads organs I gave you when you were still in your mother's womb. I did the same with many of your ancestors." The old Crone chuckles.

"How old are you?" Jet asks.

"You shouldn't ask a woman her age," the Crone says in jest. "I am older than one hundred and fifty seasons," she replies. "Prince Jet and Princess Ellaria. You hold a special place in my heart. My daughter was your great-grandmother. She was the light of my life."

"Our great-grandmother?" Jet asks, surprised.

"My daughter was growing stronger with magic as she aged," Crone says, holding back tears. "A young wizard caught her fancy. They married and had children. I watched them grow old and pass to the Spirit Realm. I couldn't help them. My magic wasn't strong enough. I have been blessed to watch our society come back to life and cursed to see all I love to grow old and pass to the spirit world."

The Crone sits on a bench covered with furs and throw rugs. "Come to me, Jetamine and Ellaria. Your presence alone makes this old Crone happy." She takes Elle and Jet's hands. "This war will not be easy, children. Many folks from these lands will lose all they have, including their lives, to the evil that approaches. We must band together to fight this evil. I am not sure we can defeat Azaz and his minions, but we must stand against them," the Crone says.

Her voice is cracked and dry, but carries, sharp as a two-edged sword. "The gifts I gave you at birth are meant to awake around your sixteenth year. We can no longer afford to wait for your gifts to mature fully. But even as they grow, remember this: they are born of love, and love is their greatest power. Use them wisely— to protect, uplift, and serve those who need you most. Love will awaken the true strength within your gift."

The Crone is our great-great-grandmother. Elle thinks as the Crone takes and holds her hand.

With each gift I give, I feel my strength fading. I only hope I have enough left to share with them all.

She tells the group, "The gifts I'll give you are seeds now, but they will grow and flourish. Elle and Jet, your powers of reason, understanding, and inner strength will develop quickly. You'll be able to think faster and mature faster than the others. I don't know when your power gifts will manifest or what they will be, but the stress and trials of battle will hasten their emergence." The Crone looks intently at Elle. "These people will need a leader."

"They already asked me to be their commander," Elle says. "I'm afraid I'll make mistakes." *How am I going to get out of this responsibility?*

The Crone replies, "Yes, you will make many mistakes."

The Crone stands and turns to survey the royal offspring, resting on her cane. She's hunched, her back bowed and stooped with age. Her dark green cloak is faded, tattered, and worn by time and her long life of one hundred sixty seasons.

The Crone looks at the royal offspring and commands, her voice ringing with authority, "Kneel."

The room silently obeys.

She lifts her cane, whispers words in a language long forgotten, and then slams the butt of her cane on the floor. Nothing happens.

"I grant you the temporary position of a wizard with all its rights, privileges, responsibilities, and powers. You are all too young and inexperienced to achieve this vaunted position. But we will need this power to fight the evil approaching our beloved realms."

"What will happen to our power after the war?" Wizard Crystal asks.

"That depends on how you use it and whether you survive. In the best case, you will remain a wizard, but I don't expect you to qualify or survive. Unless you excel in battle, you'll probably return to your boring lives.

Princess Ellaria and Prince Jetamine, the powers you inherited from your mother's ancestors, will imbue you with great strength and intellect. Your gifts will reveal themselves soon. You will be more potent than any mage when your powers fully mature. Your powers will grow, but I'm sorry, there isn't enough time for them to peak before evil reaches us. That will typically take many seasons,"

"Masters Eli and Nico, I elevated you both to Mage with power. Your weapons will fight for you now that you have completed your quests and earned your weapons' trust."

"How do we know they trust us?" Nico asks.

"You must have faith, young mage."

"Jenn, Strawberry, Pigtails, and Jet will accompany me to the Shores of the Southern Sea. We estimate we have ten days before it reaches us," Elle says. "Strawberry and Pigtails, King Eldrin Wingstorm will meet us at the Southern Shore and carry you to safety while we fight this war. You must stay together and take care of each other."

Elle reassures them, "You're stronger together than the sum of your parts. You must not waiver in your resolve."

"Cousin Elle… will you come for us? I'm scared," Strawberry whimpers, as Pigtails breaks into tears.

"You'll be fine. A King is taking you to a safe place. It's well stocked with food, desserts, and fun things to play with," Elle says, and hugs her little cousins.

"Tori, go to the Enchanted Isles with news to recruit them for the war. Speak to James and Jean in the Enchanted Isles. Tell them we're at war and need all the help they can send. Tell them to meet us at the gathering place on the shores of the Southern Seas. Take Princesses Abby Moonchild and Naariah with you. A rooter will show you to a hidden passage to the Isles. "I'll send attendants from a village I visited with you to help if you need them. The unicorns will carry you to the main island, but there may be trouble in the sky, so take care," Commander Elle instructs.

"Jet, send your fastest pixies to the villagers far to the south, beyond the mountains. They pledged to support us if we needed them when we gave them those tracts of land. Tell the villagers to go north until they see people riding unicorns and on mountain tops. Then go west. They will have a difficult time finding the Gathering Place. Some have never left their villages, so ask your pixies to stay with them and guide them."

"There are three villages nearby that can help with supplies," Lord Ennis interjects.

"I'll send some of my pixies to those villagers," Elle replies.

"Sill…"

Before Commander Elle can finish her question, Pixie Sill breaks in, "Yes. I know where to send the pixies. We won't let you down, Commander Elle."

"Lord Ennis, I understand there is some resentment among some villagers in the northern village. Do you know anything about it?" Commander Elle asks.

"Yes. It seems the evil force has taken control of some villagers. They're on the brink of war with each other."

"Very well. Let's hope they can put aside their disagreements long enough to help us win this war." Elle's voice carries the calm authority of a seasoned leader.

"Those of you heading to the northern village, report in the moment you arrive—and keep us updated regularly after that."

"We will, Commander," Pixie Sill says.

"Also, Sill, send a squad to Master Jean Pierre and Master James Dean. Ask them to petition King Eldrin to send his Egglets to collect all the royal children, take them to a safe place, and provide protection. The monastery is the safest place for them. It's a pity we cannot protect the village children; there are too many. But there's adequate shelter near their villages," Commander Elle says.

Chair Grace looks at Elle with soft and slightly downcast eyes. Her eyebrows are raised in the middle; she has a furrowed brow that conveys concern. "We're putting all the little royals together in one building without their parents? You know, many Tribal elders have already sent their children to the Monastery for their safety? There are rooter babies, little Throags, baby pixies - oh dear. You realize most of those kids are spoiled little … well, Hmmm," Chair Grace says to Elle.

Elle straightens. "Wait until my cousins from the realm beyond the western mountains reach them, Lord Duncan and Lady Taylor.

They go to defend the monastery, but they are kids themselves. I'll send a pixie to tell them to behave and be a good example for the other kids. Our grandfather gave Lord Duncan shoes that throw balls of fire when he kicks forward or stomps the ground. Lady Taylor is the one those monsters should fear. Her hands are so powerful, she only needs to hit one monster, and the others behind her fall dead like dominoes. We have good nannies who will have to suffer along with the rest of us. I hope they survive," Elle replies and laughs.

"Yes, the war of the Nannies may be more difficult than ours," Chair Grace says in jest, laughing.

The Crone surveys the royal offspring. "You have your assignments. I expect regular updates through your pixies. Queen Seraphina sent a squadron of unicorns to take some of you to your assignments."

CHAPTER ELEVEN
KARLEK: A CITY BENEATH THE SEA

Karlek: A City Beneath the Sea

Beneath a vast, shimmering dome at the bottom of the ocean lies the glorious city of Karlek. Crafts folk from every corner of the distant realms arrive, each bearing unique skills and traditions, to contribute to the creation of this magnificent city.

The Rooters are constructing a track encased in a long, transparent bubble that stretches from the city to the shore and other destinations. Trains will travel through it, carrying people to and from Karlek to the shores and to Hope.

"Ennis, Elle, Jet, you will enter Karlek through one of the underground passageways from Hope," Chair Grace says calmly. "An Oknoth will take you to the surface when you're ready to leave." She continues, "They are peaceful marine creatures with bone structures on their backs for passengers to sit on. The Oknoth creates a dome over its back with air for its passengers to breathe as it dives into the sea."

"Karlek is a fun place for family vacationers, honeymooners, water sports teams, and many others who use the city and its access to clear, warm water," Lord Ennis says. "Villagers come to Karlek to learn a trade, math, history, the old languages, and much more. In the past, pixies, royals, and even Sky People from Fe have visited and studied here. Our wonderful city also hosts a wizard school, a getting-well school, and a school for treating annoying tooth pain as well as loose teeth.

"The Rooters call it the city of love. It's where young and old lovers can enjoy their company and have fun together. They enjoy sporting activities, plays, and musicals for those who prefer calmer days and evenings. At Karlek, we celebrate cultural diversity through our cultural exchange gatherings, where people from different backgrounds come together to share their traditions. We've seen and met folks from realms so far away that they don't appear on our maps. These good people bring their customs, traditions, cuisines, and so many other traits to our society," Lord Ennis says. He smiles, lifting his glass. "We've seen and met folks from realms so far away that they don't appear on our maps."

"The room is full of warmth, laughter, and clinking goblets. Outside the conference room window, the lights of Karlek glow bright beneath the dome

But Elle's thoughts drift away from the celebration. *Can we hide this city from the demons?* She wonders. *Even the strongest walls will fall when the creatures from the dark attack.*

Lord Ennis continues, "In Karlek, visitors from all realms enjoy vacation sites, education, medicine, healthcare, sanitation, utilities, sports, etc. The buildings have a futuristic style, and the mix of cultures are rich and diverse. We built a museum and a temple at the city's center."

Karlek has grown since I was last here, Elle thinks. She's mesmerized by the grandeur and beauty of this city.

"We lead visitors through the winding underground passages that connect Hope to Karlek. Without guidance, travelers could easily lose their way in the vast, intricate tunnel network," he says. "I want to introduce you to a unique and tasty seafood, the Geo-duck. It's a giant long-neck clam. The flavor is sweet, briny, and crunchy. We eat it raw, steamed, or fried. We teach folks about the unique underwater cuisines made from various species of fish and seaweeds and how to prepare these delicious foods."

Elle looks at Jet and says, "It's too bad we don't have time to enjoy these delicacies."

Jet's stomach growls. *I'm hungry*, Jet thinks.

Elle turns to Lord Ennis. "I've sent pixies to summon the unicorns. They'll take us to the Gathering Place—we need to meet them above ground."

Lord Ennis looks to the group, "Follow me."

CHAPTER TWELVE –
ELDRIN WINGSTORM AND THE SKY PEOPLE OF FE

Egglets make their nests high on the sheer cliffs and soaring peaks of mountains encircling the city of Fe. They are majestic creatures with wingspans twice the length of a full-grown Rooter. Their dark brown wings are streaked with white patches, and their bodies are wrapped in soft, snow-white feathers. Their broad wings and long, feathered tails enable them to glide effortlessly through the skies. Egglets are loyal allies of humankind.

The inhabitants of Fe and the Egglets enjoy a mutually beneficial symbiotic relationship. The Fe folks breed and harvest fish for consumption, medicinal purposes, and trade with other tribes. Fish cultivated by the Fe folk are also a good supplementary food source for the Egglets during times of scarcity.

In return, Egglets provide transportation to the Fe folks, in and outside their realm, and serve as loyal companions to humans. The Egglets are remarkably strong, carry heavy weights with their passengers, and are fierce in battle.

On a busy day, hundreds of these gracious fowl fly with Fe folk on their backs, carrying small building tools, food, goods to trade, and more. The sky is filled with squawks and shouts as the Egglets and the Fe Folk talk to each other in loud voices to be heard over the wind noise as they fly.

The Crone assigns the tribe of King Jake-kin and Queen Mistykin of Willow World to lead and support the inhabitants of Fe. The king, queen, and Lady Joy will later depart for the monastery to meditate alongside the other royals, while their tribe stays behind to work with the inhabitants of Fe and the Egglets.

A lone unicorn and a small group of pixies arrive with Joy. Her stature exudes a calm authority, naturally drawing the attention of everyone around her. A team of unicorns brings the other tribe members.

"Gather around. Our king and queen sent me to rally support

for our war efforts."

"There's going to be a great battle on the Southern shores," Joy tells the members of her tribe. "We need to prepare for war. Princess Elle, Strawberry, Pigtails, and Prince Jet are already at the Gathering Place preparing for the coming battles. We heard from a pixie that the Royals are arriving at the monastery. They'll enter a deep state of meditation to call down more magic from the heavens.

The Redland king, queen, and I will depart for the monastery shortly to join the royals in meditation, but Ladies Mercy, London, and Harlow, you'll remain to fight alongside the people of Fe and their Egglets. Lady Amberlyn is on assignment for the Crone, with Queen Seraphina and others going to the monastery. We're safe here in these valleys and mountains for now, but the darkness will invade us!" Joy says.

Joy is wearing a white gown and a finely tailored purple cloak with intricate gold patterns hand-stitched by craftspeople from the local village. Her sash is multicolored, jewelry, woven, and tied at the waist. Her appearance alone commands respect.

She looks at May. "You have spoken telepathically with King Wingstorm in the past. We need his help. Please call him."

May bows her head and goes to one knee. *Your Excellency*, she says in a mental whisper.

Your Excellency, are you here? she asks again.

Her stature exudes a calm authority, naturally drawing the attention of everyone around her. A team of unicorns brings the other tribe members.

"Gather around. Our king and queen sent me to rally support for our war efforts. There's going to be a great battle on the Southern shores," Joy tells the members of her tribe.

"We need to prepare for war. Princess Elle, Strawberry, Pigtails, and Prince Jet are already at the Gathering Place preparing for the coming battles. We heard from a pixie that the Royals are arriving at the monastery. They'll enter a deep state of meditation to call down more magic from the heavens. The king, queen, and I will depart for the monastery shortly to join the royals in meditation, but Ladies Mercy, London, and Harlow, you'll remain to fight alongside the people of Fe and their Egglets. Lady Amberlyn is on assignment for the Crone, with Queen Seraphina and others going to the monastery. We're safe here in these valleys and mountains for now, but the darkness will invade us!" Joy says.

Joy is wearing a white gown and a finely tailored purple cloak with intricate gold patterns hand-stitched by craftspeople from the local village. Her sash is multicolored, jeweled, woven, and tied at the waist. Her appearance alone commands respect.

She looks at May. "You have spoken telepathically with King Wingstorm in the past. We need his help. Please call him."

May bows her head and goes to one knee. *Your Excellency*, she says in a mental whisper.

Your Excellency, are you here? she asks again.

A mystical creature resembling an eagle with mighty wings, long feathers, and a full plumage of varied colors approaches from the sky. His wings flutter swiftly, flapping as he lands on the solid ground.

Who calls me? Eldrin Wingstorm, King of the bird realm, asks in a powerful, telepathic voice.

Your highness, it's May. I spoke with you once before when we needed help with some construction. We need your help again. The darkness and the Obligoo are approaching all the royal kingdoms. We're preparing to battle them on the shores of the Gathering

Place, but we need to get there quickly. Can you help us?

I know about the invasion. I'll send my best Egglets warriors to take you. They will stay and fight. I'll also send the remaining force to join in the battle, King Wingstorm says in thought.

"We also need the children taken to a safe place," Lady Mercy whispers to May.

Mighty King, we need to protect our little ones. Please help us keep them safe.

The King lets out a loud, piercing screech and replies, No one in this kingdom can guarantee safety against this evil. But the safest place is the monastery. It's deep in the mountains with many hidden chambers. There will be defenders at the monastery and temple, King Wingstorm says in thought.

Eleven of the King Windstorm's finest Egglet warriors fly high in the sky from their perches on the distant mountaintops. They soar gracefully, wings stretched wide, gliding on gentle whiffs of air as they circle overhead. Then dive to the camp.

His Majesty, the good King Wingstorm, sent us to carry the children to the monastery and to stay with them, the lead Eaglet says in thought.

"Thank you for coming to our aid. The five children we told King Wingstorm about are in the City of Hope. Many of the others are at the Monastery already," May says.

Yes, we are aware of where they are at this time. Your pixies gave us this information. The lead Egglet thinks, *We'll be on our way. There is no need to talk aloud to us. You need only project your thoughts.*

They leap into the sky, startling the folks on the ground.

King Eldrin Wingstorm

"We must delay the invasion," Lady Mercy says firmly, her gaze sweeping over the leaders. "Princess Elle and her people need time to prepare."

"But we have a more immediate problem. The front line of the darkness is slowly moving toward the Gathering Place. If they capture it, it'll be much easier for them to take over the entire kingdom," a pixie says to Mercy.

King Wingstorm hears the pixie's voice, then lets out a mighty shriek, calling his army to battle. Hundreds of Egglets emerge from dense trees, the peaks and slopes of the surrounding mountains.

His Majesty lets out another mighty shriek, and suddenly the entire army, with King Eldrin leading, ascends into the sky until they vanish from sight.

Unbeknownst to the king, the darkness slowly creeps towards the boundaries of Fe. This evil fog leisurely encroaches on the foothills, up the sides of the towering mountains, and slowly flows down valleys and over streams. It leaves the land stripped, trees charred, leaves scorched to dust, and once-vibrant and colorful foliage dead and blackened beneath a gray, breathless sky. Horrid shrieks, caws, and roars call from the midst of the darkness. The sounds are like cracking branches and hissing wind, as if the forest is alive and hates your presence.

It destroys trees, plants, and life, and the soil seethes with deadly bacteria. The weather is dank and dreary, and chilling winds blow. The distance looks murky and blurred. The stench is unbearable. It smells of sewage and rotting food.

The people of Fe tremble as the darkness approaches. It slithers into their lands like a silent predator.

Hundreds of pixies fly into the land of Fe. Unicorns with wings spread glide through the wind currents, carrying the Ladies Harlow, London, King Jake-kins, and Queen Misty of the Willow World.

"King Jake-kins, thank you for coming. I know you and the gracious Queen Misty can't fight the fog, but can you help us destroy any creature that emerges from the darkness?" Lady Mercy asks.

"We can do better than that, lady," he replies.

"Lady Harlow the Eloquent, we need your powerful voice. The darkness is almost upon us. Sing! For us," King Jake-kins roars.

"Yes, my lord, I know an Aria that confounds and confuses evil beings."

King Jake-kins steps next to Harlow. "Lady Harlow." His voice is calm, but his knuckles around his sword hilt are white. "They must hear your voice." The king places a hand on her shoulder. "You express in your song what they fear most — truth, and hope."

Harlow looks at Queen Misty, who nods with a soft, proud smile. "Let them remember the sound of joy."

Harlow takes a step forward, her boots sinking into the damp earth.

She closes her eyes and sings. The aria begins low and soft, like a lullaby wrapped in sunlight. It speaks of children's laughter in springtime, healing waters, and hands reaching across battle lines. Her voice climbs, rich with defiance.

Pained howls—high, ragged, furious screeches come from the darkness. Creatures shriek and turn on each other, writhing and screeching as the lyrics of hope and kindness sear through them like fire.

The mist recoils.

When the last note falls silent, the world is still.

Queen Misty steps forward, takes Harlow's hand, and raises it high. "You changed the tide, my child."

Harlow's eyes glisten. "Only for a moment."

"Yes," says the queen. "But sometimes a moment is all we need."

HRH Misty takes Lady Harlow's hand, holds her arms up in victory, and shouts, "The darkness is dissipating, and the creatures are retreating." She looks at Harlow, smiles, and says, "We won a battle, my child, but winning the war will be next to impossible."

"Lady London, we need to spread the word to meet at the Gathering Place with your followers. Queen Misty and I are going to the Monastery to join the other royals for meditation," King Jake-kins says.

CHAPTER THIRTEEN
ENCHANTED ISLE

Enchanted Isle

A stationary hurricane swirls in the distance over the ocean, creating impenetrable winds. It shields the path to enter the Enchanted Isles. The entrance is through the eye of the hurricane after a village elder from the Enchanted Isle casts a spell to grant passage into the kingdom. The winds from the hurricane will continue, but the eye will expand to allow people and magical creatures to enter. Some say this hurricane has a mind of its own.

The islands are protected by reefs that shift shape at night and can only be navigated by someone who speaks the language of the coral. Giant clams, bioluminescent squid, and sharks patrol the waters protected by the sacred reefs.

Over a thousand seasons ago, sorcerers created this twisting vortex to conceal the path to the Enchanted Isles. The ancient wizards wanted to hide the beautiful Enchanted Isles from any evil attacks.

Most people can only enter and exit through the eye of the never-ending hurricane. An ancient wizard also created a magical passageway in the mouth of a deep cave on the main island, leading to the City of Hope.

Most islands are small, and some are even tiny. They have abundant coconut, guava, and mango trees, among other fruits, which the tribes harvest for their use. Vegetables grow well in the rich valley soil on the main island, and fish are plentiful.

A beautiful blue sea stretches to the horizon, its surface glowing with shades of sapphire and turquoise. In the warm sunlight, the water sparkles and ripples softly in the breeze.

The ancestors were seafaring. No one knows their origin, but the people know they come from an ancient lineage. The inhabitants of the Emerald Isle are human, but they are small in stature.

They waged war against one another over territory, food, and treasure, sometimes over matters so trivial they were barely remembered. The battles were brutal, leaving trails of blood and countless innocents dead or defiled. These conflicts dragged on for many seasons.

Weary of the endless bloodshed, the elders of the main island reached out to the Mage Council in desperation. In response, a pixie arrived bearing a message for the elders to speak with Queen Sandra and ask for her aid.

* * *

The queen, HRH Queen Sandra, is on a bench draped with soft fur in her quiet castle. Her eyes are closed, and her breath is steady; she's in deep meditation. The stone meditation chamber is filled with soft candlelight and the scent of burning herbs.

Suddenly, a voice speaks into her ear.

"Queen Sandra," it whispers. "The Emerald islanders need you."

She opens her eyes. A tiny pixie hovers before her, glowing faintly, wings humming like a dragonfly. "They're tearing each other apart," the pixie says.

HRH, Queen Sandra's eyes furrow. She calls her fastest pixies. "Tell James and Jean they're needed in the Enchanted Isles."

My sons will take care of this problem, she thinks. "Tell Lord Jean and Lord James to help end their wars and bring peace and stability to their society. Dispatch a squadron of our finest soldiers to help restore order. Tell them to take those who are adept in battle but also fair-minded."

* * *

"The pixie from mother told us we must go to each island, take our squadron, and bring peace to the Emerald Isles," Lord James says.

Lord Jean replies, "Yes, mom trusts us with this important task but things are never easy with some of those islanders. We need to be just with the people and protect them. But some will need to be exiled. The islanders know we won't tolerate war."

Lord James Dean replies, "We need to go to each Island with our demands and a show of force, until we achieve our goal of peace. I know we'll have to exile some people if they don't accept our demand for peace."

The islanders saw how effective the magistrates and the squadrons are in bringing peace to their islands. In less than a season, they changed their ways and began trading instead of looting.

* * *

The main island rises from the ocean like a dream made real. Towering palms sway gently in the warm breeze, their fronds whispering above hibiscus and thick ferns. The air is thick with the scent of salt, fruit, and earth, and the sound of birdsong mingles with the rhythmic crash of waves on the shore. The sea around the Island glows in shades of turquoise and deep blue, teeming with life beneath its surface.

Mistress Tori tumbles head-first onto the ground. Moments later, Abby Moonchild and Lady Narriah fall next to each other. Soon, the rest of the group and attendants who joined them from The City of Hope fall like rain onto the sandy beach.

"I'm glad the hurricane pulled us off the unicorns and dropped us safely on the main island," Narriah says.

"Look at how many islands are scattered on the ocean. It takes your breath away," Abby says excitedly.

The Enchanted Isles' pristine beaches invite you to dig your feet into the warm sand. White foamy waves pound the shore, revealing sand crabs squirming to dig back into the sand from the receding wave. The weather is nice and warm year-round.

Inhabitants of Emerald Isle live in villages with huts made of woven palms and bamboo, nestled between the trees. The roofs are covered with palm leaves tied together, and woven mats cover the floor, providing insulation and comfort to the inhabitants.

The cuisine is vibrant and diverse. Pork and other meats are slow cooked in an underground oven known as an Imu. As the pig roasts, a sweet and earthy aroma of the taro leaves, banana leaves, and other native plants created by the Imu Oven fill the air. The irresistible smell of the tender, succulent, and seasoned pork, as it cooks to perfection, is a mouthwatering experience.

They enjoy a variety of diverse and flavorful cuisines, such as breadfruit, a starchy fruit that can be roasted, baked, or boiled. They have an abundance of poke from raw fish. Tropical fruits include pineapple, mango, papaya, and bananas. They also enjoy a salmon salad made with salted salmon, tomatoes, onions, and chili peppers.

A fresh breeze cools you from the sweltering heat of the day. The water is warm for swimming and diving, and it is crystal clear.

* * *

A man dressed in only a loincloth and a hat made of palm

leaves approaches. "Hello. Come, hurry; I'm Kaito, our Chief awaits you," the elder says.

"How did you know we're coming?" Princess Tori asks. "Our pixies brought news of your arrival. The network of pixies is spreading fast with the coming devastation brought by the Obligoo and his minions. The pixies are a big help by doing reconnaissance and passing messages. They can traverse magical barriers. They travel easily to the City of Hope, Karlek, and more. Our pixies frequently communicate with Commander Elle, Prince Jet, and the others in leadership," the elder says. "I've never seen the pixies this well-organized.

We are prepared to send our warriors to battle with you against the evil darkness and the hordes of despicable creatures that threaten to permeate our peaceful society. We will keep some warriors here to protect us in case the miscreants attack us. Many warriors are secluded on distant islands," he continues. "It's a pity so many splendid warriors were confined after the Ice Cream War."

"A war over ice cream? Here in this tropical paradise? How is that possible?" Mistress Tori asks, her brows furrowing in disbelief.

"A witch visited us to see how our communities growth was progressing. She told us she helped reestablish these communities after the devastation of past seasons. She brought a tub of ice cream, kept frozen by her magic. It was so delicious, word of it spread like lightning. She brought several for the other islanders. Two of our young men started a rumor that we were hoarding ice cream on the main island. It was hilarious to see them talking about it. It became a game with them, but there was no ice cream in reality. They told many islanders there was a hidden stash under a waterfall on the main island. But when other islanders heard there was ice cream, it almost caused a war."

The elder smiles and chuckles. "It was amusing to see the two young men talk about it with such excitement. They turned it into a game when they realized none existed on the Island. They spread rumors among the islanders, saying there was a hidden stash of ice cream beneath the waterfall. At first, it was all good fun, but soon others heard about the supposed treasure, and chaos ensued. It almost led to an actual war. We told them it was a misunderstanding, and when their Chief heard our story, he couldn't stop laughing. But they had already hurt many good islanders trying to get to that ice cream. So, we banished the guilty ones to islands far from us," the Elder says.

Mistress Tori glares at him. "Yes, it is funny, but let's return to the war. Okay?"

"Yes, yes, of course. Come with me," the Elder replies.

"Is the weather this pleasant all Summer?" Mistress Tori asks admiring the warm sunshine and foliage.

"We are blessed to live in such a beautiful realm. But we face challenges from some people in the outlying islands who raid our supplies at night. That's why we invited your cousins to help us. They did such a good job, we asked them to make our land their home and join the elders," he says.

"Why did you select these two magistrates to help instead of a royal or a Mage?" Mistress Tori asks.

"We heard they served in a small community in their Realm as Magistrates. Our pixie told us they were kind, just, and confident in their abilities. We were exhausted from the wasteful wars and carnage, so we called them to help us bring order to our society. Lord Jean Pierre and Lord James Dean brought their acolytes. The Bear, a strong young man, and Squire Robert, whose skill with the swords is unmatched," he says. "Look. Here comes Teva and his warriors. They'll be a big help. He's the oldest son of that generation and the strongest member of their tribe. He's also their Chief and our ally," the elder says.

Teva steps off his magnificent boat, a large ship that resembles a giant leaf woven from the bark of sky trees, and unfurls sails made from the wings of giant fallen butterflies. "Where's your commander?"

Indignant, Tori says, "Well, hello! She's at the front. Preparing for the battle."

Teva is fuming. "You have a woman leading this army? Are you crazy? I'm going to take charge."

Teva slowly turns to his warriors. He looks back at the group. Then shouts, "Prepare to depart our Emerald Isle. We're going to war!"

"At least he's on our side," the elder says.

Their huts are made from bamboo and palm leaves. In the center of their village, a long hut serves as a meeting and gathering place.

A dignified elderly woman, dressed in a feathered cloak, approaches them. "We heard about Jean Pierre and James Dean's leadership qualities. We needed them to bring order from the chaos. They and their squadron weeded out many of the guilty warmongers. They are fair in their judgment but issue harsh punishments to the offenders. Through their diligent efforts, the Enchanted Isle is now the peaceful paradise it once was. They've gone to fight in the war, but our peace endures."

Alcyra, Chief of the largest island tribe, the Alakulas, stands before many of the island's leaders. Some are in their boats offshore, while others crowd the beach.

"Our paradise is threatened by creatures from the abyss and the deadly fog approaching the lands. Several realms have already been devastated by this attack on the homelands." Chief Alcyra of the Alakula Tribe addresses his people. "There will be a great battle between the realms and the evil that approaches. We all need to join in to protect our kingdom. The battle is far now, but it'll come closer to us until it engulfs our homeland," the chief continues. "Sharpen your spears; we're going to war!"

A roar issues from the top of the hurricane as thousands of deadly winged creatures attempt to swarm the eye. They become trapped and shredded at the mouth of the hurricane, trying to breach deadly winds.

"There's nothing to worry about yet. They can't get past the hurricane's eye at this time, but they will eventually overwhelm it and open the path to our society. They may also find the secret entrances when they battle with the Rooters," Chief Alcyra says. Magical flying canoes land on the beach. "Our canoes have arrived. Send pixies to the other islands. Tell them we're preparing for war," the Chief tells his military commander. "Tell them to meet us at the Gathering Place."

CHAPTER FOURTEEN
THE BARREN LANDS

The Barren Lands

A majestic herd of flying unicorns, with their wizard riders, land gracefully on soft, grassy terrain atop a cliff overlooking a lush valley. The sky is a deep blue, and a gentle breeze touches their skin. The steeds feast on the succulent grass and seek the tallest patches of greenery, enjoying every bite.

Wizards Cynthia, Lady Amberlyn, and Jenn dismount from their unicorns and look over the cliff to the fertile valley below.

Lady Amberlyn stands on the cliff's edge, admiring the colors. Tall trees sway in the wind, a sparkling stream weaves through the undulating hills, and greenery blankets the land below the cliff. A delicate breeze brushes past her face, bringing a faint hint of fragrance from wildflowers.

"Do people live in that valley?" Amberlyn asks.

Cynthia gazes at the sky and then at the basin below. "We don't know if people live there."

She looks at the sky again, "We have a long way to the Barren Lands, but a pixie asked us to wait here. Ah, here she comes."

A regal white unicorn with shimmering iridescent wings and a mane that reflects sunlight descends onto the cliff's edge. This unicorn wears intricate hand-crafted armor that gleams like polished platinum.

Jenn runs to the unicorn as the rider dismounts and jumps into her arms, tears running down her face. "Auntie Gwynneth. I'm so glad you're safe."

Auntie Gwynneth feels warm and hugs Jenn. She holds her head to auntie's chest as tears of relief run down her niece's face, wetting auntie's blouse. "We visited some village farmers on the way. It felt good to walk on the ground that produces food. The villagers invited us to dinner. It was a lovely evening. I was never in danger, especially with Queen Seraphina looking out for me."

Auntie Gwynneth continues, "Our pixies told us it would be a few more days before you arrive, so we also visited the village of Ai in the north. There are rumors among the pixies that many of the villagers from Ai have allowed evil to enter their hearts and minds. The rumors are true. We saw serious division among the townsfolk."

Her Royal Highness whinnies.

Auntie Gwynneth gently strokes the queen's neck. "Yes, Your Highness, crossing the wasteland won't be easy." Auntie Gwynneth looks over at the valley. "Let's go."

Seraphina takes the lead, followed by the other beautiful unicorns with the three riders on their backs. Powerful hooves thunder against the ground as the group gains momentum. They unfurl their iridescent wings and lift, flying together in a pack, rising higher, following their queen, Seraphina. They ascend until they reach the cloud cover and level off.

They dive and fly over rolling hills, grasslands, and lakes at tremendous speed. The herd safely takes its wizard riders over turbulent winds. They move in a group, almost as if they are one mind, and communicate with each other telepathically in simple words.

They swoop down to skim across a lake at incredible speed. In their wake, frightened fish leap from the water, mistaking them for predators.

Seraphina leads them over a dense forest of tall birch trees. The bark's sweet, fresh aroma fills the air.

"Up. Over the mountain," she says.

The unicorns neigh, flap their wings, and soar like a stampede in the sky. The wizards hold the manes tightly as the herd soars and glides in tight formation as it flies through tight valleys, up cliffs, and over hills.

"Up," Queen Seraphina says.

They flap their wings harder and go vertically at breathtaking speed, soaring over a mountain. Each unicorn is in sync with the others in their moves and speed.

"There," the lead unicorn says.

They dive over the mountain into a dark fog.

The unicorns' survival instincts make them reluctant to land on forsaken ground.

Howling winds, uprooted trees, scattered debris, and frequent earthquakes all contribute to the desolation of the expanding barren landscape. Dark clouds cover the valley most of the day, preventing the sunlight needed for vegetation to grow. The air is filled with the smell of ash and decay.

Tortured shrieks and jagged caws of Black Buzzards fill the air, their origin unseen, as the herd flies past overhead.

They cross over a vast sulfurous swamp with a strong odor that almost overwhelms the unicorns and wizards.

Dark clouds blanket the sky above a depressing, lifeless, devastated valley. They come to a vertical mountain cliff made of sheer rock.

The ground is uneven and pitted with holes and puddles of filthy water. A mist covers the squishy ground, and each step stirs up the murky ground fog. Slithering creatures swim in the deeper pools of rancid water and crawl on the mud.

They have no choice but to land in the filthy swamp.

Chiseled into this wall of sheer rock is a door with no handle or visible way to open it.

They're surprised when the door slowly opens and slides on crushed rocks.

"We didn't open that door. Something or someone is coming through. It may be an evil creature. Prepare yourselves," Auntie Gwynneth says as she takes a long knife from the side holster in Seraphina's armor.

There is complete silence except for the sounds of the Marshglass Dragonflies and occasional cricket.

"This is the entrance to an ancient monastery. Wizards once existed in the monastery deep in these mountains." Auntie Gwynneth says as the stone door slowly opens. "They practiced ancient magic spells and communicated with other warlocks from other dimensions telepathically."

The chiseled door creaks, making a rough grinding sound of gravel crunching against rock. Dust falls from the sides of the mountain until the door is fully opened.

A tall, gangly, old mage clad in shabby clothing hobbles out of the cave to greet them.

"Hey. Hello. Hello, you arrived," the mage says in a crackling voice.

"How did you know we were coming?" Wizard Cynthia asks.

"I dreamed you would arrive, and here you are. I know the reason you came. Sadly, so few of us are left to help fight those creatures. Fortunately, villagers will fight the wicked creatures along with you and your people. Be careful with the villagers from Ai. We heard rumors that the Obligoo's followers may have infiltrated this village. We're unsure if it's the Obligoo or a darker, more sinister evil controlling the minions ravaging our land."

The man shuffles away. "Follow me. The old monastery lies deep in the mountainous caverns beyond the hall. An ancient door leading to the school and living rooms deep in this mountain is made from beams of the hardest wood in the realms, Jatoba wood," the old mage says, chuckling.

Lady Cynthia thinks, *That wasn't funny. He's a strange one.*

The old mage walks towards a large meeting room. This room is called Chapter House. It was the meeting room of the wizard councils in the past. "Stay focused and keep moving. We have much to discuss."

Dusty scrolls lay on the floor, table, and shelves. Hundreds of candles on the walls and tables provide the needed light.

Queen Seraphina whinnies.

The old mage rubs Seraphina's neck. "Yes, your Highness. You and your team can join the others in the Gathering Place. Thank you for keeping them safe. I called others to take them when they leave." He tells the group, "Follow me! Hurry."

The old mage continues, "I'm head of the Office of Magic and Headmaster of the Mage School. Sadly, the school has been closed since last summer. We had too few students. Many of our members have gone elsewhere. I can only send two mages to help with the war. They are graduates from my school. Master Eli is a forger of mighty weapons. He can create weapons that are never dull. Mage Nico is a friend of the Animal Kingdom. It's said Master Nico can talk with the animals, and they do his bidding."

Two mages walk into the Great Room following an old woman. She says nothing. She walks past the group and disappears into an adjoining room.

The old mage says, "Greetings, Masters Eli and Nico."

Master Eli joins in the conversation. "We got your message, but it was through a lone pixie."

The old mage puts his forefinger on his chin. He then taps his chin. "Hmm. I was wondering where that pixie went."

"You didn't receive my telepathic messages? Hmm. That dragon must have intercepted them. It's capable of entering our thoughts if we let it."

"You mean the Obligoo?" Jenn asks.

"No, the one that resembles a giant, dragon-like worm," he replies.

"I think he saw the Obligoo," Lady Kaylee whispers.

The old mage glares at them, his eyebrows furrowed, cheeks flushed, and nose large and pockmarked. "There are worse things in this world than that purple creature. You have much to learn, young masters," the old mage warns.

He turns and hobbles away from the group.

Lady Amberlyn whispers to the others, "Do we follow him?"

"Come with me," he snaps.

At the room's far end, a secret door lies partially concealed behind tattered tapestries and long-abandoned, dust-covered furniture. The edges are visible, but only an eye trained in magic can see the outline of this enchanted entrance to the hidden temple.

The old Mage continues, "Many of the royals, some of whom are your parents, are here meditating. Please do not interfere with them. We need the royals to devote their full concentration to calling down magic. You can wait until they take breaks from meditating. As the head of the new Mage Council, I'll assign some of the older wizards to the monastery to join the Royals for meditation. The pixies will take care of their needs."

Wizard Cynthia looks at the others, perplexed. "Did you say, the Mage Council?"

"Didn't you listen to the Crone when she visited your city?" The mage lifts his cane and jabs it horizontally at Wizard Cynthia's arm. With each sharp poke, he speaks slowly, punctuating every word, "Focus. Keep your mind on the here and now and remember the Crone's words."

"The temple door was sealed to all, long before I was born. Only the royals—or one of their heirs— can open it again. Only their bloodline can unlock the temple and cross its threshold. The scrolls are clear on this."

The old Mage continues, "Young Lady Amberlyn, the crone elevated you to Wizard. You and Lady Crystal will remain in the monastery to meditate with the other royals. Crystal, the gift of peace you possess will bring serenity to the monastery as the royals meditate."

He glances at them, smiles, and shuffles toward the front

entrance. There stands a herd of six thornycorns. "I could help you by calling these lovely creatures. They've agreed to take you into battle," the old mage says. The head thornycorn butts the old mage. "Hey, stop that. I know you're thornycorns and not creatures. You're so sensitive." The mage smiles at the group. "The thornycorns are ready to go any time you want," he says.

Master Nico interjects, "You know I can speak and understand the languages of the Animal Kingdom, don't you?"

The head thornycorn bumps the old mage with its head again.

"I know you're hungry," the old mage says. "Yes, yes, we all know you can speak with animals, young mage."

Master Nico rubs a thornycorn's neck and whispers to the animal, "There will be plenty of long green grass where we're going."

Mage Nico speaks softly to the thornycorn using kind and gentle words. He brushes the animal's neck, reaches into his pocket, pulls out a piece of fruit, and gives it to the steed.

"This thornycorn is mine."

CHAPTER FIFTEEN
THE STEPPES

The Steppes

The Steppes are an expansive region of rolling hills, grassy plains, and open landscapes. Treeless and windswept, they stretch from the Northern Sea to forested hills and lush valleys in the distant east.

The region's ecosystem has been shaped by its extreme climate, characterized by scorching summers and bitterly cold winters. Despite the dry conditions, hardy grasses, wildflowers, and shrubs flourish across the plains. Life here is rooted in a nomadic tradition, with herders moving across the landscape. Their homes are called yurts, circular, portable dwellings scattered like footprints across the Steppes.

The inhabitants are fierce warriors in battle and pastoral nomads who herd sheep, camels, and goats that graze freely in the surrounding countryside. They value family, freedom, love, and faith in their God.

The country features vast elevated land areas, including plateaus, mountains, and hills.

While much of the region is treeless, scattered forested areas can be found near rivers, in sheltered valleys, and along the edges of mountain ranges. The combined scent of larch, birch, and pine creates a rich forest aroma.

Jonathan remembers the directive the Crone gave him at the city of Hope. Lord Jonathan, I elevate you to the rank of a wizard with the title of Marquis. You will lead your tribe and the nomadic people of the steppes into battle.

Lord Jonathon sits atop his mighty steed and addresses the people of the Steppes. "Dear friends, we have known each other for many seasons. My parents have ruled these steppes with great fondness all that time. Many of you and the tribal leaders are old friends. I come to you at a time of great sadness.

The evil creature, Azaz rears its ugly head, unleashing countless minions from the Abyss.

They're bent on destroying our lands and homes. The Crone, head of the mage council, sent me to lead our people into battle against an evil that will consume our beloved plains.

He hesitates and draws a deep breath. "We must stand with the other realms, not as divided tribes, but as one people. The steppes are our home, and now our land is threatened by a darkness that seeks to claim it. If we do nothing, our lands, our way of life—everything we hold dear—will be lost."

Jonathan is interrupted by a high-pitched, sharp screech from the mighty King Wingstorm. The King majestically soars high over the Plains' army. He lets out a piercing shriek, calling the unholy Obligoo to battle.

The Obligoo and King Eldrin crash into each other, clawing and biting. They fall and roll on the hills covered with dense forest. They crush the enormous trees with their massive bodies. Tree trunks break like twigs under the bodies of the king and the giant monster, Obligoo.

They break, flying in opposite directions. Both turn and slam into each other. Blood runs down the King's neck onto his wings.

Throwing back his head, Wingstorm shrieks into the sky—a wild, piercing cry—before launching into flight after the creature from the Abyss.

King Wingstorm hovers in the sky as the Obligoo rises from the sea.

They fight with all their strength over the ocean. He grabs the creature with his sharp, powerful claws. He bites the Obligoo with his sharp beak so hard that the Obligoo screams in pain but breaks away and flies from the king. Blood pours from the Obligoo's neck as he flies into the air, splashing it on the good King Eldrin's face. The creature dives into King Eldrin's chest. But the King's muscles are tight, and his heart is strong; he withstands the attack but feels a sudden sharp jab at his side from the tail of the vile creature.

The sharp point of Obligoo's tale is poisonous. It excretes a deadly toxin when it stabs the King's side. The jab brings a searing heat that radiates from the wound, spreading like fire under his skin. A few drops of this poison are enough to shut down the king's vital organs. King Wingstorm falls backward as his wings lose their strength.

He calls out, "One last time," and thrusts his powerful claws at the Obligoo's neck, killing it.

The monster's eyes go blank.

King Eldrin and the dead Obligoo fall and sink into the depths of the sea.

"I'll come back stronger than before, and all will hear my words," the king's whispers reach Lord Jonathan at the Steppes, as death overtakes him.

Tears build in Jonathan's eyes as he realizes the demise of the mighty King Wingstorm. He wipes the tears away with the back of his right hand.

Jonathan, Marquis of the Steppes, sits on his thornycorn. We must rid the evil from our plains.

A pixie lands on his shoulder and whispers into his ear, "Lord Jonathon, Marquis of the Great Plains, Commander Elle, sent us to call the people of the steppes to war. The Obligoo is dead, but his minions remain. They are now stronger and fiercer than ever."

Lord Jonathon turns to his siblings. "Acolytes, Mia and Chloe, this beautiful land gives us life and satisfies all our needs. The rolling hills, the blue sky above, vegetation, animals, and thousands of bird species bring our kingdom a natural and spiritual beauty."

The Marquis continues. "We must protect our beloved Steppes and the kingdom from the vile creatures that plague our world. Chloe, Mia — you're of age, trained well, and passed all your exams for knighthood. Do you accept the rank of knight and your charge to the Steppes?"

Both Mia and Chloe say, "Yes."

"Should we go on one knee?" Chloe asks.

"You're funny. We kneel when the Crone asks. You only need to agree to this ranking and to lead squadrons into battle."

* * *

Fear and panic set into the hearts and minds of the steppes villagers, the pixies, and the army as they watched King Eldrin Wingstorm battle the Obligoo in the sky.

Lord Jonathan soars above the villages with his acolytes, their unicorns streaking through the sky. They shout commands and words of encouragement to the people below.

"Sharpen your swords! Gather your provisions! Follow us into battle!" the marquis cries to the people of the steppes from atop his winged steed.

The great host of the steppes begins its long march toward distant fields of war.

CHAPTER SIXTEEN
THE MONASTERY AND TEMPLE

The Monastery and Temple with the Griffin

Squadrons of Rooters, pixies, and humans arrive in waves, summoned from across the realms to defend the ancient monastery and the temple.

The Rooters, clad in chain-link armor and wielding steel weapons, take positions among the outer rocks and lower slopes. Their senses are attuned to every tremor in the earth. As they walk in cadence toward the monastery, their knee-high boots crunch against the pebbled pathway.

The leaves in the trees whisper songs as a gentle breeze stirs them. The Rooter squadron is tired from their long march to the monastery, but the crisp morning air is refreshing. The sun is rising, bringing new hope to the defenders of the monastery and temple.

Pixies zip through the air in tight, glowing clusters, their sharp eyes and nimble flight make them ideal scouts and messengers.

The humans come in disciplined units, bearing steel weapons. They build outposts, reinforce passageways, and station lookouts along every approach.

The temple remains sealed, its golden door cold, but something stirs beyond it. It's a faint rustle, a whisper of motion. Then there's silence.

Lady Kaylee touches the door with her palm. "My father told me these temple doors were always open at one time. There is magic stored in that temple. The temple was sealed when the evil ones first approached our land."

The monastery rises as an ancient edifice carved into the mountain's bowels. Its vaulted stone halls extend deep into the rock. It's a place of quiet discipline, with winding corridors and rooms for meetings, study, sleep, and the careful storage of knowledge. Torches flicker along the walls, casting dancing shadows on stone.

The wall separating the temple from the monastery stands silent, immense, and sealed. Its great doors are made from hard Lingum wood, which is dark greenish-brown and has subtle stripe patterns. The door sills are forged from golden metal and intricately decorated with unknown symbols.

"No hand has opened the Temple in centuries. When the beasts attack, they'll try to open the temple door from here," The old mage says.

The wizards, Crystal, Amberlyn, Kaylee, and Cynthia, arrive silently.

Lady Amberlyn gazes up at the vaulted ceiling, whose arches curve like the ribs of a giant ancient beast. The others look up, admiring the monastery's grandeur.

"I did not know the monastery is this large, and the architecture is this impressive," she says, looking up.

Crystal's eyes are drawn to an old leather scroll sprawled across a cluttered table. Strange glyphs mark its top edge, etched in ink and shimmering faintly, as if resisting the dust of ages. Around it lay a scattered mess of books and manuscripts, yellowed by time; their pages curled like dry leaves. A long-dead lamp rests on its side as though toppled in haste.

"I'm glad that lamp is empty. The oil could cause a fire," Crystal says, crossing the room to the table. She opens the folio. A line reads: "Love is your power."

The old mage approaches. "This is the lost folio. You will need it to open the temple. When they attack, it will be through that door," he says, pointing to the main entrance.

Crystal asks, "There are so many kinds of love, what does it really mean?"

The old mage replies, "Love is everywhere. When you show kindness to an animal, that too is love. You love your parents, your siblings, but each love is different, shaped by who they are and who you are. The Crone sealed the monastery's front door permanently with ancient magic, ensuring no one could enter or escape from that door. The only entrance now is that door. There are hidden passageways that have yet to be explored. The entrance to the temple is hidden behind the climbing roses and vines growing on the temple walls. You'll have to find it and read the spell in this folio. It'll open the Temple doors," he says.

As defenses rose, pixies whispered of a great assembly forming at the shores.

ACT 03

CHAPTER SEVENTEEN
THE GATHERING PLACE

Various villagers enjoying the Gathering Place before the battles

The Gathering Place stretches from the northernmost coast to the steppes on the opposite side of the Eastern Mountains, and to the Southern Shores. It is wisely managed by the Ladies, Parker and Danna. Under their care, the Gathering Place thrives—not just as a region, but as a living example of what can happen when the community is cherished.

In the East lies a beautiful, lush valley between two mountain ranges, filled with trees, vibrant flora, and lush vegetation. Animal life thrives in this wonderland. Flocks of birds chirp arias of hope and love in the ancient star language.

Small townships dot the realms, from the Northern Sea to the distant south. Wolves and other predatory animals live in the wild but shy away from human settlements or villages. Flocks of birds caw and squawk as they soar overhead, and the melodious chirping of nesting birds in the trees fills the air.

The Gathering Place stretches wide with open grasslands, scattered trees, and vibrant flora. Its western edge meets the shore of a calm sea. It stretches wide with open grasslands, scattered trees, and vibrant flora. Its western edge meets the shore of a calm sea.

Tribes meet at the Gathering Place for commerce, to practice religious rites, and to conduct marriages. It's now an assembly where the diverse villagers, Rooters, Wizards, Sky Folk, Villagers, Karlek, and Emerald Isle Folk meet to plan the upcoming battle.

The large influx of people gathering for war creates a good market for the vendors. However, the fear of the impending war pervades The Gathering Place. Markets bustle with activity as people socialize, chat, buy, sell, and haggle, but most are anxious about the coming evil.

Over one hundred shops form a maze-like layout that offer everything from spices and dried fruits to fresh seafood, produce, meats, building materials, and household goods.

In the vibrant atmosphere of the Gathering Place, rich fragrances fill the air, and each scent tells a story of culture, craft, or the land itself.

Teachers take their children on school trips to compete in sports, water activities, and stickles. The game of Stickles originates from the old Rooter culture. The child holds an egg in a saucer at the end of the stick. They must run from one base to another without dropping the egg. Children may not touch the runner; however, they can distract the runner using gestures or sounds. Whoever finishes first and keeps the egg intact must scramble all the eggs in a pan with beans, sweet carrots, rambutangeos, sour peaches, and ketchup.

The Rambutangeo Tangle is the name of this delicious snack. The Rambutangeo fruit can only be harvested in the moonlight to preserve its delicious sweetness. It tastes like a mix between lychee, passionfruit, and honey. The aftertaste leaves a cooling tingle on the tongue. The children enjoy this sweet appetizer before dinner. First bite goes to the winner.

Thousands of villagers, Rooters, apprentice wizards, Throags, and pixies come together at the Gathering Place during these thrilling events. The pixies use the occasion to reunite with friends and far-flung kin, their laughter filling the air. Even the Pixie Queen arrives to greet her subjects and witness the grand performance put on by the Throags and their pixie partners. It is a time of joy and celebration for all.

But as the final act ends, a quiet shift takes hold. The playful sparkle in the pixies' eyes dims. War has come. Their cheer gives way to urgency—fear lingers, but there's no time to dwell. There is work to do.

Vendors sell a wide range of items, including woven baskets, plants, armor, and weapons. Behind the vendors is a village where talented blacksmiths, weavers, metalworkers, tailors, and many other skilled artisans create their pieces for sale. Villagers from many other townships bring items for sale or trade. The only currency is small gems, which can be used for everyday items. But most barter. Some large, precious jewels circulate in the villages from the mines in Hope. But they're difficult to sell in a barter economy. Kiosks of various colors and sizes sit side by side, with vendors hawking their wares.

The Gathering Place, a hub of tradition, trade, and culture, houses every guild. Among the many that have taken root here are the Merchant, Artisan, Herbalist, Hunter, and Fisher Folk Guilds, which shape both the economy and the cultural identity of the tribes.

Eli grasps his hammer, its head glowing with a soft, magical light. "I'll begin forging weapons for the army," he says. "We'll need every blade we can muster against our foes." He turns eyes serious but kind. "Lady Danna, the Crone, sent me a pixie. I'm to take you as my apprentice. I need a forge assistant. You offered to take more responsibility at the right time for me. I'll teach you swordplay and defense. Do you agree to taking this position?"

Lady Danna smiles. "Yes, Mage Eli. It would be an honor to work with you and learn the Forge Master's craft from you."

"Lady Danna, you must continue your wizardry studies and oversight of this place. The scrolls and spells you master will benefit in later seasons - if we survive. I know your sister will support us, working together."

"It's too bad you're at minimal strength, but we knew the gifts would mature slowly. Let's begin by making a powerful short sword you can keep at your side."

Mage Eli sits with Prince Jet and tribal elders at the gate to the market. They discuss military tactics, defense, and preparation for the inevitable attack on the Gathering Place.

Prince Jet approaches them and stands tall, looking like a true Prince of the Red Realm.

He speaks to the elders with an air of confidence. "I surveyed the gathering place. We have a defined exit through the valley in the east for children and the infirm. Some villagers started packing, anticipating the war."

"I'm impressed with the level of discipline the Throags display in training. They will be awesome in battle," Jet says. He continues, "Commander Elle will arrive here soon."

"Take a seat, young prince," a village elder says.

Mage Nico stands tall in the courtyard, surrounded by unicorns, thornycorns, and creatures of every kind. His voice is calm but firm as he speaks words of courage, preparing them for the battles that lie ahead.

I'm glad I cut all the hair off my head. I feel lighter and stronger. It won't get in my face in battle. I'm surprised they enshrined my hair under glass, Nico thinks.

"This vest allows me to send messages to animals at far distances," he explains to the anxious creatures, his voice steady and reassuring. "I'll call as many allies as I can to join us in this fight. We will be a formidable force. Unicorns, this is the great battle we dreaded for so many seasons. Your ancestors knew this evil would one day invade. They bred you through the generations to be the powerful unicorns you are today."

Loud whinnies fill the barn. Unicorns swing their heads joyfully at the words from mage Nico.

The proud winged Queen of the Unicorns, Seraphina, flies Commander Elle to the Gathering Place. They're flanked by four of the queen's strongest unicorns.

Elle approaches the elders at the front gate, feeling eyes of admiration and respect from the villagers.

"Tell the people to rest, but be diligent. We expect to be attacked by midday tomorrow. Now show me your defenses," she says with confidence.

The Gathering Place Map

Southwestern Shores

The Southwestern Shores becomes the central location for the main battles. Here, Elle's and Jet's elite warriors fight alongside the villagers against the evil Azaz and his minions.

The Battle in the North

Teva and his warriors, joined by many villagers whose farms had been destroyed, prepared for combat. The destruction of their homes unites the villagers and warriors in a common cause, strengthening their resolve to fight.

CHAPTER EIGHTEEN
THE WAR OF AZAZ: THE KINGDOM'S LAST STAND

"Every one of them must be destroyed," Azaz hisses, his venomous whisper slithering through the minds of his wicked minions.

His eyes burn with cold, malevolent fire as he gazes upon the distant lights of the mortal realm.

Azaz was once beautiful and beloved by all. But he became proud and wanted more. He wanted to rule all the kingdoms and realms, but the people rejected him long ago. A group of early wizards exiled him to the deep evil realm at the bottom of the deepest ocean.

Darkness engulfs the shore as a murky fog slowly approaches from the sea. Gray, bulbous clouds obscure the rising sun. Thunder explodes overhead, and bolts of lightning flash across the sky.

General Ennis stands a full five feet tall atop a cliff overlooking the Gathering Place. "Warriors, prepare your shields, both large and small. We will soon march to battle."

The Rooter army erupts in cheers, their swords clashing rhythmically against their shields. Villagers join in, their voices rising in a loud, spirited celebration.

They await the coming battles. Some tremble in silence, while others wear a mask of false pride.

Thousands of malicious creatures burst forth from the ocean's depths and begin their trip to the shore. The unbroken stream of minions flooding the land feels endless.

The Oozemorans are among the many creatures from the realm of evil. These gelatinous entities are giant pustular sacks of entrails that move like a glob of gelatin. They roll over their adversaries to devour them into their glutinous bodies. The Oozemorans immediately digest their prey.

Nasties are short, smelly, and have razor-sharp teeth and scales. They crawl on four legs and have threads between their toes, which allows them to swim underwater.

A frightening creature, the fearless Mocktok, twice the size of the tallest king, emerges from the ocean's waves. It stands with its shoulders bent, an angry scowl, and sharpened fangs to tear the flesh off its adversary. It stomps onto the beach, splashing water with each step. The Mocktok lifts its arms into the air, letting out a fearsome roar.

All the creatures from the Abyss fear and feel the pure hatred of the evil demon, Azaz.

At the command tent, Jet arrives riding a mat made of his threads, this floating thread mat works well and is fast. "I'll stay to help, Elle," he says.

"Jet, this is a dangerous place. You should be with the kids," she shouts.

Elle hears a voice whisper, Trust him. Your brother is your strongest ally.

He replies, "I can fight. My powers are growing fast, and I received my gift."

"Okay. I trust you, but if…"

"Yes, I know, big sister. I'll call if I need you."

Teva and his warriors arrive at the shores of the Gathering Place in long, powerful boats shaped like canoes but larger, reinforced to carry many men across treacherous seas. Crafted with ancient magic, the vessels can soar through the air, effortlessly crossing vast distances.

Teva stands tall at the prow of the lead vessel, a striking and menacing figure against the rising mist, but his heart is broken as he remembers his childhood.

Those buzzards wiped out my village. I'm going to avenge you, my family, he thinks.

Teva's nostrils flare as he walks on the shore. His eyes blaze with resolve, and his jaw is tight. His muscles are tense, ready to strike, and the air around him feels charged with anger.

He arrives with his warriors, walks to the command tent, stands with hands on hips, and states in a loud, arrogant voice, "I am Teva. I will take charge."

Tribal leaders, gathered in their command tent, consult the battle map, ignoring Teva.

"Our pixies tell us they think a large force will attack midday tomorrow," Elle says to the tribal leaders and wizards looking at the map. "They are converging here in the distant north," Elle says, pointing to a spot on the map.

What do I say to this man? Who does he think he is? Elle's temper flares.

Jet's fists ball at his side as his anger escalates, but he controls himself. Who is this guy?

Teva, his hands on his hips, bellows an order, "I am the only one who can lead this army to victory."

Jet's eyes narrow into a sharp stare as he glares at Teva.

Teva looks down at Elle.

Commander Elle takes charge of the problem. "Sir, we're honored to have you fight alongside us in this war. But I am in charge; if you don't like it, you can return to wherever you came from." He's such a creep. "Or you and your warriors can cover our Northern front, now!"

Elle points towards the north as her eyebrows are furrowed, her lips tighten, and she glares at Teva.

Teva is shocked and embarrassed.

Jet's jaw is tight with anger. His glare softens as he looks at Elle with pride.

The room is stunned into silence.

"I won't explain myself to you again, Mr. Teva. You can take your army to our Northern front now or return to where you came from," Commander Elle says. *Oh, God! Did I say that?*

Teva wonders, *How can someone so young question me with such strength? She can't be over thirteen seasons. Maybe it's an adult spirit in her body? Or a witch possesses her, and that's the reason she's so strong in her personality?*

"Very well! My warriors and I will defend and secure our lands in the North," he replies with arrogant pride.

Teva and his warriors

Teva walks out of the command tent, his face is crimson, embarrassed from having been put down by a young girl in front of the tribal leaders.

Teva, his army, and the survivors from the shattered realms have become a formidable force against the creatures of darkness on the northern shore.

"Look," Teva says, pointing to the shore.

An Oozemoran rolls out of the crashing waves onto the beach. Its viscous body forms legs to stand and walk on. It consumes a squadron of twenty of Teva's finest warriors. He directs his archers to shoot arrows of fire into the Oozemoran's body. It slows the creature but does not stop it.

Mages Eli and Nico soar over the encroaching Oozemoran.

"We've got this, Lord Teva," Mage Eli shouts.

He takes an enchanted spear from his side and throws it into the advancing gelatinous creature. It pins the creature to the sand as Mage Nico casts a light so bright that it blinds the creature. The Oozemoran casts about wildly, thrashing its arms as it struggles to unpin itself. Blind and disoriented, it strikes out in every direction.

Mage Eli remembers a past lesson on gelatinous creatures. He shouts, "The creature will turn into a gel, then melt from the spear and the blinding light. Look," he says, and points to the creature.

Its gelatinous body slowly becomes liquid until it is a glob floating and dissipating on the crashing waves.

Teva calls his people to battle. "They come earlier than we expected. Prepare for war," he shouts to his army and the villagers who have joined them. He orders his lead pixie, "Tell Commander Elle the invasion has begun."

The First Wave

"It's the terrible Nasties," a warrior shouts.

"Lord Ennis, they're early. Help them at the beach with the rooter army but leave a squadron here and be sure you have plenty of Barkelite," Elle shouts.

Commander Elle looks at Princess Tori. "Tori, go with Lord Ennis. He will need your help. Use your power of Chaos to confound the enemy. Ladies, Abby Moonchild and Naariah, you know the Root people well. You go with the army and fight alongside them," Elle instructs.

The power of her ancestors builds within her. The confrontation with Teva boosted her self-confidence. More importantly, her brave act unleashed magic, empowering her gift.

Sparks fly from her fingertips. I'm shooting sparks from my fingers. This must be my gift.

A rooter shouts, "A giant Mocktok is on the beach." "Swarm it," Lady Naariah yells.

Hundreds of Rooters rush over and climb on the Mocktok's body. They stab and chop the monster with their axes and knives over and over. The creature casts many of the attackers off its body, but the onslaught continues with fresh waves of Rooters, slashing and stabbing the evil creature. The constant stabs drive the creature to its knees. It swings its powerful arms, but there is no one to strike. Green blood flows from the thousands of lesions the Rooters inflict on it.

"I'll tie it with my threads," Jet shouts as he swings his flying mat around the creature. He shoots strong threads, binding the creature's arms.

They pull the mocktok to the ground as waves of more Rooters converge. As it crashes, the mocktok emits a painful and final howl. The Nasties and the Rooters clash in battle over and around the dead Mocktok's bloody body on the sandy beach. The Nasties retreat into the sea with the demise of the creature.

"Elle, I'm feeling the powers Dad spoke about," Jet says. "I can create a flying carpet with my threads. It flies as fast as anything we have in the sky. The ancestor's power and gift are pouring into me now. The royal's meditations are working. What was that creature on the shore?"

"It's a Mocktok. Most are twice the size of our parents. But with its massive, hairy legs and arms, this monster is the largest the pixies tell me they have ever seen," Jenn interjects.

"Stay close to me," Elle replies. I hope I'm doing the right thing. "Jet, I want you here behind the front with me," Elle continues, "I've seen your powers grow. You watch my back, and I'll watch yours. The ancestors told me to trust you."

"I only have my threads. How can I help?" Jet asks. "We're at war. You will have two gifts by the time weenter battle. threads and a second gift. They will manifest faster in the heat of battle and when we meditate. Try meditating."

How did I know it would manifest faster in battle? "You ask me to meditate at a time like this?" Jet replies, laughing, "Okay, I'll close my eyes."

"It was a wise decision to bring the thornycorns," Mage Eli, the Forge Master, says to his brother, Mage Nico, who talks to the animals in the realm. "Their wide wingspan allows us to glide quickly to the front on the slightest breeze."

"Yes, they are wondrous beasts, and they are deadly with their horns," Nico replies.

"Look, there's the command post. She's probably in there," Mage Eli says, pointing.

He directs a flock of winged warriors from Fe toward the command post, each bearing sacks on their backs filled with weapons of war he forged.

"The battle has begun in the North. We took out an Oozemoran with Teva's help," Nico reports to Elle.

Eli places some weapons on a table. "Commander Elle, we brought swords, shields, bows, arrows, and a few other enchanted arms for the tribe's leaders and for those protecting this command. I only had time to create these weapons."

Standing beside Eli, Nico says, "I assigned Egglets to fight alongside each tribal leader."

Commander Elle, Prince Jet, Masters Eli and Nico, and Lord Ennis gather around a large table, focusing on the battle plan spread across the map.

"Commander Elle, where do you want to deploy my army?" an excited Lord Ennis asks.

"The pixies on reconnaissance report the dominant force is coming straight for us. Take your army and hold the front." As Elle extends her finger to point to the front, a bolt of lightning shoots, tearing a hole in the tent and blowing a tree outside to splinters.

Oh my God, I'd better be careful. I need to learn how to control my gift.

"Send a squadron to the Monastery to protect the royals. They are meditating, calling for more powerful magic for the army," Elle says.

"What about the children?" Lord Ennis demands.

"The children are safe in the monastery, for now," Elle asserts.

Lord Ennis stands before the silent ranks of his warriors. "Brothers and sisters," he begins solemnly, "many of you have already given so much to protect our homeland. Some have lost parents, grandparents, siblings… all to the devastation we've endured when the nasties invaded our homeland. And now, once more, I must ask you to stand ready… ready to sacrifice everything, even your lives."

A low murmur of fear ripples through the army.

Above them, swarms of pixies hover, wings glittering in the light, waiting for orders from their human and rooter allies.

The only sounds are the rhythmic crash of waves on the shore and the distant calls of seagulls—Kee-ow, kee-ow—echoing overhead.

Lord Ennis continues, "The evil approaching us will consume all we have and are. We must be diligent and firm. This evil will attack from land, sea, and air. We must confront it. It is a battle from which we cannot be deterred. Look at the Rooter standing next to you. Most have already suffered grave personal loss from those early battles. Remember the parents and the grandparents you lost when the Nasties attacked our City of Hope. Consider the fate of your children if we fail.

"It's time for you to rise again and be ready to sacrifice everything to protect our homes and families. You know the evil we face. So, prepare your large and small shields and march out for battle," Lord Ennis says as the army cheers.

The Villagers

"Look!" Jet exclaims. "More villagers are coming to join the fight."

They arrive in a caravan of wooden carts armed with axes, plows, swords, and knives, prepared to battle to protect their homes.

A unicorn pulls a cart as one villager, and his wife walks beside it. "Did you bring all the medicine?" the village woman asks.

The farmer walks next to the cart, deep in thought. "Don't bother me. I'm thinking about how we can escape if our army falters."

"We're not going to…" she replies, then hesitates.

"Yes, I brought all the medicine and bandages we collected."

The unicorn, the farmer, and his wife walk on the grass towards the Gathering Place with the medical supplies.

The air is buzzing with pixies flying from camp to camp, delivering messages.

"Jet, divide the villagers into four groups—one for the northern front, one for the southern front, and one for the Monastery. Leave a squadron here," Elle yells. "I need you to lead the villagers in battle."

Is my little brother getting taller? He's growing up fast, she thinks.

Jet feels a surge of strength. Warm tingling runs from his chest to his arms, fingertips, and legs. A tiny droplet of fire falls from his fingers and immediately fizzles away. He feels warmth in his hands, but no one notices the tiny balls of fire. The balls of fire do not affect the threads he used to create the mat. But he can only use one at a time.

"How are the Royals? Are they safe?" Lady Amberlyn asks Lord Ennis.

"The Royals are safe at the Monastery. The Crone called them to meditate for more potent magic for the army. The children are also safe in the monastery. King Wingstorm arranged their protection," Lord Ennis replies.

The ocean churns, giant waves crash against the shore, and a tornado appears in the sky. Blue skies and sunlight shine through the hole the tornado unveils. But it disappears as quickly as it appeared, leaving a small opening for the sun to shine through the dismal clouds. The dark clouds drift away from the sunlight and then slowly return to cover the hole.

Evil Retreats

"Did you create the tornado?" Lady Amberlyn asks Elle.

"No. One of the young ladies studying wizardry foresaw a window opening in the sky. We don't yet know what it means, but she's convinced it's a sign of hope," Elle replies.

The minions retreat into the forests, and those that can fly go into the dark clouds. "Why are they running away?" Lady Mia asks.

"No, I don't think they're running away. There's something more sinister still here," Lady Leah says, shuddering.

An eerie still descends on them. No birds sing, and only a few insects are trilling, chirping, or buzzing. All is still except for the distant waves hitting the shore.

Suddenly, they hear a cheer from one of their cousins in the distance, and the entire army at the front lines rejoice and dance. They are celebrating what they think is the defeat of the minions. The cheering grows louder as they hug and congratulate one another.

But the darkened clouds remain and slowly return, creeping closer to the army. People stop dancing, singing, and cheering as they grow quiet, and panic seizes the group.

Pixies fly in circles around and over Commander Elle. They stay in formation, awaiting her orders. They communicate telepathically with each other in the Star Language. Pixies, the stars, and children are the only ones able to speak and understand this heavenly tongue.

Commander Elle turns to her elite pixies. "Carry this message of strength to the five gathered clans—the Rooters, the Sky folk of Fe, the warriors of the Steppes, the Emerald Isle kin, and the army of the Villagers. Tell them: prepare yourselves. This war is far from over."

Mountain Throags descends from the highlands, their tiny wings buzzing.

Their leader flies to Elle and says in a commanding voice, "We'll fight."

Elle replies, "Good. Leave a squadron here. The rest of you defend the North."

A voice whispers to Princess Elle, don't underestimate the Throags because of their tiny wings. They are mighty in battle.

"Wait," she calls out to the Throags. "Protect our front instead and leave a squadron with me," Elle orders.

"More of our cousins are arriving, Commander Elle," Mistress Parker says.

I feel the power from the ancestors getting stronger, Elle thinks.

Lady Parker eyes the Throags skeptically. "They don't look very intelligent."

Elle responds, her gaze fixed on the creatures, "They are sharp minded and fierce in battle. Those massive shoulders, scaled skin, fangs like daggers, powerful hands, and small but mighty wings make them formidable. Don't underestimate them, they're among our most powerful and clever allies."

"I'm glad they're on our side," Parker replies.

A raspy voice slithers into Jenn's mind, mocking. *Where is your commander now? Does she even know what she's doing? She's just a child. You can't rely on her.*

Jenn clenches her jaw. I know what you are, evil. Stay out of my head!

She shivers from a chill crawling down her spine. She shakes off the sense that unseen eyes are watching her, judging her every doubt and fear.

"Elle, you look older and taller," Jenn says.

Deep in thought, Elle replies, *"The sudden onset of this war is causing our gifts to manifest earlier. That may be the reason."* Elle thinks, will we be strong enough to fight the creatures? What do I do now? I wish my dad were here. Her eyes tear up.

The Dame's voice whispers into Elle's ear, soft as a gentle wind, "You can do this, my dear Ellaria. Trust yourself… and trust Jetamine. He's your strongest ally."

The enemy forces crawl onto the beach. They wait until thousands stand together as hundreds of flying creatures soar above.

"Who's leading them? The Obligoo is dead," Lady Leah says, searching the sky. "There must be another demonic creature controlling them."

"Lady Danna and Mistress Tori, I want you both at the front. Send a squad of the Rooter's best bowmen and women to clear an area in the mountain for the archers, then flood the attackers with fire and poison arrows when the battle begins," Commander Elle orders. "Lady Danna, I want you to go with Tori to focus your fire on the leaders."

"Mistress Tori, take your army and protect our southern flank," she says.

"Wizard Kaylee, Lord Ennis is sending a squadron to protect the Royals. Go with them."

Jenn's Sacrifice

A swarm of sinister black buzzards breaches the front line, diving straight for Elle and her small, exposed band of soldiers. They're outnumbered and outmatched. But before the creatures strike, Jenn unexpectedly charges in—riding a unicorn—at the head of villagers and Rooters mounted on Egglets. They plunge into the chaos, shielding Elle with fearless resolve. Steel and spirit clash in a desperate stand. One by one, Jenn and her ragtag force fall—battered, broken, their spirits crossing into the next realm— but not in vain. They hold the line long enough. Reinforcements arrive. Elle is saved.

The War in the Skies

Fairies are among the many wicked creatures. These once moral creatures converted to the ways of the Obligoo under promises of prosperity and power. They are half the size of humans, ethereal, with wings discolored by blotches of red. They carry a sword or a bow.

A group of fairies flies out of the darkness to attack the Sky People. Wizard Joy casts a blinding spell. They crash into one another. The fairies fly sightless and screech in fear.

"Let's go," Lady Joy shouts. "Fly like a flock."

From opposite skies, the Sky People descend. One group is astride mighty Egglets, the other gallops in on unicorns. They charge together into the heart of the blind enemy.

Lady Joy shouts, "Sword-bearers slash through the enemy ranks. Archers, lose your arrows." By morning's end, hundreds of foes lay dead.

The Rooters War

Lady Naariah and the Root army stand ready to fight. Their shields and razor-edge swords are infused with Barkelite.

The Nasties emerge from the ocean depths by the hundreds to crawl out to the front.

The Rooter army collides with the Nasties in a brutal clash of steel and fury. A thick, glistening slime coats the Nasties, which shields them from the Barkelite's effects. Swords and shields slam against the Nasties hardened, grotesque bodies, but the slime dulls every blow. The battlefield echoes with cries of pain as Rooters fall by the hundreds, overwhelmed by the relentless swarm.

A pixie flies to Elle with a message from Lord Ennis, "We need help at the front."

Elle turns to Jet. "Send villagers to help the Rooter army at the front."

Jet flies over the embattled Rooter army. He swings his flying mat to the army of villagers marching towards the Southern Shore.

"This way," he shouts to the villagers, pointing west. As he points, a ball of fire blazes from his fingers. It disappears, but the entire army of good villagers sees it. They break out in cheers when they see Prince Jet shoot balls of fire from his fingers.

Jet swings his mat toward the Nasties, and the entire Southern Army of villagers runs hard behind him.

A voice whispers, "You can do this."

I can do this... but how? he wonders, raising his hand.

Instantly, a relentless inferno erupts from his palm as he calls upon his gift, engulfing the Nasties in flame—hundreds turn to ash in moments.

Around him, villagers and Rooters charge forward, finishing the rest of the creatures with fierce determination. They drive the attacking forces back. Many of the enemy retreat into the darkened clouds, others vanish beneath the waves or disappear into the sky. For a moment, it seems like a victory.

But it doesn't last.

A massive swarm of buzzards gathers, swirling together like a storm of malevolence. They form a cloud of pure evil.

From sea and sky, thousands more emerge, led by the dark force himself, Azaz.

Buzzards dive at the brave Egglets and Unicorns, scattering their ranks. Many sky warriors fall, their spirits crossing into the next realm.

Then, with a roar, a flood of Nasties, more than ever seen before, descends upon the Rooter army.

The Inner Monastery

197

Inside the monastery, chaos reigns. Children race through the halls, shouting, laughing, arguing, and sometimes tumbling into full-blown scuffles. The Throags' kids participate in the activities but hold back their strength. Egglet children hop wildly, their high-pitched skreeee rising into a grating vaiii! that echoes painfully off the stone walls.

The royal offspring are the noisiest. They blast their horns, hurl balls at each other, topple vases, and scatter ancient artifacts. Toys fly overhead, glass shatters, and magical trinkets blink erratically in protest. About forty-five children fill the space: Throags, Egglets, Rooters, Noble Born, the Village Elders' kids, and even Lady Taylor and Lord Duncan, from the distant land of Angels, cousins of Prince Jet and Princess Elle.

Five nannies move through the chaos like battle-worn generals in a War Zone, each armed with a tray of snacks, a stern voice, and nerves hanging by a thread. They weave between stampeding children and airborne toys, desperately trying to maintain order.

One nanny chases a pack of giggling Rooter kids who stole a basket of candy-coated bubble gum, whose bubbles float and don't pop unless poked. The room teems with rainbow bubbles drifting into hair, eyes, and open mouths.

Meanwhile, the young Throags try to bribe the Egglet children into carrying them to the roof, since their wings haven't yet developed strong enough to take them that high. Another vigilant Throag stands guard by the stairwell, arms outstretched, blocking a determined group of royal boys from charging into the forbidden catacombs with nothing but toy swords and wild ideas.

"Not the study rooms!" cries a third nanny as two girls, a mischievous Throag and the daughter of a noble, dash past her, clutching a glowing scroll swiped from a scholar's desk.

The nanny gives chase, dodging a ball thrown by the village elder's sons just before it hits her... only to stumble backward and almost topple an ancient, fragile vase.

That was close. *Who knows what kind of magic is stored in that old vase?* The haggard nanny thinks as she cradles the delicate artifact.

The fourth nanny stands over the stove, organizing lunchtime. She holds a wiggling Rooter child in one arm, talks to her pixies, and stirs the pot of ketchup and moon berries with her other hand, all at once.

"Chew your food before you fly!" she shouts to the Egglets, but her comments are lost under the shrieking laughter, magical trills, and the unmistakable blast of a war horn outside.

"Everyone to the Chapter House. We have food, and more toys await," she shouts.

Meanwhile, the fifth nanny sits in the corner, rocking slightly, her arms wrapped around her knees, and clutching a half-eaten sandwich.

"It's not forever...it's not forever," she mumbles in a daze, rocking back and forth. "It's only until sunset, and then I can go to bed." A glitter trail floats past her head.

Despite their efforts, the tide of youthful magic, mischief, and madness surges on, chaotic and, oddly, beautiful.

"Children, pay attention," the lead nanny shouts.

Suddenly, the chaos halts.

At the arched entrance of the Chapter House, His Majesty King

Mortimer Aetherwright and His Royal Highness King Stirling Fredrickson stand tall and commanding at the entrance to the Chapter House—their noble silhouettes framed by the flickering glow of enchanted candles and wall-mounted torches.

Inside, the children freeze mid-mischief. One boy knocks over a stack of scrolls from an old desk. Another spills a glowing liquid onto an ancient tapestry.

King Mortimer's gaze sweeps over them, stern yet not unkind. When it comes, his voice carries the weight of centuries and the echo of tradition.

"This is a sacred place," he says, his tone even and commanding. "The Wizards' Council once gathered here to conduct matters of great importance. They made decisions that shaped the very fabric of our realm." He steps forward, the ornate buckle of his cloak catching the light. "Children do not misbehave in these halls. We trust you will honor this place with the dignity it deserves."

Beside him, King Stirling Fredrickson gives a single, slow nod of agreement, his eyes settling on each child. The silence that follows is not born of fear but of reverence. For the first time, the children sense the history beneath their feet.

King Fred looks towards his children. "Princess Strawberry and Princess Pigtails, settle down and mind your nannies."

Shaking his head and surveying the mess, King Mortimer says, "Your nannies are going to tell you what to do to clean this mess. I hope you didn't break something important. You kids are lucky your mothers aren't here."

Now quiet and calm, the children gather the toys and clean up the spilled jam and nectar. There are occasional whispers and a muffled giggle, but the storm has passed for now.

The Inner Monastery

Hordes of evil creatures swarm the Monastery outside while the children and their nannies clean the inner abbey, unaware of the battle taking place. Black Buzzards dive from the skies, shrieking as they strike. Below, snarling Nasties scuttle at alarming speed, launching a ferocious assault on the party.

The defending party feels a jolt of fear when they see the number and ferocity of the buzzard and the Nasties' attack.

Lady Crystal jumps onto Queen Seraphina, the majestic Queen of the Unicorns. "Follow me!" she shouts to the defenders.

A squadron of Throags attacks the Nasties and mutilates them. The Throags are mighty warriors. The Egglets, each bearing sky folk on their backs, surge into the air behind her.

Queen Seraphina thrashes her head from side to side. With each swipe, her enchanted horn shreds all those buzzards it touches.

The attackers retreat.

The defenders stand poised on hills flanking the road to the monastery, their eyes scanning the horizon. From above, swift-flying pixies flit back and forth, constantly updating Lady Crystal on the enemy's approach. Overhead, Egglets with Sky Riders circle the monastery in rotating shifts, ever vigilant, ready to meet the coming darkness in battle.

The Northern Sea

Teva's warriors, strong, fearless, and bound by honor, gather in formation on the grassy field. At their head stand Lords Jean Pierre and James Dean, side-by-side with Teva, their eyes unwavering and blades gleaming. The waves crash on the shore, and the battlefield extends far to the west between the ocean and the Mountains.

The Front Collapses

Shades of past corrupted wizards and unicorns fly into the fray. These wicked wraiths, with their hoard of nasties, from the darkness, flood the seashores, reach the grassy plains, and overwhelm the good armies. But the army holds its ground, despite so many Rooters, Villagers, and Throags passing to the spirit realm.

Mistress Tori and Lady Danna ride into the battle on a chariot pulled by two strong unicorns.

"These unicorns are stable and will lead us to the main body of the enemy," Mistress Tori shouts to Lady Danna. "I will use my power of chaos while you use your power to hold off the Nasties and Buzzards."

Lady Danna uses magical arrows fashioned by Mage Eli. Mistress Tori drives the evil ground forces into confusion with her spells of Chaos. The Rooters' devastation of the Nasties brings a short-lived reprieve from the battle.

The brave hold the enemy back until they fall, outnumbered and overwhelmed. Many good folks fall by the score as they run from the collapsed front.

But Elle jumps on Queen Seraphina, lifts her sword to the sky, and shouts, "Let's rid our land of this evil."

We can't win. There are far too many, Elle thinks fearfully.

Her unicorn whinnies and shakes its head, then leaps as Elle jumps on, grasping its golden mane. Both know they will not be able to drive the enemy back, and they will pass to the spirit realm this day.

Commander Elle leads the remaining forces rapidly toward the beach for a final, fatal confrontation with the enemy.

"Fight, fight, fight," Princess Elle shouts. The power of her ancestors builds within her.

"Elle, I got my gift," Prince Jet shouts. "I can raise fire."

Jet destroys evil with balls of fire. He casts an inferno of raging fire from his hand, destroying everything it consumes.

The remainder of the army clash swords against shields, then run into battle. Sky people fly above on the backs of giant birds. Their arrows are precise. They kill their target every time. But most of the skilled fighters are gone or wounded. They understand that winning this battle is impossible, and losing means certain death.

No matter how skilled or diligent the forces of good are, they cannot overcome the hordes of the enemy. Soon, they are overwhelmed.

The Temple

A thunderous roar rips through the air as the Temple's ancient doors, marked with pulsating runes, shudder and slowly grind open. It reveals a curtain of fine, twined linen with blue, purple, and scarlet yarn that divides sacred magic from a dying world. The curtain shreds. Its pieces fall to the ground.

Behind the curtains, an ancient scroll is wrapped in leather. It has a patina, a soft sheen, that comes from age and use.

A powerful magic grows from the scroll. It fills the sky, giving the defenders confidence and strength. The attacking minions flee, fearing the good magic. But more importantly, this magic fuels the resurrection of King Wingstorm to a mighty Griffin.

The ocean roars, the ground shakes, and water becomes a vortex.

A mighty Griffin bursts out of the turbulent sea, fueled by the prayers and meditation of the royals. The Griffin flies high and out of sight. It returns, howling and shrieking. It dives into the darkness. With a single swing of his wing, it scatters the minions and sends thousands back to the void. He sends hordes of evil minions into the Abyss, including the Nasties, Untonne, fallen fairies, and wicked apparitions.

Fear not. I'll sweep this evil with the broom of destruction, declares the almighty Griffin telepathically to Lady Joy.

The darkness coalesces into a wicked creature resembling a dragon, a mighty being far more deadly than the Obligoo.

The Griffin extends its wings, dives at the demonic creature, grabs it with sharp claws, and casts it to the abyss in one stroke. The creature, Azaz, resembles a lowly worm trying to escape in fear, but cannot escape its fate.

The Griffin

The evil creature's downfall is so complete that those who see him are astonished at his humiliation.

The brutes that remain will bother the decent folks for many seasons to come. However, the villagers now have weapons and the Griffin, if they summon it, to defend themselves.

"Azaz, the evil one, recruited some villagers from AI to fight for his cause. But when the Temple's doors were open and its sacred curtain was torn apart, a wave of magic poured forth, dissolving much of the hatred from their hearts."

CHAPTER NINETEEN
EPILOGUE

*Which way? the easy road to the Temple or the difficult
road to the shadows*

The Gathering Place is quiet now—a field of peace once more, not battle. Unicorns graze in the tall grass, children laugh and chase one another, and traders open their stalls beneath the morning sun. The kingdom is healing.

Though sorrow lingers for the friends they've lost, joy quietly returns. The people find comfort in knowing that the griffin has vanquished the terrible beast, and light has prevailed over darkness once again.

The wind stirs the ivy on the monastery's stone walls. The vines, with scents of jasmine and mint, are calming and clean, like a recent rain on a stone path.

From within, faint laughter and the rustle of students' voices echo beneath the vaulted ceilings. Where there was once war and worry, now there is quiet purpose. The monastery lives again, not as a fortress, but as a sanctuary of light, learning, and magic.

Princess Elle walks the garden path beside the Monastery and temple, her fingers brushing the petals of blooming flowers.

She wears a flowing gown of powder blue, light as silk, with a pale gold sash at her waist.

The sword at her side hums faintly, not with danger, but with the promise of peace.

Behind her, Prince Jet swings gently from a tree, his boots landing softly on the grass.

"My pixies say the storm over the Enchanted Isles is calm now," he says, brushing a leaf from her shoulder.

"There are still secrets out there," Elle says. "Places where danger hides."

Prince Jet wears a deep indigo tunic with silver stitching like lightning. His pants are dark and easy to move in, his boots worn but strong.

He grins. "Then we'd better get ready."

He takes her hand, and together they walk toward the stables. Two unicorns wait, their manes braided with threads that shine like stars, pawing the ground as if they know a journey is near.

It's twilight. Above them, the clouds part, revealing a cluster of glowing stars in a strange, new shape.

"Look," Elle says. "Even the stars are calling." Jet looks up.

"Do you think it's a map?"

"Maybe," Elle says. "Or a warning."

The sword hums again—this time harder and faster.

"My sword is trying to tell me something. Look, Elle," he says, pointing to the Monastery. "The temple and the monastery are glowing with light. But behind us, the path is swallowed by shadows." He straightens, voice steady. "I think this is the choice: we can go back to safety… or we can move forward and face whatever comes. I say we go."

And far beyond the Enchanted Isles, something moves. Their story isn't over.

Not yet.

ABOUT THE AUTHOR

Ricardo Anaya is a Vietnam veteran, storyteller, educator, proud grandfather, and Founder of Council for Education at Travel USA. His writing reflects his Christian faith and a belief in purpose, sacrifice, and redemption. The Gathering  Place is his fantasy sequel to The Land of Lakes and Forests, inspired by the truth that real magic lives in those who choose to serve—even before they believe they are ready.

3

Down the street from Pylus' apartment, a rundown building was remodeled into a small bar. A raggedy sign hangs over the door reading THE SPOT. A handful of regulars can always be found inside with a few newbies every now and then. Pylus enjoys the company there, mostly because none of them watch Champion, so they have no idea who he is outside of their interactions in the bar.

Two other people sit with drinks in hand when Pylus walks in. Freddy, the bartender, wipes down the bar as he chats with the two customers. One is an older man in his sixties, the other a young man about half his age. Jerry and Jerry Junior, everybody calls him JJ, the father and son duo that stop in every day after their shift at the factory two blocks away.

"Hey, boys," Pylus says as he pats Jerry on the shoulder and takes a seat next to him.

"Well, look what the cat dragged in," Jerry says, giving Pylus a pat on the knee, "How are you doing, son?"

"Not bad. Just living life."

"Aren't we all?" Says Freddy as he pulls out a cup, "The usual?"

"Yes, sir," says Pylus.

"One club soda coming up," he says, thumping the bar.

"Don't you ever try something new?" JJ asks.

"I can't, alcohol is toxic to me," Pylus responds, "Found that out the hard way. Took one sip and had to be rushed to a hospital."

"Is that 'cause of the dog in you?" Jerry asks.

Pylus nods, "Sure is. Same reason I can't eat chocolate anymore."

Having been born in 1990, Jerry remembers the entire downfall of humanity. He was part of the American Human Forces that combated the progressing hybrid armies while America finished working on its own hybrids. For a long time, he hated all hybrids. It didn't help that his wife was killed by one during the war. JJ was only a teenager.

The first time Jerry walked into The Spot and saw Pylus, he almost attacked him. Luckily, Freddy saw him coming and jumped him before anything happened. Once Jerry calmed down, Pylus apologized to him on behalf of all hybrid kind. Slowly after that, a friendship started to form. Still, talking about his hybrid side made Pylus uncomfortable when Jerry was around.

Jerry, JJ, and Freddy weren't Pylus' friends per se; he didn't let himself have many friends anymore, but they were kind to him and accepted him.

Just then, the door to The Spot opened, and a large crowd started making their way in. The late shift had just ended at the factory.

"That's our cue," Jerry says, standing up, "See ya, pup," he says, patting Pylus on the shoulder.

"Have a good one," Pylus responds.

Jerry and JJ weave their way through the flood of twenty or so people coming in. Aside from Pylus and Freddy, they don't like people. Another reason why Pylus doesn't consider them to be friends.

Freddy leans on the counter and taps Pylus on the shoulder, "Glad you're still with us, man."

Freddy knows what Pylus does for a living, but never watches the fights. He says he prefers not to watch because violence isn't his thing. "Too much in the streets already," he always says to Pylus.

"Thanks, man," Pylus says.

A couple of hybrids walk in with the tail end of the crowd. They see Pylus and give a quick nod before walking over to their usual corner. Being a hybrid walking around in public is usually a rarity, but in this section of town, all the washed-out celeb hybrids find their home. Those who got tired of the fame or burned out on booze and drugs eventually make their way here to be forgotten by those they were once adored by. People in this section just don't care about the hype of the world and would rather forget about most of the last fifty years. It's a perfect place for Pylus to hide out without raising questions or attracting eyes from Champion watchers.

"Hey there, stranger," a voice says from behind Pylus. Freddy's raised eyebrows let him know it's someone new to The Spot. Pylus's own eyebrows raise when he sees the owner of the voice.

"What brings you here, Miss Ordonston?" He says as the reporter takes the seat next to him, "Do I have my own personal reporter slash stalker?"

She smiles sweetly at his joke, "Aren't they the same thing? No, my sister just bought an apartment down here, so we came to celebrate with a couple of her friends."

Pylus lifts his glass to her, "Congratulations to your sister."

"What's your drink, sweetheart?" Freddy cuts in.

"Martini, please," Miss Ordonston responds.

"Coming right up."

"So, Mr. Brek," she starts before Pylus cuts her off.

"Please, call me Pylus. This isn't an interview. We can be casual here."

"Alright, Pylus," she continues, smiling, "I have to say I'm surprised to see you here. Most Champion contenders are never seen in public."

"Most Champion owners treat their contenders like animals," Pylus says with a hint of venom.

"Really? Where did you hear that? Do you know any personally who are?" Her curiosity sounds genuine, but she's still a reporter. Pylus knows he needs to be careful, or he might get in trouble with some of the other contender owners who prefer to keep their abuse hidden.

"No, I don't. I've just heard. . . rumors. Forget I said anything," he says quickly.

"All right then," Miss Ordonston says with a shrug, "Can I ask you something not as a reporter?"

"Sure," Pylus says.

She looks him in the eyes, and he sees the reporter in her fall away, "Are you ever scared when you go into a fight?"

Pylus looks at her for a moment before answering, "I used to be. Not anymore."

"What changed?"

"I got used to it," he says, sipping his club soda, "Like a soldier in a war, death and fighting have become a way of life. Ask anyone who was in the AHF during the Hybrid War, and they'll probably say the same thing."

Miss Ordonston scrunches her eyebrows together, "That's so sad."

"It's the world we live in, Miss Ordonston."

Miss Ordonston lays her hand on his arm and leans in, "Please, Pylus. If you insist on me using your first name, the least you can do is use mine. After all," she smiles slightly, "We can be casual here."

"All right. . . Leifa."

She smiles a smile that brightens her eyes. They are deep blue, like the deepest parts of the ocean, and are about as mysterious and concealing.

"Do you enjoy being in Champion?" She asks, leaning back in her seat.

"Ha! No, no, I do not." Pylus laughs, "But I don't have any choice unless I win Ultimate Champion."

Leifa looks at her drink as Freddy sets it down in front of her. She takes a small sip, followed by a deep breath as if she's trying to work up the nerve to say something.

"What's your influence?" She finally asks.

"Twenty-eight percent," Pylus responds.

She nods her head at his answer, "Just below thirty. That's why you get to use weapons in Champion."

"Sure is. Really, the only reason I've done as well as I have in all of my fights."

"Why do you say that?"

"Because while my hybrid change gave me some good perks, they're not great for one-on-one confrontation with other animals. Wolves are pack creatures after all, and I don't have a pack."

A strange silence falls on the couple for a moment after Pylus's response. He begins to wonder if he said something that made her uncomfortable when, finally, she speaks again.

"Do you ever get tired?" She asks, staring into her drink.

"Of what?"

Her eyes move from her drink to Pylus' face, "Of fighting."

Looking into the deep blue of her eyes, Pylus sees something he's never seen from a reporter before. Sympathy. For a moment, he's lost in her gaze. He's never known anyone to be sympathetic to a Champion contender.

"I... uh," he clears his throat and shifts his gaze to his own drink, "I don't, actually."

"Really?" She seems suspicious of his answer, "Is it because you enjoy it?"

He looks into her eyes again, "No, it's because I have a reason to live after Champion."

"What reason is that?"

Pylus finishes his drink and holds it up to Freddy, "You know what I don't get, Leifa? You came here with your sister to celebrate, but you've spent your whole time here talking to me. Normally, someone would say a nice hello and return to their party, but you seem like you would rather stay here."

"Maybe I just can't get enough of your golden eyes and wolfish grin," she teases with a mischievous smile.

Pylus smiles back, "Going from serious reporter to flirtatious bar girl, eh?"

"Maybe," she says, leaning on the counter, "Or maybe I'm trying to throw you off guard so I can get a better scoop from you."

"A better scoop?" Pylus raises an eyebrow, "I didn't realize there was going to be an article on me."

"Well, there's plenty to write about when it comes to you," Leifa says, "The only hybrid of your kind, the longest living Champion contender, and the only one who didn't have a terminal illness."

Pylus's eyes snap up from his newly filled drink, "You did a background check on me." It's not a question. No one was supposed to know that Pylus was an exception to the terminal illness rule for hybrids. Without going into detail, he pulled some strings with people he knew and got the hybrid transition despite being healthy and young. In order for anyone to know about his situation, they would have had to do some very thorough digging, like someone who had something to gain from knowing as much as they could about Pylus. That type of person is a dangerous one.

Shock fills Leifa's deep blue eyes, "Well, I just. . ."

"I see," says Pylus as he stands and throws a few bucks on the counter for Freddy, "Enjoy your celebration, Miss Ordonston."

"Pylus, wait!" Leifa says, rising from her seat.

"You know, it's not the fact that you did a background check on me that I don't like," Pylus says, turning halfway around, "It's the fact that everything you have done since you walked in here was to get something out of me. I don't know what it is that you want to know, but until you want to have an actual conversation with me. . . don't talk to me again."

"Oh, and one more thing," he says as he turns to leave, "Your sister must have left without you. There are no other women in here."

After leaving The Spot, Pylus makes his way briskly to a small café a mile away. He doesn't feel angry at what happened with Leifa. Mostly, he feels disappointment. Just another reporter looking for some hot new story. They're all the same. *Why would anyone care to get to know a hybrid anyway?* He thinks. *We're just a means for entertainment, right?*

Up ahead, a neon sign outside a little old building reads BECKY'S. Outside the little café sits a grubby figure smoking a cigarette. Wisps of white hair poke out from underneath an old grey beanie. A long, white beard cascades down his chest and rests on his small, round belly. If dwarves were real, this man would be one. A jacket covered in mud hangs loosely on his shoulders, literally being held together by threads. Beady eyes stare blankly at the pavement in front of him as if reliving some long-lost memory.

"Hey George," Pylus says as he gets close.

The grubby man's eyes flick to Pylus, losing all blankness and filling with a bright twinkle.

"Hello, my boy," he says, clasping Pylus's hand tightly in both of his, "Life been well to ya now?"

"Can't complain too much. How is it for you?"

"Can't be bothered with what doesn't matter now, can ya?" He says with a lopsided grin.

George was a pig farmer before the world went to Hell. He was born in Ireland, then moved to Canada when he was ten, then to South Africa when he was fifteen, and ended up in the United States when he was almost thirty. Most of his thirties were spent traveling until he met Gloria. "The love of my life and only star in my sky," as he says. She was the only child of a pig farmer from a small town in Wisconsin. After meeting her, George fell in love with her and the small-town way of life and eventually married Gloria and took over the pig farm. Pylus hears the story frequently and could tell every detail that will come up. Yet, he still enjoys hearing it.

Being ninety-four, George is a little on the crazy end of the sanity scale, but his mind is still as sharp as a tack. It doesn't keep him from speaking in strange riddle-like sayings.

"Can I buy you a meal?" Pylus asks as he puts his arm around George's shoulders and leads him inside.

"You can buy me anythin' ya like that don't give a grievance, don't ya know?" George responds, slipping his arm around Pylus's waist.

Pylus smiles as they walk towards their usual booth. George is one person who really helps Pylus forget that there is a whole world out there full of messed-up people and places. When he's with George, it seems like the only thing that matters is finding happiness in the plate of steak and eggs that gets brought out. That's the reason Pylus let himself be friends with the old man.

"Hiya, Pylus," greets a waitress as she walks past.

"Hi Ellie," Pylus says, smiling, "Been busy tonight?"

"Nothing more than usual," she returns the smile, "How goes it, George?"

"Got me feet below me instead of above me," George calls over his shoulder.

Before Pylus and George can fully take their seats, Ellie is standing at their table ready to take their order. With black hair and dark lipstick, Ellie stands out in a crowd and fits the outcast stereotype that George and Pylus slide into. Wearing all black adds to her uniqueness, but everyone who knows her knows she has a heart of gold.

"The usual for you boys?" She says, looking at George.

"You've been knowin' me well now, darlin'," George says with a wink.

Ellie winks back and scribbles on her order pad, "What about you, sweetie?"

"The usual is great," Pylus responds.

"Coming right up." She gives Pylus her signature waitress smile, the one that brings the big tips out of the male customers, and touches his shoulder gently, "Glad to see we get to have you for another day."

"So am I," Pylus says.

Ellie smiles again and walks back to the kitchen, glancing back at the pair before disappearing behind the doors.

When Ellie is out of hearing range, George leans over the table and whispers, "Now what's got to bump ya to get that slug brain of yours to let in a little common sense and ask that girl to go on an outin' with ya?"

A laugh of surprise bursts from Pylus. "What makes you think she would want to go on 'an outing' with me?" he asks.

"You as dumb as you are scary?" George asks with an eyebrow raise. "Every time that sweet lass lays her eyes on ya, the band strikes up its merry tune, and Michael Bublé turns up the romance."

"Who's Michael Bublé?" Pylus asks.

"Don't change the subject."

Pylus half sighs, half laughs as he sits back in his seat, "Look, George, I'm not looking for any kind of romance in my life right now. You know what I have to do for a living. Can you imagine me starting some sort of relationship, then getting killed a week later, and her watching me die?"

George narrows his eyes in the way that means he knows Pylus isn't telling him the truth. "Listen here, boy, you got a life to live, and the more you keep holdin' onto whatever is holdin' ya back, the sooner you're gonna lose every chance for somethin' better."

For the first time since meeting George, Pylus realizes the old man is completely sane. Kooky may be his default personality trait, but what everyone sees as crazy is just a façade to hide how truly perceptive George can be.

"You really think I should take a chance with it?" Pylus asks George.

A sly grin slides across the old man's lips, "You bet your last award-winnin' sow I do."

Pylus opens his mouth to ask another question when two plates slide between them.

"Two steak and egg platters," Ellie says, "One medium rare for George and one raw for Pylus."

"Thank you, darlin'," George says. His eyes meet Pylus's, and he motions with his eyebrows towards Ellie.

Pylus clears his throat, which has suddenly become quite dry, "Hey, Ellie. What time are you off tonight?"

She glances at George, then back at Pylus with a quizzical look, "Nine, why?"

"I, um, was wondering," the napkins suddenly become very interesting to Pylus, and he starts playing with the corner of one, "If you, um, if you don't have any plans, would you, maybe like to join me for a, um, late-night stroll?"

Her raised eyebrows concern Pylus. Did he mess up? Does she think he's joking? Is she going to say no? This is why he never tries to get to know people. He never should have listened to George!

"A late-night stroll?" Ellie says slowly with an eyebrow cocked. Then she breaks into a warm, beautiful smile, "I would love to. See you at nine."

Pylus and George watch her walk away before George slaps Pylus's arm with the back of his hand, "Atta boy! Now was that so hard?"

Pylus shakes his head to clear the surprise from his face. He hadn't actually expected Ellie to say yes to his invitation.

Looking to George, he grunts, "Yes."

"You ain't no Shakespeare, I done give ya that. But ya got your point out. If she weren't so smitten with ya, I doubt it would've worked." The twinkle in George's eye is brighter than normal.

"Thanks," Pylus mutters, "I think."

4

At 8:50, George and Pylus make their way out of Becky's and stand on the sidewalk. George pulls out his pack of smokes and lights a fresh one.

"Well, son," he breathes out with his first cigarette puff, "best be on my way. Gloria doesn't like me out late no more, how it be and all."

"Tell her I say hi," Pylus says.

"Yup, as always," George flicks his hand over his shoulder as he walks away down the street.

Laughing to himself, Pylus turns his face upwards to look at the sky. Too many lights make it impossible to see the stars like he used to be able to back home, but looking up still brings some sense of peace. He closes his eyes and breathes in deep through his nose. It's quiet tonight. Being a work night, everyone returned home already to get some rest, leaving the streets empty. This sector of town often gets forgotten with all the hustle and bustle of the higher-end areas, which means most of the time, things are pretty slow going and quiet. A nice reprieve for Pylus from the insanity of Champion.

Lost in the stillness of the moment, Pylus doesn't notice someone is with him until he feels a delicate arm lace its way through his. He opens his eyes to see Ellie smiling up at him.

"Shall we?" She asks.

"Of course," Pylus smiles back.

Becky's Cafe is only a couple of blocks away from the River Scenic Walkway that was built two or three years into the Rebuild. A floating walkway overhanging the river, with flower beds on both sides filled with different flowers to commemorate the lives of those who were lost during the war.

This city used to be called Pittsburgh in the state known as Pennsylvania. It was part of the United States of America. Now it's called the Shank Settlement. The western half of the city has occupants and the Champion arena, while the eastern half remains barren and destitute. As more people come into the settlement and as the population grows, the rebuilding progresses East more and more each year. Aside from a couple of factories, Becky's is about the furthest East progress has gone.

"So, what convinced you to finally ask me out?" Ellie asks as they make their way onto the walkway.

Pylus looks at his feet sheepishly, "George kept telling me to take a chance," he mutters.

She laughs a sweet little chirp that makes Pylus smile, "Well, I guess I owe him one now."

"Why is that?"

Her eyebrows rise as if to say, "really?"

"Maybe because I'm not very good at hiding when I have a crush on someone," she says, her eyebrows still raised.

"Who do you..." Pylus starts before the realization hits him, "Oh... I get it now."

Ellie laughs a full, joyful laugh as Pylus turns his head away, an embarrassed grin on his face. Ellie pulls herself into him, bumping him sideways a little, making him join in with her happy laughter.

"Could you really not tell?" Ellie asks.

Pylus shrugs in response, "I'm really not known to be too observant when it comes to women. I mean, I haven't had a girlfriend in years."

"Is that by choice or circumstance?"

He shrugs, "More so circumstance, but a little by choice. I have a hard time letting people get close to me or wanting to get close to anyone."

"What about George? You seem pretty close with him," Ellie says.

Pylus smiles at her sideways, "There's always exceptions to the rule."

"I guess that's true," she says, rolling her eyes to look forward, "I told myself I would never fall for a handsomely rugged man who likes to fight again."

"Again?" Pylus asks, "Sounds like there's a story behind that."

She shakes her head and makes a face, scrunching her nose in a cute, schoolgirl way, "Not really. My ex was a guy with a short temper who liked to fight anyone who stood up to him. One day, he came home and… that person was me. He beat me unconscious. When I came to, he was asleep on the couch watching Champion, one of your fights, actually. I grabbed as much as I could carry and ran out the door. Never looked back." Her eyes drift over the river. A deep sadness that doesn't suit her normally happy demeanor fills her eyes.

"I'm so sorry," Pylus whispers, "Any man who treats women like that deserves to be thrown into the arena full of Ferals."

"Wow, that's a pretty strong opinion," Ellie says, looking at him.

"I used to have a sister," Pylus says, "I had to protect her from a lot of goons who wanted to use her like that."

"Ah, makes sense," Ellie says, "What happened to her? If you don't mind me asking."

"She died about a year before I became a hybrid," He says after a moment, "She was diagnosed with terminal breast cancer. There were a couple of offers to become a hybrid, but she turned them all down. She said she would rather leave this world in peace than earn her living in it through chaos."

Ellie's grip on his arm tightens as she leans her head against his shoulder, "I'm so sorry. I lost my twin brother, too. He tried to become a hybrid, but it wouldn't take. His heart wasn't strong enough for it."

They stop walking to look at each other for a moment. Some new connection passes between their shared silence. A connection of losing one close to you and never really healing from it. Pylus smiles a sad smile as a tear rolls down his cheek.

"Do you ever wonder if your brother would be proud of you if he could see you now?" he asks, still looking at her.

Her eyes shift to the side, then back to his, "I think he is proud of me, and he can see me now. I don't believe he ever really left me." Softly, she brushes the tear off his cheek, "I don't think your sister has really left you either."

For a moment, looking into her eyes, Pylus feels something he hasn't felt in a long time, hope. "Why do you believe that?"

She studies him intently but. . . softly, "Because it's easier than believing that they're gone forever."

"I guess that's a good reason," he says as he starts walking again.

"What do you believe in, Pylus?"

He thinks for a moment, "Nothing really. Ever since turning, I've just been focusing on surviving. I never really think about what will happen when I die or when others die."

"Then why do you do your little ritual after you win every fight?"

He looks at her quizzically, "You watch Champion?"

"Only for your fights," she says with a smirk, "Now answer my question."

"Wow, you don't just have a crush on me. You're obsessed." His comment is met with a hard shove from Ellie, separating their arms for the first time since they started walking.

He laughs as he stumbles away for a couple of steps before coming back towards her. When he is close enough, she smoothly slides her arm back around his like it is meant to be there.

"Punk," she teases, "Now answer my question or I'll throw you in the river."

Pylus takes a deep breath and looks forward. He can just make out the Champion Stadium on the other side of the water, right at the point where two rivers merge.

"I do the ritual more for me than for my opponents," he starts, "I tell them that the fight wasn't in anger and that I hold no animosity towards them. I do it to keep myself grounded. I don't enjoy fighting, and I don't want to. A lot of the other contenders relish in the fame and the thrill of the fight, but I don't want to give in to that side of me. I've killed for revenge before, but never pleasure. I want to stay as human as I can."

Ellie tilts her head, "I'll be honest, Pylus, if it wasn't for the bright, yellow eyes, fluffy mane, and long canines, I would believe you were one hundred percent human. Not just because of how you would look, but because of how you act. You are the most genuine person I've ever met, and you don't expect anything from anyone."

"Why would I?" Pylus asks.

Ellie smiles and shakes her head, "There you go again. Most people see others by what they can gain from them or how they can use them. But you seem to see people as just... people. You don't expect anything from George; you just like him. You never thought of how you could use me, even though I am 'obsessed with you', as you say."

Pylus laughs and rolls his eyes, "Oh my gosh. That's never gonna be lived down, is it?"

Her eyes twinkle with mischief as she teases him, "Not until the day I die."

By now, the couple had made their way to a lookout at the river convergence. A little gazebo built looking across the dark water to the Champion Stadium. Pylus leans against Ellie slightly to get her to turn into the Gazebo. He rests against the railing with his forearms when they reach the edge. Ellie rests her chest against the railing and lets her crossed arms hang over the edge.

"Pylus?" She asks after a quiet moment.

"Yeah?"

She hesitates before asking, "Why did you become a hybrid?"

"For all the adoring fans," he answers immediately.

A hard punch to the shoulder knocks a chuckle out of him. He looks over to see Ellie fighting not to smile back at him. Thanks to his wolf eyes, Pylus can still make out all the details of her face in the dim light. For the first time, he takes a moment to really look at her. She's pretty. No, that's not right. She's beautiful. Her features are delicate but still sharp enough to give her good definition. Her dark eyes hold an intense vibrance as if she is seeing the world for what it is, but still looks for the beauty anyway. As she smiles at him, her nose scrunches at the bridge, giving her the silly schoolgirl look that fits her despite her dark attire.

Man, he thinks to himself, *I am dense.*

It was over a year ago when he met Ellie for the first time, and he never gave her a second look after that. Actually, he never really gave her a good first look, to be honest. But tonight, walking and talking with her, he can see her in a new light.

"You don't have to be so closed off with me," Ellie whispers, bumping into his shoulder softly. Butterflies erupt in his chest. His silence isn't because he is staying closed off; it's because he has momentarily lost the ability to speak.

"I, uh, I wasn't ready to die yet," he says, finally answering her question, "There was still something more for me to do."

Her eyes gaze into his with a softness that both confuses and calms him. He's never had someone look at him in such a way before. She makes him feel safe. Earlier that night, with Leifa Ordonston, he felt like the flirting and conversation were pointed towards an objective. Now with Ellie, he feels like there aren't any ulterior motives. She cares about him and listens to him with the intent to do just that. . . listen.

"Have you done that something yet?" she asks softly.

He shakes his head, "No. Not yet. I have to get out of Champion first."

"Well," she says, "I hope you live long enough to find out what it is."

Pylus already knows what his reason for living is, but it's not something that he is ready to open up about with anyone. Not even Ellie. However, maybe that will change. For half a second, he feels the need to tell her that not being ready to die was a lie. He wasn't dying when he transitioned, but the truth would be too much for her right now.

Instead, he lets his eyes fall to the dark water below them as he says, "You know, they say that those who don't survive the hybrid transformation were too pure to go through with it, as something in their soul kept them from allowing it to happen. If your brother was anything like you, then I would bet that is the reason he didn't survive. He was too good to live the life that we have."

Ellie lets out a soft breath. Truth be told, she had never talked to anyone about her brother before. Her brother was her last family member, and his death still affects her every day. When the hybrid process didn't work, she thought that it was because he didn't have a strong enough reason to survive. Her brother was the strongest person she knew, and his not surviving made her question if he wasn't everything she thought he was. Now, hearing what Pylus thinks, the memory of her brother feels. . . healed.

Taking a deep breath, she slides her arm down through Pylus' and laces her fingers into his. He turns his head to look into her eyes. "Thank you," she whispers. Tears were running freely down her cheeks.

Pylus smiles and closes his eyes. He leans his head forward until it meets Ellie's. He breaths in deeply, taking in her scent. Roses mixed with coconut and something else he can't identify. It must be her natural scent. Pylus' heart rams against his chest, fighting to get free. Feeling her forehead against his sends goosebumps up and down his spine. The back of his neck bristles with excitement as her free hand finds his face and traces his jawline. The butterflies from earlier swarm through his chest and stomach in a whirlwind of emotions that he thought were lost to him. He knows what comes next, and he welcomes the movement of his chin as it starts into something he hasn't done for a very long time.

"Well, isn't this sweet?" sneers a sticky voice.

A figure stands behind them, a single light at the opening of the gazebo illuminating him. Stringy black hair falls in front of a long, worn face with beady eyes and a crooked nose from taking one too many punches. His jaw sits slightly higher on one side, making him look like his head is cocked at all times.

"What do you want, Amos?" Ellie spits, straightening up.

The man, Amos, holds his hand up in a "I don't want any trouble" gesture. "I just wanted to find you to let you know I'm sorry for everything that's happened." The dark grin that's been on his face since he showed up gets a little wider as he talks, "I'm taking off soon and wanted to make amends."

"How did you find me?" Ellie asks.

The newcomer shrugs nonchalantly, "I stopped by Becky's, and someone told me you were heading towards the walkway, so I took a chance."

Ellie opens her mouth to say something else, but stops herself when Pylus steps closer to her and puts his arm in front of her slightly. She looks at him and sees the fight in his eyes, glinting dangerously.

"If all you wanted was to make amends, why did you bring friends with you?" He asks.

Amos's smirk slips a little at the remark. His eyes shift to the side, and he nods. Two men step out from behind the pillars on either side of the opening.

"You got a pretty good sixth sense," Amos says, narrowing his eyes at Pylus, "What did you say your name was?"

"I didn't," Pylus growls.

Amos rolls his head to the side, "I know, that was your chance to say it. It's called common courtesy." Cold eyes and a tight mouth are all he gets in response.

"Not much of a talker, I see," Amos says, all traces of a smile gone from his face, "That's alright. I'm not here to talk to you anyway. Look, Ellie, I really wanted to tell you I'm sorry, and maybe we could try to fix things between us."

Ellie's mouth drops open in shock, "Are you kidding me? You want to fix things between us? Do you think it's as easy as that? You beat me unconscious and left me on the floor. If I could have gotten out of the settlement, I would have, but moving to the other side was the best I could do."

"I know I haven't been the best person in my past," Amos says, looking down, "but I'm really trying to make a difference now, before I don't have a chance."

"You're sick," Pylus says.

Amos looks surprised at the forthright comment, "That's a little judgmental considering you've never met me before."

"No, I mean, you're literally sick. I can smell it on you. You're dying," the last two words come out in a whisper.

Amos' jaw drops in utter disbelief, "How do you know that?" he whispers slowly.

"Holy crap," says the friend on Amos's left, "That's Pylus Brek."

All three of them look at Pylus in shock. The attention makes him uncomfortable, but he keeps his face steady and unreadable.

"It's true," says Amos, "I don't know what's wrong, but I'm dying. I can feel it. I can't go to the doctors because of my history with the law. It's been almost two years since you left me, Ellie. I've thought about you every day, and I've struggled to make myself better so I could get you back. Now that I'm dying, I just want to spend my last however long with the person that means the most to me. You."

Ellie's jaw moves up and down, but no sound comes out. Tears brim in her eyes. In the quietness, Pylus can hear her heart beating. It's fast. Really fast.

"I'm sorry, Amos," she says finally, "but I'm not coming back to you. I'm willing to be your friend as long as you're around, but I can't be with you again."

The pain in Amos's eyes almost makes Pylus sorry for him. He really thought that would work. His face, however, doesn't read like a heartbreak; it looks like his pride is hurt.

"Alright then," he says, reaching behind his back.

"NO!" Pylus yells as he turns to block Ellie with his body. He's only fast enough to get his hand in front of her when the gun goes off. His hand explodes with pain as Ellie falls back, a small, dark hole in her chest.

The world turns red. Pylus strikes. Three slashes happen in quick succession. Just three. Afterward, Amos and his two friends lie on the ground, their throats agape and bleeding out, their lifeless eyes staring at the sky in frozen horror. Pylus kneels with Ellie in his arms, blood covering his hands. His blood and the blood of the three goons on his right, Ellie's coating his left as he holds it against her chest.

"Ellie!" he says frantically, "Ellie, stay with me!"

Slowly, her hand lifts to stroke his face, "It's okay, Pylus. I'm not scared," her eyes twinkle with unshed tears. She smiles her beautiful smile once more, "Thank you for today. It was the best birthday I've had in a long time."

Tears fall freely down Pylus's cheeks as he watches Ellie's hand fall in slow motion to rest on the ground.

"Ellie," he whimpers, pulling her close to him and resting his cheek against hers, "I'm so sorry."

5

"Out of my way! Where is he? Move!" Reggie pushes his way through the crowd of emergency responders and reporters, searching for Pylus. Finally, he sees him sitting with his back against the railing of the gazebo, a small blanket draped over his shoulders. Blood covers his clothes. His right hand is wrapped in stark white bandaging. The blood puddle in front of him holds his gaze. Anyone who looks at him can tell he's not there; his eyes are too distant, so much so that Reggie wonders if he'll come back.

"Pylus?" Reggie says gently as he kneels next to him. "Pylus."

"I couldn't save her, Reg," Pylus responds without looking at him, "All the training and fighting. I can *kill* multiple people easily, but I couldn't *save* one person." Reggie gently places his hand on Pylus' shoulder as he keeps talking, "I could save myself just fine. Killing them after the first shot wasn't hard. But I couldn't get her out of the way fast enough."

"Listen, kid," Reggie says quietly, "Sometimes no amount of training can stop a bullet. And sometimes, no matter how much we do, it still isn't enough. But as long as we do everything we can, nobody can blame us for what happens after."

Pylus doesn't react to Reggie's words. His eyes have shifted and are locked on a white, lumpy sheet a few feet away. A single tear rolls down his cheek and drops to the ground. Reggie's heart pounds in his chest. Words want to come out but get stuck in his throat, creating a lump he can't swallow. How do you help someone who believes they're the reason a friend is gone?

"Pylus, look at me," Reggie finally says, hoping to find the words before they come out of his mouth. Pylus slowly moves his gaze to meet Reggie's, "There are things that happen in life that we can't stop, no matter how hard we try. When those things happen, we grieve what we lose, then do everything we can to make sure it doesn't happen again. This wasn't your fault. You did all you could. I'm sorry it wasn't enough to save that poor girl, but if she could talk to you, I bet she would tell you that she doesn't blame you."

"I think she did tell me," Pylus whispers.

"Then you need to forgive yourself, kid. You did all you could. No one can ask for more."

Pylus knows he's right. The words he's shared with Reggie will probably have more meaning in a couple of days, but for now, he lets the pain live in his chest. Like most people, Ellie doesn't have any family left to grieve her, so he will.

"Let's get you home, kid."

Pylus lets Reggie help him to his feet and guide him to the car. His eyes stay on the sheet covering Ellie's body until he can't turn his head back any further. He drops his gaze to the ground to avoid looking at any of the reporters taking hundreds of pictures and asking just as many questions. All their words blur into white noise that disorients him. The slamming of the car door creates a welcoming shield for his ears. Leaning his head back, he stares out the window with no more words to say.

Reggie understands his needs without asking. No more words come from him either, even though Pylus is sure he's dying to say something. Instead of trying to ease Pylus' conscience, Reggie simply reaches over and holds his hand, an unusual show of affection for Reggie, but Pylus welcomes it.

When the car pulls up to Pylus's apartment building for the second time that night, nothing is said as Pylus steps out and closes the door. He doesn't look back as he makes his way up the front steps and through the front doors. As he makes a beeline for the stairway, Mrs. West steps out of her front door.

"Oh, good evening, Pylus dear. How was. . ." her voice catches when she sees his blood-soaked clothes and the pain in his stance, "Oh no, honey, who did you lose?"

Pylus lets out a ragged breath that shakes his body, "A special friend."

"Oh, my dear," Mrs. West says as she opens her arms and pulls Pylus into a warm hug, "I'm so sorry."

Part of the boulder that had been sitting in Pylus' chest breaks off during the kind gesture from Mrs. West. He's touched by the genuine sorrow and empathy she has for him and the kindness shown. Time stops for him as he lets the stress of the last hour fall away with the safe embrace of his elderly neighbor.

"Thank you," he chokes out.

"You are so welcome, my dear."

In his apartment, Pylus makes his way to his bedroom in the dark. The bathroom light is the only one he uses as he scrubs off the now dried blood. When he's done, the light goes out, plunging the apartment into darkness once again. He makes his way to his bed, collapsing onto his mattress. Sleep comes to him quickly, and he welcomes the dark reprieve.

***

Eight people stand around a fresh hole in the ground with a simple casket suspended over it. There was no funeral. Just a graveside service. The man standing at the head of the casket introduced himself as the religious leader of the church Ellie attended. He's currently speaking of how Ellie was quiet and liked to keep to herself in church, but would always come and talk with him after services. Her sweet spirit always made his day brighter. She had that effect on people.

Pylus stands to the side with Reggie and George next to him. George wears a nice suit that has probably been in a closet for the last thirty years. His mangy hair and beard are groomed in such a way that Pylus had to do a double-take when he first saw him. On the other side of the casket stand the other four workers from the diner. Two cooks, another waitress, and Becky, all in their early forties. All attendees are simple people in simple clothes.

Most funerals these days are this way. A small gathering of people around a grave to remember the life of a person who would be forgotten quickly once all in attendance passed on with their own simple funerals and small gatherings.

"Ellie always said that she didn't fear death," the man from the church says, "She said her faith in her creator helped her to look forward with courage. That way, she was able to live each day fully. Her example was nothing short of inspiring."

Pylus tries to swallow the lump that forms in his throat as the man speaks. Ellie was inspiring. She always had a smile on her face and a light around her. The more Pylus thinks back on his memories of her, the more he sees how brightly she shone in his life. Her influence on him was almost imperceptible, mainly because he was too caught up in his own darkness. Somehow, though, her light still found its way into his life, and just when he was finally about to let it illuminate his world, it was stolen from him. It seems, to him, every time he gets a flicker of a light in his life, something has to come along and snuff it out.

"If any of you would like to participate, you are welcome to," the church man says, pulling Pylus out of his thoughts. George and the workers from the diner bow their heads with the church man.

"They're praying," Reggie whispers, answering Pylus' unspoken question.

Pylus had never prayed before. In fact, he never really saw anyone pray before. He watches the faces of those bowing their heads. George looks peaceful, the other waitress looks heartbroken, both cooks look tired as if they haven't slept well since they got the news of Ellie, Becky holds her clasped hands to her lips, tears falling in waterfalls from her eyes. As the church man prays, a tear rolls down his cheek as well. In that one tear, Pylus sees more pain than in all the rest of the pain he has seen since this service started. This man cared for Ellie more than any of them could understand. Pylus admires his strength. Being able to hold his composure enough to perform this service despite the heartbreak he must be feeling.

"Lord, we ask for peace from thy hand to settle the restless hearts of those who grieve the loss of this wonderful young woman, and peace for her soul as she returns to thee. In thy son's name, amen." As the prayer is ended, those who had joined in it lift their heads and dry their eyes, muttering their own quiet "amen."

The diner workers each take turns going to the casket and saying their goodbyes before walking out of the cemetery. After they have all left, George steps up and puts his hand on the casket gently. Bending forward, he places a soft, adoring kiss on the lid.

"Thank you for being the first one who was ever kind to me," he whispers.

As he turns around to walk away, he puts his arm around Pylus's waist and leans his old head on his chest. The show of affection surprises Pylus. Like Reggie, George has never been one to initiate physical contact unless it was in a gruff, friendly manner. Gingerly, Pylus puts his arms around his old friend. George's whole frame shakes against him. At first, he thinks George is having a heart attack until he hears the quiet sobs. Whatever part of Pylus's heart was still intact shatters completely. The pain of George's sobs hits him like a battering ram. Time stands still for Pylus as George cries. Reggie and the man from the church stand with their heads bowed and their hands folded, giving George his privacy as he grieves. Pylus had no idea Ellie meant so much to George. Truth be told, he didn't know George could feel this strongly about anyone after all the loss he had suffered. Pylus hadn't been through nearly as much as the elderly man, and yet he had shut himself off to everyone. Why would George keep giving himself the chance to be hurt?

"She was the daughter I always wanted," George whispers.

It occurs to Pylus that George never talks about having kids. Either it was too painful, or he and Gloria had never had any. Quite possibly it was both. George had known Ellie for a while before Pylus met him, and he liked to tell slightly exaggerated stories of Ellie pulling him off the street and paying for a meal because she thought he was homeless. "Nicest flower in the whole darn meadow," as George would put it.

George takes a deep breath as he pulls away from Pylus, "Pop on in for a spill later, will ya, kid?"

"Sure thing, George," Pylus croaks, his throat tight with emotion. His friend nods and pats Pylus on the cheek without looking at him.

As George shuffles away between headstones, the man from the church steps up to Pylus with a compassionate smile. "Pylus, right?"

"Yes, sir," Pylus nods.

"My name is Billie Oliver. I didn't get a chance to properly introduce myself before the service," his eyes fall to his shoes as he continues, "I just wanted to tell you that Ellie spoke of you often. She told me what you do for a living and how she was amazed that you were still such a kind and caring person," his eyes find Pylus' again. The compassionate look he has is underlined by something else. Almost respect, "She said you were the sweetest person she had ever met and that she wanted to be like you."

Pylus moves his mouth but can't get any words past the surprise caught in his chest. Giving up, he looks at the ground and lets out a deep breath. Oh Ellie. Sweet, caring, pure Ellie. The girl whom Pylus thought was the epitome of human kindness wanted to be like... him? A beast?

Billie places his hand on Pylus's shoulder and gives him a gentle shake, "Son, I can see what you're thinking. If there was anything Ellie was perfect at, it was judging character. You may think you're less than a good person, but if Ellie says you are good, then I believe it, no questions."

What was happening? Pylus had come here to remember Ellie and grieve her loss, and here he was getting comfort and counsel from a stranger who knew him vicariously through Ellie's stories. Stories of how good of a person he is? If only they all knew.

"Thank you, Billie," he says softly.

Billie gives his shoulder one last squeeze before going to Ellie's casket and saying his goodbyes. He stops by Pylus before he walks away, "The church we meet in is a couple of blocks south of Becky's. Feel free to stop by anytime. I'm always there."

As Billie walks away, Pylus feels like some of the comfort he was feeling leaves, too. Reggie pats his arm softly and tells him the car will be waiting and to take his time.

He stands alone with Ellie, just as it was when this whole thing started. Of course, back then, it was a beautiful dream; now it's a waking nightmare. Slowly, he steps up to the casket and places his hand on it. The wood is warm under the midday sun, the last warmth he will feel from what could have been a wonderful experience.

"I'm sorry, Ellie," he whispers.

A warm breeze ruffles through his being and seems to circle his face and lift his chin. He gazes into the blue sky as the wind embraces him. As it kisses his ears, he swears he hears a voice whispering to him. Some petals from a bouquet on top of the casket flutter up into the wind, suspended momentarily in front of him before they stream away across the cemetery.

***

"No, it is not happening," Reggie says forcefully into his phone as Pylus gets into the car, then smashes the end call button multiple times as if it'll get the point across to whomever he was talking to.

"What's going on?" Pylus asks.

"Nothing you need to worry about," Reggie sighs, rubbing his eyes, "Just business stuff."

"Reggie, I am your business."

Reggie's fingers stop rubbing his eyes, and Pylus hears him suck in a quiet breath, "Got me there. Okay, one of the other Champion owners called and wants to set up a fight with you."

"Okay," Pylus says slowly, "Why is that such a big deal?"

Reggie lets out a deep breath before answering, "Because they want to do a double header."

Sometimes, to amp up the excitement of the Champion games, owners will agree to have an event, known as a double header, where their contender fights two opponents instead of one. The solo contender fights one hybrid in a one-on-one match, then immediately after the first fight, if the solo contender won, the second fight begins with a fresh opponent. It's a grueling match for the soloist but brings in almost three times the amount of revenue of a regular match, especially with a high-up and well-known contender like Pylus.

"Set it up," Pylus whispers, looking out the window.

"Pylus, you just went through a rough situation and lost a friend. You should take some time to recover." Reggie argues.

"I don't need to recover Reg," Pylus says calmly, "I need a distraction."

Reggie let's out another sigh, "Kid, running away from your grief only ends up making it worse. It's better to let the pain be there and run its course."

"I'm not running from my grief. Ellie watched all of my matches because she cared about me and wanted me to make it out," Pylus explains, "I'm tired of contending, Reg. It's time to go

43

Ultimate so I can do just that." Pylus can feel Reggie looking at him, but keeps his eyes out the window.

"You sure about this kid?"

"Yeah. I am."

Reggie waits until after Pylus gets dropped off to make the call. The whole drive home, he kept telling Pylus he didn't have to do the double header and that he could take a break for a while if he needed. Pylus was unmoved. He needed to get on with life. In his mind, you don't take a break when you lose someone. You keep going with life and take the memory of those you love with you into everything you do. At least that's how he has done things so far.

Pylus changes out of his second-hand suit and makes his way towards George's home. He had never actually been there, but George had told him the address in case he was ever in the area and needed something. The apartment building the address leads to is much nicer than the one Pylus lives in and is very well-maintained. The grass and bushes on the outside are impeccable. The stairwell leading up to George's apartment is full of paintings of all varieties. Pylus finds himself drawn towards the open mountain ranges and forests. They remind him of simpler times.

The shiny 308 on the door reflects the light brightly. It's obviously been polished recently. George must be much better off than he lets people believe. Pylus knocks on the door and waits for an answer. When none comes, he knocks again. Still no answer. Turning the handle, he pushes the door open slightly and calls for George.

"Back here," he hears from inside.

He closes the door and makes his way through the nice but mostly empty apartment. Two bookcases full of books sit on the wall to his right. A recliner and coffee table take up the middle of the room, and a decorative table sits on the far wall, covered in pictures. Two doorways sit open to his right. One is on the wall with the bookcases, and the other is on the wall across from Pylus, that one leads to a kitchen and dining room. The other must lead to the bedroom. Pylus walks through it to find George laying on a bed staring at the ceiling.

"Hey kid," he says quietly, and by the tone of his voice, Pylus knows something is wrong. "You made it just in time."

"What's going on, George?" Pylus asks, afraid he already knows the answer.

"Oh, you know, son, time comes calling for all men, and none can run longer than he done got."

Pylus grabs a chair from the foot of the bed and sits down next to George. He watches slow, ragged breaths barely lift George's chest. It feels like everything inside of him has turned to stone. George's heart beats faintly, all the strength that had carried it this far, gone.

"You know, son, you and Ellie were the only family I had left. Like the kids I always wanted."

"What about Gloria?" Pylus asks. George always told him he had to get home before Gloria got worried. *Where is she now?* He wonders.

George smiles softly and closes his eyes, "Gloria passed on ten years ago."

Pylus blinks his eyes in confusion, "Why do you always say you need to get home to her then?"

George lets out a deep breath before he answers, "Because her memory still be here. I've never let her go. When I come home I be stepping back to all the memories we made. All the pictures and scrapbooks keep her alive in my heart, and her spirit still dances through these rooms, teasing me like she always done."

"That's beautiful," Pylus whispers.

"You don't have to let the ones you love go, Pylus."

Tears fill Pylus' eyes. He didn't think he had any left. "What are you telling me, George?"

Another deep sigh, "I've felt it coming like a dark storm in the summer days. . . Only I'm not worried about this one. . . Old things gotta quit at some point, wouldn't ya know. . . And I'm old. . . So very old. . . I don't want ya crying for me, boy. . . I know you just lost Ellie. . . but it's my time. I'm happy to go. . . be with my sweet Gloria again. . . I'll even tell Ellie. . . you miss her," he says with a smile. His breaths get shorter with each word he speaks.

"Thanks, George," Pylus says, his voice breaking. He reaches up and takes George's hand in his. George gives him an encouraging squeeze.

"I was worried. . . You weren't gonna. . . make it in time," George wheezes, "but. . . wouldn't you know it. . . I got to see. . . my son, Pylus. . . one. . . more. . . time."

Tears fall from Pylus's eyes, and he has to bite his lip to keep from crying out. He doesn't have much time, and he's not going to waste it.

"Thank you, George. I will *always* remember you," he says.

The corners of George's mouth pull up into a sweet smile. He takes a deep breath and lets it out. His heart beats twice, then stops.

6

Four days after Ellie's funeral and two days after George's, Pylus stands under dim yellow lights that flicker on and off with the pounding of feet above him. He stands in his normal fighting get-up, cut off jean shorts with one of his knives sheathed on the back. The only addition is a small bandage around his right hand where his bullet wound still heals. The cool concrete feels good on his bare feet. Strung around his neck, a leather band holds two rings. One is George's wedding ring that he always wore, and the other is the ring Ellie was wearing when she died. Pylus slipped it off her finger before the officials had arrived. Eyes closed, he takes a deep breath and holds the two rings in his hands. He stays that way until he hears the doors at the end of the hallway start to open. Before he opens his eyes, he lifts the rings to his lips and gives them a soft kiss.

"Lend me your strength," he whispers as he opens his eyes.

Reggie had called him the night before and told him the details of the fight. Typical double header. The first is with a rookie contender and the second with one who has been in for almost a year. They want to make sure Pylus makes it to the second round for a better show.

Going to George's funeral had Reggie pushing Pylus to take a break again. Pylus was stubborn and told him he needed to keep going now more than ever.

The morning of the fight, Reggie had pressed him again, "Pylus, with all the press you've had from Ellie's murder and now losing George, I just don't want you to do anything reckless," he reasoned.

"Don't worry, my head is clear," Pylus reassured him.

Reggie's eyes held a trace of doubt, "I trust that kid, I'm just worried."

"I get it. You don't want to lose your best fighter. "

"No," Reggie said, "I don't want to lose my best friend."

Just before walking into the arena, Pylus stops, "I won't let you down, Reg," he whispers to the empty hallway.

"PYLUS BREEEEEEKK!!" The announcer shouts as Pylus enters the arena. "AAAND HIS OPPONENT! HOPPEEER!!"

The crowd goes wild as a slender figure literally hops out onto the opposite end of the arena. He's smaller than Pylus, and his legs make up for two-thirds of his height. It's hard to tell from this distance, but it looks like his tongue is hanging from his mouth. The arena has a row of columns on each side of varying heights, with the middle completely open. Hopper squats down, eyeing Pylus. Suddenly, he jumps and soars thirty feet to the column closest to him, landing on top easily.

A frog or toad, it seems, Pylus thinks to himself. He pulls his knife from its sheath and walks towards the center of the arena. Hopper jumps from column to column, stopping on the tallest one closest to Pylus' end. Pylus stops when he is in line with the column but still in the center of the arena. From here, he can see Hopper's skin practically glowing yellow. Something in Pylus' memory tickles his mind. What is so significant about this color?

When Pylus first became a contender, he got as many books about animals as he could get his hands on. Every night, he would spend hours studying the most common hybrid animals to give himself an advantage in the arena. Frogs and toads weren't very common because they had no offensive abilities, and most of the best defense they had was in evasion or swimming. Except. . .

Golden Dart Frog! Pylus remembers, scrutinizing Hopper's fluorescent hue. One of the most toxic animals in the world. Its skin is poisonous to the touch as long as it eats certain insects that boost its potency. Pylus would bet all his money that Hopper's owner made sure he kept up on those insects.

"Pylus Brek," Hopper calls down from his perch, "It's an honor to face you. May the best hybrid win."

"Let's see what you have," Pylus calls back with a smirk.

Hopper gives him an amused smile. He leans back slightly, then launches himself off his perch. He flies through the air above Pylus. As he gets directly over Pylus, he shoots his tongue straight down. His trajectory is sound and his aim pristine; however, Pylus is faster. Hopper's tongue flashes just to the side of Pylus' head as he ducks to the side. Before Pylus can get his knife up to cut the tongue, it pulls back to Hopper's mouth as he lands.

"That's some impressive jump distance," Pylus says, "Most dart frogs can only do short hops."

"You've done your research," Hopper says, raising his eyebrows.

Pylus shrugs, "I've always liked learning about animals. Your tongue is also longer than it should be, relatively speaking."

Hoppers looks even more surprised when he speaks, "I had multiple types of frog DNA mixed with mine. That's why I can jump far. The tongue is just a weird side effect of the transition. Sometimes it doesn't retract fully, so it hangs out of my mouth." Said tongue suddenly flicks out straight towards Pylus. He dodges barely, but is too slow with his knife again.

"Is your tongue toxic, too, or just your skin?"

"Just my skin as far as I know," Hopper says, shooting his tongue out again. Pylus dodges again but brings his knife up in time to nick the tip of it before it pulls back.

"AH! Geez!" Hopper yells, holding his tongue.

"I would say sorry, but that's not how it works here," Pylus says.

Hopper nods, "Yeah, unfortunately. Wish I didn't have to kill you, but such is life."

Hopper doesn't wait to finish his sentence before he lunges at Pylus, who dives to the side and rolls to his feet. Before he can move again, Hopper's tongue is out and sticks to his wrist. Frogs can lift double their body weight with their tongues, and Pylus is only slightly bigger than Hopper. One hard tug is all it takes to lift Pylus off the ground and over Hopper's head. Pylus slams into the ground on the other side of the frog hybrid. Out of breath but not dazed, Pylus pulls against the tongue and flips around to face Hopper. Luckily, his knife hand is free. He brings it around quickly and slices through the tongue as he feels it start to tug his arm again.

"AAAAAAAHHHHHHHH," Hopper screams as he jumps backward. He lands thirty feet away on his back with his hands to his face.

Pylus sprints towards where the frog man lays. His long wolf legs propel him forward quickly, and soon he's on top of Hopper. For having just had his tongue cut out, Hopper responds surprisingly fast. Rolling over his shoulders, he dodges Pylus' knife but only by inches. He stays crouched and eyes Pylus with a new look as blood runs from his mouth and down his chin. Murder is written in his eyes. It's a look Pylus has become very familiar with. Most contenders he gets this close to have that same look. Hopper uses the distance to his advantage and jumps straight at Pylus as if to bear hug him. Pylus bends backward, Hopper sailing over him, both toxic hands inches from his bare chest and face.

Pylus doesn't let his back stay on the ground long. Kicking his legs, he pinwheels on his shoulders and puts one hand on the ground, then rotates his hips so his feet land underneath him. Hopper had hit the ground in a roll and now faces Pylus over his shoulder. As soon as Pylus takes his first step forward, Hopper jumps again in a smooth back flip over Pylus, just like Pylus wanted.

Planting his front foot, Pylus turns his shoulders with his knife leading the rotation. The knife leaves his hand half a second before Hopper lands. As Hopper's feet hit the ground, he is met with the point of Pylus' knife in his chest. He lets out a deep grunt and stumbles backward two steps before sinking to his knees. The knife sits right in his diaphragm, half the blade sunk in.

"Nice throw," Hopper chokes out as he struggles for breath.

"Thanks," Pylus says quietly.

The crowded stadium falls silent as they realize Hopper isn't dead yet and Pylus can't get close to him without being poisoned. They watch with bated breath to see what happens next.

"You know..." Hopper says, "my first few fights... got me thinking... I could do pretty well here. . . but then. . . I heard. . . I was going against you," He tries to take several deep breaths before continuing, "Honestly. Can't say I'm mad. . . to lose to you. . . you're as good. . . as they say."

Pylus kneels in front of Hopper, being sure to keep just out of his opponent's reach, "You fought well."

"Thank you," a peaceful smile spreads across Hopper's face as he lifts his eyes to the sky, "I'm not mad I lost. For the first time. . . since I became a hybrid. . . I felt respected." He drops his eyes to

Pylus' and gives him one more smile. He takes another deep breath and closes his eyes, rests his blood-soaked chin on his chest, and breathes out his final breath. Pylus listens to his heart as it stops beating before bowing his head and reciting his honorary farewell.

After his ritual, Pylus stands and twists his knife out of Hopper's chest, careful not to touch his skin or blood. He can feel his own blood running down his back from spinning in the dirt. His shoulder is sore from being slammed on the ground, and his wrist is rubbed raw from Hopper's tongue, but otherwise, he feels good and ready for the next round.

Turning to face his next opponent, his breath stops as he sees the door already open and no contender in sight. Quickly, he scans the area around the door, then bolts for the columns when he doesn't see anyone there. Fifteen feet from the columns, a shadow passes over him. He brings his arm up just in time to have it grabbed by claws of some sort that lift him in the air and drop him from twelve feet high.

Agility and luck favor him today as he lands on his feet and rolls to a crouch. He scans the arena and still sees no one. His roll has brought him closer to the columns, so he breaks for cover again. The shadow returns as he takes his first step. Too late this time. Pylus dives as soon as the shadow catches his eye. He feels the claws kiss his lower back, but misses the grab. A less-than-graceful roll puts him safely behind the column. He presses his back to it, feeling the blood from his shoulder and now lower back sticking to the stone.

"Where are they?" Pylus hisses.

The arena appears to be empty. He checks the tops of all the columns he can see, but still can't pinpoint his new opponent. Cautiously, he makes his way around the column to the open arena side. Still no sign of movement. From here, Pylus can see all the columns on the other side, but no contender.

"Pylus Brek," sneers a voice from above.

Whipping around, Pylus drops into a crouch and pulls his knife to guard his face. A terrifying figure perches on top of the column he was just hiding behind.

His legs are covered in feathers and end in sharp, taloned feet. Instead of arms, large wings extend from a bare torso and drape over the edge of the column. His face is a normal human face with a shaved head and a malicious sneer.

"You know I told Hopper he didn't stand a chance," the birdman says. From the look of him, Pylus guesses he's part golden eagle. Probably a high-end midbrid. "Have to be honest, though, he lasted longer than I thought he was going to."

Slowly, Pylus begins backing towards the center of the arena, keeping his knife up and ready. The birdman makes him extra uneasy. Not just because of his ability to fly and razor-sharp talons, but because he reminds Pylus of Amos, Ellie's ex-boyfriend and murderer.

"Seems like the only contenders you've been up against lately are mediocre at best," The birdman continues, "Obviously, Hopper was a warm-up to prep you for a real challenge. I bet our owner was glad to be rid of him, honestly."

"Do you always *squawk* on like this?" Pylus asks, letting his anger at Ellie's death direct itself at this arrogant prick.

Birdman's cocky sneer turns to an offended snarl, making his resemblance to Amos even more apparent, "Alright then, that's what you want? Get ready, Pylus Brek."

With a piercing screech, Birdman leaps from his perch and dives at Pylus, talons out. Time slows as Pylus waits for his moment. He can see the details of each feather. The sun glints off the tips of the razor-sharp talons closing in on him. Timing is going to be everything for this to work. Each heartbeat brings the moment closer and closer until it's right on top of him. Time to move.

In one quick motion, Pylus arches his back, drops his shoulders, and slices his knife inches above his face, barely catching the back of Birdman's ankle, whose back talon catches Pylus across the forehead. Dust flies up around both contenders as Pylus lands on his back and Birdman slides into his landing.

"That's it?" Birdman calls out, "The *great* Pylus Brek? Seems to me like you are just really good at dodging. You got that fancy knife and don't even know how to use it right."

"You sure about that?" Pylus asks.

"Am I sure about that? I'm still standing, aren't I?" As if to prove his point, Birdman takes a step forward only to have his leg give out from under him. "What? Why won't my leg work?"

"You don't know much about poison dart frogs, do you?"

Birdman looks up, confused, "Poison what?"

"Poison dart frogs have toxic skin," Pylus explains. Pacing like a teacher in front of a foolish student, "Their toxicity is so potent that it can cause total paralysis in less than three hours. Given Hopper's size compared to a normal dart frog, I would say his poison will paralyze you in a matter of seconds."

Birdman's wings shake under his weight as he falls forward, barely catching himself. After a couple of seconds, they give out, and he falls to his side convulsing.

"H-how did y-you. . ." Birdman stutters.

"When I killed Hopper, the toxins from his skin stayed on my blade," Pylus brandishes the weapon. "I cut your heel with the same blade; now his toxins are going through your bloodstream. Your body is fully paralyzed, and in a few seconds, your heart will seize up, and you'll die. The worst part of your situation is you didn't last nearly as long as Hopper did."

Hatred burns in Birdman's eyes until they roll back in his head, and his convulsing stops. Pylus listens to his heart stop without sympathy for the fallen opponent. He stands without reciting his ritual farewell or signaling his victory and stalks back to his entrance. The cheers of the crowd seem distant and dull as he walks across the arena. He passes by Hopper's body on the way and slows to look at the peaceful smile still on the dead hybrid's lips. He hopes that when his day comes, he can find that same peace as he moves on from this world.

The darkness of the tunnel embraces Pylus like an old friend and brings the comforting silence that he has come to crave. Today, the silence holds more comfort than ever before.

His knife clangs to the ground when the doors close. Something is wrong. He feels so conflicted. This is his life. This is all their lives. It's kill or be killed. It's *Champion*, the price to become a hybrid. It's just how the world works. Isn't it? No matter how he thinks of it, killing Hopper feels wrong. Maybe in another life, they could have been friends.

The fight with the birdman was strange, too. Killing other contenders had never been anything personal before, but with the birdman, it felt like it was. In fact, it was almost. . . enjoyable. It made him sick to think about the satisfaction he felt watching the birdman's feeble struggle to survive.

Was he getting a conscience? After all the fighting, all the killing, now he was starting to feel sorry for those he faced. Or was it just the genuine adoration from Hopper that was making him feel this way? In only a couple of short minutes, he had made a connection with the frog man that had never been a part of any other fight. Every other contender came in with only one thing on their mind: death. But Hopper found something more to focus on: excitement for life. His outlook on a bleak situation reminded Pylus of Ellie. No matter what situation they were in, they looked for something good to focus on.

Maybe it was the losses that were making him think this way. Death had always surrounded him, but he had usually been the wielder of it. Now he was a lone soldier left over from a burst of Gatling gun fire, alone to stare at the bodies of friends who weren't so lucky.

Pylus leans his forehead against the cool cement wall. Anger and frustration burning in his chest. When did everything start getting so muddled? It used to be a cut-and-dry lifestyle. Suddenly, everything is confusing and contradictory.

"Mr. Brek," says a voice behind him.

Pylus turns his head on the wall and looks at who spoke to him. Reggie's driver and personal assistant, Travis, stands behind him in his tailored suit. "Mr. Reggie sent me to pick you up and bring you to his office."

"No press conference?" Pylus asks.

Travis shakes his head, "Mr. Reggie thinks you would be better off not appearing in public, given recent events."

"Probably smart," Pylus agrees, "Alright, I'll go get cleaned up and meet you at the car."

Picking up his knife, Pylus makes his way to his waiting room. He takes extra care to wash his knife, without letting it touch his skin, thoroughly before putting it away. He packs all his things quickly after his shower and self-medication treatment and slings his bag over his shoulder. Every time before this, he felt confident and collected walking down these halls after a fight. This time, he feels like a hypocrite and a murderer.

Travis opens the door for him when he reaches the car. Just before ducking in, he notices someone watching him. Leifa Ordonston, half concealed in a doorway. She doesn't look away when he makes eye contact with her. Her usual flirtatious gaze is cold, almost calculating. A shudder runs down Pylus' spine as he ducks into the vehicle.

The drive to Reggie's office is a short one from the arena, and soon Pylus is riding the elevator up to the eighth floor in the fancy business building. The elevator doors open to a short hallway with a door on each side and one at the end. Pylus makes his way to the one at the end of the hallway and knocks twice before walking in. Reggie sits behind his simple oak desk, staring out his floor-to-ceiling windows. He looks troubled.

"Reg?" Pylus asks quietly.

Reggie snaps his head around as if broken out of a trance, "Oh, Pylus. Thanks for coming. I've got something important to talk to you about."

"Does it have to do with the three guys I killed *that* night?" Pylus asks.

"What? Oh, no. All three of those goons were wanted for murder, so the officials said you did them a favor by dealing with them. After all, the penalty for murder is death." Reggie gives him a small smile, "Anyway, the reason I had you meet me here is because..." A knock on the door cuts Reggie off. "They're early," he mumbles as the door opens.

"Hey, Reg," a short man says as he walks in. Dark hair sticks up in all directions from his head, and a well-groomed beard covers his jaw. He has to be around Reggie's age, maybe a couple of years younger. "Sorry, I'm a bit early."

"Pylus, this is Jefferson Rye," Reggie says without standing. In fact, he looks rather annoyed.

Pylus turns and offers Jefferson his hand, "Nice to meet you, Mr. Rye."

Mr. Rye takes his hand in a firm grip and pumps it vigorously, "It's a real treat to be meeting *you*, Pylus. I hope you will consider my offer."

Pylus pulls his hand back in shock, "Offer?"

"I haven't told him yet, Jeff!" Reggie says with a hand over his eyes.

"Told me what?" Pylus asks, utterly confused. Was Jefferson Rye another Champion owner? Was Reggie actually going to trade him?

"Ah, sorry about that," Jefferson says, looking sheepish, "I can step out for a second if you need."

Reggie shakes his head, "No, no, you might as well stay and help me explain it to him."

"Explain what?" Pylus asks again, worry rising in his chest. *Would* Reggie actually trade him? After all they had gone through together? What about all the stuff he told Pylus about wanting a better life for him?

"Calm down, Pylus," Reggie says as he stands and walks around to the front of his desk, "Jeff here is the owner of J.R. Genetics, the biggest plant genetic altering company on this continent and possibly the world. His company is the reason why crop production has increased so drastically over the last ten years and why we are able to supply enough food to every settlement without most of the farmers around."

"Ah, Reg, you do care about my career," Jefferson says with an annoyingly sweet voice.

Reggie rolls his eyes, "He's also my kid brother."

It suddenly occurs to Pylus that he has never known Reggie's last name. Now that he thinks about it, he can see the family resemblance. Jefferson got the feast of the hair genes while Reggie got the famine, but their eyes and nose are the same. Jefferson has the same bright look in his eyes that Reggie always has. Except for right now, Reggie's eyes hold a new weight behind them.

"The thing is, Pylus," Jefferson says, ignoring Reggie, "I'm looking for some new... talent to hire onto my security detail. The last few recruits have been... less than ideal."

"So, what does that have to do with me?" Pylus asks.

"He wants you to be his new security guard," Reggie says.

Pylus blinks several times, not comprehending the new information, "... What?"

"I want you as my new security guard," Jefferson repeats.

"Yeah, I heard that," Pylus says, still looking at Reggie, "What I'm asking, Mr. Rye, is why would you want a hybrid on your security detail? Especially since you're such a high public figure."

"Well, like I said, my last few recruits haven't been making the cut," Jefferson says, "I blame it on lack of experience and under-training. I guess I could have taken the time to train someone, or I could just find someone with experience. But then I thought, a Champion contender has oodles of experience. And as luck would have it, I happen to know someone who is involved with Champion and has a *very* experienced contender in his ranks."

"Okay, but I'm still confused," Pylus says, looking between Reggie and his brother.

Jefferson lets out a deep sigh, and the brightness of his eyes seems to leave with his breath, "Alright, full disclosure, I want you to be my *daughter's* personal bodyguard. The last seven bodyguards she has had only lasted a month at most before they were... removed from service. There has been an increase in attacks on my daughter. Someone either wants to hold her for ransom to try to ruin my company, or they want her dead. It's gotten to the point where I won't leave her in one place for very long. I'm always moving her around when I'm not traveling, and I take her with me every time I do have to travel."

"My brother believes with your experience and... abilities as a hybrid, you could protect my niece better than the regular human bodyguards he has been employing over the last few months," Reggie adds, looking more and more tired as the conversation progresses.

"And you're just willingly going to go along with this?" Pylus asks.

Reggie shrugs, "Family comes first, Pylus. Plus, Jeff says he will compensate me for my loss. But in all honesty, kid, I want you to have a better life, and I think this is the best way for you to get it. You were saying how contending isn't for you anymore. Senseless killing has never really sat well with you anyway, but with this, maybe you can find a more meaningful life."

Pylus drops his gaze, "I... don't know what to say. Thank you, Reggie, I guess."

Reggie pats him on the shoulder, "Don't thank me yet, you don't know what you're getting yourself into."

"When would I start?" Pylus asks Reggie's kid brother.

"I will have someone get your stuff tonight if you accept," Jefferson says.

A small gasp escapes Pylus, "That soon?"

"I know it's sudden," Jefferson says, "but every second counts when it comes to keeping my daughter safe."

"Alright," Pylus says, "Can I have a few minutes to talk to Reggie?"

Jefferson nods, "Of course. I'll just wait outside."

Pylus waits until the door clicks shut before he turns back to his friend. "Okay, Reggie, I feel like I'm drowning here. This is too much information all at once."

"I know, kid, it's a lot," Reggie says, looking at the ground, "Especially with everything else that you have on your mind right now. But think of it this way," he lifts his eyes to Pylus', "you have been beating yourself up over not being able to save Ellie. Maybe someone is giving you a second chance to save a life."

Reggie studies Pylus for a moment, then softly touches the bandage on his forehead, "Nearly got you today, didn't they?"

Roiling emotions bombard Pylus' heart at the concern and grief in Reggie's eyes. The man's hand lingers on his bandage for a moment before dropping to his shoulder. Reggie lowers his head as a tear falls to the ground.

Pylus lets out an exasperated sigh, "For two years, things have been the same for us. I fight, I win, we celebrate, and move up in the world. But in less than a week, everything has changed. The life that I've known is about to be gone. Not that it's been much of a life, but all things considered, it's been a good one because of you. I can never repay you for all you've given me, Reg."

Reggie pulls him into a tight hug and holds him. Time stops as they embrace, the action saying everything they can't. Eventually, Reggie backs away, leaving his hands on Pylus's shoulders and says, "Pylus, if you really wish to repay me, protect my family."

7

In only two hours, a group of Jefferson Rye's assistants packed up everything in Pylus' apartment and hauled it away to his new home. Now Pylus stands in his empty apartment.

For the last hour and a half, Pylus stood alone, reminiscing on the nights he had spent in this room reading about animals or meditating. He thought of the first time he met Mrs. West and how she had invited him in for tea. He remembered coming home from all his fights and laying in the middle of the floor to stare at the ceiling and question the decisions that led him to this point, then forget everything and shut down his thinking. Something about letting his mind go blank and doing nothing helped him cope with the fact that he had just taken a life. Maybe this new change will help him find some closure for everything else he has done in life.

At the base of the stairs, Mrs. West waits for him, tears filling her eyes, "Oh my dear, I'm going to miss you."

"I'll miss you too, Mrs. West," Pylus says, giving her a tight hug. Tears well up in his eyes as she squeezes him tighter than her frail frame would suggest she could.

"Please promise me you will take care of yourself out there?" She says into his chest.

"Of course, I'll be sure to come back and visit you."

"You mean that?"

He squeezes her tightly again, "I sure do."

Mrs. West keeps her arm around his waist as she walks him to the big SUV waiting for him outside. She dabs her eyes with a little white handkerchief all the way out. Pylus gives her one last embrace before climbing into the backseat and closing the door.

The drive takes him further south in the settlement than he's ever gone before. It doesn't take too long before they turn onto a road almost completely obscured by thick trees on both sides.

Multiple twists and turns lead deeper into the thicket. After the second or third turn, there's no chance of seeing the main road. A mile later, the trees clear out to reveal a comfortable-looking cabin in the middle of a small clearing. A tall spiked fence surrounds the cabin in a threatening-looking circle. The SUV pulls up to a small gate and stops.

The driver turns back in his seat to look at Pylus, "You have to walk the rest of the way."

"Um, okay," Pylus says. Warily, he opens the door and steps onto the gravel drive.

As he steps up to the gate, it opens quietly. It's big enough for the SUV to fit through, so why is he walking? He waits until the gate stops moving before he starts his trek across the open area between him and the cabin. As he walks, he keeps his head forward, but his eyes move about, taking in everything he can. Hidden all around, security guards watch his movement. One behind the chimney, two inside the front window on the left, and the top one on the right, two in the trees to the left, three to the right, and those are only the ones he can see. He can smell several more, further in the trees. Seems like Mr. Rye has plenty of security patrolling around. *Why does he need me?* Pylus thinks.

The guards in the windows back up out of sight as Pylus gets closer to the door. He steps up the two front steps carefully. Standing on the porch, he takes a deep breath. He can smell coffee brewing inside, some sort of odor-concealing spray probably covering all the security guards, and a sweet perfume. Letting his air out, he rolls his shoulders and knocks on the door.

A little speaker next to the door crackles to life before he finishes his knock, "State your name."

"Um, Pylus Brek."

The speaker stays silent for a moment, then crackles, "State your business."

"I'm the new security guard for Mr. Rye's daughter. This is where the car he sent for me dropped me off."

Again, silence for a moment, "When the door opens, go through it and into the room on your immediate left. Do not linger or deviate, or you will be shot."

Pylus starts to second-guess his decision to accept this job. He jumps as the door buzzes and swings open slightly. Remembering the threat about lingering, he quickly walks in and turns left without so much as glancing around the interior of the house. As soon as he crosses the threshold of the door to the room, it slams shut behind him. He whips around to find the security guard he saw through the window earlier standing behind the door, waiting. He hears movement behind and turns to see two more guards step out from behind a bookshelf and the drapes. One of them steps behind a desk that sits in the middle of the room and sets a silver briefcase on it.

"Step forward, please." He says opening the case and turning it to Pylus. Inside is a complicated-looking computer-like system.

Pylus steps to the edge of the desk and looks from the case to the guard.

"Place each finger individually on the scanner here," the man says, pointing to a little square at the front of the case, "Start with the thumb of the left hand. You will hear a beep when each fingerprint has been recorded. When you do, lift the finger off the scanner and wait two seconds before starting the next one." When he finishes speaking, he leans back, folds his hands in front of him, and stares at Pylus. Even though Pylus is a full six inches taller than this man, he still gets the chills looking into those eyes. He gets the feeling this guy would rather kill him on the spot than take his fingerprints. Granted, the majority of humans feel that way when face-to-face with a hybrid.

Thirty seconds and ten beeps later, the briefcase is turned around, and the guard types something on it before flipping it back to Pylus, "Look in here for the retinal scan."

Pylus takes a knee and stares into the little lens. A bright light flashes quickly, making him flinch back and rub his now watering eye. He hears the briefcase turn and the guard type again, followed by the briefcase turning back once more.

"Look here for a picture. Don't smile and don't blink."

Thankfully, the camera doesn't use a flash to take the picture. Three clicks indicate the photo has been taken. The guard flips the briefcase around and closes it, then walks over to a machine in the corner that has started purring. It whirrs as something starts coming out of the bottom of it. The guard walks over and grabs it as it finishes. He clips it to a lanyard of some sort, then turns and hands it to Pylus. It's a laminated security badge with the picture of Pylus and a barcode.

"This card grants you access to the safe rooms and emergency exits. It also labels you as an official member of the Rye security detail. Keep it on your person at all times. This way." With a quick step and a stiff demeanor, the short guard steps past Pylus and moves across the room briskly.

Pylus follows the guard through the door he came in. The two other guards fall into step behind him, making him feel like he is a person of importance or concern.

Out in the entryway, Pylus takes a quick look around. A simple hallway leads down to two more doors on the far end of the house. On the opposite side of the hallway, a staircase leads to an upstairs area. The group crosses in front of the stairs and into the room directly across from the one they were in.

"Take these in there and change," the guard says, handing Pylus a pile of neatly folded clothes. Pylus takes the clothes and steps into the little changing room that would serve as a closet for a normal house.

The pristine white shirt feels strange on his skin. He's never had anything this nice before. He moves his arms over his head and can feel the shirt stretch nicely, his necklace with the two rings on it making a slight protrusion. He fingers the rings gently before continuing. He ties the tie sloppily, having only had to do it a couple of times in his life. The sleek black suit coat is a little snug, but he thinks it will manage. He takes the new security badge and clips it to the inside pocket of the coat. Immediately, two problems arise from his new outfit: the trousers are too short, and they have given him shoes to wear. Due to his longer-than-usual feet and thick pads on the bottoms, shoes have always been an issue for him since he became a hybrid. He found it easier to just go barefoot everywhere and feels like shoes weigh him down. With no other options, he tucks the white shirt into his faded jeans and steps out.

"These don't fit," he says, handing the trousers and the shoes back to the guard.

"Very well," the guard says, "Replacements will be found as soon as possible."

"Don't worry about the shoes. I'm made to be barefoot," Pylus says, which earns him a disapproving scowl from the guard.

"Where is your ID card?" The guard asks with more annoyance in his voice than before.

Pylus pulls open his jacket to reveal the card hanging from his inner pocket. The guard nods approvingly, then walks past him and out the door. Pylus follows with the other guards in tow. Out in the hallway, the smell of perfume from earlier is stronger. He glances up the stairs in time to see the blur of a figure disappearing around the corner.

The lead guard takes him down the hall to a doorway that opens to another staircase leading to the basement. They make their way down to a cement hallway with multiple doors off each side. The group moves to the last door on the right and walks in. Inside, the walls are literally covered with guns. One wall is completely made up of pistols, and two more are full of semi-automatic rifles. The wall with the door they came through has shelves stocked with ammo. Pylus is somewhat familiar with guns, but couldn't name the ones they had here. These are too high-end for him.

The lead guard takes one of the pistols down and sets it on a table in the middle of the room. "This is your EDC. It is your responsibility to keep it clean, loaded, and operational at all times. We have been told you are proficient with knives as well. You will be permitted to carry any of those that you wish as long as they do not impede your movement and you can conceal them. Do you prefer a hip or a shoulder holster?"

"Shoulder," Pylus responds, "My knives will sit on my hips."

The guard nods and walks over to a cabinet underneath the pistols and opens a drawer. He removes a box and sets it on the table next to the gun. One of the guards from behind Pylus sets a box of ammo down next to the other items.

"Show us how you handle your weapon," the head guard instructs.

Pylus picks up the gun and examines it for a second, getting familiar with the feel and buttons. He pulls the slide back and locks it in place to check the inside of the barrel. Using the button just above his thumb, he drops the magazine and catches it with his free hand. The spring in the magazine is stiff as he loads in ten gleaming bullets, then slides the magazine back into place with a crisp click. He presses the release button next to his pointer finger, and the slide racks a new bullet into place smoothly.

"Locked and loaded," he says, placing the gun back on the table, being sure to point the barrel away from everyone.

The guard actually looks impressed, "Very good. Remove your jacket and put on your new holster."

Pylus does as instructed and places his new suit jacket on the table. The holster is authentic leather, he can tell by the smell, and is stiff from sitting in the box. It creaks as he unfolds it, the buckles clinking together in a cheery tone. It only takes a minute to get the holster situated comfortably and the gun strapped in. The guards give him two extra mags to fill and strap into the opposite side of the holster. When he replaces the jacket, the gun imprint can be seen easily through the fabric.

"That will get fixed," the lead guard says when Pylus examines the print. "Rogers and Phillips will take you to the range and test your ability, after which you will be shown to your room, where you will find your knives and all your other belongings. You will then be brought to Mr. Rye's study and introduced to your new charge, and will from thenceforth be considered her protector and will be obligated to keep her safe, no matter the cost. Welcome to the force, Brek." And with that, the man walks out without so much as a second glance.

Pylus watches the guard as he walks out, then turns to the other two standing to the side. "Which of you is Rogers?"

One guard with buzzed black hair steps forward and nods.

"Then that makes you Phillips," Pylus says to the other guard.

"Yeah, that's me," he says as he steps up and pats his comrade on the shoulder, "Lighten up, Rogers. He's just like any other recruit. Sorry for all the stiffness around here. Brit takes his job very seriously, and Rogers here is nervous around hybrids."

"Don't worry," Pylus says, "I only bite certain people."

Rogers stiffens at Pylus' comment, but Phillips laughs and puts his arm around Pylus' shoulders to guide him back out of the room.

"I think you'll be just fine here," he says as they walk down the hall, "most of the guys aren't as stiff as Brit. Just take the job seriously enough to keep everyone safe, and you'll be fine. Oh, and try not to die in the process. This way." He opens a door just a couple down from the room they were in and walks through.

A small shooting range spreads out in front of them. It only has three stalls, but it has to be fifty yards long at least. This simple-looking cabin holds a lot of secrets.

Phillips grabs a paper target of a human head and torso and hangs it from the clip in the center stall. A push of a button sends it out a little way.

"We'll start you at fifteen yards and see how you do. Shoot five shots as quickly and accurately as you can," Phillips says as he hands Pylus some earplugs and steps behind him.

Pylus takes a deep breath and steps up to the shooting line. Unholstering his new gun is a strange feeling. It reminds him of drawing his knives, but the weight difference and finger placement throw him off. He raises the gun with both hands and sights in his target. BANG, BANG, BANG, BANG, BANG. After shooting, he holsters his gun and steps back. Phillips brings the target forward.

"Two in the chest, one in the stomach, one in the shoulder, and one just to the side of the head. Not bad. What were you aiming for?"

"Center mass," Pylus says, pointing to the center of the chest.

Phillips nods, "Let's try twenty-five yards this time."

Again, Pylus steps up to take his shot at the fresh target. This time, he gets three on the chest and two misses. At thirty-five yards, he gets one on the chest and one in the shoulder, with two just barely missing and one not even hitting the target. The last target is sent out to fifty yards, "just for fun," as Phillips puts it. One shot hits the target right in the forehead. The other four miss completely.

"Pretty good for someone who hasn't had any formal training," Phillips says, looking at the last target, "You've definitely shot before, though."

Pylus nods, "Before I became a hybrid, I used to go shooting with a buddy of mine."

"How long ago was that?"

"Over three years," Pylus answers sadly.

"Well, you haven't lost much," Phillips says, clapping him on the shoulder and walking out.

After refilling his magazines, Pylus follows Phillips with Rogers trailing behind. They make their way back to the main floor, then up to the second level. Phillips leads them to the last door in the hallway and walks in. It's a simple bedroom with a single bed and a closet. Another door to the left leads to a small bathroom. All of Pylus' things are already in the room. His book boxes lay in the corner while the ones holding his clothes and knives are sitting on the bed.

"Grab what knives you want, then we'll take you to see Mr. Rye," Phillips says.

Pylus walks to one of the boxes on the bed and pulls out a pair of blades from the several knives within. They're shorter blades, only seven inches total length. Not the ones he would use in Champion, but big enough to do damage and still be hidden. He quickly attaches them to his belt, one on each side, and turns back to his escorts. They leave the room and take him to the first door on the same side of the hallway. Phillips knocks lightly before entering. Jefferson Rye sits behind a very fancy desk, looking over a stack of papers. Behind him, large windows show the woods surrounding the house and the final rays of sunshine disappearing beneath the horizon.

"Ah, Pylus," he says, standing, "Glad to see you made it and have gotten settled in." He shakes Pylus' hand vigorously and smiles up at him.

"Thank you, Mr. Rye," Pylus says, forcing a smile.

"Brit wasn't too rough with you, was he?" Mr. Rye asks, "He tends to be a little uptight with the new recruits."

"No, he was fine. Just doing his job."

"Good, good! Come take a seat with me for a minute before my daughter comes."

Pylus pulls out one of the immaculate leather chairs and takes a seat.

"Pylus," Mr. Rye starts suddenly serious, "I am so very grateful to you for accepting my invitation. I need to warn you, however. My daughter is a bit of a free spirit. Many of her past security guards have expressed frustrations with many of her... antics. I hope that your abilities as a hybrid will help to keep those behaviors in check.

"That being said, I give you full permission to do what you think is necessary to keep my daughter the safest. Within reason, of course. But I won't be having you report in every day or have surprise checkups on you or anything of that sort. I feel my daughter's behavior has a lot to do with me being around and her trying to get a rise out of me. She's much like her mother in that sense. Anyway, my brother told me good things about you, Pylus, so I'm going to trust you to use your best judgment and keep my daughter safe." He leans forward and gives Pylus a stare that makes his blood run cold, "Don't disappoint me."

"I won't, sir," Pylus says.

Mr. Rye stares at Pylus a second longer until a knock on the door pulls his attention. Brit, the guard who led Pylus around, comes in with a young woman.

"Ah, there you are, sweetheart," Mr. Rye says as he stands and walks over to the young woman. "Pylus, meet my daughter, Ella."

Pylus's heart jumps to his throat. Ella? What are the chances the person he is supposed to protect has a name ridiculously similar to that of the person he couldn't protect? Cruel irony.

Pylus stands and offers his hand, "It's a pleasure," he manages.

"The pleasure is mine," Ella says, shaking his hand with a smile. She's a tiny little thing. Her head barely reaches Pylus' sternum. Dark auburn hair cascades over her slender shoulders. Her light green eyes look at him with both awe and interest. She's pretty, but looks like she's still a teenager; the way she holds herself suggests she's older, though. Perhaps that just comes from having such a prestigious father.

"Well, I have some work I must attend to, so why don't you two get acquainted?" Mr. Rye says, "And Ella, be nice."

Ella rolls her eyes teasingly and smiles sweetly, "Oh, Dad. When am I not?"

Mr. Rye glances at Pylus with a look that says, "Good luck."

Pylus smirks as he follows Ella out of the office. The rest of the guards exit as well and walk down the stairs.

"See ya around Pylus," Phillips says as he walks away.

"See ya," Pylus responds.

Ella has moved to the door between the office and Pylus's door. She grabs the handle, then turns to look at Pylus, "I'm pretty tired tonight, so I think I'll just go to bed. See you in the morning."

"Okay, uh, sleep well," Pylus says. She smiles at him and disappears into her room.

Pylus walks into his own room and lets out a deep sigh. He didn't realize how tense he had been the whole time. Hopefully, this isn't a new thing. So what, she has a name similar to Ellie? She's not Ellie. Ellie is gone. She's gone because he couldn't do enough. The same won't happen with Ella.

A click from the next room catches his attention. He can hear something sliding, then what sounds like someone grunting. Someone's going through the window of Ella's room! Pylus jumps across the room to his own window and throws it open. He slips through the opening quickly and comes face to face with. . .

"Ella?" He says, looking at his new charge, halfway out her own window.

She gives him a sheepish smile and a quiet, "Hi."

"What are you doing?" He asks.

"Shhhh," she hushes him, "My dad will hear you." She climbs the rest of the way out of her window and starts to close it behind her.

"What are you doing?" Pylus repeats.

Ella looks at him like it's obvious, "I'm sneaking out."

"Are you nuts?" Pylus asks in disbelief, "You know there's someone coming after you, right?"

"Oh, relax," Ella says as she works her way past Pylus, "I can take care of myself. I'll be fine."

"You're not going anywhere." Pylus grabs her arm and stops her from sneaking any further across the roof.

If looks could kill, Ella's would take Pylus out ten times over, "Take your hand off me, or I will tell my father you tried to take advantage of me."

Pylus tightens his grip on her arm and leans in until his nose is just inches from hers, "Go ahead," he growls.

Surprise washes over her face and leaves her speechless. Something Pylus gets the feeling doesn't happen very often.

"In fact," Pylus says, "why don't we go tell him right now?"

He begins pulling her across the roof towards the window of her father's study.

"No, no, no! Please, please don't!" Pylus stops and turns to look at her, "I'm sorry! I'll go back to my room. I promise!"

Pylus looks at her for a second longer before releasing her arm and opening her window for her. "In you go."

With a look of defeat, Ella crawls back into her room and closes the window and the blinds. Pylus crawls back over to the window of his room, waits a moment, then slides it closed without going inside. Almost immediately, Ella's blinds are pulled back, and her window slowly starts to slide open. She tries her best to be as quiet as possible. When the window is open enough for her to sneak through, she sticks one leg out and starts to pull herself back onto the roof. She's about halfway again when she sees Pylus and freezes, her eyes wide.

"You know something interesting about me," Pylus says, "I can hear heartbeats. That means I can tell when you are lying to me."

"Isn't that just convenient?" Ella spits at him, pulling herself the rest of the way onto the roof and sitting to lean against the wall.

"You do realize that multiple people have died to keep you safe, don't you?" Pylus asks.

"That's their job," she replies with a sneer, "When they're protecting the daughter of an important person, getting injured or killed just comes with the territory."

"Yeah, it's their job, but that doesn't mean their life is worth any less. They're still people, and some of them probably had families that they left behind."

"If they can't take the heat, they shouldn't play by the fire. Besides, I didn't ask them to protect me. That is all, my dad," she rests her head against the wall, looking at the stars.

Pylus stares at her for a moment, "You should consider yourself lucky to have someone who cares about you that much."

Ella rolls her eyes at him, "Oh yeah, I am so lucky to have a dad who is paranoid so I can't go out and have any real friends. I can't even go outside my own house without some big, scary guy with a gun behind me every step I take."

"Better than being killed," Pylus points out.

"At this point, I really don't know if it is."

Pylus pulls back as she had just slapped him across the face. "You are the most selfish brat I have ever met in my life! You have a dad who will give you literally anything you could ever want when the majority of the people left on this forsaken planet don't even have a family to go home to! Most of us lower-class people don't remember our parents. We've spent most of our lives doing whatever we could to survive, and here you are acting like safety is a nuisance! Let me tell you, I didn't go through my hellish life just to sit and babysit some pompous twit who doesn't even realize how good she actually has it."

"How good do I actually have it?" Ella retorts, sitting forward, "Do you have any idea how boring my life is? I have never had any friends, ever, and I never get to get out and do anything with my life!"

"I couldn't care less," Pylus says, "If boredom is your biggest problem, you have it better than everyone else in this world. Yes, I've had friends, but I've also watched most of them die! Yes, I could do anything with my life, but most of the things I had to do involved surviving just one more day in the hopes that tomorrow might hold something slightly better than what I was going through. Yes, I don't know what it's like to have an overprotective parent trying to control me because I never even knew my parents! So, forgive me if your little whining session about how hard life is doesn't bring tears to my eyes!"

Ella moves her mouth like she is trying to say something, but can't get it out. She looks like he either genuinely hurt her or shocked her with his lack of compassion. For a moment, Pylus feels ashamed. He knows part of his rant came from the things he's been trying to deal with over the last few days, but then again, this girl has no idea what hardship means.

"Why are you so mean?" Ella finally asks.

He looks her in the eyes and says, "Because I've lost too much and seen too much to be sympathetic to someone who has everything and still wants more."

She shakes her head and turns to look out over the open yard. Tears roll down her cheeks, and she bites her lower lip to keep it from quivering.

"I never wanted this life," She whispers, "The one thing my dad can't give me that I want more than anything is freedom. Not just freedom to leave the safehouse, but freedom to have a life. I want to be able to make my own decisions, even if that means living with the consequences. I'm tired of being told where I can go and what I can do with no room for argument or compromise. It's like I'm property, not a person. In trying to protect me, my dad has made me a bird in a cage. Just another pretty thing for him to show off when it suits him, but locked up and hidden away all the rest of the time."

Now it's Pylus' turn to be surprised. The way she sees her life sounds disturbingly similar to being a Champion contender. No decisions, no real life, just doing what other people tell you to do, and trying to make it through each day without losing your mind.

Letting out a deep sigh, Pylus sits next to Ella. "How about this," he says after a minute, "I'll make a deal with you. If you take it easy on me with the sneaking out, I'll start working on your dad to let you go and enjoy some new experiences, as long as I am accompanying you, of course. But I will do my best to be less of a big, scary guy with a gun."

Ella's gaze snaps from the empty yard to his face, "You would do that?"

"Yeah," Pylus says, "If it makes my job easier, then I'll gladly do it."

"Why the sudden change of tune?" Ella asks warily.

Pylus sighs, "Let's just say I have some understanding of being trapped somewhere and not having control over your life."

Ella nods like she knows exactly what he is talking about. "Okay then," She says, "I won't sneak out anymore and will play the perfectly obedient daughter for a time. But if you don't convince my dad..."

"Then I will personally help you sneak out," Pylus cuts in.

"Really?" She gasps.

"Really, really."

She looks at him for a moment, impressed. He offers his hand to her and, after a moment, she shakes it. They sit there together for a time, like the calm after a storm. She examines his face like she's trying to find some sign of deception. Eventually, she nods her head, satisfied.

"I guess I will see you in the morning then," she says, turning and climbing back through the window.

"Sleep well, Ms. Rye," Pylus says.

"You can drop the formalities, Pylus. You did call me a selfish brat and a pompous twit already tonight," she says with a wink and a smile.

Pylus laughs sheepishly, "You're right. Sleep well... Ella." He has to work to get the name out, but she doesn't seem to notice.

With one last smile, she closes and latches the window, then draws the curtains closed. Pylus hears her get into bed and shift until she's comfortable. It only takes a couple of minutes before her deep breathing lets him know she is asleep. He starts to move back towards his window when he hears something behind him. He turns to see Mr. Rye's head sticking out of his office window with a tired look on his face.

"Come chat with me, Pylus," he says.

Pylus swallows hard, "Yes, sir."

It feels wrong to climb into his new boss's office through the window. Pylus is half tempted to go into his room and come in through the doorway, but decides it is better not to keep Mr. Rye waiting. He steps through the window and stands up straight. Mr. Rye's laptop sits open on his desk, and on it is a security camera screen.

"Take a look at this, Pylus," Mr. Rye motions to the laptop. "What does it look like?"

Pylus already knew what it was the moment he saw it, "It's the roof right outside this window."

"That it is. I have this camera set up as an extra precaution to protect my daughter's room and my office. It alerts me whenever there is movement on the roof. As you already know, there was a lot going on out there tonight." The same cold look that he gave

Pylus when he told him to protect Ella at all costs is back and just as cold.

Pylus takes a deep breath before he responds, "I was just doing my job and keeping your daughter safe, sir."

Mr. Rye doesn't say anything to that, just continues to stare. Seconds drag by as Pylus waits for some kind of reaction to let him know if he did the right thing or if he was going to have the shortest career as a security guard ever. Slowly, the corner of Mr. Rye's mouth curls upward. He nods a little and holds his hand out to Pylus. Tentatively, Pylus reaches out and shakes it.

"Pylus Brek," Mr. Rye says, "You just earned yourself a pretty bonus."

"A what?" Pylus asks.

"A bonus, son," Mr. Rye repeats, "As soon as the motion detector let me know you two were on the roof, I slid the window open a little and listened to everything you said. I have to say, kid, you got guts. Any other man would have you buried alive for talking to his daughter that way, but I've wanted to say that to her for a long time now, so thank you."

Pylus swallows the nerves that had bunched up in his throat, "Um, you're welcome. I guess."

"And about her going out for some 'new experiences' as you called them," Mr. Rye continues, "Can you promise me that you will keep her safe no matter what?"

Pylus nods slowly, "Either that or I'll die trying."

Mr. Rye smiles approvingly, "Then you have my full permission to start taking her out on little trips around the safe house. Just make it seem like you actually had to work to convince me before you do. Ella doesn't know I have the camera set up out there, and I would like to keep it that way in case she turns back to her more rebellious nature. That girl shifts moods quicker than Champion goes through contenders."

"I'll do my best, sir."

"Have a good night then, Pylus," Mr. Rye says as he takes a seat, "You can leave out the door, unless, of course, you prefer the window."

Pylus chuckles at the joke and makes his way out of the office and to his room. He closes the door behind him and turns on his light. All the boxes of stuff still lie around the room. He takes the ones on his bed and places them to the side. When his bed is clear, he takes off his weapons and his shirt and tie before he lays down and quickly falls asleep.

8

Six o'clock the next morning, a single ray of sunshine peeks through the curtains, right into Pylus' eyes. He cracks one eye open and rolls over to escape the harsh light. A single bird sings outside the window. Slowly, more join in until the trees around the house are alive with morning calls. Pylus always enjoyed listening to birds in the morning. Since he moved to the Shank Settlement after becoming a hybrid, he hasn't been able to hear them as well. A smile works its way across his lips as he stands to get ready for the day and listen to the birds sing. He splashes some water on his face to help him wake up a little, then walks back into his room and starts to dress. As he finishes buttoning up his shirt, a knock sounds on the door. He opens it to see Phillips standing there holding some new clothes.

"Morning," the other guard says, stepping into the room, "Try these on."

"Morning," Pylus says as he takes the new trousers. They fit perfectly. The new suit coat also fits perfectly over his weapons, concealing them nicely.

"You ready for your first day?" Phillips asks as Pylus tries on the new clothes.

"Can't be any wilder than last night was."

"Oh really?" Phillips raises his eyebrows, inviting an explanation.

"I caught Ella trying to sneak out," Pylus says as he picks up one of the shoes Phillips brought, "I'm not wearing these."

"That's fine by me, at least I can tell Brit we tried, but they didn't fit," Phillips says, tossing the shoe over his shoulder. "So, what happened with Ella?"

Pylus shrugs, "Not much. She tried to sneak out through the window. I heard her leaving and stopped her before she could. We had a little chat, and at the end she agreed to stop sneaking out."

Phillips' jaw drops, "She actually agreed to that?"

Pylus rolls his head side to side, "Yeah, sort of. I have to convince her dad to let her go out every now and then and enjoy life a little more by herself. Well, by herself with me guarding her the whole time, that is."

"Do you think you'll be able to get the big man to agree to that?"

"Already have. Mr. Rye pulled me into his office after Ella went to bed. He has a camera that watches those windows," Pylus nods to his window and the roof where he caught Ella, "He saw and heard the whole thing and agreed to let her go out if I'm with her."

"Impressive," Phillips says, "I didn't think we would ever find anyone who could tame that girl."

"We'll see if she keeps up her end of the deal," Pylus says with a chuckle.

"That we will. I hope I'm not around if she doesn't, and you're left with the blame."

"I think it would be better for me to get taken out before that point."

"I think so too. Well, I'd better get on to my actual job," Phillips says, picking up the shoes he brought and opening the door, "See ya around."

"See ya."

Pylus follows Phillips out the door and watches him go down the hall to the stairs, then listens at Ella's door to see if he can hear any movement. Nothing but deep breathing. He walks back into his room and rummages through his boxes until he finds what he's looking for. An old copy of War and Peace. The one thing he brought with him from his life before the Shank Settlement. Currently, he is reading it for the third time.

Flipping through the pages, he walks back into the hall and positions himself next to Ella's door so he can hear her if she starts to move. Two pictures fall out from between the pages that were set in to hold his spot. He picks them up and holds them in his hand while he reads.

***

"Morning, Pylus." A voice calls a couple of hours after Pylus had begun to read.

"Morning, Mr. Rye," Pylus says, looking up.

"I see you're a man of literature," Mr. Rye nods towards the book.

"It's a better way to pass the time than most things," Pylus says.

"That's true," Mr. Rye nods, "If you're waiting for Ella, you're going to be waiting a while. She usually sleeps in until noon."

Pylus raises his eyebrows, "Really? What time is it?"

Mr. Rye pulls his sleeve up and checks his watch, "Eight twenty-seven." He says, "Do you not have a watch?"

Pylus shakes his head, "Never needed one."

Mr. Rye nods a little, "Why don't you come with me?"

Pylus puts the pictures back in his book and stands to follow Mr. Rye into his office. When he walks in, a small case has been placed on the desk. Inside are twelve beautiful watches. All different colors and models, and Pylus can tell that all are very expensive.

"Go ahead and pick one," Mr. Rye says.

"Really?" Pylus asks. These are the nicest watches he has ever seen, let alone held or been given.

"Of course. I can't have you running late when you're in charge of my daughter, especially with the schedule I tend to keep."

Pylus looks at all the watches again, then picks up a seemingly simple black one with gold numbers. He slips it on his wrist and clasps it in place.

"Good choice," Mr. Rye says, "That is one of my favorites."

"Thank you, sir," Pylus says.

"Don't mention it," Mr. Rye gives him a friendly pat on the shoulder, "Enjoy your book and your new watch."

Pylus nods as he steps back into the hall. Mr. Rye closes the door behind him at the precise moment Ella's door opens.

"Good morning," Ella says through a yawn. Her hair is a mess, and her eyes are still half closed. Her baggy shirt and sweats are ruffled from sleep.

"Morning," Pylus says, "I was told you usually slept in until noon."

She gives him a sarcastic smile in response and walks past him towards the stairs. Pylus follows after her with a grin.

"I'm used to staying up late trying to sneak out or figure out a way to sneak out," she explains, "Last night someone convinced me to actually go to bed at a decent time."

"I see," Pylus says, "Does that mean last night you didn't come up with any ideas on how to get around our agreement?"

"Nope. I'm a woman of my word, Pylus," she says, starting down the stairs.

They reach the bottom and turn to head down the hallway, only to find Brit there. He must have just come up from the basement.

"Good morning, Ms. Rye. Pylus." He says formally. If he's surprised by Ella's abnormally early appearance, he doesn't show it.

Ella gives a small wave without looking and continues down the hall.

"Morning, sir," Pylus says with a nod.

As he passes Brit, he is stopped by Brit's strong hand on his arm, "Keep her in your sights. She's a slippery one."

"I will, sir, but I don't think we'll have any problems."

Brit nods and continues on his way. Pylus follows Ella down the hall and through a door on the opposite side from the one that leads to the basement. A modest kitchen and dining area spread out in front of him. It looks like he just walked into the perfect pre-war family home. The only things missing are family pictures and inspirational quotes decorating the counters and blank walls. Ella grabs a banana and folds herself into a chair at the table, pulling her legs up underneath her in a way that makes Pylus' legs hurt just looking at her.

"You can sit down," Ella says through a mouthful of banana, "All the food is free game if you're hungry."

"Thanks," Pylus says, snagging an apple from a fruit basket. He walks over and sits in the chair just across from Ella.

"Nice watch."

Pylus glances down at his new accessory, "Oh, thanks. Your dad let me borrow it."

"I recognize it. He used to wear that one a lot."

"Used to?" Pylus asks, tilting his head.

She studies the table while she answers, "It was one my mom got him for a wedding anniversary gift. He stopped wearing it when she passed away."

"I'm sorry." That sounded lame, but Pylus didn't know what else to say. Parents were a foreign concept to him. Having never known his, and then watching all of his parental figures get taken out of his life. What else could he say?

Ella looks up from studying the table and studies his eyes instead. After a second, she gives him a soft smile, "Thank you."

They finish their breakfast in silence. Afterward, Ella announces she is going to her room to shower and get ready for the day. Pylus makes her promise she won't try to sneak out the window again, then settles down in the hallway with his book. He pulls the pictures out again and looks at them.

One shows pre-hybrid Pylus with a girl who looks similar to him. Pylus has a goofy look on his face that the girl is laughing at. The other picture is again of pre-hybrid Pylus and a different girl. Only this one shows him and the girl looking deeply into each other's eyes, lost to the world but not each other. He smiles sadly and puts the pictures down to continue his reading.

Thanks to his new watch, Pylus knows it's an hour and a half later when Ella emerges from her room looking and smelling like a completely different person. Her hair is pulled back into a tight braid, and she wears outdoorsy clothes like she is planning on going hiking. Her half-closed eyes are now open and bright, taking in everything they see. For some reason, she put on a copious amount of perfume too. Pylus raises his eyebrows at her over the top of his book.

"What?" She asks.

"Going somewhere?" he asks.

"There are a few nature trails that go through the woods around here," she says innocently, "I want to go check some of them out. I assume you talked to my dad about that this morning when he gave you the watch."

"Sure did. He put up a bit of a fight, but in the end decided some small outings would be okay." Pylus closes his book and stands up, "Let me put this away, then we will head out."

A refreshing breeze blows through the open yard as the two make their way towards the front gate. Yesterday, the gate was left unguarded when Pylus arrived. Today, three individuals stand by it. Two of them are off to the side having a conversation, while the third guards the opposite end of the gate. The one standing by himself notices Pylus and Ella first and clears his throat loudly. The other two stop talking and turn to face them. It's Brit and Rogers.

"Out for a walk, Ms. Rye?" Brit asks when they get close.

"Yes, we are," Ella says, "We were actually hoping to go and enjoy the beautiful scenery around here. I've heard a couple of the guards talking about some nature trails close by, and I wanted to go check them out. If that's okay?" She smiles sweetly and bats her eyelashes in a way that would make any schoolboy agree to anything she said. Brit, however, is no schoolboy, probably never was.

"Ms. Rye," Brit says in a way that makes Pylus think they have had this conversation before, "You know how dangerous it is for you to be out and about."

"I know, but now I have a new security guard with some extra special abilities," she motions to Pylus, "I promise not to try and ditch him like I did the last one. Although even if I did, I think he would find me pretty easily. I'm wearing my Charming perfume today, and I doubt his wolfy nose would lose that scent very quickly."

Brit looks from Ella to Pylus, then lets out a deep breath, "I have your word you'll stay close to Brek at all times?"

"Absolutely."

"Alright then," he says finally, "Don't be gone too long or we will send a search party after you."

Ella clicks her feet together and snaps her hand up to her eyebrow, giving Brit a rigid salute, "YES SIR!"

Pylus can see the physical struggle from Brit as he fights to keep his eyes from rolling at Ella's exaggerated display before he steps to the side and lets them pass. Rogers opens the gate for them. As Pylus passes Brit, the older man nods to him, then glances at Ella. Pylus returns the gesture and follows his charge out the gate and into the woods beyond.

"You're a big talker, aren't you?" Ella says after five minutes of walking in silence.

Pylus chuckles and shrugs in response. He keeps his eyes searching the trees around them and his nose trained on the breeze that blows through occasionally and clears away enough of Ella's perfume for him to get a scent of everything else around.

Ella rolls her eyes, "Well, I don't like the feeling of being escorted by a robot, so how about a game?"

"What kind of game?" Pylus asks warily, scared of the answer.

"We take turns asking each other one question, and it has to be answered honestly."

"A get-to-know-you game?"

"Yup!" she says enthusiastically, "If I have to spend every minute with you lurking around me, then I want to know you. And know if I can trust you."

Pylus looks at her skeptically, "Your dad trusts me."

"My dad trusts that you can protect me," She says, "That doesn't mean he trusts you personally."

"Valid."

"So, are you going to play?" She asks, looking at him.

Pylus sighs, "Fine."

"Perfect!" Ella practically jumps for joy, "First question, why don't you wear shoes?"

He can't help but smile at the randomness of the question. But it is fitting for Ella's personality, "Ever seen a dog wearing shoes?"

"Only when they are pets," Ella says.

"Wait, what?" Pylus asks, perplexed.

Ella looks at him in surprise, "Have you never seen anyone put shoes on their pets?"

Pylus shakes his head, "No, that's absurd! Why would you waste money on something as useless as clothes for animals?"

"Lots of the higher class do it," Ella says, "They pamper their nasty little rat dogs and dress them up like dolls or something. I guess they're pretty good at spending money on useless things."

"Well, I don't get to associate with many of the higher class," Pylus says, "Most of the dogs I know are strays or owned by people who have a hard enough time getting clothes for themselves."

"Ah, that makes more sense," Ella says, "But you didn't really answer my question."

"I can't find shoes that fit right," Pylus says, "My feet are longer and slimmer than normal. Plus, I really don't need them. I have thick pads on the bottom of my feet like dogs do, so they are pretty tough."

"Huh, interesting," Ella says.

Silence falls over the two as they continue walking. After a couple of minutes, Ella pokes Pylus in the ribs, "It's your turn to ask a question. "

"What if I don't have any questions?" He asks.

She frowns at him and gives him a "yeah, right" look with her eyes.

"Okay, fine," he says with another sigh, "What's your favorite color?"

Ella bursts into a high-pitched laugh and stops walking to hold her stomach.

"What?" Pylus asks, confused.

"That's the question you are going to start with?" Ella asks, wiping a tear from her eye.

". . . Yeah. . . Why is that so funny?"

"Because of all the questions you could ask someone, you go with the most childish question ever," She shakes her head and starts walking again, "Green. My favorite color is green. What's yours?"

"Yellow."

"Really?" Ella wrinkles her nose, "Are you serious?"

"Yeah." Pylus says, "Why is that surprising?"

"Because you don't seem like someone who would like yellow," Ella says, "You seem more like a black or red type of person."

"Am I that dark and broody?"

Ella smiles mischievously, "Oh, definitely."

Now it's Pylus' turn to roll his eyes.

"Why do you like yellow?"

"Nope, it's my turn for a question," Pylus says.

Ella smiles to herself, "Oh, that's right. Go ahead."

Pylus turns to look at her, "Why do you always try to sneak out? Aside from feeling like a bird in a cage. I just can't wrap my head around the fact that you would want to get away from a life where you never go without."

Ella slows a little and stays quiet for a bit before she finally answers, "I guess it seems silly, doesn't it? As you said last night, I'm a girl who has everything she could ever want, from a father who loves her more than anything else in the world. And yet, I feel like a prisoner. I'm the pretty porcelain doll that sits on the shelf but never gets played with. Too delicate to touch. My dad has seen all the worst in the world and doesn't want me to see any of it.

"I understand why he feels the way he does, but all the things he has seen have blinded him to the beauties that are out there. If he were here with us, he would be complaining about how we're so exposed and how we need to get somewhere safe instead of seeing how beautiful the trees are and how peaceful it is out here. So, I guess to answer your question, I want to experience the beauty of the earth and have time to see the best things the world has to offer."

For the first time since they started their walk, Pylus looks up and actually takes in the trees and the surrounding vegetation. Ella's right, it is beautiful and peaceful. Concourses of birds sing and call to each other through the treetops. A small breeze blows through, shaking the leaves of the plants, rustling them serenely. The thick foliage has completely separated them from the safe house, making it seem as though they are lost in the depths of the forest.

"Does it really not bother you that your guards got killed protecting you?" Pylus asks.

Ella glances at him with a wary eye, "To be honest, I didn't even know they died until recently. I was always out of the area when they were killed, and no one mentioned why I got a new guard the next day. I figured it was just because they failed at keeping me out of dangerous areas or something and got fired. But my dad makes it seem like such a big deal, even though he has at least three guards get killed a month protecting him. Brit has only been in charge for a little over four months. His successor took a bullet for my dad coming out of an international meeting. I've grown up hearing about this guard dying this way, and that guard died that way. I guess I just figured it was part of the territory and never thought much of the actual guys who were dying. Plus, I was never close to any of them. You're the first bodyguard I've been able to talk to."

Pylus raises his eyebrows in surprise. Surprise at the answer Ella gave, so matter-of-fact, and surprise that it made some amount of sense to him.

As the pair continues their walk, they step into a small clearing where the sunlight falls to the ground unobstructed. Its warmth lands on the pair and pushes out the chill from the breeze. Soft grass covers the clearing, and Pylus curls his toes into it. He hasn't felt grass like this in a long time. It's not the short-manicured stuff that surrounds the cabin. This is wild, long, unhindered, and beautiful, just like Ella said.

"I think," Ella continues, "the main reason would be because I feel like I never have a chance to live. I'm always told where I can go and what I can do, and I always have to have some stick-in-the-mud bodyguard by my side. At least this time the stick-in-the-mud is a little more lenient." She bumps him with her shoulder and gives him a smile, "I just want to have the chance to make a decision for myself. I said last night that I would gladly deal with any consequences from my actions. But first, I need a chance to make decisions that have consequences."

They reach the other side of the clearing and step back onto a trail that starts to circle back towards the cabin. The breeze has died down, and the birds' singing picks up in volume as they flit through the trees after one another.

"I'm just tired of being kept under such tight control," Ella says softly, "Have you ever felt like that?"

Pylus shakes his head, "No. My life is more like a coyote. I've had to scavenge and struggle to survive, but I've never really been tied down until I became a contender. Even then, I still had my freedom."

"You must think I'm being overdramatic and ungrateful then," Ella says, wiping her eyes, "It's not that I don't love my dad and realize how much he does for me. I just wish to have a life outside of whatever house we happen to be living in at the time. I want experiences outside of the guards and the paranoia of when the next kidnapping is going to happen. I want to live without the stress, even just for a little bit."

"It does get tiring being stuck inside," Pylus agrees.

A strong gust of breeze causes a shudder to run down Pylus' spine. He looks around at the trees surrounding them and listens to the leaves rustle. By now, they had made their way back to the clearing where the cabin sits. Ella stops a few feet shy of the tree line and puts her hand on Pylus' arm to stop him.

She turns to face him fully, "Thank you, Pylus."

"For what?" He asks.

"For getting me out here," she says, "I've tried to come out here multiple times, and they wouldn't even let me out of the gate. You must have been pretty convincing when you talked to my dad and got him to let me have some freedom."

"I just reworded what you said to me last night. Told him you felt like you were stuck in a cage," Pylus says, scratching his neck.

She smiles the truest smile Pylus has seen from her yet. It reaches her eyes and lights them up with true happiness.

"Thank you again," she says, giving him a kiss on the cheek before walking out of the trees and towards the gate.

Pylus watches her go for a moment, then squats down behind the bushes.

"Keep a sharp eye out. We're not alone out here," he says in a low voice to the guard camouflaged in the bushes, then he stands and follows Ella.

9

The moment Pylus steps through the front door, Brit is next to him with another guard.

"Ms. Rye," the head guard says quickly, "I need to speak with Brek for a few minutes. Johnson here will accompany you until we are done."

"Oh, um, okay," Ella says with a confused glance at Pylus.

"This way, Brek," Brit grabs Pylus by the arm and practically drags him down the hall, to the basement, and into the weapons room. The door is shut as soon as they enter. Mr. Rye and two other guards stand waiting around the table.

"Alright, Brek," Brit says, stepping to the right side of the table, "Tell us about this person in the woods, how you knew they were there, and what you can tell us about them. None of our perimeter scouts saw anyone or have seen anyone since you gave that warning."

"I could smell him," Pylus says, "It was a scent coming from deeper in the woods than where the guard I spoke to was."

"How do you know it wasn't one of our guys?" Asks the guard on the left.

Pylus looks at the guard, "Do your men carry cyanide on them?"

"How do you know what cyanide smells like?" Asks the other guard.

"I wasn't always a hybrid," Pylus says vaguely. "Anyway, that's not important. What is important is that there is someone walking through the woods with poison, and he was dangerously close to getting to your daughter, Mr. Rye."

"We are scanning the woods already," Brit says, "So far, there's no sign of anyone being out there besides you and Ella."

"Look to the northeast of where I talked to the guard," Pylus says, "That's the direction the wind was blowing from. Probably fifteen to thirty feet away."

"You can tell all that from the smell?" Mr. Rye asks. It's the first thing he's said, and Pylus simply nods his response.

Mr. Rye raises his eyebrows, "Is that also how you know it was a man?"

Pylus nods again, "Men and women have distinct scent differences when they sweat."

"Impressive," Mr. Rye says.

Brit cuts in, "Were you able to detect anyone else?"

"Only your man in the bushes."

"Are you sure?"

"Positive."

"If it's one man, he may be a scout or a very highly trained hired assassin," Brit says to Mr. Rye, "But if what Brek says is true and he is carrying a dose of poison, we have to assume the latter."

Mr. Rye looks down at the table and leans forward onto his hands, "What do you suggest, Brit?"

"For now, act normal," Brit says, "Wait and see if they make a move. It's likely they have no idea Brek was able to pick up on their scent, and if we panic, we'll give away our advantage. We are scheduled to head out in two days. We can double the security rounds and limit the amount of breaks each guard gets. If nothing happens between now and the time we are scheduled to leave, we will continue as planned. If they do make a move, we get to the cars and move to the next safe house."

Mr. Rye studies the table intently as Brit studies him for any sign of approval. The other two guards keep their eyes up, watching the door as if they expect the mysterious wood dweller to walk through.

"Alright," Mr. Rye sighs. His eyes flick up to Pylus with that same steely look that is becoming common during their conversations, "Are you still confident you can protect my daughter?"

"Yes, sir," Pylus says.

"Good," Mr. Rye lowers his eyes, a tired look in them, "Brit, get Pylus a headset and run him through the evac drill."

Brit nods, "Yes, sir."

Mr. Rye exits the room with the other two guards in tow. Brit moves to the same set of drawers he got Pylus' holster out of. He opens one lower down and pulls out a small walkie-talkie and a corded earpiece.

"Clip this to your holster and run this up your back and into your ear," he instructs as he holds up various parts of the setup. Once Pylus has it in place, Brit starts showing him how to work it, "Turn it to frequency three. It will ask for a PIN. Push the button on the earpiece and say three, five, five, two."

Pylus does so and hears a computerized female voice ask for a pin, "Three, five, five, two," he says and waits until the voice lets him know access has been "granted."

"Push the button on the earpiece to speak," Brit says, showing the button on his own equipment, "it will connect to every com in a half-mile radius."

"West side is clear," a voice says in Pylus' ear, making him jump.

"You'll get used to it," says Brit dryly, "Let's show you the garage."

They walk out of the weapons room and down to a door next to the shooting range. It opens into a small garage that holds two very beefed-up SUVs. A dark ramp goes up on the other side. It must have a secret exit somewhere in the yard.

"This is the unit you will bring Ms. Rye to," Brit motions to the car on the right. "You will bring her here if an emergency arises. A guard will be here with the door open for you. Make sure Ms. Rye gets in first, then follow her. The guard outside will close the door for you. If there isn't time for you to get in, get out of the way and devote yourself to making sure no hostiles get through that door."

"Yes, sir," Pylus nods.

"Very good," Brit moves past him to the hallway, "The code word for this operation is 'freedom flight'. Once that command sounds, do everything in your power to get Ms. Rye here as quickly and safely as possible. Remember, if it is required to give your life, that is a sacrifice we are willing to make. Now, return to your charge and stay vigilant."

Pylus can hear Ella from the bottom of the stairs. She's talking to the guard in the kitchen. She asks his name and where he's from but doesn't get an answer. Pylus gets to the top of the stairs and walks into the kitchen. Ella is standing on the counter, looking through the top shelf of a cabinet. The guard stands at the doorway with his hands behind his back and eyes straight forward.

"I'll take it from here, soldier," Pylus says, clapping him on the shoulder.

The guard nods and does a crisp about-face and makes his way out of the kitchen.

"Charming guy," Pylus says when the guard is out of hearing range.

Ella looks back enough to roll her eyes, "I couldn't get a single word out of him. Not even his name. I mean, you're pretty stuck up, but at least you'll indulge my questions. He wouldn't comment on anything! How weird is that?"

"Pretty weird," Pylus agrees, "What are you doing?"

"Making lunch," she says, hopping down with a large bowl in her hands.

"You can cook?"

She shoots him a glare and opens the freezer, "Yes, I can cook. You think just cause I'm a rich guy's daughter, I have someone cook for me?"

"Um. . . Yeah," he says sheepishly.

She smiles at his discomfort, "My dad has hired chefs before, but I like to make my own food. It's fun to create something with just a few ingredients."

"So, what are you going to create today?"

"Chicken fajitas," she looks back at him mischievously, "Want to help?"

He shrugs and takes off his jacket, "I've never been much of a cook, but I can follow directions."

She gives him a nice smile this time, "Good. Take these peppers and onions and slice them."

After some slicing, sizzling, and spicing, the fajitas are done. Once the tortillas are warm, the two sit down at the table and start into their lunch. The meat is a little too cooked for Pylus, but the rest of it is delicious.

"Okay, I have a question," Ella says, "Since you are part dog, does that mean you can't have certain things like chocolate?"

Pylus nods as he tries to finish his mouthful of food, "As far as I know, the only things I *can't* have are chocolate and alcohol. Everything else has been okay, though."

"Is there anything from the other side?" she asks around a bite of fajita, "Like can you have some things that humans can't?"

He nods again, "I can eat raw meat and drink puddle water without any side effects. That counts as two questions by the way."

Ella rolls her eyes, "Fine. You can do two then."

Pylus smirks at her annoyance, "First, where did you learn to cook?"

The happy twinkle in her eyes dims a little, and her smile falters, "My mom taught me. She loved to cook, too."

There is a sadness mixed with joy in her eyes as memories of her mother dance in front of her on the table. Pylus can almost see young Ella in an oversized apron, standing on a stool. She tries to hold a bowl steady as she stirs its contents. An older version of the Ella he knows stands just behind her, smiling and offering encouragement.

"How old were you when she passed?" He asks.

"Thirteen," she breathes out, "Old enough to remember but still young enough to forget a lot. Did you know anything about your parents?"

Pylus shakes his head, "No. They left my sister and me at an orphanage when I was two."

Ella perks up slightly, "You have a sister?"

"...Had."

"Oh," she says quietly, slouching back into her chair, "I'm sorry."

Pylus gives her a small smile, "Thanks."

The rest of lunch goes by in silence as they both live in the memories of loved ones lost. Once they finish their food, they clean up the dishes and put them away. Ella takes some food and puts it on a paper plate to take to her dad. She tells Pylus that if she doesn't make sure her dad eats, he will go days without food. A very goal-driven man indeed.

Pylus waits in the hall as Ella goes into her father's office and gives him his lunch. He hears Mr. Rye talking on his phone to someone about "the gala" that is going to happen in the next week. He assures the person that they will attend and that the presentation will go as planned. Ella kisses him on the head and walks back to the hall, closing the door behind her. She walks over to Pylus and leans against the wall next to him. They stand there for a few moments, comfortable in the quiet.

"What do you do for fun?" Ella asks, breaking the silence.

"I don't have fun," Pylus answers. It sounds like he is just keeping up the brooding, mysterious type persona, but it's the truth. It's been a long time since he did anything someone would classify as a good time.

Ella looks at him with eyebrows raised, "Are you serious?"

"Yeah," he says with a laugh, "I was a contender for two years, and before that I was busy just trying to survive."

"So, you don't do anything to pass the time? You just stare at the walls?"

He nods with a shrug, "Sometimes."

"Oh my gosh," Ella laughs, "That is so sad."

"It is, isn't it?" he says, joining in her laughter.

"So, what would you do when you weren't staring at walls?"

"I would train a lot. And read."

"That suits you," she says as she looks him up and down, "It fits your boring personality."

Pylus chuckles as he rolls his head away from Ella, "Well, you know, keeping up appearances is *very* important to me."

Ella laughs, "Oh, I can tell. What do you like to read then?"

"A little bit of everything," he says, "I read a lot of adventure fantasy when I was a kid, then switched to thrillers and mysteries. When I became a contender, I read a lot of animal biology books and war books with some fun reads scattered throughout. Right now, I'm reading War and Peace. Ever heard of it?"

He turns to see Ella looking at him with a deer in the headlights look. She shakes her head a little, "Nope. Never heard of it. I also would have never guessed you were a nerd."

Pylus smiles and rolls his eyes, realizing he does that a lot around Ella. It's almost like that's the basis of their relationship.

"Were you able to bring any of your books with you?" Ella asks.

"Actually, I was," Pylus says, gesturing to his room, "I'll show you some if you want."

Ella shrugs and follows him to his room. They walk in, and Pylus pulls his boxes of books open. There are six filled to the brim with books. He only has eight boxes in his room, and he can tell that Ella is more than a little surprised that the majority of them are filled with literature.

"What?" He asks, "I *really* like books, okay?"

"Obviously," she says.

Pylus smiles and starts rummaging through his collection. Reading for pleasure is a nearly dead hobby. Finding new books is a rare event, and Pylus cherishes every book he is able to get his hands on. Ever since he was a kid and learned how to read, he has loved books and kept all of the ones he found over the years. After he became a contender, and Reggie gave him some freedom, he searched out every traveling merchant and trade shop he could, looking for new books. He was lucky enough to find one in the settlement who had a love for them like he did and kept a large collection of them. When he had first found them, he bought half of their inventory right then and there. It was only ten or twelve books, but that was like gold to Pylus.

"Here," he says, handing Ella one, "Try reading that."

"Moby Dick?" She asks sardonically.

"You know it?"

"Never heard of it," she holds the book and flips through the pages carefully, like something might jump out at her.

Pylus smiles at her discomfort, "It's the story of a monster whale during the 1800s, when people used to hunt them for blubber. An obsessed captain swears he will bring down the white whale and devotes his life to catching it."

"Oh yes, as a person actively being hunted, why wouldn't I want to read a book about an obsessed hunter?" Ella says, handing him the book back.

Pylus' face drops as he takes the book back, "Leave it to you to make that connection. Okay, hold on then." He crouches and digs through two more boxes before popping back up, book in hand, "Aha! Try this one."

"The Secret Garden?"

"A young girl has to go live in her uncle's mansion and feels trapped because she's not allowed to explore it," he says, "But then she finds a secret garden that was abandoned years before and makes it her own little sanctuary."

Ella looks from him to the book and purses her lips, "Hmm. Alright, I'll give it a try. But if I'm going to try one of your hobbies, I want you to try one of mine."

"Sneaking out isn't a hobby, you know," Pylus teases. He moves as Ella throws a halfhearted kick at him.

"I have actual hobbies, you know!"

Pylus rights himself and stands up, snickering to himself. If he can keep getting reactions like that out of Ella, this job is going to be a lot more fun.

He holds up his hands, "Alright, I'm sorry. What hobby did you have in mind?"

Ella's scowl is replaced by a grin, "Follow me."

After dropping off her borrowed book in her room, Ella leads Pylus to the main floor, down the hall, and into the basement. They walk into the gun range and through a door to the side that Pylus hadn't noticed his first time in here. They step into a smaller range, only about fifteen feet wide and twenty yards long. Ella walks to a set of double doors on the opposite wall and opens them up to reveal four bows and several arrows hanging there. Opening a smaller set of doors under the first, Ella pulls out a large cube target and hands it to Pylus.

"Go put that on the green line."

He does what he's told and puts the target halfway down the range on a green line painted on the floor. When he gets back to Ella, she has slung a quiver around her waist and filled it with arrows. She studies the bows, trying to decide which one she feels like shooting.

"Are you familiar with bows?" She asks.

Pylus shrugs, "A little. I know a couple of different styles of bows, but I haven't shot one since I was a kid hunting rabbits."

Ella turns her head sharply, "You used to hunt rabbits for fun?"

"For food."

"Oh," she says quietly. Another reminder that she has no idea what growing up in the real world is actually like. "Well, let me show you my favorite."

She pulls down a dark green compound bow and hands it to Pylus, "This was my first compound bow. Fifty-pound draw. It took a while before I was able to pull it back, but I've gotten used to the weight now."

"It's beautiful," Pylus says, turning the bow in his hands, "The one I shot as a kid was a compound too. I think it was only thirty pounds, though. Something meant for kids but worked well enough for small game."

"Let's see if any of your skills stuck around," Ella says as she takes the bow out of his hand.

Stepping up to a big red X in the middle of the floor, she draws an arrow and nocks it in place. She pulls the string back as she takes in a breath and rests her hand by the corner of her mouth. Pylus realizes he is holding his breath as he watches her sight down the arrow. An old habit from hunting with other kids. All is quiet for two heartbeats, then Pylus hears Ella start to let her breath out and anticipates what is coming next. The bow string twangs as Ella releases it, sending the arrow streaking down the range. In the blink of an eye, the arrow is gone and reappears in the target. A perfect bullseye.

"Your turn," she says, handing him the bow with a proud smirk.

Pylus looks at the bow in his hand with a sigh and pulls an arrow out of the quiver on Ella's hip. He steps up to the X and places the arrow. He takes a deep breath and draws the string back. His muscles perk up at the old but familiar motion. Muscle memory takes over as he sights down the arrow. He focuses on the target and lets his air out. The thrum of the string sounds like welcoming an old friend back from a long trip. His heart jumps at the thrill of feeling the arrow skim past his hand. It buries itself deep in the target with a hearty thud. His shot landed just inside the widest circle of the target. About six inches from Ella's.

"Not bad," Ella says, stepping up, "Looks like you still have some skill after all. Want to try the recurve next?"

For the next couple of hours, they try each of the bows and cycle through all the arrows. Ella always hits the bullseye or just outside it. Pylus hits it every now and then. Every time he does, Ella congratulates him the same way one would a small child showing off a finger painting.

"Can I ask you something?" Ella says as they gather the arrows from the target.

"Is this part of your game?" Pylus asks.

She smiles and shakes her head, "No, it's not."

"Okay, what's up?"

Her eyes study the point of an arrow she just retrieved, "You've done fight training, right? Like hand-to-hand combat and stuff?"

Pylus nods, "Yeah, why?"

"Well, I...." She shifts uncomfortably, "I was wondering if... if you could train me some?"

"What?" Pylus asks, surprised.

Her eyes lift from the arrow to look into his, "I want you to teach me how to fight. Or at the very least, how to defend myself if it comes to it."

Pylus moves his jaw a couple of times, trying to get words to come out. Finally, they come, "Sure. But why?"

"Well," she plays with the arrow in her hands, "since you're going to try and convince my dad to let me have more freedom, I think him knowing that I can defend myself might help ease his worries. It will probably help convince him to let me do more than just go on a nature walk. Also, I want to feel less helpless."

That's actually a really good idea, Pylus thinks, "Alright, I'll pitch the idea to your dad tonight."

Ella's face lights up with excitement, and she squeezes the arrow in her hands, "Thank you!"

"Brek report in. Where are you?" A voice says in Pylus' ear. Brit is calling over his intercom.

"One sec," he says to Ella, then activates his com microphone, "This is Pylus. Ella and I are at the archery range."

"Two guards are waiting for Ms. Rye in her room. Drop her off there, then meet me at the gate. Two minutes," the com goes quiet after Brit gives his instructions, and Pylus doesn't expect him to be waiting for an answer.

"Brit needs to see me at the gate," he says to Ella, "I'm supposed to drop you off at your room, then go meet up with him. Sounds urgent."

Ella raises her eyebrows and unclips her quiver, "Better get moving."

Two minutes later, Pylus stands at the gate waiting for Brit. He sees him walking out of the tree line. Brit motions for Pylus to follow him and starts walking towards the spot where Pylus and Ella had come out after their nature walk earlier that day. Brit stands at the tree line and waits for Pylus to catch up to him.

"This way," he says, stepping into the trees.

He leads Pylus through the foliage, weaving in the direction of the scent that Pylus caught. About two hundred feet in, they meet up with four other guards, all heavily armed. Brit points to a bush in the middle of the group. Pylus can see a small strip of cloth hanging from one of the thorny branches.

"Smell that and tell me if it's the same scent you caught from our uninvited visitor," Brit says.

Pylus walks up to the bush and takes a deep breath. He smells the flowers and the wetness of their leaves. Another breath. Again, the flowers are mixed with something else. Moving in closer, he takes another deep breath and closes his eyes. Flowers again and another scent. The same one as before. The stranger from the woods.

"That's it," he says, turning to face Brit.

Brit says nothing, but the lines around his face deepen. "The guard you gave the warning to came scouting this way immediately after giving us the news. He saw someone out here, but they fled before he could get a good look at them. He tried to pursue, but they moved too quickly and lost him. Be vigilant. I doubt they went too far."

"Yes, sir," Pylus says. He opens his mouth to ask if they need anything else when he catches something on the wind. The skin on the back of his neck bristles, and his muscles tense. "He's close," he whispers.

Brit's eyes get wide, but the rest of his body suggests nothing is wrong. "Find him," he says quietly.

Pylus nods and starts walking back towards the cabin as if nothing is wrong. He waits until he is a hundred feet or so away from the others, then ducks under a low branch and drops to all fours. He creeps along, keeping low to the ground. Thanks to his longer-than-normal arms and extended feet, this is as comfortable as walking upright is for him. Keeping his nose to the air, he catches onto the scent and adjusts his direction of travel to follow it. Soon, he can hear the voices of Brit and the other guards running through security precautions. Pylus can tell they are false reports. *Smart move, Brit.* He continues to creep past the group and head further into the trees. The scent is getting stronger the further in he goes.

A twig snaps up ahead, stopping Pylus. He listens closely and can hear someone moving quietly through the bushes. Whoever it is moves well through the thick growth, obviously experienced with moving through heavily wooded areas. The steps move closer and closer until they are pretty much on top of Pylus. If it wasn't for a big bush in front of him, the stranger would see him. The scent is strong as ever now. It's definitely the smell from earlier, but there's something off.

Pylus flexes his arms and legs, preparing to attack. If he can catch them by surprise, it will be much easier to take them in. He rocks back until most of his weight is on the balls of his feet. Quick and deadly, that's the goal. Now!

He pushes off hard and rips through the bush, hands extended. His claws grip flesh, and he sees a coat made of the same material that was caught on the bush. His prey starts to pull and tries to run from his claws. Using his momentum, he swings his feet to the other side of the body and uses the motion to pick the figure up and throw it into a tree a couple of feet away. The body slams into the tree and falls to the ground, its spine shattered.

Pylus can't believe his eyes. The coat drapes over the body. It's an old army-style piece, khaki in color. The arms are empty and tied around the chest of the one wearing the article of clothing. The coat definitely has the same scent that Pylus has been smelling, but the body doesn't match the shape that would fit into it. The one laying on the ground in front of him is a small deer. He's been tricked.

10

"Brek! Come in, Brek! Did you get him?"

Pylus stares at the deer, not hearing Brit call him. *Who is this guy?* Obviously, someone with some kind of training who was also expecting Brit to use Pylus' hybrid senses to find them. He's either done his research and scoped the area thoroughly, or there is an inside man within the guards.

He knew I was part of the guard detail and that I had pegged his scent.

"Pylus, answer me!"

The use of his first name snaps Pylus out of his trance. He fumbles with his earpiece, "Yes, I'm here. The guy gave me the slip. Used his jacket as a distraction. Tied it to a deer and took off."

"Alright, Brek, try and find the scent again then rep-," Brit's commands are cut short. Pylus listens to the silence for a second, wondering if Brit is getting more information or if he has just lost focus.

"Pylus," Brit says over the com, a sense of dread in his voice that puts a pit in Pylus' stomach, "a dead guard was just found near the backside of the house. His uniform is missing."

Fear grips Pylus' throat, squeezing the air out of it. His blood turns cold, and his limbs go numb. "Ella," he whispers.

Twigs slash his face as he races back towards the house. A flash of color blurs past him, Brit and the others. He doesn't even glance their way. The only thing that matters is getting back to Ella.

"PYLUS!" Brit roars through his com, "You get to her and get her out of here! If he gets in your way, *end him*!"

Pylus doesn't waste time responding; that was already his plan. He drops to all fours, using his wolf attributes to run faster. In seconds, he is back at the fence surrounding the cabin. He doesn't slow down or bother going to the gate; instead, he takes two bigger steps and leaps the fence in a massive jump. Crossing the yard to the cabin takes less than a second. Using a raised flower bed as a foothold, he launches himself onto the roof of the porch just outside his and Ella's rooms. A scream from inside tells him he may already be too late. One step is all it takes to get him close enough to throw himself forward and through Ella's window, shattering it. He flies into the room, glass all around him. Another scream breaks out. He lands on the bed and rolls off the side, landing in a crouch. Glass litters the floor, cutting the hand that he puts on the ground to steady himself.

"Pylus," Ella whispers from behind him.

He doesn't turn to look at her because the person everyone has been looking for is standing right in front of him. A wicked-looking dagger hangs loosely from the man's fingers. Behind him, a hand belonging to someone else lies just inside the doorway, a puddle of blood surrounding it. Pylus pulls one of his own knives from his belt and lunges at the man. The man leaps back and swipes Pylus' knife out of the way with his own. Using his free hand, Pylus pulls his other knife and takes another swipe at the man. The man leaps back again with impressive speed. They stare at each other for a moment, sizing up the threat the other poses.

The man wears a mask covering the lower half of his face and a cap low on his head, almost obscuring his eyes. The suit he stole from the guard hangs limply from his frame, too big for him. He must have slipped the hat and mask on after he got inside. Cold, beady eyes meet Pylus' and linger for a moment. There is nothing behind those eyes, just a dark emptiness, soulless.

Pylus moves to rush the man again, but he jumps out the shattered window and runs across the roof. Dropping his knives, Pylus pulls out his gun and fires off three rounds. All three miss as the man drops off the roof. He quickly covers the distance from the cabin to the gate. The poor guard standing at the gate barely has time to register the shots and recognize the target fleeing across the yard. A quick slice across his neck ends his life and leaves the man in the mask with an open getaway.

"FREEDOM FLIGHT! FREEDOM FLIGHT!" Brit screams through the coms.

Pylus turns and looks back at Ella. She crouches in the corner on the other side of the bed. Her hands cover her ears, and tears stream down her face. Her breathing is fast and ragged with sobs and halfway spoken words. Pylus holsters his gun and one of his knives. He keeps the other drawn and ready. In one jump, he clears the bed and lands next to Ella. He doesn't bother saying anything to her. She's so scared that nothing is getting through to her right now. Instead, he puts his arm around her and half-guides, half-drags her to her feet and out the door.

Both guards assigned to Ella while Pylus was gone lie dead in the hallway. Their throats slashed open, and their empty eyes stare. Pylus wishes there was some time for him to take care of them, but his first priority is to the living, a lesson he learned a long time ago.

They make their way down the stairs and through the hallway. Other guards rush to the doors and windows, watching for any movement.

In the basement, things are less busy but no less intense. The only people around are the ones waiting at the SUV for Pylus and Ella. The pair rushes into the underground garage in time to see the first SUV screeching up the ramp and out of sight. A guard stands holding the back door of the second vehicle open, his gun drawn and waiting. Pylus ushers Ella into the backseat and hops in right behind her. The door slams shut, and tires scream as the driver hammers down on the accelerator. They shoot through the garage and up a ramp, popping up on the backside of the house from a camouflaged exit.

A hidden gate opens in the fence, and the driver heads through onto a barely visible path. Trees fly by, and Pylus wonders if this driver is trying to finish the job the masked man couldn't. Soon, they take a sharp turn onto a paved road. A radio comes to life in the console at the front of the car.

"Transport Two, come in. Are you out Transport Two?"

The driver picks up a radio mic and speaks into it, "This is Transport Two. We are out and on the move. Both targets made it safely. Over."

"Good. Meet at rendezvous point seven. Check in every hour until arrival. Do not stop except for necessities. Over."

"Roger. Over and out."

"Where is rendezvous seven at?" Pylus asks.

The driver flicks his eyes to the rear-view mirror, then back to the road, "It's in the Lakes Settlement. About seven hours away."

"How many times will we have to stop before we get there?"

"Unless we have an emergency, we shouldn't have to stop at all. These vehicles are top of the line in fuel efficiency and are equipped with a secondary gas tank."

Pylus nods approvingly, "Good. Is there anything you need from me?"

"You do your job and let me do mine."

Pylus looks over at Ella. She's curled up in a ball next to him, her head resting on the door with her hands still over her ears. She has her eyes squeezed shut tightly, and silent tears run down her cheeks. Carefully, Pylus reaches out and grabs her arm, giving it a gentle pull. She sits up without any resistance. He puts his arm around her shoulders and lets her head fall to his chest. Her body shakes profusely, but she still doesn't make a sound.

After some time, her shaking subsides, and her breathing falls into a slow, calm rhythm. By now, the sun has set, and the landscape outside falls under the shroud of night. They left the Shank settlement behind an hour ago, and now all that they see through the windows is dark nothingness. Pylus feels his eyelids getting heavy and tries to keep his head from dipping into a slumber.

"You can take a load off, kid," the driver says, eying him in the mirror, "We have another few hours until we get to the rendezvous point."

"How are you going to stay awake?" Pylus asks.

In response, the driver holds up an aluminum can with PEAK printed on it. A high-energy drink that a lot of contenders use to get amped up right before a fight.

Pylus smiles and lets his head lay back against the seat. He tries to keep Ella as comfortable as possible and find a comfortable spot for himself. After a few minutes, he slips into a deep, empty sleep.

***

Hours later, Pylus is awoken by the purr of the engine being cut. He looks out the window and sees they are outside a modest house, again surrounded by a tall fence. Other houses can be seen off in the distance. The landscape is mostly flat with a small hill rising just behind the last house that can be seen.

Bringing his gaze back into the car, Pylus looks at Ella to see that she is already awake. He can tell by the faraway look in her eyes that she is still in shock. She hasn't come back to them yet.

Gently, he sits up and opens the door. He steps out onto the driveway and then helps Ella out. Keeping his arm around her shoulders, he scans the area and quickly walks her towards the door, where Brit and a group of other guards are waiting. As a group, they move from their position on the porch and surround Pylus and Ella. The two are led into the house and through a lavish entryway. The ceiling must be at least twenty feet high. Like the house in the Shank Settlement, appearances are deceiving.

The group moves into a hallway on the opposite side of the entryway and continues to the last door on the right. Brit opens the door and ushers Pylus and Ella through before following. The rest of the guards take their place outside.

Mr. Rye paces inside the room with Rogers and Phillips standing on either side of the big, covered window behind him. He stops as soon as Ella enters the room and rushes to his daughter. Fresh tears well in her eyes as her father moves to hold her, and this time, Ella lets the sobs come out. Pylus steps back into the corner to allow them some privacy. Brit steps back with him and places his hand on Pylus' shoulder.

"Well done, Pylus," He whispers.

Pylus doesn't respond. He just watches Mr. Rye embrace his daughter. Feelings of nostalgia and longing tear at his heart, and memories he thought he had moved on from invade his mind. Familiar faces long since forgotten swim in front of him again and beg for his attention. He fights to keep them away, but that seems to only make them more persistent.

"Pylus," a voice pulls him out of his mental battle. Mr. Rye stands in front of him with his hand outstretched, "Thank you for saving my daughter."

Pylus reaches out and grasps the hand offered to him. Mr. Rye covers Pylus' hand with both of his and brings it to his forehead. "Thank you," he whispers, his voice thick with emotion.

Not knowing what to do, Pylus puts his free hand on Mr. Rye's shoulder and gives him what he hopes is an encouraging squeeze. After a moment, Mr. Rye stands up and takes a deep breath.

"Well," he says, "we have had a few very eventful hours. Pylus, will you take Ella to her room so she can get some rest? Brit, you and I have *a lot* to discuss."

Mr. Rye gives Ella one more tight hug as Brit opens the door and Pylus steps up to lead her to her room. As he gets close, Ella leans into him and wraps her arms around his midsection. He puts his arm around her shoulders again and walks with her and the rest of the guards who were in the hall to a room on the second floor.

"Your room will be that one," one of the guards says, pointing to the next door over. "Can you take it from here?"

Pylus recognizes this guard as the one who was watching Ella while Pylus was briefing Brit on the intruder he smelled. His gaze holds a hint of fear, mixed with relief. If he had been the one asked to take Pylus' place again, he probably wouldn't be here right now.

"Yeah, I will be okay, thanks," Pylus says. As one, the group turns and leaves Pylus and Ella.

With Ella still latched onto him, Pylus opens the door and leads her into the room. It's much bigger than the cabin they had come from, but it has the same layout. A big bed sits against the wall to the right with the door to the bathroom on the left. The wall straight across from the door has two windows on it. Each one has bars across it that Pylus guesses were recently added. The curtains are also drawn tight, making the room feel smaller.

Pylus leads Ella over to the bed and pulls the covers down for her. She lets go of him and sits on the edge of the bed, her eyes still far off and unfocused. Pylus takes off her shoes and jacket and lays her back. After pulling the covers over her, he turns to leave. Before he can, Ella grabs his wrist. He looks back at her. She keeps her eyes on the wall, still with that faraway gaze.

"Please don't leave," She whispers.

The fear in her voice breaks Pylus' heart, "Alright," he says.

He lays on the ground next to Ella's bed after removing his coat and weapons and checking the windows to make sure they are locked and secure. Ella scoots over so she can see him over the edge of her bed. They lay in the darkness for a few minutes, neither able to sleep nor wanting to talk. The ticking of the clock on the nightstand counts the moments of sleeplessness with each deafening tick.

Ella, still in shock, tries to find something to focus on, but everything seems fuzzy and far away. Her body is numb, and nothing seems real. Images of the two guards getting their throats slashed, and the man with the soulless eyes keep flashing through her mind, causing her to curl up and try to hide. The sounds of the men choking to death on their own blood echo through her mind along with the sickening sound of the knife slicing through their flesh. Every horrible detail becomes increasingly vivid with each retelling, revealing itself over and over again.

Pylus's mind keeps seeing flashes of the man, too, but for different reasons. There was something off about him. His scent was unique. Every human has a unique scent, sure, but they are all distinctly human. This guy was human, but also something else. He smelled like. . . death.

Laying in the dark, Pylus hears Ella shift and gasp on the bed every few minutes. Every time she does, he tenses and starts to sit up, only to realize she's reliving the horror she just experienced. He knows the feeling. She isn't dreaming exactly, but keeps seeing warped images of the events she witnessed. Most likely, the ones she keeps seeing are not as bad as what she actually saw in person. Her mind's way of dealing with the shock.

When Pylus dealt with things like this, he remembered the numbness and the recurring fear made fresh with every memory. His mind wandered through clouds of thought with no substance, trying to find a way to cope with the trauma it had been forced to endure. Every now and then, a strikingly vivid image would emerge from the haze, startling the mind and pushing the fear to a new level.

Once Ella stops moving, Pylus thinks she has fallen asleep, until something touches his arm, making him jump a little. He realizes it's Ella's hand and breathes a sigh of relief. He lifts his forearm so it's propped up by his elbow and bumps Ella's hanging arm. She wraps her hand around his wrist and squeezes tightly. He gives her a reassuring squeeze back. A relieved sigh comes from the bed, followed by gentle breathing a few moments later. She finally found some reprieve. Pylus lets out a sigh of his own and closes his eyes. Some deep breathing exercises help him calm his mind, and in a few minutes, he's asleep as well, still holding Ella's arm.

***

Morning brings a soft sort of silence with the sun's warming rays. Pylus slowly opens his eyes at the sound of an unfamiliar bird chirping. He listens for a moment, trying to understand why things seem so out of place. His arm feels funny, and when he turns to look at it, he sees Ella's hand still holding onto him. Everything from the day before rushes back to him in a tidal wave of memory. He closes his eyes against the onslaught for a moment until the slideshow slows down, then he turns to look at Ella. He can just make out part of her face over the edge of the bed. Her steady breathing tells him she's still asleep. Not wanting to wake her, he stays put and tries not to move too much. Every few seconds, her hand tenses on his arm. She must be dreaming. Hopefully, it's something better than the events of the previous night.

Suddenly, Ella's entire body jumps, her head shooting off the pillow. Her eyes scan the room wildly like a cornered animal, searching for a predator she won't find. Pylus sits up quickly and puts his hand on her shoulder.

"Hey, hey, it's okay, you're safe," he says soothingly as he moves onto the bed with her, "I'm here, you're safe."

Her eyes lock onto him, and the wild look slowly fades away. She lets out a sigh of relief and closes her eyes. Her head falls forward onto his chest as she takes deep breaths to calm down. Pylus moves his hand from her shoulder to hold the back of her head. Memories of doing this to his sister when she had nightmares flood his mind.

The memory of his sister shocks him. He hasn't thought of her for so long that he almost forgot he comforted her this way. Looking down at Ella, he can almost see his sister again.

He notices Ella is still holding onto his arm. The skin on her fingers is white where they are gripping in terrified desperation. Her other hand holds her sheets to her chest with the same intensity.

"Don't worry," Pylus says, "I won't let anything happen to you."

"I believe you," Ella whispers.

Her grip on his arm and the sheets relaxes as she rolls onto her back to stare at the ceiling, keeping her hand on Pylus' arm. The emptiness has left her eyes. She is now fully aware, immersed in her grief and fear.

"Do you think they had families?" She asks.

"The guards?" Pylus guesses. She nods in response, "I don't think so. Anyone who has someone to go home to wouldn't take a job like this one, where they never get to go home."

Ella is quiet, and Pylus wonders if that helped her feel better or made her feel worse. Finally, she says, "They have no one to mourn them then. No one to remember them."

Her comment catches Pylus off guard. He didn't expect this girl, who had several personal guards get killed, to be so concerned with the memory of two people whom she didn't know. Maybe it was just that this time she had been close to being a memory as well.

"No, that's not true," Pylus says, "They had friends here. Other guards. That was their family. They will be remembered by those who knew them."

A tear slides out of Ella's eye and runs down into her hair, "I didn't even know their names, Pylus. I couldn't even tell you what they looked like. I didn't care about them until I saw them lying on the floor and knew they couldn't protect me anymore. How selfish is that? They are dead, and the only thing I can think of is how there is no one there for me."

Pylus tries to think of something to say to comfort her, but can't seem to remember how to speak. He can't procure a single word in his mind.

"It was different this time," Ella continues, her voice heavy with regret, "With the other guards who got killed, I had gotten out before it happened. I was safe, but I later heard that they hadn't made it out. I didn't know until days, even weeks, later for some of them. It was still a shock, but my dad loses guards frequently enough that it wasn't lingering.

"This time, though, I watched them die. I saw the fear and pain right before their life left their eyes. After the first guard was killed, the second one fought back but didn't last long. I saw what was going to happen to me, and all I could do was scream and curl up on the ground. At least the guards faced their end fighting. But if that's what happened to all of the others and I didn't even give them a second thought, then I..." she breaks off and covers her face with her arm as she is overtaken with silent sobs.

"Shh, come now," Pylus says, putting his hand on her head and rubbing her forehead with his thumb, "You can't blame yourself for being ignorant. You've never been faced with that sort of thing before, so how could you feel for your past guards when you didn't realize what was actually going on?"

A small part of Pylus doesn't believe his words. He knows Ella's indifference to her past guards being killed had more to do with her selfish outlook on her status and life and less to do with not fully understanding what death was like. But now wasn't the time for her to get a lecture. The truth of life had hit her full force, and now she had to grieve not only for the two guards she had watched die but also for the guards in her past that she hadn't given a second thought to, and lastly for her callousness.

"I could have still shown a little more remorse for them or asked about how they died," she whimpers, "I didn't even care enough to find out how they died. I was so selfish. You were right with all those things you said about me on the roof after all. A selfish brat and a pompous twit."

Pylus licks his lips and swallows hard before he talks again, "We can't change the past. We can only learn from it and commit to change in the future. I know what it's like to have regrets, and I know what it's like to learn from them. It takes time, but eventually you will move on and become a better person because of this, if you want to be."

Ella stares at the ceiling quietly. Her eyes starting to get the faraway look again before they move to Pylus, "I guess you're used to stuff like this after being a contender."

"Actually, I was used to it before," Pylus says.

"Really? Why?"

He gives her a sad smile and says, "That's a story for another day."

"Okay," she whispers, "So after the first time, how did you recover?"

Pylus looks down at her hand on his arm, thinking how to respond. He'd never really thought about it much. Hasn't ever really had to. His life has been a whirlwind of tense situations for the most part. Trying to remember the first experience with death is difficult, like trying to catch a specific fish out of a constantly moving school.

"Honestly," he finally says, "in my case, I don't think I ever recovered. I went from one situation to another and just got used to it," Ella's face falls, and tears rim her eyes. "But for you, it can be different. You're not going to be faced with this every day like I was. It will be hard for a couple of days, especially with the guilt, but you'll learn that tragedy happens, and we can't change that. All we can do is mourn those we lose, then live for them when they can't do it for themselves."

Ella's green eyes sparkle with tears. The hurt behind them evident, crushing Pylus' heart. If he could take her pain away and put it on himself, he would because he knows how to handle it, but that is only wishful thinking.

"You don't have to go through this alone," he continues, "I'll be here to help you."

One corner of her mouth pulls up slightly, "Thank you, Pylus."

"You're welcome," he says with a smile.

"Well then," Ella says softly, sitting up and letting go of his arm, "guess I better get ready then."

As she swings her legs over the side of the bed, Pylus stands and offers her his hand. She takes it and stands next to him. Before walking to the bathroom, she gives him a tight hug that holds more meaning than just gratitude.

"I'll just be outside," Pylus says.

She nods and goes into the bathroom, closing the door slowly. Pylus walks to the hallway and closes the door of the room. He sees someone to the side; Phillips stands outside Pylus' bedroom door with his hand raised as if about to knock. Phillips gives him a confused look, then raises an eyebrow as he looks at Ella's door. His eyes move back to Pylus, and the other eyebrow joins the first one.

"I was just making sure she is doing okay," Pylus explains.

Phillips nods his head with his eyebrows still raised, "Yeah, okay. Anyway, Brit wanted me to tell you that Ella is not allowed to leave the house today and that we will be leaving tomorrow morning, so be ready."

"Leaving for where?"

"The Ryes have an investor gala in the St. Louis Settlement tomorrow night, then we're moving west for more corporate gatherings and charity events. It's gonna be a long couple of weeks, so enjoy your day off."

Pylus chuckles, "I didn't think I got days off with this job."

"Day off is used loosely around here," Phillips says with a smirk and one last glance at Ella's door, "Don't have too much fun." He pats Pylus on the shoulder, then heads off to his other duties.

"It's not..." Pylus starts, but decides that it won't make any difference to Phillips.

He leans against the wall as Phillips disappears from view. He can hear the shower running in Ella's room and some other distorted sound. He focuses his hearing to try to figure out what it is. The sound keeps changing as he listens, growing louder and quieter randomly. The pitch keeps changing, too. When the sound starts to swell, he realizes what he hears. Ella is singing. Out of curiosity, he cracks the bedroom door so he can hear better. She's singing a song he doesn't recognize, but the melody is nice, and her voice carries it well. She continues for another minute before switching to a new song. Again, Pylus doesn't recognize it but likes how it sounds. He listens to the words and is touched by the emotion in Ella's voice. Whether it's the strain from last night or the feel of the song, he can't tell; all he knows is that listening to it makes him long for something unknown. The shower turns off as the song comes to an end, and Pylus closes the door softly.

For a few minutes, Pylus can hear Ella shuffling around in her room, opening drawers and making her bed. When she enters the hallway, she's wearing an outfit for working out, her hair pulled back into a tight ponytail, still slightly damp from her shower.

"Going for a run?" Pylus asks.

"You tell me," She responds, "you're the trainer."

Pylus's eyebrows almost shoot off his face, "You want to train? After what happened last night?"

"*Especially* after what happened last night," she says somberly, "I felt so helpless and weak yesterday. I don't want to feel like that again. Besides, I could use something to keep my mind off that. A way to blow off some of the stress that I can't seem to think myself away from."

"Fair enough. Where do you want to train? I've been given orders not to let you leave the house."

"There's a training room in the basement. Come on." They fall into step together and make their way down to the room.

Unlike the cabin, the house's basement is normal sized. It consists of two rooms. One has mats on the floor and a variety of training equipment for martial arts and other forms of combat training, while the other is a full weight room. A couple of other guards work out in the weight room, but the training room is empty. Ella walks to the middle of the mat and starts stretching. Pylus steps to the side and removes his jacket, weapons, and holsters, placing them on a bench.

"So, what are we going to start with?" Ella asks, "Arm bar? Knife attack? Full nelson?"

"Your stance," Pylus says, stepping onto the mat.

Ella makes a disgusted face, "My stance?"

"If you want to fight effectively, you have to be balanced. The way you're standing now," he gives her a hard one-handed push to the shoulder, knocking her onto her backside, "Worthless."

"That was mean," Ella scowls at him.

Pylus offers his hand to her and helps her to her feet, "Best way to teach is to demonstrate."

They spend the next few hours going over Ella's stance and guard. By the time they stop for lunch, Pylus has started teaching her how to defend against different attacks. He steps towards her and acts as if to push her. She redirects his arms with a well-placed block and gives him a good punch to his chest, followed by a light back knuckle to his forehead.

"Very nice," Pylus says, "You learn quick."

"Thanks, I've always been pretty athletic," Ella responds.

"Let's get some food, then we can pick back up later if you want," Pylus puts his holsters and weapons back on and carries his suit coat over his arm.

After a quick lunch of peanut butter and jelly sandwiches, they resume their training. Ella listens intently to Pylus' instructions whenever he corrects her or teaches her something new. Her drive is impressive and almost scares Pylus sometimes, but he knows how she feels. The weight of being utterly helpless in a dire situation can change a person. They either succumb to the thoughts of being weak and worthless or they decide to change and become unstoppable. Ella is becoming the latter. The hours sneak away from them as they focus on training. Before they know it, night has fallen.

"Brek, where are you?" Brit calls over Pylus' com.

Pylus is surprised that he forgot about his com and how comfortable it has become, "I'm in the training room with Ella."

"Training room? What are you doing there?"

"...Training," Pylus says after a moment.

The other side of the com is quiet for a minute, and Pylus thinks he can feel the anger coming from Brit, "Listen here, wise guy, I don't need any of your sarcasm after the trip we've had the last couple of days. Now what are you really doing?"

"We are actually training," Pylus emphasizes, "Ella wanted me to teach her some self-defense."

"Oh," Brit goes quiet for a bit, "Well, I guess that is a good idea. Well done, Brek. But it's getting late, and we have an early day tomorrow. Finish up and get some rest. We leave at 0830."

"Yes, sir," Pylus says in the most sarcastic voice he can. He doesn't have a problem with Brit, but sometimes he thinks he is wound a little too tight.

"Brit has called a curfew on us," Pylus says to Ella.

"Big boss man always has to ruin the fun," Ella says, rolling her eyes.

Pylus laughs as he gathers his gear and heads out the door behind Ella. They talk about what Ella has learned so far and where she can use it as they make their way to their bedroom doors.

"Thank you, Pylus," Ella says when they reach her door.

He gives her a small smile, "You're welcome."

"I guess I will see you tomorrow bright and early."

"Guess so. You going to be okay in there?" He nods toward her bedroom door.

She looks back at the door and contemplates her answer, "I think so. Just don't panic if I come wake you up in the middle of the night."

"Alright. Sleep well, Ella."

"You too."

11

Pylus wakes to his watch reading 6:12 AM. Rubbing his eyes, he sits up in his bed and stretches out all the stress that had been accumulating since he started this new job. Yesterday's training and last night's shower made for the perfect recipe for a good night of sleep. Taking a deep breath, he steps out of bed and walks into his closet.

Jefferson Rye runs quite the operation. Before Pylus even arrived at the house, clothes were already set out for him in his closet. The person in charge of wardrobe is efficient and precise. He puts on his slacks and shirt but leaves off the tie and jacket. Stepping back into his room, he walks to the foot of his bed and sits on the ground with his back to the mattress. Since all of his books were left at the cabin in the Shank Settlement, he has nothing better to do for the time being, so he closes his eyes and takes deep breaths.

Meditating has always been one of Pylus's favorite activities in the morning. Most nights, he is barraged by nightmares all night; meditating helps him clear his mind of the painful memories he is forced to relive. After the nights when nightmares spare him their company, he still meditates and finds that it helps him have a better outlook on the day. All in all, it gives him time to sort through the things he is dealing with and prioritize each emotion he is experiencing. A beneficial skill to have when his occupation is killing.

A small knock on his door pulls him from his breathing. He checks his watch, 7:17 AM. Confused, he stands and moves to his door. He opens it slowly and peeks out. Ella stands in the hallway looking impatient and flustered in her pajamas.

"Come to my room. Now," she says, then disappears before Pylus can say anything.

Pylus doesn't know if he's more surprised at the way Ella is acting this morning or the fact that she is awake and alert this early. Scratching his head, he puts on his weapons and jacket then steps into the hallway and down to Ella's room. She paces back and forth at the foot of her bed, chewing on a nail. When she sees Pylus, she rushes to him, grabs his arm, and pulls him to her bed.

"Sit down," she says as she pushes him backward, not giving him the option to stand even if he wanted to. "Okay, wait here, I really need your help."

More confused than ever, Pylus watches her rush into the bathroom and hears lots of movement. Ten seconds later, she comes out carrying a red dress in her left hand and a dark green one in her right.

"Which one should I wear to the gala tonight?"

Pylus stares at the dresses, then at the flustered girl holding them. "I... don't know."

"Oh, you're right," Ella says, "You need to see me wear them in order to tell which is better. One sec!"

She rushes back into the bathroom and closes the door with a bang that makes Pylus jump. He rubs his eyes, convinced he's dreaming, but when he opens them, he's still on Ella's bed.

"What is happening?" he asks himself.

Not even a minute later, the bathroom door clicks open, and Ella steps out wearing the red dress. It's tight around the torso and flows from the waist down in a puffy but elegant curtain. The sleeves just cover her shoulders, leaving the rest of her arms and the line of her collar bones exposed. A ruffled sash is tied around the waist with a quaint little bow on the back.

"I think I'll leave my hair down with this one and wear black heels," she says as she spins, causing the dress to fan out around her. "Okay, now I'll put on the green one."

Pylus starts to say something, but she's already gone, the bathroom door separating her from his objection. This is way out of his area of expertise, not to mention his comfort zone. Fashion has never been his strong suit, and he hasn't ever cared. Survival has always been more important. When faced with life-or-death situations, he can react and process information flawlessly. Right now, his brain doesn't seem to be working properly at all.

The door opens again, and out steps Ella in the green dress. Its emerald silk fabric shimmers as she moves. It's a beautiful sleeveless dress that hugs her body all the way down, but doesn't reveal too much. The skirt is slit to her knee and parts slightly with each step.

"I'll pull my hair up with this one and wear my diamond necklace with matching earrings, but I haven't decided which shoes yet." She pulls her hair up and holds it with one hand as she strikes a couple of poses, "What do you think? Which one looks better?"

Saying something would be the correct way to respond to this situation, and Pylus knows that, but no matter how hard he tries, nothing comes out of his mouth. The craziness of the situation, combined with the surprise of how pretty Ella looks in the dresses and the bewilderment of why she asked him for his opinion, keeps his mind from functioning the way it is supposed to.

"Well?" Ella asks, looking at him, her eyes almost pleading, "Which do you like better?"

"Um... the uh..." he clears his throat and tries again, "The green one." His voice sounds like a ten-year-old boy in his own head. He feels like one, too, trying to talk to a pretty girl.

Ella looks over at the full-length mirror she has resting against the wall and examines herself, "Yeah, you're right. It looks better with my hair color than the red does. Thanks!" She says with a smile, then disappears into the bathroom again.

That must mean his job here is done. Shaking his head, Pylus stands and moves to the door. He can hear Ella messing around in the bathroom, probably doing her hair and getting ready. He makes his way back to his room, puts on his holsters and weapons, followed by his suit coat, still leaving off the tie, not caring if anyone has a problem with it. He's not cut out for this type of judgment. Determining the safety of a situation or chasing down an assassin? Sure, that is easy. Trying to help a woman decide what to wear? No way.

A sound from the hallway catches his attention. Someone is coming up the stairs, quickly. Pylus steps into the hall in time to see Brit round the corner.

"Ah, good, you're ready to go," Brit says as he covers the distance between him and Pylus in three strides.

"Do you always walk so fast?" Pylus asks.

"Yes," Brit replies curtly, "Now we leave in twenty-five minutes. You need to make sure Ms. Rye is up and ready to go. Be at your transport vehicle at 0830. It's a four-hour drive to the gala. Any questions?"

"What's a gala?" Pylus asks, feeling, for the second time in mere minutes, like a little kid.

Brit scrunches his eyebrows together, "You don't know what a gala is?" Pylus shakes his head in response, "It's a big party for people involved in a certain organization. Lots of times, they are fundraisers for charities or big company projects."

"Aren't things like that usually at night?"

"Yes, but this one has two parts. The first, from noon to four, is for all company members in the area. The second, from six to ten, is for company investors and asset holders only. The big wig party, if you will."

Pylus flicks his eyebrows up, "Sounds like a big deal."

"It is," Brit nods, "so be on your best behavior and try to keep Ms. Rye under control."

A groan escapes Pylus before he can catch himself, "I'll do my best, sir."

A hint of a smile brushes across Brit's face, and his eyes flick to Pylus' missing tie before he nods and turns to head back to the stairs without saying another word. Pylus listens to him walk down the stairs and away through the house. The sound of his weirdly brisk steps is replaced by another, sweeter sound. Ella's singing echoes from her bathroom. Pylus recognizes the song she's singing. It's a slow, storytelling song about a young man moving to what used to be New York City and struggling with the winter months.

Making music is often considered a dying art in this day and age. Many songs from pre-war times are still available for those who have preserved their technology or have access to it. For the majority of people, though, music is a rare gift, and Pylus is no exception.

When he was a kid, he lived in a place that had some old music devices saved so that he could listen to music from the past with the other kids. All the music came from the 2010s and 20s and was stored on things called CDs. Little metallic discs that had to be put into a stereo device and plugged into an electrical source. In his later years, when he had moved to the larger settlements, he was introduced to small handheld devices that stored music. One simply had to plug headphones into it and push play. Some even had speakers to play music without headphones. These devices had to be charged to work, but could easily be taken anywhere. He was told cellphones used to be able to store music on them, too, but the ones used now don't have that capability.

Ella's singing stops abruptly. Pylus snaps his head up, listening for any sounds out of the ordinary. Nothing. He can't hear any movement. Just as he is about to walk into the room to make sure everything is okay, he hears the shower turn on. He lets out the breath he had been holding and leans against the wall. The events of the past couple of days have him on edge.

Drifting off into his own thoughts of what a gala will be like, Pylus doesn't notice the shower turn off a few minutes later until he hears Ella say, "Pylus. If you can hear me, will you come in here for a second?"

Intrigued, Pylus opens the door and steps into the room. "Ella?" he asks, not seeing her.

"In here," she says from the bathroom.

Pylus steps over and pokes his head through the doorway. Ella sits, wrapped in a towel, on a stool in front of her mirror with her hair pulled up in a messy bun. She has her elbows on the counter and leans in close to the mirror as she applies some sort of makeup to her eyes.

"What do you think?" She says, leaning back and turning to face him.

"Of... what?" He asks.

"My makeup," Ella laughs.

"Oh. It looks nice," he says sheepishly.

Ella rolls her eyes and turns back to the mirror. She pulls a pin out of her hair, and it cascades around her shoulders.

"You, sir, are a man of eloquence," she teases.

Pylus frowns, "I didn't get much chance to practice my speaking in the arena. Too busy trying to stay alive."

"I guess that's true," Ella says. She pulls parts of her hair up and turns her head from side to side, "Don't go too far. I want your opinion when I get my hair figured out."

Pylus sighs quietly, "Alright."

He makes his way over to the foot of Ella's bed and sits down. His eyes drift along the bare walls and ceiling, looking for any interesting details. Meanwhile, Ella flicks on a blow dryer and hums to herself as she dries her hair.

"Do I make you uncomfortable, Pylus?" Ella calls out from the bathroom when she finishes drying her hair.

"What?"

"Do I make you uncomfortable?" She repeats.

"Not you yourself," He says, "Asking me about what you should wear and how your makeup looks does a little bit."

"And why's that?" Even though Pylus can't see her, he can hear the proud smile in her voice.

"I'm not the best source to go to for fashion advice."

Ella's laugh rings through the room, "What's so hard about it? You look at me and tell me if you think I look pretty or not."

Pylus leans forward and rubs his hands together, "In my experience, a girl who is pretty without makeup will still be pretty with it."

"You think I'm pretty without makeup?"

"...Yes."

Ella's head appears in the doorway, half her hair in a bun, while the other half hangs wildly around her head. She gives him a strange look that he can't read.

"What?" He asks.

"Nothing," she replies, "It's just not very often you meet a guy who will tell you if he thinks you're pretty without having an ulterior motive."

"Ulterior motive? Like what?"

"You'll find out today," she says vaguely and disappears behind the wall again.

"You mean at the gala?"

"Yes, sir. The great gathering of creepy old men and their thirsty understudies."

Pylus notes the venom in her voice, "Now I'm confused. When showing me the dresses, you seemed so excited to go today, but with the way you talk about it, you make it sound like it's torture."

"I enjoy the dancing and the food and the sweet old ladies. You know, the party stuff," she says, "The things I hate are the investors who always come on to me even though they are much, much older than me, and their young, aspiring apprentices who make even more moves on me."

That makes sense. A good party is fun until someone decides to ruin it by invading your space. Not that Pylus knows what parties are like. Things like galas are reserved only for the highest class of the broken world.

"They can't all be that bad," Pylus ventures. His inquiry is met with a sharp laugh that screams, 'You couldn't be more wrong.'

"We live in a world full of scum and back-biters, Pylus. Most of them are the ones running the world," her voice drops to a darker tone, "These people didn't get to the top by making friends and being a good person."

"How does your dad survive?" Pylus asks. If what Ella says is accurate, someone like Jefferson Rye would get eaten alive.

"My dad is a special case. He's kind and genuinely wants what's best for humanity. But don't be fooled. Anyone who crosses my dad or tries to go behind his back quickly regrets it. If they're around long enough to figure it out."

Icicles run through Pylus' veins. Jefferson Rye puts on a good show of compassion. Good enough to make Pylus believe in him, even though they have only had limited interaction with each other. He can't say that he's surprised, though. He knows firsthand that to survive in this world, everyone needs to have a little bit of a dark side and a willingness to do what it takes to get where they want to go. The thing that scares him is how casually Ella said what she did. A terrifying thought runs through his head. *Were my predecessors killed while doing their jobs or for not doing their jobs?* He quickly shakes the thought out of his head. Jefferson Rye wouldn't be the kind of employer to kill off his security detail just because they made a mistake.

"For the most part, my dad is an honest, moral man," Ella says, pulling Pylus out of his dark rabbit hole, "He only gets nasty if someone else starts it."

"Good to know," Pylus mutters to himself.

The conversation dies as Ella focuses on her hair. Pylus lays back on the bed and stares at the ceiling, thinking about what Ella just disclosed to him. How much could he trust these people? Up until now, he had felt safe with his new job. Sure, it's been a busy couple of days, but at least the people have treated him well despite him being a hybrid. But what if it was all just for show? Not wanting to think about that anymore, he racks his brain for something to ask Ella.

"What was that song you were singing earlier?" He asks, remembering the pleasant tune.

"I don't remember the name of it, but it's an old folk song from the 2010s," Ella replies from behind the wall, "My mom used to sing it to me when I couldn't sleep at night."

"It's nice. I remember hearing it before, but not enough to know it or any of the lyrics," Pylus says, wondering what it would be like to have a mother sing you to sleep. "You have a beautiful voice, by the way."

"Ah, thanks. I don't get to sing for other people very often. My dad always says I have a good voice, but he's my dad, so he's obligated to say that."

"I can tell you he wasn't just saying that because he's your dad."

"You have a lot of experience with music and good singers?"

Pylus smiles, "No, but I know your voice doesn't hurt my ears, and I enjoyed listening to it."

Ella's head appears back in the doorway, "Well, now that I know that I'm gonna sing so much, you'll regret saying it."

Pylus lifts his head off the bed to look at her, "When I get tired of it, I'll just gag you."

Ella snickers, "That'll sit well with my dad."

"He would probably thank me," Pylus shoots back.

Ella sticks her tongue out at him, but smiles before pulling her head back behind the wall. Pylus smiles and lays his head back down. He looks at his watch; it's 8:00. So much for the boring mornings he thought he was going to have to endure. This is much worse. He hasn't been late with Brit's schedule yet, but he thinks it might start becoming a regular thing with these galas and Ella's insistence on making her appearance something remarkable.

"Pylus?" Ella's subdued voice drifts out to him.

He sits up, thinking something is out of place, "Yeah?"

It takes her a moment to respond, "Can I ask you something personal?"

He sits back on the bed. He didn't realize he had started to stand.

"You can ask, but I might not answer," he replies.

"Wouldn't expect anything less from you. But here goes," she takes a deep breath before asking, "Do you remember *anything* about your parents?"

Taken aback, Pylus stares at the bathroom doorway. Where had that question come from?

"Um, no. As I said, they dropped me off at an orphanage with my sister when I was around two. The only reason I know that is because I was told. My earliest memories don't start until about five years old."

"You were dropped off with your sister," Ella repeats, not as a question.

"Yeah."

No sound comes from the bathroom for a moment. Then Ella asks, "How old was she when she passed?"

Pylus has to think for a moment. He knew his sister was roughly two years younger than him, but they had never had birthdays that they were aware of. At the orphanage, they used the day they were dropped off as their birthday and estimated their age.

"I think she was around twenty-two," he says.

Ella is quiet for several moments. She had moved out from behind the wall when Pylus answered her question, a strange look on her face.

"That's so young," she whispers. If Pylus didn't have enhanced hearing, he didn't think he would have heard her.

Over the years, he had forgotten how young his sister was when she passed. Dying young was just how the world worked for those in Pylus' social class. If you lived past your thirties outside a settlement, you were doing pretty good. If you lived longer than a couple of years in Champion, you were doing fantastic.

Pylus and his sister had been through so much together that it seemed like they were older than their actual age.

"Was she your only family?" Ella asks quietly, back behind the wall.

"By blood, yes," Pylus answers.

"What was it like having a sibling? I've always wanted one."

A full minute passes before Pylus can think of how to even start a response to the question, "It's an ever-evolving life. As kids, when things were good, we would be friends for five minutes, then be at each other's throats over a toy or a rule in a game, or something silly like that. Then, we'd go back to being friends two minutes later. She was simultaneously the most annoying thing on earth and the best friend I could have asked for. When the other kids were rude, we had each other's backs. No one picked on my little sister but me."

"That is both the sweetest thing I have ever heard and the most concerning." Ella cuts in.

"It's just how kids are most of the time," Pylus says with a shrug, "but things changed when we got older. As we began learning how the world really works and how cruel people can be, we clung to each other. After all the hardships that come with surviving the broken world we live in, you realize that family is the only sure thing you can count on. My sister became my reason to fight and live, and I became hers. She was my best friend and my strongest supporter in whatever life threw at us. Having a sibling is the greatest gift."

The room falls into silence once again when Pylus finishes speaking. He can't hear any movement from Ella. Time seems to freeze. The only indication of it still passing is the ticking of the clock on the nightstand. It's almost deafening in the somber quietness.

"A part of me is glad I didn't have to grow up in the same world that you did," Ella eventually says, "but part of me wishes I could have been your sister. She was lucky to have a brother to care about her as much as you did."

"I was lucky to have her there to take care of me," Pylus says. A tear rolls down his cheek, but he is quick to wipe it away.

Ella lets out a deep breath. Something inside her chest longs for the type of connection that Pylus had described with his sister. She had always felt as if she was missing something in her life, but never knew how to fill it. Now she did. She wanted a sibling. Wanted a big brother to make her feel protected and safe. Wanted a sister to show her the love she lost when her mom died. Her dad was the only person she could think of whom she was truly close to, and even then, he worked so much that she barely had time with him. If she had a sibling, then she would have always had someone around to help make life a little sweeter.

Shaking those thoughts from her mind, she stands and closes the bathroom door so she can change into her dress for the gala.

On the other side of the door, Pylus stands and starts walking back and forth across the room. He is antsy to get going to this gala and get it over with. The idea of being at a large gathering with a killer tracking Ella makes him uneasy. Hopefully, the man from last night hasn't figured out where they are or where they are going. However, if there is a rat in the security...

"Ten minutes to load out," A voice says over Pylus' com.

Glancing at his watch, Pylus is surprised to see the time. It didn't seem like he had been talking to Ella that long. He hurries over to the window and looks out at the driveway. Men stand around each vehicle looking out at different angles, most likely keeping a watch for any suspicious characters. Brit goes to each man individually. He says something to them, and they nod in response. It looks like they won't be taking any chances with the loadout.

"How do I look?" Ella asks from behind Pylus. He hadn't even heard her open the door.

Turning around, his eyes go wide, and his mouth drops slightly. The woman standing in front of him is no longer the same girl he has been guarding for the last two days. Her auburn hair is curled and pulled up in a very stylish bun. The dark lines around her eyes give her the look of a woman who hides a vast amount of wisdom, accentuating the shades of green in her eyes. Beautiful diamond earrings hang from her ears, and a necklace with multiple loops of diamonds hangs around her neck. The light glints off each priceless stone, making it seem like she is shimmering. Dark lipstick contrasts with her fair skin, drawing attention to the mischievous grin she wears and the beauty of her jawline and lips. The dress that looked nice earlier looks incredible now. It accentuates the right parts without being gaudy and tantalizes the eye with the rest. The deep green gives an added depth to her eyes, making them pop. The very demeanor of her stance makes her seem like a woman of admirable reputation that anyone would kill to be close to.

"You, uh... look... nice," Pylus stumbles through his compliment.

The mischievous grin grows into a full, radiant smile. The look she gives would be akin to someone watching a new puppy chase its tail.

"You're sweet," Ella says, then turns and walks to her closet. She picks up a pair of white high heels and sits on the edge of her bed to slip them on. When she finishes, she stands and turns to Pylus, wraps a white shawl around her shoulders, and says, "Shall we?"

12

Four hours and ten minutes later, the two-car caravan had driven halfway back to their original safe house. Currently, it makes its way down a heavily wooded road, winding back and forth with the serpent curves that cut through the trees. Every now and then, a river can be glimpsed through the woods. Thick foliage shrouds the road in shadows as the tree branches curve over the top, creating a natural archway. Fitting for a special event like a gala.

The car ride had been uneventful. Ella had told Pylus all about previous galas she had attended and all the people he just "had" to meet if they were at this one. Pylus had let his head rest back on the headrest and drowned out most of what Ella had told him. As far as socializing goes, he only has room for a couple of people in his life at a time. Making acquaintances hasn't been part of his vivacity the last few years, and now doesn't seem like the time to change that. He can play the charming public figure if needed for fans or the press, but for his private life, he feels less is better. Why have a thousand people who know you when you don't have one person who knows you well? Not that he gives many people the chance to know him well, but the ideology still stands.

Just as it seems like they will be driving through trees forever, the thick foliage suddenly stops. Pylus shifts in his seat to look out the front window and gawk at the view. A massive clearing takes up the tip of a peninsula sticking out into a small lake. The river he thought he had seen earlier was actually part of the lake wrapping around this small landmass. At least a quarter mile of land had been cleared, and right at the point of the peninsula stands a lavish mansion overlooking the south-east part of the water.

Castles were something that Pylus had read about but never seen pictures of or really had any idea what they looked like. He could imagine they looked something like this. Completely made of stone with four rows of windows climbing all the way up the side. Spires rise from each corner in rounded towers that look like they should hold a stolen princess or a ferocious dragon from one of the books he has read. A broad staircase leads up to large, beautiful double doors with elaborate metalwork surrounding the windows.

Cars line the sides of the cleared area, with more lining the driveway, dropping off guests at the front door who make their way into the building. Men in dark suits stand ready on the staircase, presumably security. Most of the people getting out of the cars are wearing suits and dresses of the same quality level as Pylus's suit, but some are far better. A clear distinction between company workers and investors.

Soon, the car in front of them pulls up to the entrance and stops to let its passenger out. A fine-tailored valet opens the back door and steps to the side, stiff and proper, as Mr. Rye exits the vehicle. Brit exits from the other side and follows close behind as the man of the hour walks up the stairs, chatting leisurely with everyone he passes.

Next, Pylus and Ella's car pulls up. The chauffeur opens Ella's door, and Pylus follows Brits' example, opening his own door. He walks around the back of the vehicle and steps up next to Ella.

"Excuse me, sir," the valet says. He's a young man in his early twenties with slicked hair and a clean, childish face, "You forgot your... shoes."

"I don't wear shoes," Pylus says.

The young man looks perplexed and stammers for a minute before nodding awkwardly and moving to the next car pulling up.

The sheer magnitude of the building in front of Pylus strikes him as he cranes his neck to see the top of the spires some fifty feet in the air. Something brushes his hand, drawing him from his marveling. Ella slips her hand into his, gripping his fingers tightly. Her face is whiter than usual, and her mouth is a tight line, distorting the way her lipstick accentuated her lips earlier. Pylus realizes she hasn't said a word since they entered the clearing. He had been too caught up with the building to realize her change of character. Her eyes are wide and stare up at the massive doors as if they're the gaping jaws of a waiting monster. They may as well have been, considering what they might be hiding. The smell of fear pours off Ella, and her heart beats quickly. Pylus can feel a slight tremble in her hand as she grips his.

"Ella?" He says gently, "Are you alright?"

"What if he's here?" She whispers.

Understanding hits Pylus like a slap in the face. This whole time, Ella has been playing the strong, excited card when in reality, she must have been terrified. If the man who is after her was able to corner her in a safe house, how easy would it be for him to catch her in a large crowd? It had already occurred to Pylus and the security detail that the assassin might be at this party. They had prepared mentally for the outcomes and knew to keep themselves on high alert. They felt confident that they would be okay.

Ella, on the other hand, didn't know this. The thought of the assassin being at the party was one she had avoided since she didn't have the confidence of safety. Now, being face-to-face with the actual possibility of facing her murderous stalker again tore her apart from the inside. The fear she had been masking with excitement broke free of its shackles, invading her mind and rampaging through her. Her vision narrows to the open maw of the mansion doorway. The longer she looks, the more convinced she is that she can see two dark, dead eyes looking back at her from the dark corners inside. Her breathing shortens and quickens as her heart rate rises. The doors continue to morph into the evil smile she imagines the assassin had on his face as he watched her wither in the corner. He might even be watching her now!

"Hey, listen to me," Pylus says, stepping in front of her to block her view of the mansion. He tries his best to keep his voice calm and gentle, "As long as I am next to you, you will be safe, alright? Don't leave my side, and you will be alright. I promise." Ella's eyes are out of focus like the day the attack happened but slowly she settles her attention on Pylus as he talks, "Do you trust me?" He asks.

Her eyes latch onto his, suddenly fully present as she whispers, "With my life."

The rapid thumping of Ella's heart starts to slow. Closing her eyes, she takes three deep breaths. She pictures the scene from her bedroom the day before. The assassin was looming over her with his bloody weapon. The hand of the guard was lying limp inside her door, blood slowly pooling around it. The fear and certainty of death crushing her from within. And Pylus. Appearing like an avenging angel with a score to settle. She sees the look of fury in his eyes as she remembers him fighting the assassin. His power and graceful maneuvering that came from years of training and fighting for his own life. She remembers the ferocity he had. The drive to live, to fight... to protect *her*. She can see the concern in his eyes when he comes to her. She can hear the worry in his voice that matches the gentle solicitude he shows her now. Knowing that he is right here with her brings the fear back under control. She knows he will do everything to keep her safe. He's already proven that, but more importantly, he has shown her that he cares about her, and that is what motivates him to do his job well. Not money or notoriety. Genuine care. When she opens her eyes again, they are bright and shining. A small smile plays on her lips, bringing out the confidence she always had.

"Let's get this party started," she says.

"Alright," Pylus says, matching her smile, "After you, my lady."

He steps to the side to let her walk first, but she keeps a hold of his hand and pulls him with her, keeping him by her side. Together, they walk up the ten steps to the front door and enter the mouth of the beast.

The first thing to hit Pylus is the noise. A mob of indistinct chatter assaults his ears. Outside, he couldn't hear it as much, but inside the massive ballroom, sounds reverberate off the stone walls and hardwood floors mercilessly.

The second thing that hits him is the smells. Thousands of different scents all around him. Most are subtle and easy to ignore, while others seem to cram themselves into his nostrils and go ten rounds with his senses. Perfumes and colognes pollute the air while delicious fragrances from various foods draw the nose to their origin with tempting insistence.

The third, and probably the most impressive, is the sights. Hundreds of people dressed in the finest formal clothes available. Colors dance before Pylus' eyes that he didn't even know existed. The cheapest of the dresses that he sees makes him feel like his simple security suit got picked up from a drunk outside The Spot. Light from the setting sun trickles in through the high windows, igniting the colors in a brilliant vibrance and reflecting them onto the walls.

"Oh, they have Éclairs!" Ella exclaims, dragging Pylus over towards the food table.

Food platters sit on a row of tables sixty feet long at least. Everything looks exquisite, and Pylus can only name two or three of the dishes he can see. Ella immediately reaches for the dish piled with fluffy things that look like elongated rolls topped with chocolate. She picks two up and hands one to him excitedly.

"Here!" She says like a kid sharing their favorite candy.

"I can't eat that," Pylus says.

Ella's face drops into a pout as she asks, "Why not?"

"I can't eat chocolate," Pylus reminds her.

"Oh, that's right," she says with a huff, "Well, I guess I'll eat these two, then I will have you try my second favorite treat here."

Without another word, Ella devours the two treats, looking none too ladylike in the process. The sight of this young woman in an elegant party dress stuffing her face with chocolaty treats makes Pylus smile. Ella sees him watching and smiles like a little girl on Christmas morning. Her inner child has come out to make the most of this impressive event. Mainly the treats.

Ella looks away and wipes her mouth with a napkin, then glances back at Pylus. Her eyes narrow slightly, like she's contemplating a difficult question, "You have a nice smile. You should show it more."

Pylus gives her a look that says she's being silly, "I will if you keep eating treats like that."

"What's so funny about it?" She asks, putting a hand on her hip.

"Oh, nothing," Pylus shrugs and turns away, "Just seeing you be all proper in your fancy dress and scarfing down sweets is a funny sight."

Ella sticks out her tongue in response, "Maybe if we find a treat you can actually eat, you'll be the same. Now come along, boy. Let's find something that won't make your little tummy hurt."

"Haha, you're so funny," Pylus says sarcastically.

Ella smiles and grabs his hand, dragging him further down the table of food. Everything they pass smells amazing, and Pylus keeps slowing to linger on certain ones. Every time he does, Ella pulls his hand impatiently. Eventually, they make it to the opposite end of the table, Pylus making a mental note of all the things he wants to go back and try. Three platters of the same dish take up the end of the table they stand next to. Glazed roll looking things glisten on the plates with red jelly stuff peeking through slits on the top.

"What are these?" Pylus points to the nearest plate of treats.

Instead of answering, Ella smiles and hands him one, "Just eat it. It's one hundred percent dog friendly. . . I think."

Hesitantly, Pylus lifts the treat to his mouth and takes a bite. Gooey sweetness explodes in his mouth, the softness surprising him. It's like biting into a cloud filled with jelly.

"Holy crap," he says around his mouthful of food, "What is this?"

"It's a raspberry Danish," Ella says.

Pylus takes another bite and closes his eyes, "I've never tasted anything this good."

"I'm glad you like it," Ella says as she grabs one for herself.

After two more Danishes, Pylus reminds himself he is supposed to be doing a job. He quickly scans the crowd around him, but doesn't see anything suspicious. His gaze drifts further and further into the crowd with every sweep. Nothing to worry about, it seems. He makes eye contact with Brit across the room, who is scanning the people just like Pylus. They nod to each other and continue their observations. Everybody around Pylus and Ella seem oblivious to their existence, much to Pylus' liking.

"Ella!" Calls a voice to the side of where the pair stands. Both turn to see a little old lady shuffling through the crowd towards them.

"Mrs. Mead!" Ella calls back joyfully. She rushes over to the old lady and embraces her warmly.

Mrs. Mead places her hand on Ella's cheek as they part and looks at her like a proud grandmother, "Oh my, how lovely you look this evening," she says lovingly, "How have things been for you, my dear?"

"Oh, you know," Ella says nonchalantly, "same thing day in and day out. Not much happens in my life with these guys around." She jabs her thumb at Pylus with her last statement. He grins and shakes his head a little.

His smile fades when he looks at Mrs. Mead. Her eyes have settled on him, and the look she gives him is just short of deadly. He didn't think cute old ladies were capable of such contemptuous expressions.

"I'm surprised your father would employ such individuals to keep you safe," Mrs. Mead spits, keeping her eyes on Pylus, "considering their history of violence."

"Mrs. Mead," Ella says in a consoling tone, "Pylus is different. He's not a bloodthirsty killing machine like you think all Hybrids are. He's kind and loyal and has already done so much for me."

Mrs. Mead leans in and whispers to Ella, presumably so Pylus can't hear, but little does she know, "Believe you me, girl," the old lady says coldly, "Once those things get a taste of innocent human blood, there's no stopping what comes next." She pulls away and gives Ella the "You'll see" look before walking away without giving Pylus another glance.

"I'm so sorry," Ella says, blushing as she faces Pylus.

"Don't worry about it," he says, "I've had plenty of hate for what I am. You get used to it."

"It's just that she lost her husband to a hybrid just after the war," Ella continues, "They were the biggest contributors to my dad when he was starting his companies. They're good people who are just misled in their beliefs. I—"

"Ella," Pylus cuts in, "It's okay, really. You don't have to worry about me hating her. I don't reciprocate the feelings people show me when it comes to being a Hybrid. My kind decimated the world in the war. It's natural for people to feel disdain for us. We just have to show them that now we aren't the same. If they want to see it, they will. If not, they can let their hatred eat away at them. But that won't change me."

Ella sighs heavily, "You're right. To be honest, I agreed with her for a long time. I thought Hybrids were terrible and should be eradicated. But then I met an old Midbrid who fought in the war. He told me that after the first week of being in the war, he had seen enough and had spent the rest of his time finding humans to save and escort to safety. He told me that just because you were part animal didn't mean you lost your humanity. I've never met someone as kind and gentle as he was, until I met you. Ironically, the nicest people I've ever known have been part of the group that is hated the most by the world."

"That's always how it goes," Pylus says.

A hand on Pylus's shoulder makes him jump and reach for his knife. He relaxes when he sees Mr. Rye holding his shoulder and smiling, "Sorry to scare you, Pylus, but I have someone who would like to meet you."

A short Asian man steps out from behind Mr. Rye and nods his head, "Pylus, this is Mr. Yen." Mr. Rye introduces the newcomer, "He's one of our constituents from the Chinese Republic and is a big fan of the Champion circuit here. When I told him I had hired you as Ella's new guard, he said he just had to meet you."

Mr. Yen takes Pylus' hand in both of his and bows his head again, "The pleasure is mine, Mr. Brek."

Pylus puts on his best social smile and follows Mr. Yen by bowing his head, "Always nice to meet a fan. Do they have a Champion circuit in the Chinese Republic, Mr. Yen?"

"No, no," he says, "We put our Hybrids to different use."

A strange new smell sneaks its way to Pylus. He glances at a man standing behind Mr. Yen, who wears dark sunglasses over his eyes, so Pylus can't see where he is looking. His head is shaved, but it looks like there's a strange design tattooed on it. The smell comes from him.

"Is that use bodyguards perhaps?" Pylus asks, nodding towards the man.

Mr. Yen raises his eyebrows, "Very good, Mr. Brek. How did you know?"

"I can smell him," Pylus says, tapping his nose, "It's the human scent mixed with something else. A snake of some kind, perhaps? And please, call me Pylus."

"Consider me impressed," Mr. Yen says, turning and pointing to his Hybrid bodyguard, "This is Ming. He is a Midbrid, as you call them here. Twenty-three percent emerald anaconda."

Ming takes his sunglasses off and smiles to reveal rows of small, pointed teeth instead of human ones. His eyes are typical slitted snake eyes. Dark and terrifying.

"We only let a certain number of Hybrids be in existence at any given time and put a limit on how many one person can have in employment," Mr. Yen explains, "If any have more than thirty percent animal influence, we take their life immediately. We don't want to risk anything."

"Oh," Pylus says, "that's one way to do it."

"Everybody has their own solution," Mr. Rye cuts in, "Don't stray too far, Pylus. Mr. Yen would like to talk with you more after we speak to more people."

Mr. Yen bows again and turns to leave with Mr. Rye's arm around his shoulder. Ming nods to Pylus stiffly before putting his sunglasses back on and turning to follow his boss.

"Wow, you're world famous," Ella whispers.

"I guess I am." Pylus agrees.

"Come on, I'm thirsty," Ella says, dragging him off yet again.

13

The rest of the afternoon gala flies by in a blur. Pylus stands close to Ella as she talks with workers and shareholders alike. Her persona is completely different than the one she had on display when she was given as his charge two days ago. Here, she is a professional and mature woman who speaks about the company with ease and gets along with everyone she talks to. The way she speaks and laughs makes those around her feel like they have been friends forever, when in reality, she just met most of them that day.

"Ugh, I am exhausted," Ella says as she leans against the wall next to Pylus. She just finished speaking with one of the production managers of the local warehouse about the role he plays in the business. While it is a very important role, it is not an interesting one... except to him.

"I never would have thought you had a social limit," Pylus says.

Ella leans her head against the wall and looks at him, "Everyone has a social limit. Some of us have just been trained to keep socializing after we've reached it."

"Sounds awful."

"You have no idea."

"I think I might by the time this is all over."

Ella laughs, "Oh, these next two weeks will just be a taste of what it's like. When my dad upgrades the company, he goes to each branch individually and holds a formal party for each one that lasts two days."

"How many branches does your dad have?" Pylus asks, realizing he doesn't have any idea how big J.R. Genetics actually is.

"Around thirty, I think," Ella says, scrunching her face as she thinks, "One in each of the major settlements and a few more in smaller ones out West somewhere."

"How many people does each warehouse employ?"

"The smallest has one hundred and seventy employees, roughly."

Pylus raises his eyebrows, "That has to be the biggest company in the world!"

Ella smiles without looking at him, "It is. Dad had already established a good company base and reputation before the war. Leaning on his assets and investors, he was able to go dark until the rebuild started, then he came back full force and has grown exponentially due to supply and demand from the world. If it wasn't for my dad's efforts, the world would be a much more desolate place. Millions more would have starved."

"Ms. Rye," a voice cuts in.

Pylus and Ella look over to see a young woman in a server's uniform standing with her hands behind her back.

"Your rest suite is ready when you are. It's the first door to the left on the second floor if you go up that stairway," she points to a staircase on the far side of the ballroom.

"Thank you," Ella smiles at the server, then turns to Pylus, "I'm tired, let's go up to the room."

She takes off across the floor with Pylus close behind as they pass people from earlier. Ella smiles and says quick goodbyes. Mrs. Mead gives her a tight hug as she walks past and gives Pylus a chilling glare that could have frozen Hell. In return, he gives her a smile and a nod, hoping to appear polite, then follows Ella up the stairs and to the doorway of the room the server had mentioned.

The rest suite is lavish with multiple couches randomly spaced out and pillows filling almost every available space on them. Ella walks over to the nearest couch and throws herself onto it with a heavy sigh. Pylus takes a spot on the one straight across from her, moving several pillows to do so. Both sit back and stare at the ceiling, enjoying the time to relax and do nothing. A few minutes go by before Ella breaks the silence.

"Is it my turn to ask a question?" She asks.

Pylus lifts his head off the back of the couch to look at her, "You're still playing that game?"

"Well, yeah. We have nothing better to do," she says.

"I have no idea who asked the last question."

"I'm going to say it was you then," she adjusts herself so she can look at him better, "So, how old are you?"

Pylus chuckles and lays his head back, "That's your question?"

"Yeah. Why is that funny?" Ella asks.

"I don't know. Same reason you thought me asking your favorite color was funny. I would have guessed that question would have been one of the first ones you asked."

"You would think, but it wasn't. So, answer it."

Pylus grins at her snooty demand, "As I told you with my sister, I don't know my actual birthday, but I think I'm around twenty-seven." He glances at her to see how she reacts. A simple eyebrow raise is all he gets.

"I would have guessed you were older with how grumpy you are," Ella says.

Pylus snorts at the comment, "You think I'm grumpy?" Ella just shrugs in response, "Whatever. I guess it's my turn for a question, so how old are you?"

"Why don't you guess?"

"I hate guessing games," Pylus says, closing his eyes.

Ella makes a face at him that he doesn't see, "Boring."

"Well, it's also confusing," Pylus shoots back, "When you socialize at the gala, it seems like you are around my age, but when we were back at the safe house, your maturity suggested you were sixteen. Twelve, when you were being really insolent."

A pillow thumps into his chest in response to his comment. He smiles and wraps his arms around it like it's his favorite stuffed animal.

"For your information, I'm twenty-five," Ella sneers, then adds, "Punk."

"Twenty-five, huh?" Pylus says. For half a second, it's not Ella he's sitting across from.

"Do you think about your sister often?" Pylus bolts upright and looks at Ella.

"What?" He asks, shocked that she can read his mind.

Ella is taken back by the burst of energy, "I, um... I asked if you think about your sister often."

For a couple of seconds, Ella doesn't know if Pylus will answer the question or just get up and walk out.

Finally, he looks at the ground and says, "I used to. For the first year or so after she died, she was all I could think about. Eventually, though, I pushed all those thoughts away until I stopped having them. I haven't thought of her much the last couple of years."

"Why?"

"Why what?"

Ella looks at him sadly, "Why did you push the thoughts away?"

A big sigh precedes Pylus' answer, "Because for years we were there for each other, she was always by my side, my constant. When she died, I was lost. I couldn't function alone, didn't know how to. Remembering her just reminded me of that over and over again. So, I had to restart and live my life as if I had always been alone. It made it easier to survive."

"But you had to forget about your sister?" Ella says in disbelief.

Pylus shakes his head, "I never forgot her. I just accepted that she was no longer a part of my life and moved on."

Ella's jaw drops, "How could you do that?" She whispers.

"It's what helped me survive," Pylus says defensively, "I didn't have anyone to protect me like you did."

Regret fills Pylus immediately after saying what he did. Ella's open mouth closes into a tight line. He expected anger to fill her eyes, but he can only see disappointment.

"I'm sorry. I shouldn't have said that," he says quietly.

Ella holds up her hand and shakes her head, "It's okay. You're not wrong." Tears fill her eyes, and her voice cracks as she continues, "Losing my mom was the hardest thing I ever went through, and I think about her every day. But I never thought about that as a luxury I got. It makes sense that you would have to push through your pain, given the situations you were in. I was spoiled with a father who took care of me when I was at my lowest and with the chance to let my grief take over. I actually got to mourn my mom because I was safe with my dad. You didn't have anyone and didn't get the chance to truly grieve for your sister, and it breaks my heart."

This time, Pylus' jaw drops open. He thought she was disappointed in *him,* but now he realizes she was disappointed in herself. She thinks of herself as selfish for being allowed to properly mourn her mother. Her true sympathy for him leaves him flabbergasted for a few moments.

"I.... uh," He clears his throat, "I appreciate your sympathy. I'm touched by how much you care, but please don't feel guilty for having a better situation than I did. I wish I didn't have to leave the memory of my sister behind me, but it was what I needed to do at the time. I wish more than anything I could have had what you did to appropriately mourn my loved ones."

"Ones?" Ella asks, looking in his eyes for the first time since he snapped at her.

"That's a story for another day," he says gently.

"You sure have a lot of stories for another day."

"In my defense, we've only known each other for a couple of days," Pylus reminds her.

"I guess that's true. So, are any of those books good?"

Pylus turns around to look where she is pointing. In the back corner is a bookshelf full of books that he didn't notice before. He walks over and starts examining the options. Halfway through the small library, he pulls out a book and walks it over to Ella.

"Here, it's the same one I lent you back at the safe house."

"Really? Oh, good!" She snatches the book from his hands and flips through the pages until she finds the spot she had stopped at, "I had started reading it when you were called out to help Brit, but got. . . interrupted." Her eyes trail away as she sees the dead guard falling through her doorway.

"Hey," Pylus says, tapping her leg, "It's in the past. Time to start working away from it."

"You're right," she says, shaking her head, "Good thing I got a good distraction." Pylus smiles as she sits back and delves into her book.

After finding a book that seems interesting, Pylus sits back on his couch, ready to read until the next gala begins.

***

"These are the galas that I hate," Ella says, eyeing the men and women entering the ballroom. She and Pylus had joined the growing crowd of investors and owners for the second gala. They had reclaimed their earlier spot on the wall close to the food tables. Pylus snacks on three different types of meat dishes while Ella eats some fruit.

"Are these the ones you always get the creepy old guys and desperate young bucks at?" Pylus asks after swallowing a mouthful of food.

Ella nods and says, "I give it another thirty seconds before someone comes up to me."

Pylus scans the crowd. Aside from Ella, beautiful young women are not in the present company. In fact, the only women present are the wives of the older gentlemen. Even the female servers have disappeared. Ella must not be the only one who gets advances from the men.

"Why do you come to these things if you don't like them?" Pylus asks.

"For my dad," she replies, "These things are as hard on him as they are on me. He'll come up to me soon for a break from visiting or to vent or simply for a hug. As I said before, these people aren't the kindest or most trustworthy."

As if prompted by a thirty-second cue, a man in his late fifties strides toward the pair purposefully. Pylus watches him warily.

"Ella, my dear," the man says, opening his arms wide, "How are you this fine evening? You look ravishing as always."

Ella smiles a tight-lipped smile when she responds, "Thank you, Mr. Blane."

Mr. Blane puts his hand on Ella's shoulder and kisses her cheek; in his other hand, he holds a glass of an alcoholic beverage. It seems it's not his first glass.

The man is at least an inch taller than Pylus and looks to be in great physical shape. Graying hair covers his head and falls to his shoulders in a fancy haircut. His face is clean-shaven but still rugged somehow with a prominent jawline and a scar running from his chin to the bottom of his ear. When he smiles, perfect teeth gleam in the light. He would be a pleasant-looking man if it weren't for his eyes. Cruelly dark and mysterious. Not mysterious in the sexy romantic novel way, but like a person hiding something sinister. Treacherous.

"I have to say, Ella, you get more beautiful every time I see you," Mr. Blane continues, "You look more like your mother every day."

"Thank you," Ella says with a gracious head nod.

"Your father was telling me about the recent scare you had," Mr. Blane says, "Are you doing alright?" The hand he placed on Ella's shoulder remains there. Almost as if to keep her from running off.

"I'm doing fine, thank you," Ella says, "Things would be much different if it hadn't been for Pylus." She gestures to him with a genuine smile.

"Ah, yes, Pylus Brek," Mr. Blane's persona changes as he straightens and eyes Pylus, "I've seen you in Champion. Quite the fighter."

Despite the compliment, Pylus feels insulted, "Thank you, sir."

One of Mr. Blane's eyebrows goes up, "And a gentleman. Consider me impressed."

Pylus forces a smile, "I've had lots of practice with reporters."

"I see," Mr. Blane turns to Ella, "Well, I'm so very glad you have a bodyguard who can do his job well this time."

Ella tenses slightly at the comment but keeps a good face. Pylus can smell her anxiety and hear her heart pounding. This guy may put on a good "just a concerned friend" show, but he makes her uncomfortable. *Very* Uncomfortable.

"Well, I better be off to socialize some more, but I will circle back around," with a charming smile that doesn't reach his eyes, Mr. Blane makes his exit.

Once he disappears into the crowd, Ella drops her head onto Pylus' arm and groans, "See what I mean?"

"He definitely thinks you're beautiful," Pylus says. "His heartbeat was all over the place, and he smelled. . . excited."

"Excited?" Ella asks, "You can smell that."

"Only when someone is excited in a certain way."

"Like what?" Pylus glances at her and raises his eyebrows, "Oh... like that." She says, then makes an exaggerated dry heave.

Pylus smiles, "What's the matter? Don't like older men?"

"Not that much older," Ella says, disgusted, "He's older than my dad."

"That would make family dinners uncomfortable."

"Among other things."

"Heads up, you got another one coming," Pylus nods to the side at a young man strutting over to them.

The kid has to be nineteen at most and two inches shorter than Ella. His suit is one of the nicest ones present and has been tailored to accentuate his arm muscles, not that there is much to work with. He smirks as he makes his way towards them, leading with his chest and swinging his arms by his side.

"Hello there," he says, stepping up to Ella and extending his hand, "My name is Chester Sandstrom." he plants a small kiss on Ella's hand, "And you are?"

"Ella Rye. It's a pleasure."

"Oh, believe me," Chester says with a chuckle, "the pleasure is all mine. Who might this strapping young man be? Your boyfriend, perhaps?" It's obvious he's joking.

Ella, however, slips her arm around Pylus' and smiles up at him, "Yes, he is."

The shock on Chester's face matches how Pylus feels, although he is able to contain it better than the ambitious young man. He smiles at Ella, hoping he is playing along well with the charade.

"Oh, forgive me. I'm Pylus Brek," he says, reaching his hand out to Chester, who tentatively shakes it, "Wonderful to meet you, Chester."

"Pylus Brek? As in the Champion contender?" Chester asks, narrowing his eyes.

"The one and only," Ella says proudly.

"I see. So how did you two meet then?"

"I fought for her uncle in Champion," Pylus says, grateful that it's the truth. "He became a good friend of mine when I started making a name for myself. One day, as we were talking in his office about my future in Champion, Ella and her father stopped by for a quick visit – "

"We stop in to see my uncle whenever we are close to the Shank Settlement," Ella cuts in.

"Lucky for me, they did," Pylus continues, "Ella and I became friends instantly, and Mr. Rye was kind enough to buy my freedom from his brother so Ella could have a friend and a protector to travel with." Making things up on the fly was not Pylus' strong suit; however, this lie was coming to him remarkably well. "After spending two or three whole days together, we realized that there was something more than just friendship." He looks at Ella to drive the point home. She looks into his eyes, and for a moment, he thinks she is actually in love with him. Her acting is good enough to fool him, even though he knows the truth.

Chester stares at them with a dazed expression, his chest no longer puffed out, as if someone had stuck him with a pin. He clears his throat when it is obvious Pylus and Ella aren't going to continue, "So, how long have you been together then? I seem to recall you having a fight just a few days ago."

"That's right," Ella says quickly, "It was that same day that my father and I visited my uncle. Our decision to be something more than friends is a recent one, as of today. We actually haven't told anyone but my father yet, so if you don't mind keeping it a secret for me." The innocence in her voice has Pylus convinced he needs to keep the secret as well. He has to remind himself that there was nothing to tell.

"Uh, of course. Your secret is safe with me." Chester offers a half smile before turning and walking away.

Once the boy is far enough into the crowd, Ella and Pylus burst into a fit of snickering laughs. They try to control themselves and keep quiet, but the relief of the stressful situation ending fuels their giggling. Ella covers her face with her free hand and lays her head on Pylus' shoulder again. Pylus has to hold his hand over his mouth to keep his enjoyment contained.

"What's so funny?"

The snickering pair instantly stops their laughing fit and turns to the inquisitor. Mr. Rye looks at them with eyebrows raised and an amused smile of his own.

Pylus lets out a sigh of relief as Ella starts talking, "We just diverted a young man's interest in me."

Mr. Rye's amusement turns to inquiry, "And how did you do that?"

Ella and Pylus look at each other. Hesitantly, Ella speaks up, "We told him that Pylus and I are. . . dating."

Agonizing seconds tick by with Pylus and Ella holding their breath, waiting for Mr. Rye's reaction. His face is blank as he looks back and forth between the two. Just when Pylus thinks the man is never going to say anything, Mr. Rye throws his head back and lets out a hearty laugh and claps Pylus on the shoulder.

"That is brilliant!" he bellows, "I knew hiring you was a good idea, Pylus!"

Pylus and Ella simultaneously let their breath out in a relieved laugh. Mr. Rye chuckles to himself and keeps a hold of Pylus's shoulder.

"I'll have to keep the rumor going," Mr. Rye says, giving Pylus another big thump on the back.

"Mr. Blane is the only one who knows Pylus is actually my bodyguard," Ella says.

Mr. Rye makes a face and brushes his hand in front of his nose like he's shooing a fly, "Oh, that's an easy explanation. Guard turned lover isn't uncommon after all. But now you'd better act the part. People's eyes are going to be on you."

"Don't worry," Ella says, leaning into Pylus, wrapping her arm around his and resting her cheek on his shoulder as she smiles up at him, "I've already thought about that."

An almost proud smile spreads across Mr. Rye's face, "My little actress," he says fondly. "Anyway, the reason I came over was because Mr. Yen is asking about you, Pylus. He was wondering if you would mind sitting with him for a moment. He's very curious about your hybrid abilities."

"Oh, no, not at all," Pylus says.

"Wonderful," Mr. Rye smiles, "This way then." He slips his arm around Pylus's shoulders and leads him across the room. Ella keeps a loose hold of his other arm, keeping up a good act.

Mr. Yen stands close to the main doors of the building. He and Ming stand close together, talking fervently. It seems the conversation is a very private one. Just as Pylus suggests, they come back in a little bit; Mr. Rye calls out to the pair. Mr. Yen looks at them and smiles pleasantly. He shakes Pylus' hand with a bow as he gets close.

"Pylus, thank you for coming to speak with me again," he says.

"No problem, Mr. Yen," Pylus says, "Mr. Rye says you have some questions about my influence."

"Yes, yes," Mr. Yen says excitedly, "Forgive my inquiry, but you are the only canine hybrid in the world that I have heard of, and I can hardly contain my curiosity."

"Well then, fire away," Pylus says.

"Oh, where to begin?" Mr. Yen asks, rubbing his chin, "How about with your abilities. What changes have you experienced with the influence? And how much influence do you have?"

"My influence is about twenty-eight percent," Pylus begins, "that's why I'm allowed to use weapons in Champion. It's low influence for a midbrid, but since I'm the only canine hybrid, they don't know if my influence has had a stronger effect than it would for other canines."

"What do you mean stronger effect?" Ming asks. It's the first time he's spoken, and his deep voice surprises Pylus.

"Well, when they talk about influence percentage, they only mean how much of the DNA has changed," Pylus explains, "However, what they can't measure is how strongly the change happens. For example, two lion hybrids have the same influence percentage, and both have increased strength and smell, but one of them has a sense of smell far stronger than the other.

"Scientists believe the strength of the change is determined by the strength of the previous DNA and abilities *before* bonding with the animal's DNA. So, if a human had a stronger sense of smell before being influenced, then they will have a stronger sense of smell compared to other hybrids of the same influence and percentage."

Ming nods his head and strokes his chin deep in thought, "And since you are the only canine hybrid, they can't accurately measure how strongly the change has affected you comparatively in regard to the animal chosen for you?"

"Correct," Pylus says, "They can only measure my change against my non-hybrid abilities to see how much has been influenced."

"So, what abilities do you have then?" Mr. Yen asks again.

Pylus's ears twitch slightly at a buzzing sound before he answers, "My hearing and smell are both heightened. They are actually stronger than any known canine species; however, that might be just a random spike in the influence. One canine hybrid might only have the same sense of smell as a lab. Another might be closer to a bloodhound. It just depends on them.

"Another more obvious change is my teeth," he opens his mouth slightly to show his elongated fangs, "my fingernails and toenails are now claws, my eyes changed color, the soles of my feet are padded like dogs, so I never have to wear shoes, and some other, less prominent physical features. Before the change, I was five feet eight inches tall as a human. Now I'm six foot two. My muscle density is higher, making me faster and stronger than an average human. I pretty much have the strength of a bodybuilder without the size. My arms and feet are significantly longer, making it easy for me to walk or run on all fours."

Mr. Yen looks at his own arm, then at Pylus', "Ah, yes, I see. Most human arms only reach to mid-thigh. And those are the long ones. Yours reach to your knees. I'm surprised I didn't notice before. It looks natural the way you carry yourself."

"Thank you," Pylus says with a smile, "It's more noticeable if I crouch or if I walk on all fours."

"You sound like a werewolf," Ella says, and Mr. Yen lets out a soft, amused laugh in response.

"Pretty much," Pylus says, "Just without the full moon stuff. The weirdest ability I have is being able to see in the dark because I'm not colorblind like wolves are. It was quite disorienting at first."

"Interesting," Mr. Yen says with one hand on his chin. He studies Pylus intently as he speaks, "Exactly how good is your hearing and smell?"

Pylus focuses for a minute, separating the different sounds and smells before saying, "I can hear your heartbeat if I concentrate, even with all the commotion going on around me. As for my smell, do you see that lady with the purple scarf?” Pylus points to the woman who stands at least two hundred feet away. Mr. Yen nods as he looks to where Pylus points, “I can smell her from here. She has on a very strong rose-scented perfume to try to cover up the smell of cigarettes, but it’s not working very well. The trick is focusing my senses to pick out what I want. If I’m not searching for something, everything just fades into a buzz of white noise or a ball of fragrance. I have to clear through all the different stimulants if I want something in particular to stand out.”

“Incredible,” Mr. Yen whispers, “Can you remember certain smells for long periods of time?”

“Can’t you?” Pylus asks, “I’m sure you have plenty of smells that are familiar and that you use as references for new smells.”

“That’s true,” Mr. Yen agrees.

“Are your reflexes heightened?” Ming asks.

Pylus nods, “Probably not as much as yours, but they are faster than before. Training has also helped them improve.”

“How much did you train?” Mr. Yen asks. An almost urgent tone to his voice, like he has to know the answer.

“At least two hours a day. I practiced hand-to-hand combat, knife fighting, and grappling. I messed around with bo staffs and clubs a little, but those aren’t helpful in Champion, so it was more just for fun.”

Mr. Yen eyes him with an almost wary look, “Quite the specimen, aren’t you, Pylus?”

Pylus smiles shyly and shrugs, “Not any more than other hybrids, sir.”

“Right, of course,” Mr. Yen says with a dry smile, “Well, it has been a pleasure talking with you, Pylus. Do enjoy the rest of your night.”

“Thank you, sir.”

Mr. Yen and Ming walk away to socialize with more prestigious company, leaving Pylus, Ella, and Mr. Rye alone, Brit not too far away. Ella squeezes Pylus’ arm and whispers, “Is it just me, or did that seem more like an interrogation at the end?”

“It was,” Pylus says, “His heartbeat changed when I told him about my hearing, and he started to smell nervous, like he was afraid of being found out or something.”

"Do you think he is hiding something?"

Pylus glances over his shoulder to look at Mr. Rye and Brit, but the two men have turned away and are speaking with a gentleman several feet away.

"Most likely," he says, turning back to Ella.

"Like what?"

Pylus looks at her and sees the concern on her face, "Nothing we have to worry about right now. As you said, everyone here has a dark side. Maybe Mr. Yen has some secrets he was afraid I would figure out. Like enjoying cheap cologne when he can obviously afford the good stuff."

Ella tries to smile and looks up at him with wide eyes. He smiles at her and brushes a loose hair behind her ear, then tilts her chin with his pointer finger, "Don't worry. You're safe with me."

The fear melts from her face, replaced with a calm smile. She nods and tucks her head into his arm once again.

The rest of the gala drags by but goes smoothly. People come to talk to Ella and ask about her new "boyfriend". It gives the two plenty of opportunity to solidify their backstory and relay it to Mr. Rye when he comes over to them to get breaks from socializing. A couple of young men who haven't heard the news yet try their hand with Ella, but are politely declined as she is, in her words, "already spoken for".

As the gala comes to an end, Mr. Rye moves through the crowd, shaking hands and thanking everyone for coming. Ella takes Pylus and sneaks out while the crowd focuses on her father. They make their way down the front steps just in time to have their driver pull up, let them slip in, and drive away without being noticed. Or so they think. Pylus looks back at the lavish building to see Ming watching him from the doorway. His sunglasses are off, and his cold snake eyes follow their vehicle as they pull away from the mansion.

Pylus shudders as he turns to face out the front window. "So, where are we heading?" he asks.

"There's a neighborhood about thirty minutes away where all the houses are for the company leaders who come to these galas," Ella says.

"Do you ever stay anywhere very long?" Pylus asks.

Ella smiles, "Yes, we do. It's just the time of year when we visit all the branches of the company to assess the progress and work."

"Oh boy," Pylus whispers to himself.

Thirty minutes later, he and Ella climb the steps to a modest house in a cul-de-sac neighborhood. They walk in the front door and down a set of stairs to the basement. Ella leads him to a room at the end of the hall.

"This is my room," she says awkwardly, "Um... your room is just right there across the hall. So... goodnight, I guess."

"Goodnight, Ella," Pylus says.

She smiles a little smile, then turns and steps into her room. She takes one more look at Pylus before closing the door. Pylus shakes his head as he steps to his room. Before he can go in, Ella's door opens again, and her head pops out.

"Um... this might be weird, but would you mind... sleeping with me... again?

Pylus looks at her calmly and nods, "Sure. Let me just grab a pillow off my bed."

Ella smiles a relieved smile, "Thank you. I'll get changed quickly, then open the door for you." Her head disappears again, and her door closes.

Pylus snags a pillow off the small bed in his room and returns to the hall to wait for Ella. He only has to wait a couple of minutes before the door opens, and Ella stands to the side wearing a silky pair of blue pajamas. Her hair and makeup are still the same, though.

"Come in and pick your spot while I take my makeup off," she says.

Her room is the same size as Pylus' with a twin bed and a makeup stand in it. As far as safe houses go, this one is the most modest one Pylus has been to. He closes the door behind him and tosses his pillow on the ground next to Ella's bed.

Ella sits at the makeup stand and uses wipes to take off the stuff she took so long to put on earlier that day. She notices Pylus watching her in the mirror and makes a face at him.

"What are you looking at?"

"You look like a whole new person now." The package of wipes sails at his head in response to his comment. He catches it easily and smiles his most innocent smile at Ella.

"Oh, don't give me those puppy dog eyes," she sneers.

"Why? Are they working?" Pylus asks, putting the wipes back on the stand.

Ella sticks out her tongue at him and turns back to the mirror. She starts pulling pins and hair ties out of her hair. Pylus watches in amazement as the number of things getting pulled out turns into a small mountain on her stand.

"How many of those things do you have in there?" He asks.

Ella gives him a side smirk, "The price of beauty."

"Seems too high to me," he says, "Especially when you are already naturally beautiful."

"Oh, that's so sweet," Ella says, putting her hands over her heart, "But it's fun to get all dolled up for special occasions. It makes me feel more put together. Almost like a mask of confidence."

"Hm. I don't understand it," Pylus says, taking off his jacket and laying it on the ground next to his pillow, "Your confidence level already seems *too* high." The package of wipes returns to make another attack on his head. This time it connects. He laughs and tosses it back to Ella.

He removes his weapons and holsters and lays them on the floor, then he himself lays down. Soon after, Ella turns off the light and crawls into her bed.

"Hey Pylus," her voice says in the darkness after a moment.

"Yeah?"

"Did you really have a good time tonight?"

"I enjoyed the food."

Ella laughs, "Well, I guess that's one good thing about the party." She goes quiet for a minute, then speaks again, "Hey, thanks for being my boyfriend tonight."

"Anytime."

She stays quiet for a moment, but her heartbeat tells Pylus she has something more to say. Eventually, it comes out, "Can we just keep the charade up for all the parties we have coming up?"

Pylus fingers one of the rings he has around his neck absentmindedly. Ellie's ring. The girl he wanted to be his actual girlfriend, and the one Ella is reminding him of more and more the longer he is with her.

"...Sure," he says in a quiet voice.

"Thanks," she whispers. Pylus can hear the smile in her voice and smiles back even though she can't see him. Soon, all is quiet, and they both drift off to sleep.

14

Seven days mesh together in a mess of driving and parties, talking and eating, playing boyfriend and bodyguard at the same time. Between galas and travel time, Ella insists on continuing her self-defense training as soon as they get the chance. They spend late nights working on technique and catching up on sleep in the long car rides. By the time the eighth day rolls around, Pylus feels exhausted and sick of being in a car. They've traveled across the continent from the East Coast to the West Coast, zigzagging to different settlements. So many new places and people. It's all a bit overwhelming. Handling a press conference every few days after a fight is one thing, but at these events, there is always someone who wants to talk. Most want to talk to Ella, but some like to talk to both of them, and Pylus is done with all of it.

The fake boyfriend charade has become so commonplace that Ella and Pylus walk out to the car holding hands and often hold hands during the long car rides. Multiple times, Ella has fallen asleep on Pylus' shoulder after a late night while they drive to their temporary residence.

Currently, Pylus sits in a rest suite after a particularly long afternoon gala. Ella sits beside him with her head, of course, on his shoulder. She dozed off a couple of minutes ago, only seconds after sitting down. The rhythm of her heartbeat and slow breathing is calming. After days of hustle and bustle, it feels nice to just sit and relax. Pylus feels his eyelids grow heavier the longer he listens to Ella sleep. His head lolls to the side, pressing his cheek onto the top of her head. Luckily, today her hair is down and doesn't have all the little metal things in it that she uses to hold it up.

Just as Pylus is about to close his eyes and follow Ella's lead, footsteps echo softly in the hallway. He usually wouldn't give a second thought to someone walking down the hall, but these footsteps sound like someone *trying* to be quiet. Suspiciously quiet.

The footsteps are slower than they should have been for someone walking normally. They sound as if the one making them is walking sideways. Each step takes longer to land than it should. Since the floor in the hallway is hardwood, there should be more echo from each step, but Pylus can only hear when the shoe touches the floor. A soft whisper of rubber on wood. Not the slightest reverberation of sound after. The steps slowly make their way down the hall, then stop right outside their door.

Pylus focuses his hearing; someone just outside is breathing slowly, calmly, and somehow menacingly. Taking a deep breath, he smells Ella's perfume and hair products, the leather of the couches and fabrics of the pillows, and the sweat of a man, but it's strange. There's something familiar about the scent, but it keeps getting covered with the stench of lots of cologne.

The trick to having a heightened sense of smell is figuring out how to sift out the scents that aren't relevant. However, no matter how much he concentrates, he can't get a strong enough whiff of the man's main scent to remember where he smelled it from. Was it Ming? Or one of the other guards he knew? Maybe it was the attendant that had brought them here. He had the same cologne but not as much. Then again, all the male attendants must have shared a cologne spray because they all smelled the same. This one still seemed off. Like something he remembered from his first day as Ella's bodyguard.

Opening his eyes, Pylus watches the door and kicks himself mentally for not locking it. Carefully, he draws his pistol and rests it on his lap, trying to stay as quiet as possible. Moments pass by slowly. Just as he thinks the person outside might leave, the handle of the door slowly starts to turn. Pylus lifts his pistol to aim.

Suddenly, more people can be heard coming around the corner down the hall. Hurried footsteps heading in the opposite direction tell Pylus their "visitor" is leaving. He lets out his breath and rests his gun back on his lap. The new, regular-paced footsteps stop outside their door. Someone knocks quietly before turning the handle and opening it. Mr. Rye walks in with Brit and another guard close behind.

Brit raises his eyebrows at the gun on Pylus' lap, "Trouble?" He asks quietly.

"Almost," Pylus responds.

Mr. Rye hurries to the coffee table in front of Pylus and sits down, looking worried. "What happened?"

Pylus quietly recounts the experience with the mysterious visitor he heard. He makes sure to include the strange smell and the calm breathing, suggesting the man was a trained operative.

Brit sits down next to Mr. Rye, "Could you tell what they smelled like?"

"Sort of," Pylus says, crinkling his brow, "I couldn't get a good smell since they were wearing lots of cologne. The same cologne all the male attendants wear, actually. But it was off. Not perfectly human. Like the smell from the assassin back at the Shank house. I think it might have been him."

Mr. Rye and Brit look at each other in a silent conversation. Brit keeps his face stern and unreadable; Mr. Rye, however, looks nearly frantic.

"He caught up faster than we thought," Brit says.

"Would you be able to recognize this smell again if you got close to it?" Mr. Rye asks, turning to Pylus.

Pylus nods, "I could recognize the cologne easily, but as I said, all the attendants have it on. I could probably find the underlying scent as well if I'm close enough to the guy."

"We saw a man wearing a server uniform turn the corner at the end of the hall when we came up the stairs," Brit says, "Makes sense, he has the same cologne as the other workers."

"A server? Not an attendant? What did he look like?" Pylus asks, nearly sitting up before remembering Ella sleeping on his shoulder.

"Short, bald head, pale, probably late twenties or early thirties, athletic but not stocky," Brit rattles off, "That's all we could see before he was out of sight. Didn't get a good look at his face. Definitely clean-shaven, though."

"Alright," Pylus sighs, "I'll keep an eye out for him and alert you if I see anything."

Brit gives him a curt nod, "Good man."

"That's not why you came here, though, is it?" Pylus asks.

"No," Mr. Rye says, a shadow passing over his face.

"A kitchen worker was found dead behind the manor," Brit says, "They didn't have any leads on who did it, but after what you told us, I think we can be pretty certain it was the same guy."

"Holy crap," Pylus breathes out, "How did he kill them?"

"Why does it matter?" The other guard asks. He still stands next to the door as if he's waiting for the server to come back.

"Because if I know how the guy likes to kill, then I know what to expect when he comes for Ella," Pylus explains.

Ella stirs in her sleep, reminding everyone to keep their voices down. Pylus softly strokes her hair, and she settles back onto his arm.

"The only wound they found on the body was a small hole on the side of the neck," Brit says, "It wasn't deep. Maybe half an inch. Something that small would have to be incredibly precise to kill someone."

"Or poisoned," Pylus adds.

"That's highly possible."

Mr. Rye stands and walks to the window. He places his forearm on the wall and his other hand on his waist; his shoulders slump as if the weight of the whole world sits on them.

"There's something I need to tell you, gentlemen," he says, looking out the window. "It's not something you'll be happy to hear."

Brit and Pylus make eye contact, then look back to Mr. Rye, "What is it, sir?" Pylus asks.

"I suspect the person who is targeting Ella. . . is one of the investors."

Brit stands up quickly, "What makes you say that, Mr. Rye?"

A broken sigh comes from the dejected man, "Because I recently changed the process of delegations. It makes it so that there is a significantly slower return to investments, but the use of the money is more secure and will be more profitable by the end of the next decade."

"Why is that such a big deal?" Pylus asks.

"For most of the investors, it wasn't," Mr. Rye says, rubbing his chin. But almost half of them wanted to keep things as they were. Higher returns are quicker but less secure in the company. When we voted on it, the majority ruled in favor of the change, but only by one vote." Mr. Rye rubs his eyes with one hand and continues, "After that meeting, investor relations have been rocky at best. Out of the twenty-five investors, twelve of them haven't talked to me since, and most of them have been at one of these galas. Seven of those twelve are here today."

"But Mr. Rye," Brit says, "How can you be sure one of them is targeting your daughter?"

Another heavy sigh, "I hold the power to make ultimate decisions without the investor's input. The only reason I have meetings and votes is to give them a feeling of importance and worth within the company. So, if I wanted to change a decision previously made, I could without the consent of the investors." Mr. Rye breaks off like he can't keep going.

"So, if someone wanted to coerce you into retracting that decision, holding your daughter as ransom is a sure proof way to get you to agree," Pylus finishes for him. A nod confirms what he said, "Why would they be so adamant about changing it back, though? How much of a difference is it?"

"Roughly eight million dollars," Mr. Rye says.

"A year?" Brit asks.

Mr. Rye finally turns from the window, "A month."

Brit's jaw drops in sync with Pylus'. That's more money than either of them can even fathom, and that's how much these men are making in a month. No wonder they all have massive mansions all over the place. With a recovering economy, that much money would give a person the ability to have anything they wanted. Except that power was just recently taken away from them, relatively speaking.

"How much are they making now per month?" Brit finally asks after a minute of gawking.

"Only nine hundred thousand," Mr. Rye says.

"You think they are all angry enough with you to go to such drastic lengths to get the decision changed back?" Pylus asks, getting a sad nod in response, "Seems a little over the top to me, but then again, I've seen first-hand what people will do to get what they want."

"We all have," Mr. Rye says as he sits back on the coffee table, "and it gets even worse when it comes to money. The pettiness of humanity is more evident when one believes money is power. Amazing what little scraps of paper can turn people into."

Brit slowly takes a seat next to his boss, "It's a dog-eat-dog world, sir. Men as high up in the global economy as your investors are sure to be ruthless enough to pull something like this."

"Who were the investors that disagreed with the decision?" Pylus inquires.

"You haven't met any of them yet, thankfully," Mr. Rye says, "Mr. Yen, however, was the deciding vote. He was on the fence for a long time but finally decided to side with me. I think he still has a little resentment for the decision, though."

"Mr. Yen seemed to be strangely interested in my abilities as a hybrid," Pylus recalls, "After telling him about what I can do, his bodyguard, Ming, seemed to be keeping a close eye on me."

Brit stiffens, and Mr. Rye clenches his hands together. "They're supposed to be here tonight," Brit says.

"What about Clive Blane?" Pylus asks, "When Ella and I talked with him, he seemed to have an almost predatory interest in Ella. Not to mention he seemed to detest me without having even met me."

"Clive is an odd character," Mr. Rye says, "But he was one of the ones that sided with me and has been one of my longest-standing friends in this business. He may be strange and make others uncomfortable at times, but he is with me all the way."

"Pylus," Mr. Rye says quietly. Leaning forward, he fixes Pylus with his hard stare, the one that makes Pylus' blood run cold, "Don't let anything happen to my daughter tonight."

Pylus meets his gaze confidently, "You know I won't, sir."

With a stiff nod, Mr. Rye stands and walks to the door. Brit follows after giving Pylus an almost sympathetic look. The other guard eyes him, then turns to follow the two men back into the hallway. With a soft click, the door closes, and Pylus is left alone with Ella's soft breathing again.

The conversation that just happened runs through his mind on repeat. Now they have an idea about who might be behind the attacks on Ella. There's no way to know for sure, but Mr. Yen's strange interest in Pylus and Ming's watchful eye have him questioning. But in the end, Mr. Yen had sided with the decision, so he couldn't hold too much animosity, right?

Then there's Clive Blane. Aside from being a creepy man with no personal space, he didn't seem to have too much malicious intent towards the Ryes. In fact, he seemed to treat them almost as if they were family. Him being the sketchy uncle that made everyone else feel gross. Mr. Rye had defended the man himself.

The other investors that Pylus hasn't met yet are all possible suspects. He'll have to be extra careful every time he meets someone new tonight. Then there's the fact that the assassin showed up to tonight's gala, which can't be a coincidence.

Now Pylus has four things to worry about. Keeping up the boyfriend charade, identifying the assassin, watching for any investors giving unnatural amounts of attention to Ella, and most importantly, keeping Ella safe through all of the pandemonium that is bound to break out sooner rather than later.

Ella stirs against his shoulder, pulling him off his thought train. She stretches her arms out and sits up. The remnants of sleep sit in her half-open eyes. How her hair stayed looking good after taking a nap on his shoulder is a mystery to Pylus.

"Morning," he says.

"Hi," she says with a groggy smile.

"Have a good nap?"

"Yes, sir. I dreamed about my dad and Brit and you, though, so that was weird," Ella says with a yawn.

"Oh, really? What happened?"

"Nothing much. You three were just talking, but I couldn't tell what any of you were saying."

Pylus sighs with relief. The last thing he needs is Ella being paranoid and bolting at the first sign of trouble.

"Do they have any good books here?" Ella asks.

"I'll check," Pylus says, standing.

The rest of the break is spent in peaceful quiet… sort of. Ella reads, Pylus worries. He sits with a book in his hands to seem like he's normal, but his mind flits through everything he now knows. Sooner than either of them wants, it is time to go downstairs. Pylus takes a deep breath before walking out of the room. Here goes nothing.

Things already seem different as soon as Pylus and Ella enter the ballroom. The usual jovial chorus of voices is a dull rumble instead of a boisterous discord. All of the guests have broken off into their own little groups where they talk quietly with one another. Some steal wary glances at others, while some shoot a look and shake their heads. The whole scene has a murder mystery feel. Tense and waiting.

Pylus quickly scans the crowd, looking for any servers that match the description of the assassin. Only three are in the room at the moment, all three with full heads of hair. A bald server shouldn't be too hard to pick out in this crowd.

Mr. Rye stands against the far wall, speaking to a group of people. Good to see he has some friends here in the wolf den. Hopefully, having associates who are less hostile towards him will keep the others away.

Mr. Yen stands just to the side of the group talking to Mr. Rye. His eyes shift from the group to other guests until they find Pylus and Ella. The Chinaman's gaze settles on the pair for a second longer than it does with other guests before moving on across the crowd.

Other wandering eyes keep landing on Ella as she makes her way down the stairs. She must sense something is going on. Her heart rate rises with each step, and she keeps taking deep breaths.

Out of the corner of his eye, Pylus sees movement from the kitchen area. He glances over in time to see six bald, clean-shaven servers walk out. All of them roughly the same height and build. That can't be a coincidence.

Pylus reaches up and pretends to scratch his ear so he can press the speaker button on his com, "Brit, check out the kitchen help."

From across the room, he sees Brit look at the servers. The bodyguard's eyes get wide, and his jaw clenches. He looks over to where Pylus and Ella descend the stairs and says one command with his eyes, "Don't leave Ella". Pylus nods and turns his gaze back to the servers, none of whom pays them any attention and moves about doing their server duties. Everything would seem normal except for one thing. The bald servers move close to all the exits and stay in those general areas. Only one doorway stays unguarded; it leads to a balcony that hangs over a forty-foot cliff overlooking a river.

Looking back to Brit, Pylus can tell the head guard has already noticed as well. They make eye contact again, speaking wordlessly. Each man knows his duty. Brit whispers something to Mr. Rye, then steps to the side and touches his ear.

"Be on high alert," Brit says over the coms, "We may have some unwanted company. Keep your eyes on any bald servers near you."

Pylus knows that there are only four guards here with the Rye's, including him. He's sure if Brit had known Mr. Rye's theory about a rouge investor being the mind behind this whole thing, there would have been more.

Pylus keeps his eyes moving from one server to another. Simultaneously, he scans the crowd for anyone watching Ella closely. He finds someone. Waiting at the bottom of the stairs is Clive Blane. He smiles his sickeningly charming smile as Ella gets closer, his scar standing out prominently under the rooms lights. Despite what Mr. Rye said about the man, Pylus still feels defensive around him.

"Dear Ella, you get lovelier each day," Blane says. Pylus can smell the liquor on the man's breath from ten feet away. It nearly knocks him out when they get closer.

"Thank you, Mr. Blane," Ella says without a smile.

"A little birdie told me a surprising rumor," Blane says, leaning in, "Apparently, your guard here is a little more than that."

Ella forces a small smile, "You heard right. We were trying to keep it a secret a little longer, but... word got out quickly."

"Congratulations, young man," Blane says, turning to Pylus, "Keep a tight grip on her or I might sneak in and snag her." With a wink at Ella, he turns and walks away. Pylus watches as the man meanders through the crowd, smiling and shaking hands before walking out the front door. Must need a smoke break.

A shudder runs down Ella that transfers to Pylus, causing the skin on the back of his neck to tingle. Ella's grip on his arm tightens, and her breathing accelerates.

"Come with me," Pylus says. He puts his arm around her shoulders and leads her to the balcony. The cool air is refreshing for both of them. They take a couple of deep breaths at the railing, trying to shake the creeps that came with talking to Clive Blane.

"I don't know how long I can do this," Ella whispers. She stares at the water running down below them.

"Is it really necessary for you to be here right now?" Pylus asks.

"No. But I can't leave my dad," Ella says, "Sometimes I feel like he needs me to be here. Especially since my mom isn't around for him anymore."

A shiver shakes Ella's body as a breeze blows through. Without thinking, Pylus takes off his suit coat and wraps it around her shoulders.

"Thank you," she says, giving him a strange smile.

"What?" He asks as her look lingers on him.

"Nothing. Just funny how much of a gentleman you can be. It doesn't fit your cold, cut-off persona."

"I did have a sister at one point," he reminds her.

"I guess that's true. She taught you well then."

"It wasn't just her. I've had other women close to me in my life. Even dated a couple."

Ella fakes a gasp, "Pylus Brek had a lover?"

"Oh, shut up," he says with a smile.

"I guess I shouldn't be surprised," Ella says, "You play the fake boyfriend role so well, it makes sense you have experience."

"Thank you, I guess."

A calming silence falls over them as they watch the river rushing below. Pylus is thankful for the somberness of the party tonight. The quiet conversations don't carry out onto the balcony, so they can almost forget they are there. Almost. Pylus keeps glancing over his shoulder, watching for bald servers.

"Pylus," Ella says, "Can I ask you something?"

"I'm pretty sure it's my turn for a question, but I guess you can have it," he teases.

Ella shakes her head and chuckles, ". . .Why did you become a hybrid?"

Pylus gives her a confused look. That was a random question for the situation. Caught off guard, he momentarily forgets that she wants an answer.

She bumps his shoulder softly with her own, "You don't have to be so closed off with me."

Suddenly, it's not Ella standing next to him on the balcony, but Ellie. Instinctively, he reaches up and touches the rings around his neck. He can see Ellie's dark hair and delicate features as he stands with her in the gazebo. Those eyes that seemed to comfort and confuse him all in the same moment. He can feel her moving closer to him when a voice yells from behind them. Her ex, Amos, has arrived, and Pylus knows what is going to happen. He tries to scream at Ellie to run. Tries to move to protect her, but it's like she can't hear him. Then it hits him. She can't. She's not there. It's not Ellie, it's Ella.

The world snaps back into focus. Ella stands in front of him, looking into the ballroom, confused and scared. The yell he heard is still going on and is coming from the crowd inside. He turns to look the same way Ella is. It's hard to tell what's happening, but something is obviously wrong. Voices are calling out, no longer socially but worried, terrified even.

There's something going on at one end of the room just outside of view. Suddenly, a scream from the opposite end rings out. Then another from the side opposite the balcony. Confusion and growing panic seize the crowd. Heads swivel back and forth, looking for the problems. The bald servers snake their way through the crowd, looking as if they mean to fix whatever it is that is scaring the guests.

More screams fill the air, and all control the frightened guests were holding onto dissipates. People start moving in all directions, trying to get out of the ballroom. Whatever is going on, they don't want anything to do with it. Through the moving surge of people, bodies can be seen lying on the ground, dark pools of liquid spreading out from them. Someone is killing the guests. Pylus grabs Ella's arm and starts to move towards the pandemonium. They have to get out of here.

Two steps towards the door are all he gets before a figure moves into his path. Pylus stops and puts his arm in front of Ella. One of the bald servers stands in his way with a twisted smile on his face and no life in his dark eyes. The smell of cologne is unmistakable. It's the same one from upstairs with the same underlying scent Pylus remembers. Pylus growls menacingly. It is definitely the same assassin from the safe house. The eyes never lie.

Pylus crouches and gets ready to fight when another bald server joins the first. Then another. And another. Soon, all six of them block the doorway. Pylus backs up with Ella until they are against the railing. Even with his training, six on one is a rough fight. Especially against six who are definitely experienced fighters.

"Brek! Where are you?!" Brit screams into his coms.

Five of the servers pull bloodied knives out from under their vests. The sixth, the assassin they have run into before, cracks his neck and smiles even wider.

"Pylus! Answer me!" Brit continues to yell through the coms, "Someone get eyes on Ella."

Behind the group of assassins, the ballroom rages in absolute chaos. People trample each other trying to get out, while those whose loved ones were killed kneel next to the bodies to cry and wail. People trip over each other and fight their way through the crowd.

With a slight nod from the lead assassin, the group slowly steps towards Pylus and Ella, fanning out in a semi-circle. Pylus draws his gun. Just as he clears his holster, a knife slams into his hand. Reflexively, he drops the gun and shakes his hand. Luckily, the blade had hit broadside, only cutting his hand slightly but still serving its purpose. Pylus' gun clatters to the ground next to the thrown knife. This is bad. Pylus could attack and maybe take out two of them before the others jump on him, but that would leave Ella exposed. The chances of getting out of this alive with Ella are incredibly low and keep getting lower. Unless. . .

"I'm with you, Pylus," Ella's shaky voice says in a whisper, "I can't do much, but I can do something."

Pylus glances at Ella, her terrified pale face. She clings to his outstretched arm. Her eyes are wide with fear, but also clear and willing to fight. Pylus can't help but feel proud. By now, the assassins have moved within ten feet of them, nearly close enough to attack.

Time slows as Pylus steels himself to do what he is about to. He takes a deep breath, flexes his hands, and lets his air out. He hopes this works. Turning quickly, he wraps his arms around Ella, yanks her off the ground, and rolls over the railing of the balcony into the open air.

***

When Pylus failed to respond to Brit, Phillips had been sent to find him and Ella. Getting through the crowd had been difficult. He felt like a salmon swimming upstream with bears lining the river. Eventually, he resorted to dropping his shoulder and rushing through people in football fashion. He had to find Ella, and he did, just in time to see Pylus jump off a forty-foot cliff with her in his arms.

"Brit," He says grimly into his coms, "we have a situation."

15

From the balcony, one would think the river was moving slowly. It wasn't. Pylus and Ella hit the water feet first, rocketing downstream with the aggressive current. By the time Pylus can pull himself and Ella to the surface, the mansion is far behind them, just little dots of light on a vast, dark canvas. Ella clings to Pylus' neck as she gasps for air. Her breath comes in rapid bursts, mingled with whimpers and shrieks, every time Pylus sinks too low. After a couple of attempts to reach the edge, Pylus realizes it's useless. The current is too swift and strong to make any progress. With few other options, he lies back and lets his feet guide him down the river.

"Ella," he says loudly. She looks at him like a cornered animal, "Calm down. I've got you... but I need your help. You need-" his head gets sucked under water as they drop around a rock. He pops back up sputtering and spitting out water, "You need to put your. . . feet downstream. . . Hold onto me. . . try to float by my side."

She nods and pulls her feet around so they're pointing the same way as Pylus'. Her grip doesn't lessen, but it does shift off his chest, making it easier to keep his head above water.

"Good, good," he says, his face splashed with water, "We'll float until the water slows... then we'll make our way to shore."

"Look out!" Ella screams.

Pylus turns in time to see something big and dark coming at him from the side. He pulls his arm up in time to block his head, taking most of the impact with his shoulder and bicep. The object detours off his arm, pushing them further into the river, then heads downstream away from them, scraping its way along Pylus' arm. He tries to push it away when his hand catches something sticking out of its side. He realizes the thing is a large log. He quickly grabs the branch he felt and hangs on, nearly ripping his

165

shoulder out of its socket to do so. When he can, he pulls up as hard as he can and slings his arm around the top of the log, then pulls Ella over to it so she can do the same. After several failed attempts, Ella finally gets situated with Pylus on the downstream side of their new ride, watching for rocks.

"You okay?" Pylus gasps, turning slightly to look at Ella.

She nods. The wild look in her eyes is gone now that she has something safe to hold onto. They stare at each other for a moment before Ella breaks into a smile and starts laughing. Pylus can't help but join in.

"What were you thinking?" Ella asks through her giggles.

"Get away from the guys trying to kill us," Pylus says.

"Well. . . it worked." More laughter.

After a few moments, they gather themselves and try to analyze their surroundings. Dark trees line both sides of the river. Surprisingly, there aren't many boulders in the river that they can see.

"How long do you think we will have to hang here?" Ella asks.

"Maybe we don't," Pylus says, reaching as far over the log as he can. He finds a good stub to hold on the opposite side and hoists himself onto the slick top. Surprisingly, the log doesn't roll as he climbs on top of it. *It must have a large branch underneath*, he thinks. When he gets himself steadied, he reaches down and lifts Ella on top as well. They sit facing each other as they straddle their makeshift boat.

"This is much better," Ella says, "I can almost pretend we're on a pleasant outing just floating in a river."

Pylus chuckles and shakes his head, "Beautiful evening, isn't it?"

Ella laughs and leans forward, resting her head on Pylus' shoulder. Pylus wraps his arm around her and squeezes. He can't believe they made it out of there without a scratch. Well, without any serious scratches. The lacerations on his shoulder and bicep from the initial impact of the log are long but mild. The sleeve of his shirt is in tatters, though.

"So, what do we do now?" Ella asks without lifting her head.

"Wait for the river to slow, then get to shore. After that, find a settlement and see if we can get to a phone."

"A phone?"

Pylus nods, "Brit had all of us memorize an emergency number to contact if we ever got separated from the group. It's for a phone that he always carries with him. After I contact him, he will instruct us on how to get back with the group or give us a rendezvous spot."

"What if we can't find a phone? I'm not sure where we are, but large settlements are pretty scarce out here," Ella says.

"Then we do plan B. The company will proceed with the planned schedule of events. They probably won't attend anything given the situation, but they will still follow the same route on the same days and at least make an appearence," Pylus explains, "All we have to do is figure out where we are and where the closest stop will be that gives us the most amount of time to meet up with everyone else."

Ella nods, but as she sits back, her face says she's totally lost. "Okay, I think I got it."

"Okay, simplified version," Pylus says, scratching his head, "Get to shore and find people, ask if they have a phone. If there is no phone, start walking."

"... Oh boy," Ella sighs.

Pylus reaches over and puts his hand on her shoulder, "Don't worry. I'll get you back to your dad."

She gives him a halfhearted smile and nods. Silence takes over as they both slip into their own thoughts. The sound of the river is soothing yet daunting at the same time. This river is deep and lacks many boulders, which gives the water a gentle rippling sound as it courses through the land. However, the depth is unknown, and the swift current makes it precarious. Every now and then, there's a break in the trees lining the shore, but no sign of a road or any bridges that Pylus can see. This area must be mostly deserted.

After what feels like ages of floating, the river slows enough for Pylus to guide their log over close to shore. When they're ten feet away, he slips over the side into the water. It's deeper than he expects, and he loses his footing slightly. Ella screams as his head slips under the water.

"I'm okay," he sputters, popping back up, "Just got surprised."

Once he gets his balance, he finds the water up to his chest, meaning it would still be over Ella's head. He holds tight to a broken branch of the log and starts walking it closer to the shore. He uses the downstream current to his advantage and works at a diagonal angle, getting closer and closer to land. When the water is to his waist, the log sticks into the mucky bottom of the river and stops, proving his theory of a large branch underneath. Pylus helps Ella off as the current takes the back end of the log downstream and soon pulls the rest along. The pair stands and watches their saving grace disappear around the next bend.

Soaked and sore, they splash onto the riverbank and stretch, working out all the stiffness from riding in the same position in cold water on a near-Autumn night.

"Alright," Pylus says, rolling his neck, "From the mansion the river carried us mostly south and a little west. The next destination of the company is going to be in the Desert Province, South of where we were. If we head in that direction," he points through the tree line, "we will be going in the same direction as your dad and will hopefully find people who can help us."

"S-s-sounds g-good," Ella says through chattering teeth.

"We'd better move fast," Pylus says, wrapping his arm around her shaking shoulders.

The suit coat Pylus gave Ella is only slightly damp, but her dress is still soaked and offers little warmth. Pylus can tell the cold is starting to take its toll on Ella, as her steps are robotic and jagged, although that might be due to the stiffness working its way out. When they are only a few feet into the trees, she starts to shake slightly; however, Pylus knows it isn't due to stiffness and starts to worry.

"We have to find some shelter or some way to warm you up," Pylus says, more to himself than Ella. He sniffs the air a couple of times, trying to get a scent of people. He doesn't smell anything human, but he does smell something that might be of help. Cows. Usually, where there are cows, there are people. And shelter. "This way."

The trek to the source of the smell takes longer than Pylus would like. The night is getting colder, and Ella's shivering is worsening. Every step seems to be an increasing effort for her. Several times, she stumbles over her own feet not lifting high enough. The longer they walk, the more she leans on Pylus, and the shakier her breathing gets.

"Come on, Ella. Almost there," Pylus encourages as he picks her up and cradles her against him. Her body rattles in his arms, shaking him as well. He can feel her temperature dropping rapidly and sees that her eyes are closed. Holding her close to his chest, he begins to run. "Ella, talk to me. How are you feeling?"

A shuddering breath answers his question, "S-so. . . c-c-cold," she whispers eventually.

That's all the encouragement he needs to break into a full sprint, dashing through the foliage as fast as he can. Trees blur into a mixture of shapes and blobs. His eyes fall out of focus as he relies on his nose to guide him to help, hopefully. The scent of livestock gets stronger as he pushes on, but so does Ella's shaking. Pylus moves faster than he ever has before. Silently, he pleads for it to be fast enough. They can't have survived this long just to be killed by a little cold weather.

Suddenly, the tree line stops abruptly, opening to a massive meadow. Five or six cows stand a little way off, surrounded by wooden fences. In the distance, a small cottage can be seen at the other edge of the field. A small light is on in one of the windows, drawing Pylus to it. Without slowing, he changes his course from the cows to the cottage and pushes himself as fast as he can. The meadow seems to be getting bigger the longer he runs. Seeing the destination makes it seem that much further out of reach.

Finally, the door to the house is right in front of him. He kicks it a couple of times, willing it to open. Agonizing seconds tick by, each one seems to take a little more life out of Ella. Her lips have darkened to a deep blue while her skin is getting paler. He says her name and gets no response. She's unconscious. He kicks the door again and calls out.

Footsteps can be heard cautiously approaching the door from inside. The handle turns slowly, and a crack of light appears.

"Hello?" Pylus almost yells, "Please, we need help! She's freezing," and he angles Ella towards the door for the owner to see.

An eye peeks out from the crack and examines him. It flicks from Ella to Pylus and back again.

"Ya ain't one-a dem hooligans been stealing cows, is ya?" The eye asks in a creaky, old voice.

"No, sir," Pylus says hastily, "We were just travelling through and got lost in the woods."

"Hmm," the eye says and studies him for a moment longer.

Just when Pylus thinks the door is going to slam in his face, it slowly begins to open further. The eye that had been inspecting him is set back in an old, weathered face. A matching one appears as the door opens, separated by a large, wrinkled nose and a tight-lipped mouth. The man is short with a mess of white hair flopping around his wrinkled features. He wears a "don't mess with me" expression and stands in the doorway holding a sawed-off shotgun to emphasize the threat.

"No funny business, ya hear?" The old man asks.

"Yes, sir."

The man gives a satisfied nod and steps to the side, "Lay 'er in there," He points with his gun to a small living room where the light is coming from.

Pylus steps past him with a quick "Thank you" and rushes to the little room. A small couch and a bookshelf are the only things in the room. A fire crackles in the fireplace, giving the only light in the house. Pylus lays Ella on the couch and removes his suit coat from her shoulders. He throws a heavy blanket from the back of the sofa onto her. With her covered, he reaches under the blanket and blindly removes her still-wet dress, careful not to touch her in any wrong way. When he gets her dress off successfully, he lays it on the floor in front of the fire. After getting everything situated, he sits on his haunches and watches Ella. Minutes pass before she finally stops shivering and color slowly, so very slowly, starts to return to her face.

Satisfied that Ella is going to be okay, Pylus sits down with a heavy sigh and runs his hands over his head. He looks back at the old man and sees him standing in the doorway, his gun hanging loosely in his hands.

"Thank you," Pylus says again.

"Don' thank me yet," The man says, "Still decidin' if I'm gonna shoot ya or not."

Pylus shrugs, "Can't say I blame you. I doubt you get many visitors out here. Especially in the middle of the night."

"Nah, I don't," the man grunts, "Even less hybrids with big knives."

"Right," Pylus says, "Would it make you feel better if I gave you my knives?"

"Wouldn't hurt."

Cautiously, Pylus pulls his knives from their sheaths and slides them across the floor to the feet of the man. He glances at them, then uses his heel to kick them back to the front door.

"My name's Pylus by the way."

"Aight." The man says.

"Alright," Pylus repeats and turns his attention back to Ella. Her shivering has stopped completely, and her lips are slowly returning to their normal color.

"Where y'all come from?" The man asks.

"You know the big mansion north of here that sits on a cliff?" The man nods, "We came from there. Floated down the river."

"You floated the river?!" The man pretty much yells, "That'n there's over five miles away! How y'all swim that long?"

"We didn't," Pylus says, stunned that they had traveled that far. "There was a log we found and floated on."

"How long were ya in the water fer?"

Pylus has to think for a minute. His memories of the river are pretty mushy considering it was dark and his adrenaline was at an all-time high, "Probably about an hour or so."

"No wonder that girls nearly froze ta death," the man rubs his head in disbelief, "Yer one lucky sonnuvagun."

"Why do you say that?"

The man looks at him like it should be obvious, "It's the daggum middle of October, boy! We got our first frost last night!"

"Holy crap," Pylus whispers. He hasn't even noticed the cold, thanks to his wolf DNA, but now it all makes sense how badly Ella had been affected. He knows it was bad; he just hadn't realized how bad it is, until now.

"That girl probably got the first stages of hypothermia," the man continues, "Maybe the whole daggum thing! Wait here." He disappears down the hall, and Pylus can hear him rummaging around in what sounds like the kitchen. Drawers open and pots rattle as the man searches for something. "Scoot that couch closer to the fire," he shouts from the other room.

Pylus jumps up and does as he's told. The couch is lighter than he thought it would be, even with Ella on it, and he can move it easily. He stops it a couple of feet from the fire, then throws another log into the blaze. Ella twitches slightly, then settles in under the blanket.

The man pokes his head in the doorway, "Lemme know when she done woke up."

Before Pylus can respond, the man pulls his head behind the wall and is gone. Pylus turns his attention back to Ella. Her damp hair is a mess all over the couch armrest, and her makeup has smeared around her eyes. Pylus takes the edge of his still-wet shirt and starts wiping the mess off her face. It doesn't take too long to get everything off, and in a couple of minutes, Ella just looks like a girl sleeping peacefully.

"Boy," the old man calls from the kitchen, "Ya cold?"

"No, sir," Pylus calls back, "I'm fine."

"Need some dry clothes?"

Pylus looks at his now black, smudged shirt and torn pants, "That would be great, thank you."

The old man appears in the doorway with a pair of jeans and a t-shirt. He tosses them to Pylus from the door, then returns to the kitchen. Pylus steps behind the couch and quickly changes, hoping Ella doesn't choose that moment to wake up. As if sensing his thoughts, Ella stirs and starts to sit up just as he finishes pulling the shirt over his head. The shirt is two sizes too big, and he has to cinch his belt up tight to keep the pants on, but they work.

Ella gasps as she sits up and pulls the blanket tight around her. Looking around sporadically, she takes in the room and her dress on the floor.

"Pylus?" She calls out.

"I'm right here," he answers, stepping to the side of the couch and into her vision, "How do you feel?"

"Cold," she says, "and concerned. Why is my dress on the floor?"

"Oh," Pylus says, "Well, I uh. . . hmm. . . I just. . ."

"The boy done saved yer perty lil' hide missy," The old man barks as he barges into the room with a steaming cup of something. Smells like tea to Pylus, but he's not sure what kind. Something with honey and peppermint.

"I knew that much," Ella says, "But that doesn't answer the question I asked. Why is my dress on the floor?"

"You were starting to get hypothermia," Pylus says, "I had to get the wet clothes off in order to get your body temperature back up faster."

Ella gives him a look of disbelief.

"Don' worry, Missy," the old man says as he hands her the cup of tea, "Boy was a regular gentleman. Made sure you was covered so he din't see nothin' and he was sure careful not to touch nothin' neither."

Ella takes the cup of tea with one hand and makes sure to hold the blanket with the other. Her eyes dart between Pylus, who finds a sudden interest in the pattern of the couch, and the old man, who seems to be daring her to challenge his statement.

"Who *are* you?" Ella asks the old man.

"Names Chip," the man says proudly, "Chip Banks."

Pylus gives the man an annoyed look. The sudden change in his demeanor is surprising, and he wonders if it has something to do with Ella waking up. Most likely. She seems to have that effect on people.

"Nice to meet you, Chip," Ella says.

Chip gives her a quick smile, then turns and heads out of the room, "I'll be back with some clothes fer ya."

An awkward tension settles in the room after Chip walks out. Pylus' eyes flick from the couch to the floor to Ella back to the couch. Ella studies the fire intently as if she can unlock the secrets to the universe in there and sips her drink.

After a minute, Pylus clears his throat and says, "I'm sorry... for.... taking off your dress."

"It's alright," Ella says, giving him a sideways glance, "It probably saved my life."

"If it makes you feel better, I didn't see anything," Pylus says, "Or feel anything," he adds quickly.

"Pylus, really, it's okay," Ella says gently, looking him in the eye, "I'm just trying to process everything. One minute I was on a balcony enjoying the night air, then I careened off a cliff into a freezing river, where I ended up sitting on a log floating down said river, only to make it to dry land, pass out, and wake up naked in a strange house with a crazy old man."

"That would be disorienting," Pylus agrees.

"I'm not embarrassed or anything about what you did. It was a smart idea, and I trust you."

Pylus meets her eyes and gives her a small smile. The awkward tension evaporates from the room just as Chip walks in with a bundle of clothes in his hands.

"These belonged to the Missus, God rest 'er," he says, handing the bundle to Ella, "We'll step out and let ya have some privacy."

Chip grabs Pylus' arm as he walks past and half-drags him out of the room. His grip is surprisingly strong for an older man, and it's obvious he is not trying to be soft.

In the hallway, Chip releases Pylus and leans against the wall with arms folded. Pylus looks around to get a layout of the house.

It's a small cottage. To his right is the living room and another doorway that leads to the kitchen. On the left are two doors that open to bedrooms. At the back of the house, another door leads outside. At least Pylus assumes it goes outside. There's no window in it, so he can't be sure.

It only takes Ella a few seconds to get dressed before she calls Pylus and Chip back in. Chip has Pylus help him scoot the couch back to its original position and tells the two to have a seat, then walks out of the room again. Ella wraps herself back up in the blanket and picks a spot, leaning on an armrest. Chip had given her a worn pair of jeans and a thick sweater to wear, and in just a few seconds, she feels much warmer. Pylus sits on the couch next to her and stares into the fire. Chip comes back carrying a chair, sets it down in front of the couch, then sits slowly.

"Now," he says with a sigh, "tell me yer story."

He fixes his eyes on Pylus and waits for an answer. Pylus looks at Ella and tries to figure out where to start.

"Well," he says, clearing his throat, "Ella here is the daughter of a prestigious businessman named Jefferson Rye." He pauses to see if Chip makes any sign of recognition. He doesn't, so Pylus continues, "I was hired a few weeks ago to be her bodyguard. We were traveling through the major settlements for business parties. At the one we attended tonight, we were attacked by assassins and jumped off a balcony into the river, where we floated on a log until we were able to get to shore and make our way here."

Chip listens to everything with no emotion. If he's confused or surprised, he doesn't say anything. Pylus falls silent as he finishes his short explanation, waiting for Chip to respond.

After a few moments, Chip finally speaks, "Aight," He says, leaning back, "What's yer plan now?"

"Uh, I'm not sure," Pylus says, taken aback.

"Really?" Chip raises his eyebrows, "You haven't thought of a plan yet?"

"No. . . I mean, yes. . . We have a plan," Pylus says.

"Then what is it?"

Pylus takes a breath to center his thoughts before he continues, "We need a map. Once we figure out where we are, we can figure out the closest place for us to meet up with our group. Unless you have a phone."

Chip barks out a sharp laugh, "Definitely not. Got a map, though. Hang on a sec." He disappears once again.

"What do you think happened to everyone else at the party?" Ella asks after Chip walks out.

"Well, it's obvious you were the main target," Pylus says, "I think once we got away, the assassins probably disappeared while everyone else ran around in a panic for a bit before they got out to their cars.

Ella doesn't respond. Instead, she keeps her gaze on the crackling flames in the fireplace. The light dances in her pupils, giving her eyes a distant look. It's as if she can see the pandemonium of the party again.

"Do you think my dad's okay?" She asks after a moment.

"Of course," Pylus says immediately, "Brit was already on high alert, so once things started moving, he would have had your dad out the door."

"I hope I get to see him again," Ella whispers.

"Hey, look at me," Pylus says as he shifts to face her with his whole body. Ella slowly turns her head to him, "I will get you back to your dad. I promise. I don't care how far I have to go or what happens, I will get you there."

Ella forces a small smile, "I know."

Pylus reaches out and takes her hand, giving it a comforting squeeze. She squeezes it back, then lifts it to her lips and gives it a soft kiss.

"Alright, here it is," Chip says, announcing his presence loudly. He carries a large folded piece of paper in one hand, which he begins to unfold as he sits down.

Pylus lets go of Ella's hand and holds one side of the map while Chip has the other.

"This is where we are," Chip points to a spot on the map, "This here is the mansion where y'all came from." He points to another spot northeast of the first spot. They had traveled much further west than Pylus had thought.

"How big of an area does this cover?" Pylus asks.

"Just the west half of what used to be Colorado."

"Do you have one of the old Western United States?" Pylus asks hopefully.

"Sure do," Chip says, standing and walking out the door again. It only takes him a minute before he comes back with the map Pylus asked for.

Pylus takes it eagerly and compares it with the smaller map. When he finds the relative spot where they are, he marks it with his finger on the big map and drops the smaller one.

"Okay," he says scanning the map, "The route Mr. Rye is going to travel will take him South to these three settlements," Pylus points to three separate areas in what used to be New Mexico, Arizona and California, "They will stay in each location for two days then head north and stop here in the Lights Settlement," what used to be Las Vegas, "They will stay there for two more days then end here in the Boise Settlement for the final company gala.

The plan was to take a day after the gala to recover before making the nonstop trip back East; however, with the circumstances, I doubt Brit will allow for the day of rest and will head back to the Shank Settlement as soon as the gala is over. That will be the closest location for us to meet up with them, and it gives us ten days to get there."

"And just how are you planning on getting there?" Ella asks.

"It's been a long time since I was out this way, but I remember most settlements being self-sufficient and not using vehicles -"

"That's still true," Chip cuts in.

"So," Pylus continues, "we walk."

"We walk?" Ella repeats. Her perplexed look is enough to tell Pylus she might change her mind about being reunited with her dad.

"Unless we can find a horse to ride," Pylus says.

"And how likely is that?"

"Pretty likely," Chip says, "Lotta folk in these parts use horses fer transport."

That seems to appease Ella somewhat, "Okay, that's not as bad."

"Even with a horse, it will take us seven or eight days to get there. Nine without one if we're able to move nonstop without anything coming up on the way, and we really push ourselves," Pylus says, tracing a path towards their destination. "Are there any large mountain ranges between here and this valley?" He taps a spot on the map labeled Bear Lake.

"Right here," Chip traces a spot with his finger, "But if ya follow this road here, you can skirt 'round it ta this valley and beeline it ta the Boise Settlement. Don' even have ta go into that valley."

"Alright," Pylus says with a sigh, "We'll head off first thing in the morning if that's okay with you, Chip."

"Long as ya don' steal nothin'," Chip says.

"Promise," Pylus says.

Chip gives him a satisfied nod, "Lemme grab ya some supplies."

"Thank you," Ella says.

He nods again and walks to the doorway, "Boy. You need a coat?"

"A light jacket would be fine, thanks," Pylus says.

Chip nods one more time, then disappears around the corner.

"How are you not cold?" Ella asks, drawing her blanket around her tighter.

"The wolf influence raised my body temperature to one hundred and two," Pylus says, "I don't really feel cold until it's below freezing, then it gets a little chilly."

"That's convenient," Ella says.

"It's nice for the cold, but it sucks for the heat. During the summer, if it gets above seventy degrees, I get really hot. The influence also mutated my sweat glands, so I can't sweat."

"Do you pant then?"

Pylus squints his eyes, thinking, "Sort of. I still pant like a human does when they're out of breath, but it's more for cooling down now. Doesn't work as effectively as it does for dogs, though. Most of the time, I just have to take a cold shower to cool down."

"Interesting," Ella mutters.

"Aight," Chip says, entering the room with a hiking backpack, "I put two sleeping bags in here and a couple of blankets. Here's a jacket for ya and a big coat for the lady. See if these shoes fit ya, miss."

He hands Ella a pair of socks and plain white running shoes. She slips them on and nods her head in approval.

"They will work fine, thanks."

Chip nods, "In the mornin' we'll set ya up with some rations and get ya on yer way."

"Thank you, Chip," Pylus says.

The old man nods yet again, his signature motion apparently, then turns to walk back out of the room, "Y'all get some rest now," he says over his shoulder.

The light in the hallway goes out, and one of the bedroom doors clicks shut, leaving the house quiet except for the crackling of the fire. Pylus and Ella sit for a moment, neither one moving. Eventually, Pylus stands up and sets another log on the fire before laying on the floor. Ella shifts around and lays back down on the couch. Without a word, she slips her hand over the edge of the couch and takes hold of Pylus'. Then, in the peaceful quiet of the night, they fall asleep.

16

Pylus wakes up to smoldering coals in the fireplace and a slight chill in the room. He is close enough to the hearth that he doesn't have to move to grab a new log and toss it on the dying fire. The coals crackle and pop as the new log disturbs them. Nothing else happens for a few seconds, then a small flame springs to life. It only takes a few minutes before the whole log is engulfed in flame. Once it is, two more join it, creating a lively fire. Pylus smiles and rests his arm on his stomach, and enjoys the warmth.

On the couch, still holding his hand, Ella sleeps soundly.

By the heavy snoring in the other room, he can tell Chip is still sleeping as well. He wonders what time it is, but doesn't bother to look at his watch. The river adventure had ruined it completely. He guesses it's around five in the morning, though. The sun will rise in another couple of hours, and it will be time to begin.

With nothing better to do, Pylus lays his head back down and closes his eyes. For the next couple of hours, he listens to the deep breaths of Ella, the crackling fire, and Chips' roaring snores. Soon enough, the sun starts peeking through the window on the far wall. Time to get going.

Pylus sits up and lightly shakes Ella, "Ella," she stirs and stretches, "It's time to go." Coincidentally, at the same time, Chip's snoring cuts off abruptly.

"What time is it?" Ella asks mid-stretch. One of her eyes opens halfway, giving Pylus an annoyed look.

"Around seven, I think. The sun is just coming up. We'd better get going before those assassins catch up."

The mention of the assassins scares all sleep out of Ella's face, "Okay, let's get going," she says, swinging her legs off the couch to put on her shoes.

Pylus stands and stretches. His joints are a little stiff from the day before, but not as bad as he thought they would be. He takes a couple of steps over to the nearest window and glances outside. Thin wisps of fog hover over the dew-covered meadow. The tree line that stretches into the distance seems to be emerging from the fog. A giant, motionless army awaiting its orders. Something white against the dark green forestry catches his eye. He squints to try and see it better, but a slam of a door draws his attention instead.

"Mornin'," Chip says in a gravelly voice.

"Morning," Pylus responds, then turns his eyes back to the forest. The mist has cleared, but the white object is nowhere to be seen.

"Y'all ready ta be on yer way?" Chip asks, stepping next to the couch and leaning on the armrest.

"Just about," Ella says as she finishes putting on her second shoe, "Thank you again for your help."

Chip waves his hand in the air like he's trying to swat a gnat, "Don' mention it. It's what my wife woulda have done, God rest her. Just don't tell no one I'm out here."

Ella smiles and nods, "Deal."

Pylus has kept his eyes on the tree line during the conversation, trying to get a glimpse of the odd white thing he saw before. He thinks it was just a deer, but he wants to be sure. Ella steps up to him with their backpack of provisions from Chip in her hand and puts her other one on his shoulder.

"Everything okay?"

He opens his mouth to answer, but stops as his blood runs cold. Three of the bald assassins step out of the tree line carrying large machine guns.

Pylus grabs Ella and falls to the ground just as the first bullets rip through the window. Chip stands quickly to make his way to the door. He takes less than four steps when a stray bullet catches him in the head, knocking him to the ground. Pylus yells his name, knowing he's already gone.

Bullets tear through the window and burrow into the opposite wall. Pylus keeps his body on top of Ella's as wood splinters rain down on them. Suddenly, the shooting stops, presumably for a reload, giving Pylus his chance. He springs to his feet and half-drags, half-carries Ella out of the room. She gets her feet under her and heads for the back door. Before she can get too far, Pylus grabs her and pulls her into Chip's room.

"What are you doing?" She yells, "We have to get out of here!"

"They want us to go out the back door," Pylus says, "They let me see them so I would get you out of the bullet's path and then run out the back. I guarantee one of them is waiting outside the back door to take me out, then carry you off."

How do you know?"

Pylus takes a breath before he answers, "Because I've used the same tactic before."

Ella's chest starts heaving with rapid breaths, "What do we do then?"

"Take a breath and trust me," Pylus says, holding her shoulders, "Just follow right behind me." He takes the backpack from her white knuckled grip and slips it on.

He gives Ella a quick smile, then dashes across the room and jumps through the single window on the opposite side. Branches slash at his raised arms and body. He hits the ground and rolls awkwardly over the backpack, glass falling all around him. Ella gingerly climbs out through the empty frame. Together, they run deeper into the trees. Pylus glances back and sees one of the assassins rounding the corner from the back of the house in pursuit. Ella's adrenaline propels her to run faster than Pylus would have thought possible, and he has to maintain a brisk pace to stay just behind her. He can hear the assassin following them, not gaining but not falling back.

Ella rushes through a wall of branches and disappears. Pylus follows closely, then stops just on the other side. Focusing his hearing, he listens to the assassin getting closer. Pylus flexes his fingers, getting his claws ready for when the time comes. The assassin bursts through the branches and runs face-first into Pylus' claws. Pylus grabs the assassin by the throat, digging into the soft flesh. The assassin's lower half doesn't stop when his throat does, causing his legs to fly up in the air. Using all his strength, Pylus slams the assassin on the ground, then rips upward, slicing the man's throat out. Without waiting to see the outcome of his actions, Pylus turns and rushes to catch up with Ella.

Using the sound of crashing branches as a heading, Pylus has to sprint to catch up. Ella's fear has taken control of her, and she is fleeing like a terrified deer. Almost as fast as one too.

Suddenly, the crashing of branches stops and is replaced with a terrified, "Pylus!"

Hearing Ella's desperate cry spurs Pylus to run faster than he knew he could. Instinctively, he switches his main sense from hearing to smell as he tries to pinpoint Ella. Once he catches her scent, he drops to all fours and tears through the forest, leaping over logs and ripping through foliage. Up ahead, he catches a glance of the dark red of Ella's sweater through the brush. In a few steps, he jumps between two trees and lands facing her. She faces him with a look of absolute terror. As Pylus moves to go to her, something hits him hard on the back of the head. He falls to the ground on his side, seeing stars. The hit wasn't enough to knock him out, leaving him coherent enough to roll when he hit the ground, but not sufficient enough to assess the situation appropriately.

His roll ends with him on his side at Ella's feet, facing another assassin. The man holds a silver pistol in his hand and points it directly at Pylus. A wicked smile crosses his face as he eyes down his prey. His finger slowly moves over the trigger and begins to tense.

The sound of the gunshot explodes through the quiet forest. Birds flee the safety of their tree branches, trying to escape the unfamiliar sound. Pylus and Ella jump at the same time. Pylus expects pain to erupt in his chest at any moment, but none comes. Instead, the assassin's head falls forward, and he collapses on the ground next to his gun. The barrel of another gun can be seen peeking out from behind a tree directly behind the bald man. Behind the gun stands. . .

"Leifa?" Pylus asks, astonished.

Leifa Ordonston steps over the body of the assassin, scanning the woods as she does, "I don't have time to explain, but I've been looking for you, and you need to come with me now," she says quickly.

"How. . . what. . ." Pylus starts.

"There's no time, Pylus, we have to go!" Leifa doesn't wait for a response. She steps past Ella and starts making her way through the woods.

Pylus stands quickly. He gently takes Ella's arm and guides her to follow Leifa. The trio makes their way through the woods briskly, and although Pylus and Leifa both scan the trees fervently as they move, there are no other signs of assassins.

Leifa leads them down a small deer trail that weaves in and out of the trees. Soon, they break through the tree line onto an old two-lane road. Two horses stand saddled and ready to ride. Leifa holsters her gun and jumps onto one.

"Can you ride?" She asks Pylus.

"Yeah," he says, quickly jumping onto the other horse's back. He reaches down for Ella and hoists her up behind him.

As soon as Ella is up, Leifa turns her horse and takes off down the road, sticking to the grass. Pylus gives his horse a quick kick and follows. Ella holds herself tight against his back as they ride as fast as the horses can run.

A crack from behind them makes Pylus turn around. The three assassins with the machine guns stand on the road watching them. One of them has his rifle to his shoulder but drops it to his side. Either they are out of ammo, or they think they won't be able to hit the riders from this distance. *Or they don't want to risk shooting Ella.* Pylus turns back forward and follows Leifa around a corner and out of sight from the assassins.

They ride hard for ten minutes before slowing to a trot. Pylus and Leifa spend the next fifteen minutes glancing over their shoulders to ensure they're not being followed. Satisfied that no one is coming after them at the moment, Pylus rides up next to Leifa.

"Start talking," he says gruffly.

Leifa gives him a side-eye glance and asks, "Where do you want me to start?"

"How about with who you are. I may not be in the loop, but I don't know many journalists who track people and shoot assassins without thinking twice about it."

"I'm not actually a journalist," Leifa says, "I work undercover for Mr. Rye. He sent me to act like a reporter so that I could scout you out before he asked you to be Ella's bodyguard."

"How come I've never seen you?" Ella chimes in.

Leifa turns and looks at Ella with a condescending eye roll, "Again, undercover. Your dad couldn't have everyone knowing who he had working for him when they're supposed to be sneaky. Especially his talkative daughter."

"I'm not that talkative," Ella grumbles.

"Is that how you got my background information?" Pylus asks.

Leifa nods, "We knew the basic things about your past from your hybrid records, but Mr. Rye wanted to know what kind of person you were. He already had his brother's opinion of you, but he wanted to see how you handled strangers."

"How did you know where to find us?" Ella asks. That question hadn't occurred to Pylus. He narrows his eyes and waits for the answer.

"Your dad had me patrolling the perimeter of every party you've attended so far, keeping to the shadows and slipping out without anyone noticing. When you two took your dive over the balcony last night, I was immediately sent to scout for you. I didn't get too far before I saw a group of bald guys heading in the same direction I was going. I knew that couldn't be a coincidence, so I tailed them as they searched for you and waited for an opportunity to sabotage them."

"There were originally six," Pylus says, "I killed one in the woods, and you shot one, but there were only three behind us when we got to the horses. Where is the sixth one?"

"I don't know," Leifa says with a sigh, "When they were taking up positions around the cabin, I lost sight of all but the one I followed, which was the one I shot."

"The cabin," Ella whispers, "Oh, Chip."

"I know," Pylus says gently, squeezing her hand.

"Do you know where you're heading?" Leifa asks.

"The Boise Settlement," Pylus says, "Don't you have a phone to contact Mr. Rye?"

"I did, but I broke it," Leifa says, "There's another homestead a couple of miles north of the one you were at, that's where I got the horses. While I was there getting them, I took out my phone to call and update, but a horse bumped me, and my phone fell into the water trough. Hasn't worked since."

She pulls a phone out of her pocket and presses a couple of buttons on it. Nothing happens.

"How unfortunate," Pylus says, not really surprised at the bad luck, "Looks like the trek to the Boise Settlement is our only option."

"Do you have a map?" Leifa asks.

"I think Chip put one in our pack last night," Pylus says, "We'll have to stop at some point and take inventory of what we actually have."

Leifa nods in agreement, "Let's ride for a few more hours, then we can break for the horses and figure out where we are."

"We've been heading mostly North since we got on the road, and we went pretty much directly West through the woods," Pylus says, "Shouldn't be too hard to figure out which road we're on."

"Nice sense of direction."

"Thanks."

As they continue to ride, the sun slowly makes its way through the sky. Tense minutes tick by. Pylus keeps his head on a swivel, checking all around them for any signs of trouble. Luckily, the road they are following is pretty straight for miles, giving them a good view of their surroundings. Leifa seems to relax quickly as they ride, confident they aren't in danger for now.

Ella keeps her head buried in Pylus' back for the most part. Pylus can hear her short breaths as she cries softly. Poor thing had just recovered from the last assassination attempt when this one happened. Pylus grabs her hand and gives it another squeeze. She tightens her hold around his middle, cutting off his breathing a little, but he doesn't say anything. Her quiet sobs last only a few minutes, then she slips into the same silence that holds Pylus and Leifa.

"Let's stop here," Leifa says after two or three hours, guiding her horse to a small stream off the side of the road.

Pylus follows suit and helps Ella slide down to the ground before jumping down himself. Leifa gets down as well and pats her horse before getting a drink from the stream.

"Do you think the person you got these horses from will notice they're gone?" Pylus asks as he gets his own drink.

"Not likely," Leifa says, wiping her hand on her pants, "Those assassins killed him before they moved on to where you were."

Pylus shakes his head and glares at the stream. These people have no regard for life. He can see the irony of that thought coming from him, but at least the people he has killed signed up for it.

Ella hangs back and hugs herself. Their pack lays on the ground at her feet, the old coat Chip had given her wrapped around her shoulders. Something on the ground holds her attention. Pylus stands and puts a hand on her shoulder. Slowly, she pulls her attention from the ground to look at him with tears welling in her eyes.

"When will it end?" She asks, "When will the killing end? Everyone who has died so far has been innocent. Why am I so important that people have to die for me?"

Pylus tries to think of something to say, but can't. Eventually, he just settles for, "I don't know."

Ella closes her eyes and bites her lip, "Maybe it would be better if I just disappeared. Played it off like I died then just ran away. Then no one else would die and my dad would hopefully be left alone," she opens her eyes and looks at Pylus again, "You would come with me, wouldn't you Pylus?"

For a brief moment, Pylus thinks the idea sounds ludicrous, but the more he thinks about it, the more it appeals to him. No one trying to find them. No assassins popping up out of nowhere. They could just run away to a small settlement or even the middle of nowhere and just start a new life. He could easily leave his belongings behind, as there is no one to miss him. The only friends he had are either dead or Reggie. And Ella. As annoying and spoiled as she is, Pylus can't lie and say he doesn't care for her. But so does her father.

"I get where you're coming from," Pylus says, "But think about your dad. He's already lost your mom. The only thing he has left is you. I don't have any kids, but I do know what it's like to lose everyone you think is important. When that happens, you give up on life. There's nothing to live for, so you just quit. The world is a dark and hopeless place, and all you can think about every day is getting out of it. Some days, the temptation to take yourself out is almost too strong. If you decide to disappear, then I'll be right there with you, but do you really want to put your dad through that?"

"If it keeps people from dying. And he will recover from it… eventually."

"Ella, the people who have died aren't your fault. The guards were doing their jobs. They knew what they were getting into. Chip was killed by the assassins. Same with the people at the gala."

"But they killed them trying to get to me," she whispers, tears streaming down her face.

"They didn't have to," Pylus counters, "They had the drop on us on the balcony and could have jumped me, then run off with you. And at Chip's, they could have broken in and tried to take you that way. They didn't have to be so extreme. They chose to kill. The deaths of those people are on the hands of those men, not you."

Ella nods and looks down again. Pylus gently raises her chin with his finger and looks into her eyes, trying to convey all the empathy he can into his next words.

"It's their fault. Not yours."

"Okay," Ella whispers. Pylus doesn't think he would have heard her if it weren't for his advanced hearing.

He pulls her into a tight hug as her body shakes with more sobs. They only last a minute before she takes a deep breath and pulls away, wiping her eyes.

"Okay, so what's the plan?" she says with forced conviction.

Pylus grabs the pack from the ground and crouches beside Leifa, who is pretending to examine the rocks that sit in the riverbed. He digs through the pack and pulls things out to take inventory. When the pack is empty, they have two small sleeping bags, two blankets, a map, two empty water bottles, a beanie, three lighters, a tin kettle, and a pair of leather gloves.

"Alright," Pylus says, unfolding the map and laying it on the ground, "This is Chip's house," he points to the same spot Chip showed them the night before, "We ran through the woods following this course, which means the horses would have been on this road. We've been following the road and have gone around four curves, two of which were left, and two were right. That one back there is the most recent one, which would put us about here."

He places his finger on the map showing their relative location. Luckily, the road they had been following ran almost parallel with the one Chip had suggested they take. They were maybe ten miles away from it, separated by open grassland.

"We can head straight west from here and should hit that road in three hours or so," Pylus continues, "Then we make our way through these mountains and head Northwest when we get to the other side. From there, we head through this valley and then follow the main road all the way to the Boise Settlement.

"Between here and this valley, there aren't any settlements, just a bunch of homesteads, which is good and bad. Good, because it means we won't run into too many people, but bad, because we won't be able to get many resources. Once we hit the valley, there might be a small settlement we can stop at if needed. Between there and the Boise settlement, just homesteads again."

"You think we will be able to find water and food?" Leifa asks.

"I know how to hunt and can identify certain plants we can eat," Pylus says, "There should also be streams and rivers most of the way. There are a lot of them around the valley on the other side of the mountains, but until we get to them, we will just have to get water when we find it."

Leifa looks at him with squinted eyes, "How do you know so much of the area out here?"

"I grew up in the valley we are heading to."

"Really?" Ella says.

Pylus nods, "Until I was thirteen or fourteen."

"So how did you end up back East?"

"That's a story for another day." Ella rolls her eyes.

Pylus folds the map up to put it away. "Let's get ready to head out," he says, picking up the pack. The tinkling of metal makes him stop. On the side of the pack is a long pocket he hadn't noticed before. He opens the zipper and gasps. His knives sit cradled in the pocket, waiting. Chip had picked them up and put them in his pack. Pylus had no idea when the man had grabbed them, but he couldn't thank the old grouch enough. He stands with the knives in his hands. Slowly, he slips them into their sheaths and sends out a silent thank you to Chip, hoping somehow, wherever he is now, he can hear it.

Ella gives him a small smile as she starts packing their things away. Pylus takes the water bottles and fills them with water from the river, then puts them in the pack. When all is packed and ready, they mount their horses and head off again.

True to Pylus' estimate, they find the road they need to follow almost three hours later. The sun sits directly overhead, signaling near midday. A rumbling growl sounds from behind Pylus. He turns and checks the sky, but sees no clouds and nothing moving behind them. The growl sounds again. He looks at Ella, and realizes she's holding her stomach. Another growl reverberates from her body.

"We better find some food," he says, spurring his horse forward.

"I think I see an apple tree up ahead," Leifa says.

Pylus looks in the direction she points and heads toward a lone tree standing by the side of the road. As they get closer, they can tell it is most definitely an apple tree. Most of the apples appear to have fallen and are rotting on the ground, but a few still hang on, as if waiting for them. Pylus pulls one from the branches and hands it back to Ella, who devours the fruit within seconds.

"Whoa, slow down," Pylus warns, "You'll give yourself a stomachache if you eat too much too fast."

"I know," Ella says, spitting some apple out, "but I haven't eaten since yesterday afternoon."

Now that he thinks about it, Pylus hasn't eaten anything since then either. As if on cue, his stomach lets out a monstrous growl. He grabs an apple for himself and takes a bite. The sweet juices explode in his mouth, and he has to fight his urge to scarf it down like Ella. Leifa snags an apple of her own while the horses munch on the ones already fallen.

"Make sure to pack some up for the ride," Pylus says, "Who knows how long it will be until we find more food."

"Take it easy with the water too," Leifa adds, "Two water bottles won't last that long."

Pylus nods in the direction the road is heading, "I'm sure there will be a stream in that canyon at some point. The thing about this area is there's plenty of rivers and streams."

"If you say so."

"Let's pack up as many apples as we can, then ride fast for the canyon," Pylus says, "I don't like being out in the open like this."

They quickly pack every open inch of the pack with apples and add a few to the pockets of their jackets and coats. Once full, they gallop towards the mouth of the canyon. It takes less than an hour to get there, and they are welcomed by a quick-flowing stream running below the road. They stop to give the horses a drink break and to refill their own water. Five minutes later, they begin their journey through the canyon.

"Pylus," Ella asks after some time. She has been so quiet that her voice surprises Pylus.

"Yeah?"

"Do you think the assassins are following us?"

"I guarantee it," Pylus says, "Following horse tracks is easy. Especially with how soft the ground is right now. Seems like they got a bit of rain a couple of days ago. But we do have an advantage. They will have to be moving fast or have a car that can go off-road to follow us."

"Do you think they'll catch up to us before we get to the settlement?"

"I don't know. But I'll be ready for them if they do."

"I know," she whispers.

17

Nightfall comes quickly in the canyon. The tall slopes block out the sun sooner than Pylus would have thought. Once the sun's light completely disappears, Leifa calls for them to stop for the night. They munch on a dinner of apples and river water. Not daring to light a fire, they rely on Pylus' superior night vision to find them a good spot to sleep. He finds the flattest spot he can and rolls out the sleeping bags.

"You two can sleep," he says, "I'll take the first watch."

"Sounds good, wake me up in four hours," Leifa says as she crawls into a sleeping bag and falls asleep in seconds.

Ella slowly gets into her sleeping bag and settles in. Taking one of their blankets, she puts it under her head as a makeshift pillow. Pylus walks over and sits next to where she lays, leaning against a small tree. Ella's hand finds his in the dark, and she quickly falls asleep.

The cool night air whispers around Pylus, tickling his cheek. Crickets play their songs in the darkness, searching for each other. An owl calls out from somewhere in the night, low and quiet as if it doesn't want to draw too much attention. Despite their precarious situation, Pylus feels peaceful. It's been a long time since he has sat under the stars and listened to the symphony of the nighttime inhabitants. The owl calls out in the distance and is answered by the chirp of a fox. A beautiful night indeed.

Pylus leans his head against the tree trunk and closes his eyes. He remembers cool autumn nights as a kid, sitting below the open night sky with his sister, watching for shooting stars. He smiles thinking of his sister, something he hasn't done in a long time. A gust of wind blows around him, rustling the tree limbs and bringing the scents of nature. He breathes deeply, searching for any scent that shouldn't be there. Nothing out of the ordinary. He can almost convince himself they're just out on a camping trip. No assassins. No crazy conspiracies. Just three friends enjoying the outdoors.

Four hours pass by without incident. Pylus enjoyed the time to himself with the creatures of the night as his company. Carefully, he slips his hand out of Ella's and wakes Leifa. Her eyes opened quickly if she had been waiting for him to shake her.

"Anything happen?" She asks, sitting up.

"No," Pylus says.

"Good," she says, stretching.

Pylus stands to go to the pack for a drink of water.

"Pylus," Leifa says. He turns with a mouthful of water, "You don't trust me, do you?"

He doesn't answer immediately, but takes his time to swallow his water, "Why would I?"

"Because I saved your life."

"Lots of people have saved my life. Most did it for ulterior motives."

"What ulterior motive would I have?"

He shrugs, "Don't know. But that's not a reason to trust you."

Leifa scrunches her nose, annoyed. "Okay, what if I told you something only a person who works closely with Mr. Rye would know?"

Pylus narrows his eyes, "Like what?"

Leifa meets his gaze, "Like his head guard is named Brit."

"Common knowledge. Everyone who has any sort of connection to the Ryes knows who Brit is."

"Fine, Mr. Rye visited you the day you won your double header in Champion. He visited you in his brother's, Reggie's, office. He had me scan the building as a false reporter before he got there."

"That's true. He did visit me that day in Reggie's office. But that's still not convincing."

Leifa sighs and rolls her eyes in frustration, "Oh, wait! The first night you were guarding Ella, she tried to sneak out, and you convinced her to follow the rules if you got Mr. Rye to let her have more freedom."

"How and why do you know that?"

"After scoping you out, I recommended you to Mr. Rye, and he wanted to show me that I gave him a good recommendation."

"I didn't see you there that day," Pylus says skeptically.

"I came by when you and Ella were on a walk in the woods," Leifa says, "When you told the guard to sound the alarm, I was sent outside to start checking the perimeter. I went out the back door as you came in the front."

Pylus eyes her without a word. Her gaze matches his, unwavering. Her heartbeat has been erratic throughout the whole conversation. Probably out of frustration, though.

"Alright," Pylus eventually says.

"Does that mean you trust me?"

"No," he says flatly, "It means I believe you. The trust will come later. . . maybe."

Leifa shrugs, "Guess that will have to do for now."

Pylus doesn't respond. Instead, he walks around Leifa and heads to the empty sleeping bag.

"One more question," Pylus says as he sits down, "How much do you know of my past?"

"Not much," Leifa says, "I know you became a hybrid without being terminally ill, and everything that has happened to you since then. Before that, you came from a small homestead just North of the Shank Settlement."

Pylus eyes her for a moment longer. Her heart had quickened when she talked about his life before he changed; she had lied. He wasn't going to pry, though. He would find out eventually. He gives her a nod, then lays on his back on top of the sleeping bag. It doesn't take long before he falls asleep.

***

She appears again. It's been weeks since she has come to him. He lays on his back staring at a gray ceiling. Like a ghost, her figure glides by his peripheral vision. His head snaps to see her, but she isn't there. Quickly, he sits up and looks around. She's nowhere to be found. Slowly, he stands, keeping his head moving, looking for any sign of her. Everything around him is gray. A flash of black to his left catches his eye, but he finds nothing. Another to his right, nothing. A sigh from behind, he whirls, nothing. He closes his eyes, takes a deep breath, and waits.

Time has no place here. His waiting just goes on and on, seeming to last forever and pass in an instant at the same time. Steps approach from behind. He forces himself to keep his eyes closed and wait. A delicate hand rests on his shoulder. Slowly, he reaches up and squeezes it lovingly. The hand squeezes back, then pulls away.

He opens his eyes and calmly turns to look at the hands owner. Her back is to him as she walks away. Her long blonde hair flows behind her. The thin, white dress she wears billows out in a silent wind that he can neither hear nor feel. Her hand trails behind her, beckoning him to take it.

Stepping forward, he reaches for it. She continues to walk further from him. He quickens his pace to catch her, to hold her hand once more. The distance between them grows. He starts to run, arm desperately outstretched, ready to pull her in and never let her go again. The harder he runs, the farther she moves away. His heart rate escalates as she fades into the nothingness that surrounds him. He tries to scream, but nothing comes out. His breathing jumps in quick spurts as he chokes out silent sobs. She's gone now, but still he runs. He can't let her go. Not again. Not this time.

A sound echoes all around in the void. It's indistinct, but he feels it drawing him. Is it her? Has she come back? The voice calls to him as the void collapses in. The gray fills his vision, and his body stops moving. He's floating through the void, following the voice. It grows closer, she's coming, he can almost feel her!

The gray void of Pylus' dream is replaced by the gray of the early morning sky. Sounds slowly make their way to his ears. Birds chirp, horses snort and munch on grass, and something rustles to his right.

"Pylus," a voice says, pulling him out of his stupor.

Leifa crouches by him, her eyes dark and warning, "We need to move."

Without another word, she stands and moves to the horses. Pylus rolls his head to the other side and sees Ella awake and packing. He sits up and shakes the last clinging vestiges of sleep from his mind. It doesn't take long to get everything packed up, and the horses saddled. After a breakfast of water and apples, they continue into the canyon.

"We should ride a little faster," Leifa says, "We took a pretty long rest. That gave the assassins more time to catch up to us."

Pylus nods, "Take the lead."

Leifa pulls ahead and urges her horse forward quickly. Pylus' horse doesn't need any prompting to keep up with its friend.

"Were you dreaming?" Ella asks after some time winding through the canyon.

"What?" Pylus asks, taken aback.

Ella looks down, embarrassed, "You growled a lot in your sleep. Were you dreaming?"

"Uh. . . yeah."

"What about?" Her tone isn't prying, just curious, and it puts Pylus at ease.

"Somebody I used to know," he says, quietly.

"What happened?"

Pylus takes a deep breath and exhales, "She was walking away from me, and I was trying to catch up to her, but the harder I tried, the further away she got. I couldn't call out to her or say anything at all. No matter what I do, she always gets away."

"Always gets away?" Ella repeats, "Have you had this dream before?"

Pylus nods slowly, "I used to have it frequently, almost every night, but last night was the first time in a while."

"That's awful," Ella says, "Is it your sister?"

"No."

"Who is it?"

He takes another deep breath before answering, "It's my wife."

Ella gasps, "You were married?"

Pylus nods slightly, "She died right before my sister. Before I became a hybrid."

"I'm so sorry," Ella says, squeezing him around the middle.

"Thanks," he whispers. He doesn't know how to respond when someone apologizes for the tragedies in his past.

Several minutes pass before Ella speaks again, "So, are you going to tell me the rest of those stories that were for 'another day'?"

Pylus smiles to himself, "Today's not that day. But soon."

A movement to the right catches Pylus' eye. He looks in the trees and sees dark blurs moving through the undergrowth.

"Take the reins," he says as he slips off the horse.

Ella starts to say something but Pylus is gone into the shrubbery before she can get it out. She watches as he appears and disappears between trees and shrubs. Everything is quiet except for rustling leaves every now and then. Then Pylus is nowhere to be seen. With the horse following the one in the lead, Ella doesn't pay too much attention to where she's going. She keeps her eyes on where Pylus had appeared the last time.

Suddenly, a snarl breaks through the trees, followed by a squeal. Branches thrash, and another squeal pierces the air, then a third, then all is quiet again. Ella searches the trees for signs of movement. She can't see anything but green and shadows. Her eyes catch movement off to the right. She looks over in time to see Pylus walk out from between two big trees, three large rabbits in his hands.

"A bit better than apples and water," he says, holding up his catch.

He hops back on the horse and drapes the rabbits over his lap. Leifa watches him with an amused smirk, then turns and continues on.

The day drags by. They take brief stops for lunch and bathroom breaks, but keep moving until the sun gets close to the horizon. When they finally stop, everybody groans and stretches their legs for a few minutes before slowly unpacking their things.

"Been a long time since I rode a horse this much," Pylus says.

"I don't think I've ever ridden a horse this much," Leifa chuckles.

"As a little girl, I wanted to take riding lessons," Ella chimes in, "I don't want to anymore."

"I'm surprised you didn't get the chance," Pylus says.

Ella shrugs, "It was at the beginning of the rebuild, and no one was really offering."

"Makes sense," Pylus mumbles, feeling stupid. He should know better than anyone what it was like at the beginning of the rebuild.

Leifa steps over and inspects Pylus' kills from earlier, "I can skin these if you get some firewood for a fire."

"Do you have experience with skinning animals?" Ella asks.

Leifa nods with a proud smile, "I grew up hunting for my food."

Ella raises her eyebrows but says no more.

"I'll get some firewood," Pylus says, heading for the trees.

"I'll help," Ella offers.

Together, they walk into the trees to start their search. Finding downed branches proves to be easy enough. The hard part is finding ones that have been down long enough to dry out. Slowly, they expand their search further from their camp. After some meager success, they come upon a dead, fallen tree with dry branches ready for the taking. Pylus breaks off the branches and tosses them to the ground, where Ella stacks them in neat piles.

"Sooo," Ella says slowly, "is it another day for one of those secret stories yet?"

Pylus chuckles as he breaks off another branch, "Depends on which one you want to hear."

"How about growing up?" she asks, "Where were you at and how did you end up in the Shank Settlement and in Champion?"

"That's a lot of time to cover," Pylus sighs, "How about I start with growing up and see where we go from there?"

"Sounds good."

"Well, where to start?" Pylus sits on the log and thinks back, "I didn't know my parents. When I was two, or a little younger, my sister and I were dropped off on the doorstep of this makeshift orphanage. It used to be a nunnery in the past. It was located in Logan Canyon, a canyon in the northern part of what used to be Utah. We are going to be going through the valley at the base of that canyon. The lady who was living there at the time was alone with her three kids when we were dropped off. For some reason, she decided to take us in, too. Over the years, she ended up taking in ten more children to care for. All of them little girls."

"How old was your sister when you got dropped off?" Ella asks.

"Just a couple of weeks."

Ella gasps and covers her mouth with her hand. "Oh my goodness," she says, sinking down onto the log next to Pylus.

"The lady who took us in was like a mother to all of us, though," Pylus continues, "Her name was Edith Wright. We had a simple life with her. She taught us how to grow a garden and can vegetables. Her sons and I taught ourselves how to hunt and trap animals. By the time I was ten, we had all the other kids living with us, and we lived a good life."

"How old were the other kids?" Ella asks.

"Edith's boys were all older than me. When I was dropped off, they were three, five, and seven. The rest of the girls were anywhere from my sister's age to just older than Edith's middle son, Joseph. So, we were all pretty close. When I left, the youngest was ten and the oldest seventeen."

"How old were *you* when you left?"

Pylus doesn't answer for a moment, and when he does, his voice breaks, "Twelve. I was twelve."

"What?" Ella says, "Why did you leave so young?"

"We had to," Pylus whispers, "One day, I was out hunting with Edith's boys. All the girls were back at home cleaning and picking vegetables. It was right when the rebuild started. People were scavenging for survival, and it opened up opportunities for awful people to run rampant. As we were scouting through the trees, we saw a group of men walking up the road. There were ten of them; they all had machetes and hatchets. We could tell by looking at them that they meant trouble. We tried to sneak away to warn everyone, but they saw us. Three of them chased us, but we knew the area and lost them easily. By the time we made our way back home, we were too late."

"We found Edith just outside the main building. She was already. . . gone. The rest of the girls had been taken, including my sister. Brock, Edith's oldest boy, was furious. He took Edith and set her in one of the storage sheds and set it on fire. Then we got our bows, all the arrows we could carry, and a few knives and took off after the girls. We tracked them for a full day and a night without stopping before we caught up to them. . ."

"Then what did you do?" Ella asks when Pylus doesn't continue.

He looks at her and gives her a sad smile, "Later. We should head back to Leifa."

"Fine," Ella pouts.

18

With arms full of sticks, Pylus and Ella make their way back to Leifa and the three hunks of meat sitting on the rocks of a makeshift fireplace. They drop their haul next to the fire pit and start stripping bark and small bits of wood for kindling. Soon, a small fire crackles with two pieces of rabbit sizzling on a rock in the center. Pylus munches on his raw meat off to the side.

"Thanks for dinner," Leifa says with a sideways smile to Pylus.

"Anytime," he responds around a mouthful.

"I wish I had some spices," Ella says, mostly to herself.

"You and me both," Leifa agrees.

Leifa pulls one of the rabbits off the cooking rock and sets it on a flatter one. She hands it to Ella, then pulls the other one off for herself. Pylus hands each of them one of his knives, which gets him looks of disgust.

"What?" he asks, "I wash and disinfect them. Often."

With a wary look, then a shrug, Leifa begins cutting into her meat. Ella stares at the knife for a moment longer, then cuts into the meat slowly, as if it might jump at her. The rest of the time passes without conversation. At the end, the trio sits and stares into the flames, lost in their own thoughts.

Finally, Ella breaks the silence, "Do you think the fire will lead anyone to us?"

Leifa and Pylus share a look before Leifa says, "Doubtful. We've been moving faster than they could have been for the last couple of days. Plus, it's small, and there are trees and mountains surrounding us."

"We can build up the rocks if it makes you feel safer," Pylus adds.

"No, it's okay," Ella says, "If you two are confident, I trust you."

"How far do you think we've come?" Leifa asks.

Pylus pulls the map out of the pack and traces the course of the road. He checks the angle of the setting sun and compares it to the curve of the road, then searches the map.

"We should be out of the canyon tomorrow by mid-afternoon, would be my guess," he says, "By tomorrow night, we should be on the other side of this town, Dragon. I've never heard of it, and last time I was in that area, there weren't any settlements."

"Shouldn't have too many problems then," Leifa says.

Shouldn't, but I'm not going to be too hopeful," Pylus says, "I'm not sure if we will have any water after this point here, so we need to make sure and fill up anytime we can."

"What about food?" Ella asks.

"I'm going to keep my eyes out tomorrow and catch anything that moves," Pylus says.

"That will only last us a day or two," Leifa points out.

"Not if I'm able to catch something every day," Pylus counters, "But this time of year, all the wild fruit trees are nearing the end of harvest. We will just have to keep our eyes open for anything. If needs be, we can survive off of water for a couple of days until we can find something to eat. Worst case scenario, we have seven days left of travel; we can survive that long without food."

"Oh, I hope not," Ella groans.

Pylus smiles at her, "I'll do everything I can to make sure that doesn't happen."

"Sounds like there's a lot of variables that can go wrong," Leifa says.

"There are," Pylus agrees, "but that's what happens in a situation like this. Everything we have to work with is unknown."

Leifa sighs heavily, frustrated, "Lovely. Well, sounds like we should move as much as we can, so I'm going to bed. You good to take first watch, Pylus?"

He gives her a nod in response. She pulls her sleeping bag over to the fireside and crawls in. It only takes her a minute to fall asleep. Ella pulls her sleeping bag over, but doesn't get in. She sits cross-legged on it and watches the fire.

"Did you get cold last night?" Pylus asks.

"A little. Nothing too bad, though."

"When you go to sleep tonight, put the cooking rock under your sleeping bag. It'll be warm, and the heat will get trapped in the bag with you."

"That's a good idea," Ella says absently.

Pylus nods and falls silent, thinking Ella has her own thoughts she wants to spend time with. He tosses two more branches on the fire and watches the sparks dance through the air.

"So, what did you do?" Ella asks suddenly.

"When?" Pylus responds.

"After the girls were taken. What did you and Edith's sons do?"

"Oh, right," Pylus says, remembering the story he was telling her earlier, "Well, it was pretty easy to follow the group since there were so many people moving in the same direction," he begins, "We followed the trail until we caught sight of them. We waited and just watched them until dark. We knew that at some point, we would have an opportunity, so we got as close as we could to their camp and waited for it.

"Eventually, one of the guys took a girl off into the woods. Brock and I followed them. The other two boys stayed behind to watch the camp in case anyone else decided to join. When Brock and I caught up to the guy, he was starting to move on the girl. Brock snuck up behind him before he could do anything, and slit his throat. We sent the girl back to the other guys, then waited for someone to come searching. Before too long, someone did, and we killed him, too. Brock covered the guy's mouth and held him while I stabbed him. We didn't want to risk more of them coming after us, so we snuck away with the girl we rescued. Of course, the other men found the bodies and were on high alert after, but that was alright. We were patient.

"Over the course of the next week, we followed the group and slowly picked them off, one or two at a time, and rescued as many girls as we could. Eventually, there were only four of them left, and they only had three of the girls. One night, when they stopped for camp, we surrounded them. They realized they didn't have a chance against so many of us, even though we were only kids, so they gave up and asked us to let them leave."

"Did you?" Ella asks when he doesn't continue.

Pylus pokes the fire with a branch as he answers, "No. We held them on their knees, and killed each one."

He tosses the branch into the fire. Sparks explode into the night, sending a flash of light outward. Ella watches the light flicker against Pylus' skin and eyes. The emptiness in his face makes her heart hurt.

"After that, we made our way from place to place until we found one we liked a few miles north of the Shank settlement," Pylus finishes.

Ella waits a moment to be sure he's done before asking, "Is that where you stayed until you became a hybrid?"

Pylus nods, "At least my sister and I and a couple of other girls did. Edith's boys left after a couple of years, with most of the girls, to return to the nunnery. Said they needed to be closer to their mom."

"Why didn't you go back with them?"

"I liked the place we found. It was a small homestead, only a few families. The man in charge was named Marshall. He was a good man, and he basically took us in as his own children. They were kind-hearted people who took care of their own. It . . . felt like home."

"Sounds nice," Ella says quietly.

Pylus smiles to himself, reminiscing, "It was. When I was nineteen, I married one of the girls that I grew up with and stayed there until she died. Shortly after her, my sister passed. Then I moved to the Shank Settlement and became a hybrid. And that's my story."

Ella looks at him, saying nothing. Something twinkles in her eyes with the light of the fire.

"You've had quite a life, haven't you?" She finally says.

"I guess," Pylus snorts, "I'm just grateful I've had a life. Lots of people haven't been that lucky."

"That's true," Ella agrees.

Suddenly, Pylus's head snaps to the side, his eyes wide and flicking from shadow to shadow. Shifting to a crouch, he creeps towards the trees.

"What -" Ella starts, but is hushed by his raised hand before she can get her question out.

Pylus stops moving a couple of feet from the tree line. A low growl rumbles through his chest. Ella follows his gaze towards the trees, but can only see darkness. Then, out of the shadows, shining with firelight, two eyes reflect. They move closer, staying fixed on Pylus. Ella holds her breath as a nose emerges from the inky blackness, followed by a long snout, light gray fur, shining eyes now a dark brown, pointed ears, and a narrow head. The rest of the wolf slowly materializes from the shadows, its head low and tail down. It sniffs the air towards Pylus and sways its head back and forth, examining him.

The creature stands a head taller than Pylus does in his crouched position. It has to be nearly four feet tall. Ella has never seen a wolf before, but she can still tell this one is big, even by wolf standards.

The beast pushes its muzzle forward towards Pylus and lets out a small whine. Pylus responds with a similar sound. The wolf tilts its head and steps up to smell Pylus, who keeps his head down and stays still as the wolf circles him. When it gets in front of Pylus again, the wolf sits and gives him a small lick on the forehead.

Pylus lifts his head enough to be nose to nose with the wolf. The creature looks back to the trees and huffs. Three more wolves move from the shadows to the light, eyeing Pylus as they walk past their pack leader to the other side of the fire. The horses whinny in fear as the animals slink into the shadows beyond. Pylus and his new friend lock eyes as the other wolves disappear into the night. The wolf gives one last grunt before moving to the other side of the fire, joining its pack in the night. A soft howl calls out from the darkness. Pylus returns the call with a smile.

"Can you understand them?" Ella asks incredulously.

"Sort of," Pylus shrugs, "It's more like recognizing the inflections of someone's voice. Like how you can tell when someone is annoyed or angry, regardless of what they say. I can tell what they are feeling or what they intend based on their noises."

Ella shakes her head slightly, "Amazing."

Pylus smiles and walks over to the horses to calm them down. He strokes their noses and whispers to them in soothing tones.

Slowly, they return to their lazy munching on the grass at their feet. Pylus gives them one last pat and then turns back to the fire.

"Do all dogs act that way around you?" Ella asks when he sits back down.

"No. Some get aggressive if I'm in their territory. Others are curious like the wolves were, and some just run away."

Ella nods and contemplates the dying fire. After a moment, she asks, "Why do you think you're the only wolf hybrid?"

"Scientists have no idea," Pylus answers as he puts another branch on the fire.

"That's not what I asked," Ella says, giving him a look that says she thinks he's hiding something.

He lets out a sigh, "Alright, fine. This is *my* theory. The wolf DNA they used on me was from a wolf that I had found as a pup and raised. I had a bond with him, and he had been around my DNA for years already. I think with canines, since they are emotional animals with familial bonds, there needs to be a bond with the DNA specimen before the hybrid process can work."

"I could see that," Ella says after a moment, "Have you told anyone else your theory?"

Pylus shakes his head, "No. I don't know if I'm right, and I don't really care to find out."

Ella looks at him for a moment, "I think you just like being unique," she says with a smirk.

"You know me so well," Pylus says, sticking his tongue out.

Ella returns the gesture and giggles. Pylus smiles back, enjoying hearing her laugh again. The last couple of days have been hard on Ella, and it weighs on his mind. He misses her bubbly personality and happy-go-lucky attitude, even when she was being selfish and annoying. That brief glimpse into her old self gives him hope. Maybe they can make it through this after all.

A light breeze blows through their little camp, rustling the tree leaves softly. Pylus leans his head back, closes his eyes, and takes a deep breath, enjoying the peaceful night. Before he can take a full breath, his eyes snap open, and he stands up, looking into the darkness behind him.

"What's wrong?" Ella asks, concerned.

Instead of answering, Pylus drops to his knees and shakes Leifa's shoulder. She sits up immediately, eyes wide, searching for trouble. She looks at Pylus, confused.

"They're here!"

Three thunderous booms shake the quiet night. One of the horses shrieks and falls to the ground, its companion rearing back and struggling against the reins holding it to the tree, screaming to get free.

Two more gunshots explode in the night. The coals of the fire pop as one of the bullets hits them. Pylus grabs one of the water bottles and throws the contents onto the fire. Coals hiss and pop as the light almost goes out, and thick smoke covers the campsite. Using the cover, Leifa and Pylus take action. Leifa bolts into the trees, hiding behind one of the larger ones. Pylus grabs Ella and guides her to Leifa's hiding spot. When they are all together, the group turns and runs deeper into the woods. They run until the noise of the living horse can barely be heard. Leifa ducks behind a particularly large tree and presses her back against it. Pylus and Ella join her, glancing around their cover searching for any signs of pursuers.

"They caught up faster than I thought they would," Leifa says.

"How did. . . they catch up?" Ella asks, hands on her knees, breathing heavily.

"They're trained professionals," Pylus says, "Probably only stopped for a couple hours to sleep while we took all night. I should have known better!"

"But what-" Leifa starts, but is cut off by Pylus.

The trio holds their collective breath listening. Crickets chirp, and sounds of nightlife creep through the trees. Suddenly, the noises start to quiet down in the direction they had run from. Pylus signals to Leifa and Ella to stay put, then crouches down to all fours and disappears silently into the undergrowth. Leifa keeps her gun held at chest level, ready to use, as the noises of the night go quiet and the silence gets closer and closer. It's as if the inhabitants of the forest know something is about to happen, and they don't like it.

A scream of anger and pain breaks the silence, followed by gunshots and yells. A series of thumps and grunts echoes back to the women. Leifa tightens her grip on her gun and is about to step out from behind the tree when a body falls at her feet. The dim moonlight shining off the bald head confirms it's an assassin. The man tries to scramble to his feet but is smashed by Pylus as he jumps on top of his prisoner. Pylus flips the assassin onto his back and hauls him up by the collar of his jacket with a menacing growl. Pylus slams the man into a tree, his bared fangs inches from the man's face.

"Where are the others?" Pylus snarls.

The assassin's eyes roll in his head from the force of being slammed. His head falls forward and rolls to the side.

With a groan, he rolls his head up and smiles at Pylus, "He's coming for you," he whispers, blood dribbling out of his mouth.

"Who?" Pylus asks. When he doesn't get an immediate response, he slams the assassin against the tree again, "Who is coming!" he roars.

A maniacal cackle is all he gets in return. Pylus takes a finger and jams his claw just below the assassin's armpit. The man screams in pain until Pylus pulls his claw out.

"Who is coming?" He asks again.

"You already know him," the assassin gasps, "He's the one who broke into the safe house. Everything has been his plan."

"What is his name?"

The assassin makes a sound like he's choking on his words.

"What. Is. His. Name." Pylus repeats.

"I don't know. We just call him Sting."

Pylus growls in frustration, "Where is he?"

The man doesn't respond immediately, convincing Pylus to stab him in the side again. The man cries out and slumps as Pylus pulls his claws out of the soft flesh. The only thing keeping the man standing is Pylus's tight grip on his collar.

"The road branched. . . a few miles back. . . we didn't know which one you took," the assassin says through deep breaths, "Sting. . . and our other companion took one. . . we took the other. . . But he'll catch up to you. He always does." A smirk spreads across the assassin's face, "To be honest though. . . I'd be more worried about the company you keep."

"What do you mean?" Pylus asks.

One of the assassin's knees shoots forward in response, catching Pylus in the groin. He doubles over with a heavy grunt. The assassin pushes him over and rushes Leifa. Before she can react, he grabs a hold of her gun and rips it out of her hand. He turns quickly to point the gun at Pylus, but Pylus is faster and catches his wrist. In one swift move, he snaps the wrist, grabs the gun, and puts two bullets into the assassin's chest. The man grunts once, then drops to the ground. Pylus looks at the now-empty gun in his hand and drops it. The gun thumps to the ground simultaneously with another wet thump. This one is followed by a sharp pain in Pylus' side. He glances down to see a hand holding a short knife with its blade buried just above his hip.

19

The realization doesn't hit immediately. Pylus stares at the handle sticking out of his side and the hand holding it. His gaze follows the arm up to the face of the wielder of the blade.

"Leifa?" He whispers. Then the pain comes.

He gasps and falls to his knees. As he drops, Leifa pulls the knife out, causing the pain to rip through his whole side. Ella drops next to him and presses her hands against his wound.

"Sorry, Pylus," Leifa says, wiping her knife on his jacket, "I really didn't want it to end this soon."

"What are you talking about?" Pylus asks. It's hard to breathe, and he feels like his muscles are shutting down. *What is happening?* He's been stabbed before, several times, and it wasn't ever this bad.

"I was going to let you live until we got closer to civilization, you know, for added protection," Leifa says, "But now that we are down a horse, I figure I don't need any extra baggage."

"You're a hired assassin too," Ella says, glaring daggers at Leifa.

"Sure am," Leifa says, spreading her arms out like a magician finishing a magic trick, "And I just solidified my biggest payday."

Pylus struggles to stand, but his legs can't bear his weight. He tries several times, but his arms start shaking from the weight.

"Wondering why you can't move?" Leifa asks, "I took the liberty of applying a small amount of poison to my dagger blade. Unfortunately, it's not potent enough to kill you; it's been on there too long, but it will at least keep you down long enough for me to get away. Then, when the other assassins catch up to you, they can finish you off."

"So, all that reporter business was just to get close to me?" Pylus asks, "How did you know this would all play out in your favor?"

"Ah, are you sad my flirting wasn't real?" Leifa mocks, "My employer knew Mr. Rye was going to ask you to be little Ella's nanny, so he sent me to investigate you. They wanted to know as much about you as they could so we could find the right time to make our move. Good luck took care of the rest."

Ella gasps suddenly, "You have someone inside my dad's security detail."

Leifa gives her a wry smile, "You better believe it, sweetheart. Now, I would love to stay here and chat, but the poison will probably wear off in a few minutes, so I'd better head out while I still can."

She stands and grabs Ella forcefully by the shoulders, shoving her back towards their camp. Ella screams for Pylus and fights against Leifa to no avail. Leifa has at least five inches on her and is stronger than she looks. The knife in her hand prompts Ella to go along with her. Eventually, Ella stops resisting and trudges along with her head low. A sad howl cries out from behind them. Another answers from somewhere ahead of them.

"Sounds like Pylus is about to be wolf food," Leifa sneers.

Ella bites her tongue to keep from saying anything and keeps moving forward. When they step over the second assassin's body, presumably killed by Pylus before he brought the other one to them, Ella looks for something he may have dropped to help her. No luck. She tries to take her time as they continue, picking her steps carefully, faking a trip here and there, even falling to the ground at one point. She needs to buy Pylus as much time as possible. If she can keep Leifa busy until the poison wears off, then maybe Pylus can catch up to them.

"You are quite the klutz, aren't you?" Leifa says after a particularly exaggerated trip over a downed branch.

"It's hard to see, alright," Ella shoots back, "It's not like I can see in the dark. Do you even know where you're going?"

Leifa pokes her with the knife. Not hard enough to puncture through her clothes, but enough for her to remember it's there. "Of course, I know where I'm going. I'm a professional tracker."

"I'm pretty sure we came from that direction," Ella points to the right.

"Shut up," Leifa snarls, "I know where I'm going. I can see the coals from the fire up ahead."

Ella looks forward and sees that she's right. It's dim, but the glow of the embers that didn't get doused with water can be seen through the trees. Leifa steps ahead, grabbing Ella's arm and dragging her roughly the rest of the way. They enter the clearing to see the last log Pylus threw on fire in flames once again. The campsite looks about the same as it did when they left it. Blankets and sleeping bags strewn about. Their backpack open by the fire. The body of the dead horse lying on the ground. No... both horses lay on the ground.

"No," Leifa whispers, then raises her voice to a yell, "NO! I didn't work this hard to get stuck here like this."

"Looks like your luck ran out," Ella says with a smirk. Her haughty attitude quickly fades with a backhand from Leifa, and she falls to the ground with a cry.

"Don't think you're out of this yet, you brat!" Leifa spits, "I'll get you to my employer if I have to drag you there!"

She turns back to the two dead horses and runs a frustrated hand through her hair. Ella slowly gets to her feet, rubbing her cheek. A low, familiar grunt reaches out to her from behind a nearby tree. She glances back but sees nothing. Another bark calls out from the other side of the campground. Quick footsteps rush past to the right. Were those eyes she just saw to the left?

Leifa is too frustrated to notice any of this. She paces back and forth, cursing under her breath. Ella slowly bends down and grabs a short branch off the ground. As Leifa turns at the end of her pacing, Ella swings the branch as hard as she can. Leifa sees the movement at the last moment and leans away. The branch scratches across her cheek and opens a deep gash under her eye. She screams and tries to throw a punch before Ella can swing again. Ella drops her weapon and blocks the attack just like she practiced with Pylus. Her free hand curls into a fist and lands a punch in Leifa's stomach. Leifa grunts and pushes Ella back. Ella stumbles but catches her balance as Leifa attacks again. This time, she's too fast and catches Ella with a hard punch to the cheek. Ella falls onto her back, her face exploding with pain. Her eyesight goes blurry for a moment, disorienting her. When she can see again, Leifa stands over her with her knife in a white-knuckle grip.

"You just have to be delivered alive, not unharmed," she hisses. Dropping to her knees, she brings the knife down in a quick arc.

Ella gets her hands up in time to catch Leifa's arm and push it to the side. She kicks her hip out, keeping her hands on the knife Leifa is still holding. With a hard pull and her legs pushing against Leifa's ribs, she gets the knife in her own hand. She rolls backward, ending up on her hands and knees, the knife pointed at Leifa. Without hesitating, Leifa dives at her, ignoring the knife completely. They fall into a heap with Ella at the bottom. Together they roll and thrash, fighting for the weapon. Ella pulls it back, slicing Leifa's hand, then thrusts it forward. Leifa gasps and falls to the side. She holds her ribs as she scoots away. Ella hops to her feet, ready to keep going, but hesitates when she sees fear in Leifa's eyes. She looks down at her hand, and red liquid drips from the end of the knife. She looks back at Leifa. Blood has started to work its way through her fingers. Ella had stabbed her between the ribs on her left side. Probably not deep, but still a bad spot.

Ella sways at the sight of the blood and the realization of what she has just done. The knife falls from her fingers as she stumbles back, her breath catching in her throat. She lets out a strangled gasp as the world swirls around her. She runs into something firm and steadies herself. Two hands wrap around her waist, holding her upright. It doesn't register at first that she ran into another person. When the world stops swirling around, she remembers the other assassins are still out there, and realizes one of them is holding her up! Adrenaline bursts through her entire body. She throws a frantic elbow behind her and connects with a solid thud.

"Ah, geez, what was that for?" says a familiar voice.

Ella whips around to see –

"Pylus!" She squeals, adrenaline still pumping through her.

She throws her arms around his neck and squeezes tightly. He returns the hug with a deep sigh.

"I'm glad you're okay," he whispers. He glances up to see Leifa lying on the ground watching them. With a gentle push, he separates himself from Ella, "Start running up the road. I'll catch up."

"Yeah, okay," Ella says. She throws one more glance at Leifa, then turns and starts running, as if the entire world is after her, which today it seems like it is.

Pylus crouches and picks up Leifa's knife. He examines it, locks eyes with Leifa, and throws the knife deep into the woods.

"Seems like you underestimated what you were getting yourself into," he says, "You should have put a little more poison on your knife."

"If the horses were alive, it wouldn't have mattered," Leifa says, trying to move. A little remnant of poison had remained on her blade after stabbing Pylus. That remnant was now in her. She can feel it working through her body, keeping her down. Her attempts to move are feeble at best.

"Even if the horses were alive," Pylus says, "I still would have found you." He stands, walking backwards to the edge of the firelight, their pack and one of the sleeping bags in hand, "Goodbye, Leifa."

The false reporter watches as the light reflecting off his wolf eyes disappears into the darkness, only to be replaced by another pair a little lower. A nose and snarling mouth full of teeth emerge from the spot Pylus had previously been. Three wolves creep and growl their way towards the paralyzed woman, hunger in their eyes.

20

By the time Pylus can catch up to Ella, all the effects of Leifa's poison have worn off. It takes him longer than he expected it would to get caught up to her, even with the remaining stiffness. The stab wound doesn't help any. Neither does Ella run at a dead sprint with no signs of slowing down. Only when Pylus calls out to her does she stop and wait for him.

"I didn't know you could run like that," Pylus says when he catches up.

"Pretty easy to. . . when people. . . are trying. . . to kill you," Ella pants with her hands on her knees.

"That's true," Pylus agrees, remembering the adrenaline rush he had when he'd been hunted as a child, "Only these people aren't trying to kill you. We know from what Leifa said that they want you alive. At least you don't have to worry about dying."

Ella rolls her eyes at his comment, "That's so much better. Thank you."

Pylus would shoot back a sarcastic remark, but a sharp muscle spasm takes away his desire to talk.

"So, now what?" Ella asks, looking around.

Pylus nods down the road as his side relaxes, "We keep moving."

Ella nods and takes a deep breath before heading down the road with Pylus by her side.

By the time the sun's light peeks over the mountain tops, several miles have been put behind them. The adrenaline from the night before has finally subsided, leaving the pair enervated. Pylus carries the pack, the weight ridiculously heavy. The lack of hearty meals and sleep has been affecting him faster than he expected, not to mention the emotional strain the last couple of days have had on them. The time it would have normally taken them to walk a mile takes them almost three times as long. Ella moves slowly with her feet barely leaving the ground. A heavy fog settles in their heads, causing things to jump in and out of their vision. Pylus shakes his head multiple times to clear it, but can't get his eyes to focus. He glances up to the rocky slopes around them in search of a hidden enemy he is convinced will catch them soon. A dark abyss in the rock catches his eye instead. He rubs his eyes and looks again to be sure he is seeing right. Up the slope a few yards, a small cave sits tucked back in the rocks.

"This way," he croaks, pulling Ella behind him.

They struggle ten or fifteen yards up the slope to the opening of the cave. It stretches back into the mountain and turns after a few feet. Pylus looks back down the slope, the way they came, searching for any kind of movement. Satisfied there isn't anyone following them, he ducks inside the cave, Ella in tow. They turn the corner at the back and have to stoop to get to the furthest corner. Twenty or so feet in from the entrance, they find the flattest spot they can and settle in. The sun's light is pretty well blocked back here, making it the perfect place for a quick nap.

Pylus pulls out the sleeping bag and hands it to Ella, "Take a couple of hours to sleep, then we will keep moving."

Ella nods and situates the sleeping bag on the rough ground, "What about you?" She asks, pulling the pack under her head.

"I'll be fine for now."

She nods again and soon falls asleep. Her peaceful breathing helps Pylus to relax. He watches the dim light from the entrance shimmer and shift as birds fly by and clouds cover the sun. The sounds of nature are a dull hum that seems to seep into his bones, relaxing him further. Just sitting helps to clear his head slightly. He breathes in deeply and smells all the world around him.

A bird call disturbs the peace and startles Pylus. His head snaps up as he scans the cave for anything amiss. The first thing he notices is that the sun's light has shifted. He fell asleep! From the angle of the shadows, it appears to have been for several hours. Nearly the whole day. Ella still sleeps next to him. Rubbing his eyes, he stands and walks to where the cave bends. Cautiously, he peeks around the corner. No assassins stand at the opening. Nothing smells different than before. No concerning sounds either. He lets out a sigh of relief. Lucky, he was fortunate this time. He might not be again.

He walks over and shakes Ella awake. She groans and rubs her face. Without a word to each other, they pack up and resume their trek. Hours drag by as they make their way along the road. The sleep helped clear their heads, but only boosted their energy for the first couple of miles. Once it ran out, their speed and alertness took a turn for the worse.

By the time night falls, the canyon is far behind them. The dry, open land they now trudge through has little to offer by way of vegetation. Scraggly bushes of some kind litter the ground in patches. Pylus rolls out the sleeping bag among some of the thicker ones for Ella, who practically falls onto it.

"I can hardly feel my legs," she says.

Pylus chuckles and lays on the ground next to her, "I thought I was in good shape, but that much walking was brutal. I haven't done that much since I was a kid."

"How much further do we have to go?"

Pylus sighs, "A long way."

"You might be carrying me," Ella groans.

"Ah, don't be a wuss," Pylus says with a smirk.

"If I had any energy, I would slug you," Ella mumbles.

Pylus chuckles again and sits up, "I bet after tomorrow we might start seeing more settlements. There are a couple between here and the big valley. At least there *was*. They might not be around anymore."

"Does that mean actual food?" Ella asks.

"Hopefully."

"Ugh, I could really go for a good burger right now."

"With fries?"

She gives him the 'duh' look and says, "Can you have a burger any other way?"

"Just making sure, you're somewhat normal." Pylus teases as he stands and stretches. He works out the stiffness that has already begun to settle in during the two minutes he has been sitting down. "I'm going to walk back a little way and make sure we're clear. Maybe search for some food while I'm at it. I'll wake you when I need to sleep."

"Sounds good," Ella mumbles, already breathing softly.

Pylus smiles and heads back down the way they came. He keeps his ears perked, focusing most of his attention on the noises around him. Only nature sounds reach out to him with their chirps and cries. He walks for a few hundred yards before deciding things are good for now. *How long will it last, though?* He thinks to himself.

Soon, he makes it back to Ella with a rabbit and a pheasant he caught in the brush. Quietly, he builds a fire with the lighter that he slipped into his pocket after making the last one. Ella opens her eyes halfway when the flames start dancing, but closes them again and continues to sleep.

Pylus watches the flames while he snacks on his catch; the meat helps him feel better and more energized. His life hasn't ever been what one would consider normal or quiet, even for the post-war world they live in, but the last few weeks have been a different kind of strange for him. He has experienced the most lavish and the absolute worst living conditions of his entire life over the last week.

"How did I get here?" he asks himself.

Ghosts of his past flit through his mind as he thinks about the events of the last few months in reverse. The last breaths of George and Ellie. Reggie, with his big smile and welcoming demeanor. Being treated like a grandchild by Mrs. West.

His mind continues to pull memories back to the present, ones he had locked away for a long time. The kind eyes of his sweet wife. His sisters' incessant teasing. Marshall, the man who had taken him in. Edith and the kids he had grown up with.

The shadows on the outskirts of the firelight begin to play tricks on him. The ghosts from his mind dance just outside the light, enticing him to go running to them. Every time his eyes flick to what he thinks is a person, they disappear only to skirt through his peripheral vision on the other side, taunting him. His attention darts back and forth from one shadow to the next, hoping, praying to see someone he once knew, until he finds Ella.

For a moment, nothing moves. The ghosts of his mind stand just on the edge of his vision, waiting to see what he will do. Ella's body is lit by the fire, the light giving her skin a golden tone. Her auburn hair shines as it frames her peaceful face. One of her hands lays on the ground, palm up, reaching towards Pylus. The whirlwind of faces and memories in his imagination melts away, replaced with memories of his time with Ella. He sees her sneaking out of her window that first night, the meals that they prepared and ate together, and the stupid question game that she always likes to go back to. Slowly, a smile begins to find its way across his face as he thinks of pretending to be her boyfriend at the galas. As tiring and slightly annoying as it was, they did have fun watching the faces of everyone who found out and relished slightly in the deflated chests of every young kid who thought he had a chance.

Each slow, observed breath of Ella calms Pylus' racing mind more and more. Soon, all remnants of those he has lost have faded back to the dark corners of his mind, where he likes to keep them. A new brightness has filled his being. Something new has been growing in him that he hadn't realized until now. Through all the stubborn arguing and grating comments, Ella has planted a new feeling in him. It was so subtle, so soft as it took root in the vast emptiness of Pylus Brek. Through her random moments of genuine kindness and gentle probing into his past, Ella Rye has begun to bring life to a shell of a man. Slowly, gently, Pylus reaches his hand towards Ella's.

Suddenly, she jolts awake, sitting up with a gasp. Pylus jumps and pulls his hand back, startled. He moves to her side and takes her shoulders so she looks him in the eye.

"Hey, it's okay. I'm here with you," he says quietly.

Her eyes fix on his, and a strange flutter flits through his chest. He remembers doing this with his sister when she used to have nightmares. How similar the look is in Ella's eyes. He watches as the fear on her face gives way to relief once she remembers where she is.

"I dreamed they caught up to us," she whispers.

"Don't worry, you're safe," Pylus says.

Ella closes her eyes with a sigh. Leaning forward, she rests her head on Pylus's shoulder, causing the flutter to take off again. For some unknown reason, tears well up in his eyes.

"I'm so grateful you're here," she says.

"Me too," he says after a moment.

She pulls away from him and wipes her eyes, "Why don't you get some sleep? I doubt I'll be able to now."

Pylus nods and takes her spot on the sleeping bag. He watches as she takes another log and tosses it on the fire. The flames illuminate the haunted look behind her eyes. In such a short time, she's had to go through so much. All the money her father has, and not even she is protected from the evil the world has to offer. As his eyes close, Pylus wonders if he'll ever see the playful, mischievous look he's come to know and enjoy from her again.

21

Another day drags by. Pylus and Ella continue trekking down abandoned highways. Finding food proves to be the hardest challenge. All the settlements that Pylus remembered from his childhood have long since been abandoned. Water is easy to access with the countless streams and rivers running through the hills. But the game is scarce, along with fruit trees and berry bushes. And all the wild fruit has begun to rot from the cold weather. Hunger becomes a constant, unwanted third companion. Rabbits only fill one up for so long.

"I swear if I have to eat another tasteless rabbit, I'm going to throw up," Ella grumbles.

"Hold that thought," Pylus says as he dashes off into the bushes, returning a second later with a rabbit in his hands. He holds it up, smiling sheepishly. Ella groans and drops her head.

"Sorry," he says, "not many options out here."

"It's okay," Ella sighs, "Beggars can't be choosers. However, I would enjoy another pheasant. That actually had some flavor to it."

"I'll try my best to get another one."

One rabbit and a chilly morning later, their never-ending journey continues. The walking isn't bad for Pylus anymore. He's grown used to the repetition, and his athletic physique helps him adapt quickly. Ella, on the other hand, has never felt worse. Her legs seem to grow more enfeebled with every step. The mild ache that once lived in her calves now fills her entire lower body, clinging to her muscles like sap to a tree.

"Hold on," she gasps, bending over her shaking knees, "I need a break."

"You took a break five minutes ago," Pylus says with a furrowed brow.

Ella nods, "I know, but my legs aren't used to this much running and walking in such a short amount of time."

Pylus lets out a heavy sigh and looks at the expansive country scene before them. He puts his hands on his hips as though he's about to reprimand the mountainous terrain. After a moment, he sighs again and walks over to Ella. Dropping to one knee, he jerks his head forward.

"What are you doing?" Ella asks.

Pylus points to his back, "Hop on. I'll carry you."

"Uh. . . are you sure?"

"Just get on,"

Ella gingerly steps forward, puts her arms around Pylus's shoulders, and lifts one leg onto his side. He grips her leg in a soft but sturdy hand and stands quickly, pulling her off the ground. He adjusts her until she's comfortable, then hands her the pack he had set down. Before Ella can get it fully on, Pylus starts off at a brisk pace.

"You weren't walking this fast before." It was meant to be an observation, but came out more like an accusation.

For a moment, Pylus doesn't act like he heard her remark, but then smirks and says, "Sorry you have short legs."

"Excuse me?" Ella scoffs, trying to sound offended even though she can't help smiling.

"Hey, don't worry about it," Pylus says, "Lots of people have short legs. Although compared to most short people, you still walk slowly."

Ella snorts and shakes her head, "I'd choke you out, but then I wouldn't have a ride."

"I could use the nap," Pylus retorts.

Ella laughs softly and leans her head against his. For a moment, she can almost forget they're being hunted by master assassins, and that her father is probably sick with worry, and they only have a few days to catch up with him before. . .

No! She tells herself in her mind, *I can't think like that or I'll just bring myself down and become useless. I have to keep my mind occupied.*

"Is it my turn?" She asks out loud.

"What?"

"Is it my turn?" she repeats.

". . . for what?"

"To ask a question, of course."

Pylus turns his head as far as he can to look at her, "You still want to keep going with that game?"

"Why not? You got something better to do?"

Pylus shrugs. Ella takes that as her sign to go ahead, "Alright," she says, thinking, "Where does the name Pylus come from?"

Pylus stays silent for a moment, gathering his thoughts. "Have you ever heard of the *Odyssey*?"

Ella shakes her head, "Can't say that I have."

"It's some of the oldest historical writing we have. An epic poem written by a man named Homer during ancient Greek times. You know the people who worshipped Zeus and Poseidon, that whole crowd. The poem has twenty-four books, but the first four follow a man named Telemachus and his journey. One of the cities he visited is named Pylos. Although I'm probably pronouncing it wrong. It's where he begins his rite of passage. A rite of passage is a ceremony with multiple tests that a man must pass to reach his potential and be considered a true man. It marks a new phase of life. When I became a hybrid and started Champion, I needed a new name. Since it was a new phase of my life, it kind of became a rite of passage for me. One day, I read the name in a book and decided that was it, but I changed it slightly."

"Wait, Pylus isn't your real name?" Ella asks.

"Nope."

Ella waits, expecting him to say more, "What is your real name?"

"I'm not going to tell you," he says curtly.

"Ah, come on," Ella begs.

Pylus looks back at her, then refocuses on the road, "No."

"Please?"

"No."

"Pretty please?"

"No."

"Why not?"

"No."

"I'll give you a kiss if you tell me."

"Oh, please."

"How about I stop being so needy?"

"Is that even possible?"

"Okay, first, ouch. Low blow. Second, I promise I won't laugh."

He gives her a considering side eye, but the answer remains, "No."

"It must be really bad in order for you to be *this* adamant about keeping it a secret."

"Something like that."

Ella huffs in frustration. Honestly, his stubbornness is both impressive and infuriating. That must be why her dad likes him so much.

"What will it take for you to tell me?" She asks.

"Nothing. You can't change my mind."

Lame answer, she thinks.

"What if I guess it?" she ventures.

Pylus laughs through his nose, "Good luck."

"Game on," Ella says. She scans the sky as she thinks of the worst boy names possible. "Leonard?"

"Nope."

"Dang okay. How about Eugene?"

"Wrong again."

"Blanche?"

"Thankfully, no."

"Oswald."

"Definitely not."

"Philemon?"

"Where did you even get that one?"

"I don't know. Is it Percy?"

"You think Percy is a bad name?"

"I'm reaching for straws here, give me a break. I'd do better if you gave me a hint."

"Not a chance."

"Fine. Oh! Maybe you're one of those boys who were given a girl's name, and you hated it!"

Pylus stops and says, "Okay, what boy wouldn't hate being given a girl's name?"

"Touche. Okay, here goes. Um, Shirley."

"Nope."

"How about Stacey?"

"I knew a Stacey once. Nice guy, but no."

"Is it Ashley?"

". . .Oh my gosh."

"What?! Is that it?"

"I can't believe it."

"What?!"

"You just won't give up."

Ella groans and sinks down until her chin bounces on Pylus's shoulder. She can see the cocky smirk spreading across his face.

"You're a butthead," she mumbles.

Pylus laughs a genuine laugh, "Now you resort to name-calling? This is like being a preteen all over again."

"Keep making fun of me, and I'll give you a wet willy."

"Just remember who's carrying whom, sweetheart."

Ella growls her defeat. Pylus growls a real growl at her and refocuses on the path ahead. For a while, the only sounds are their breathing and his brisk footsteps. Ella would keep talking if she weren't so irritated by Pylus and his stupid resolve to keep his name a secret.

"Doyle," Pylus says suddenly.

"What?" Ella says, barely acknowledging him.

Pylus takes a deep breath and repeats himself, "My name used to be Doyle."

The information doesn't register with Ella at first, but slowly her eyes widen, her eyebrows knit together, and her mouth drops open slightly, "Doyle?! Your name is Doyle?"

"Used to be," Pylus corrects her.

"You're right," Ella sighs, "That is an awful name. You should have kept that to yourself."

Without warning, Pylus releases his hold on Ella's legs. Normally, her arms are draped securely over his shoulders, but at this moment, one hand is on her head and the other is only lightly touching his shoulder. Consequently, when he lets go of her legs, gravity wins. She collapses to the ground in a heap.

"Ow! Oh, come on," Ella yells after him. She stands wobbling, then half runs, half limps to catch up. "Okay, I'm sorry, I deserved that." She says, grabbing his arm.

Pylus looks at her with an accomplished gleam in his eye. Without a word, he bends down and helps her onto his back again.

After a few minutes of silence, Ella asks, "You really don't like the name Doyle?"

"I'm going to drop you again," Pylus growls.

Ella laughs and tightens her grip around Pylus' neck, "Oh, you love me, and you know it."

Pylus snorts, "Don't flatter yourself."

"But did you really just change your name because you didn't like it?"

"No," Pylus says after a moment, "Truth be told, very few people actually called me Doyle. My sister and my wife were the main ones, although they usually shortened it to D. Everyone else called me Slick."

"Why Slick?"

Pylus shrugs, "I don't know. That's what the boys I grew up with called me, and it stuck. But the *real* reason I changed my name was because I felt like I needed to leave my old self behind. I was becoming. . . something new, and that something needed to be different. The old me is long gone. Besides, can you imagine a stadium full of fans chanting the name Doyle? No. What's left now is Pylus Brek. Wolf hybrid, Champion contender, and rich girl babysitter extraordinaire."

Ella wrinkles her nose at the jab but doesn't respond. She thinks for a moment, then says. "That makes sense."

"You really think so?" Pylus asks.

"Sure," Ella says, "You were stepping into a new life, trying to get away from the past, and the best way to do that was to become someone new. Completely let go of who you used to be and never look back."

"That's pretty much it," Pylus says, "Although I didn't become a Hybrid to escape my past."

Ella cocks her head in confusion, "Didn't you become one because you were sick like everyone else?"

"No," Pylus whispers, "I never had a terminal illness. I became a hybrid for other reasons."

"What reasons?" Ella asks, scared of what the answer might be.

"Revenge," Pylus says, his voice so low it's barely audible.

Ella looks at him with uncertainty. His eyes are dark, like when he was facing down the assassins on the balcony. It's a darkness that doesn't come from killing. It comes from losing something and only appears when one is determined not to lose again. The wolf inside her bodyguard hides in those eyes, barely contained. It scares her to see it so close to the surface, but it also brings her a sense of peace, knowing it is loyal to her.

As she reminds herself of this, she whispers, "What are you getting revenge for?"

Pylus doesn't answer for a moment. The wolf in his eyes burns through the yellow swirls. It seems as though he is having an internal battle for control between his human side and his animalistic nature. Finally, he says, "My wife. She didn't just pass away. She was murdered, and I'm going to find who did it so I can end them.

"I know it was a hybrid that did it. We found hair on her that wasn't hers and checked it under a microscope. It had the altered DNA of a hybrid, but our instruments weren't sophisticated enough to tell us what kind. I figured if I got involved with the hybrid world, I could find a hybrid assassin one way or another and track down the one that killed my wife."

Ellas stares in disbelief, the new information still rattling in her mind. Everything she thought about Pylus has just been thrown out the window. The ferocity she sees in his eyes is terrifying. Far more so than the look he has when he fights to protect her.

"How did you become a hybrid then?" she finally asks.

"I knew people who did the hybrid procedure and told them my story after my wife and sister died. They knew my wife and sympathized with me and wanted to help me get revenge."

Ella drops her eyes to the road, "That's. . . insane."

"I know," Pylus says.

"Not like you are insane, just the situation itself is insane," Ella says quickly.

"I know what you meant," Pylus says softly. The ferocity has faded from his eyes, the wolf going back to sleep. Or maybe just waiting for its time to strike.

For a time, they continue on in silence. Ella, unsure of how to feel after this new revelation about the man who holds her life in his hands, replays the conversation over and over in her head. Pylus only thinks of one thing, or rather one person, his wife.

22

"If you had to choose a different animal to be a hybrid of, what would it be?" Ella asks as she and Pylus sit on the side of a road, eating a pheasant Pylus caught.

"I don't know," Pylus says around a mouthful of bird, "Probably a lion or something like that."

"How come?"

"They're strong but still agile."

"I should've guessed that. Always the fighter," Ella looks at the rising mountains that surround them. A slight breeze flows through, rifling the drying autumn leaves. "You know, I wouldn't mind settling down somewhere like this. Far away from everyone. No expectations or roles to live up to. Just enjoying your own little part of the world."

She trails off as her eyes glide along the peaks, sloping up and dipping steeply, forming a protective barrier from the cares and tragedies of the world. Her eyes fall along a particular tree line and land on Pylus. He watches her with a strange look. The yellow of his eyes has a softness that Ella doesn't recognize. They meet hers and study them gently. In any other circumstance, the focus would be uncomfortable, but the way they gaze into her is almost comforting. It's like looking at him, in this moment, he truly sees her. No walls to hide behind. It feels. . . strange, but in a good way. No one has ever looked at her without judgment like he does now.

"What?" She whispers, "Why are you looking at me like that?"

A small smile tugs at Pylus' mouth, "You just. . . reminded me of someone."

"Who?" She asks.

"My wife," the small smile falters slightly at his response. He gazes at her for a moment longer before dropping his eyes then looking deeper into the canyon.

"We should be out of the canyon in another couple of hours," he says, "We'll be in Logan by tonight. Maybe we can find an actual bed for you to sleep in."

A slight whine slips from Ella's chest at the thought of having a soft mattress to sleep on. It seems almost too good to be true. Pylus glances at her and smiles before standing and offering her a hand. With a deep breath, Ella takes the hand, ready to head towards the new city and hopefully a bed.

As the sun sets, a few hours later, buildings rise all around Ella and Pylus. Nothing big, but actual buildings. Downtown Logan has a quaint atmosphere. Old houses randomly fit in with the commercial buildings along Main Street. All the business buildings seem to have stepped out of the early 1900s. A few newer-looking buildings fit in here and there among the blast from the past. To the east, a magnificent castle-like structure sits atop a hill overlooking the valley.

"What do you suppose that is?" Ella asks, pointing to the building.

"Don't know, maybe a church of some kind," Pylus says.

"I thought you used to live here?" Ella says.

Pylus scans the surrounding buildings as he answers, "We lived up the canyon a way and never came down here. This is where all the gangs would pass through."

"Oh," Ella says, "It's a beautiful building."

"Yes, it is," Pylus agrees, looking at the building one last time. It was the only building with the windows still intact and no signs of damage. "This way." He heads towards a tall hotel on the corner of the intersection they stand in.

The building has only three floors, but compared to the smaller ones around, it seems enormous. The front doors have been smashed, and the white exterior is now a brownish-yellow. Pylus walks through the doors with knives drawn, checking behind furniture and in dark corners for anything unfriendly. Ella follows tentatively, staying tense and ready to run or fight. Pylus slowly turns his head from side to side, listening and smelling for anything.

The lobby they walk through is small and straightforward. A desk sits to their right with a hallway leading behind it. Pylus creeps across the lobby to a door that says stairs. The nearly set sun offers no light into the darkened area, making it difficult for Ella to see where she's going. She can hardly make out Pylus as he pushes the door open slowly and enters the stairwell. She hurries to catch up before the door shuts. Inside the stairs, she grabs the back of Pylus's jacket to not get separated. They make their way to the second floor and into a long hallway. Doors line both sides all the way to the end. Pylus walks to the first and puts his ear to it. Hearing nothing, he tests the handle. It's broken, and the door swings in as he pushes on it. Someone has been here before. Not surprising.

The room is small with a bathroom immediately to the right as they walk in and a large bed in the center of the room. Everything else that used to be in the room has long been pilfered. As luck would have it, the only thing left is the bed frame with an old mattress.

"Oh, thank goodness," Ella sighs, falling on the bed. A considerable cloud of dust jumps in the air, enveloping her. As quickly as she jumped on the bed, she jumps off, coughing and rubbing her eyes.

Pylus chuckles to himself, then takes hold of the mattress and flips it. More dust flies into the air, but the underside of the mattress appears much cleaner.

"Try again," he says.

Ella lies back on the bed more cautiously than before. She sighs happily, relaxing into the softness. Pylus closes the door to the hallway and turns back to find Ella already sleeping soundly. With a smile, he spreads the sleeping bag over her, then steps to the cracked window and peeks through the curtains to the parking lot below. The last rays of the sun disappear as he looks for any signs of movement. This room looks out to the back of the building, opposite the side through which they entered. Everything here is quiet.

It's strange to be so close to the place where he spent his youth. Edith and the kids she looked after haven't been part of his thoughts for many years. Tonight, he can feel the skeletal remnants of their memories calling him back to the canyon. The road that leads to it is only a block or two away. Under different circumstances, maybe he would go back and see the old nunnery. But not this time. Ella is his primary focus. He doesn't have time for sightseeing. Plus, he doesn't think he's ready to face that part of his past.

***

The night passes without incident. Pylus even lets Ella have an extra two hours of sleep. He can't bring himself to separate her from the beloved mattress just yet. When he finally does, she smiles and says she hasn't slept so well in her life. Pylus smiles and takes a turn, enjoying the luxury.

Dawn brings a heavy dew, almost a frost, on everything. Sunlight glistens on every surface as Pylus and Ella prepare to leave their room for the night. They lazily make their way into the hall and back to the lobby. Lethargy refuses to release its grip on their limbs. Having had a good rest has taken its toll on their stress-strained bodies.

The rising sun shines directly into the front doors, making the outside look like a doorway to heaven or the surface of the sun. Pylus shields his eyes as he steps into the light. When his eyes adjust, he drops his hand and looks directly down the barrel of a rifle. He holds his arm out to stop Ella from walking any further.

A man with dark brown hair and a large beard holds the rifle level with Pylus' eyes. Two more men step out from behind the first, each with a rifle of their own. One has close-cropped hair and a mustache; the other is clean-shaven with hair well past his shoulders.

"Who are you?" The bearded man asks in a gruff voice.

"We're just travelers passing through," Pylus says calmly.

The bearded man scoffs, "We've had plenty of travelers pass through before. Most of them weren't too kind as they did."

"Easy now, boys," Pylus says, holding his hands up and stepping back, "We don't want any trouble. We're not. . . Wait a minute. Brock?"

Surprise bursts across the man's face, "What... how... how do you..." he studies Pylus intently. Slowly, his eyes widen, "Slick?"

Pylus smiles, "How've you been, brother?"

"Slick!" The man, Brock, shouts. He lowers his rifle and pulls Pylus into a tight hug. Pylus lets out a hearty laugh and hugs him back tightly.

Brock pulls back and gives Pylus a good shove, "What are you doing out here? Last I saw you, you were staying with Marshall back East."

Pylus laughs softly, "Where to begin? How are you, Joseph?"

"Can't complain," the man with the mustache says, stepping forward and embracing Pylus as fiercely as Brock had.

"And you, Billy?" This is directed at the man with long hair, "You look like a hippy."

Billy smiles as he gives Pylus a hug, "You're one to make fun of appearances. When did this all happen?" He gestures at Pylus' wolf-like claws, pointed fangs, and yellow eyes.

"A couple of years ago," Pylus says with a shrug as if he just got a simple haircut, "Figured it was time for a change."

The men laugh like the old friends they are. Ella gapes at the interaction. She's never had anyone be so excited to see her or accept her as easily as these men accept Pylus' hybrid transformation.

"And who is this lovely young woman you tricked into traveling with you?" Brock asks, extending his free hand to Ella. "Brock Wright miss. Pleasure to meet you." He gives the back of her hand a gentle kiss with a wink.

"Oh. . . um. . . I'm uh. . ." Ella stammers.

"Down, Brock," Pylus says, "Just because you covered up your ugly mug doesn't mean you're any less scary looking."

"Still look a whole lot better than you," Brock shoots back.

Pylus laughs and gives Brock a shove. Brock returns the laugh as he grabs Pylus around the neck in a headlock.

"So, what brings you back through these parts?" Joseph asks, pushing his way between the two.

"And you never said who your friend is," Billy adds, smiling at Ella.

"That's a long story, boys," Pylus says, "As for her," he gestures at Ella, "This is Ella Rye. Daughter of bioengineer genius Jefferson Rye."

The three brothers look at each other, then back to Pylus with blank stares.

"Never heard of the guy," Brock says.

"Seriously?" Ella says.

"Uh, yeah," Joseph replies, "We don't care much about the rest of the world. All we focus on is our little home and our families."

Ella looks at each of the brothers, flabbergasted. They, in turn, grow increasingly confused at her surprise.

"She's hardly ever associated with someone who doesn't know who her dad is," Pylus explains, "Her dad has made food more abundant and accessible for people living within or near larger settlements. His company is the biggest reason large societies around the world have flourished since the rebuild."

"Oohh," the brothers say in unison.

"Anyway," Billy says, "What you still haven't told us is why you're here."

"Okay, I'll give you a quick recap," Pylus says. He tells the brothers about losing his sister and wife. Then, moves to becoming a hybrid, competing in Champion as a top contender, then getting hired as Ella's bodyguard. He skims over the parties and traveling until he gets to the part where they jumped off a balcony. Brock laughs at that part, saying something about "Slick and his old antics".

Pylus continues on with the assassins tailing them, meeting Chuck, running into Leifa and her betrayal, then the last couple of days leading them to Logan.

At the end of the story, all three brothers let out a low whistle. Billy shakes his head and looks back and forth between Ella and Pylus. Joseph runs his hands through his hair, looking at the ground. Brock strokes his beard, deep in thought.

"You don't stay out of trouble for long, do you?" He asks Pylus with a twinkle in his eye.

Pylus shrugs with a smirk, "Can't help it, I guess."

"Same old Slick," Joseph says.

"So, now you're just heading towards the Boise Settlement," Brock says, still stroking his beard, "Wish we had a horse to give you. That would chop your travel time in half."

Pylus shrugs again, "Since we had horses at the beginning, we'll actually be there in time if we have to walk from here. Even with all the mishaps we've run into and the extra sleeping we've done."

"That's fortunate for you," Billy says, "We do have some extra food we can send with you. It's back at the settlement a couple of miles away."

"We appreciate the offer, but we don't know how close the assassins are to us, so it would be better if we got moving as soon as we can," Pylus says.

Brock nods his agreement, as does Joseph. The two share a look, and a silent conversation passes between them. Billy looks to Pylus and rolls his eyes. Apparently, the youngest brother is used to being left out.

"When was the last time you saw these assassins?" Billy asks.

"The last two we haven't seen since Chuck's house. We know the rest are dead," Pylus says, "I wouldn't expect them to be too far behind us, though."

"That's a good assumption," a new voice says.

Brock and his brothers raise their rifles and spin to scan the streets. Pylus pulls his knives and crouches close to Ella, ready to protect her. Together, the four men create a protective circle around her, each facing a different direction. Nothing moves. Pylus strains to hear where the mystery visitor is, but can't make out anything aside from his companions' heartbeats.

"What's the matter, Pylus?" The voice says again. It's so quiet, Pylus knows he's the only one who can hear it, "Can't find me?"

Pylus sniffs the air. Nothing. Wait, there. The faint smell is hard to detect, but it's there. It seems to be coming from Brock's direction. The same smell from the woods and Ella's room that first night. It's him. *Sting.*

Across the street from the group, a bald figure steps out from behind an abandoned commercial truck. He smiles coldly, his eyes still bearing the same empty look. Brock and Pylus notice him at the same time. Brock introduces himself with a shot from his rifle. Sting ducks behind the truck before the shot goes off, barely dodging the incoming bullet.

Joseph and Billy turn to face the unwelcome guest to give a welcoming of their own. With everyone focused on Sting, all the attention is off the hotel doors, where the other assassin sits, waiting.

Seeing his chance, he rushes from his hiding place. The shifting of his weight causes pieces of broken glass to fall to the ground with a soft tinkle. Normal people wouldn't notice the sound, Pylus, however, isn't normal. The falling glass reaches his ears. In slow motion, he turns to see the assassin rushing Ella. Grabbing his charge in a bear hug, he falls flat on his back. The assassin's momentum is too much for him to change direction that quickly. Instead, he changes his target, barreling into Joseph's back, knocking him down, and sending his rifle clattering into the road.

"Jo!" Brock and Billy yell, swinging their rifles towards their brother's assailant. Before either can get a shot, Joseph recovers himself and jumps onto the assassin.

Sting rushes from behind his cover and advances on the group. Pylus yells to Billy as he rolls Ella off him and gets to his feet. Billy turns his rifle towards Sting only to have it knocked to the side. Sting throws a quick jab, connecting with Billy's eye. Billy grunts and releases his rifle. Sting drops the weapon and throws his now free hand in a hard cross punch. Billy sees the attack in time to duck out of the way. Now under Sting's guard, he pushes forward, grabbing Sting around the middle and pushing him back.

Brock swivels between his brothers, trying to find a chance to help one. Deciding his weapon is useless, he drops his rifle and moves to help Joseph, who is now pinned under his opponent.

Billy pushes against Sting, who steps backwards quickly, keeping his feet beneath him. Suddenly, Billy stops and lifts with all his strength, throwing Sting over his shoulder. With incredible agility, Sting pushes off Billy's shoulder, flipping himself around and landing on his feet. He lands nimbly only to be met with a slash from Pylus' dagger. He steps to the side so the blade misses his neck by a whisper. Pylus recovers his momentum and faces Sting with Billy by his side. Sting stands before them with a devilish smile.

"Isn't this fun?" the assassin says, rolling his shoulders.

"Shut up," Billy yells, rushing him.

Pylus moves close behind him, prepared to move at any opening. Billy throws a quick right-left combo as soon as he gets close enough. Sting blocks the blows easily and returns two hits squarely to Billy's nose. Billy yells in pain and stumbles back. Pylus ducks low around his brother and takes two swings at Sting. The assassin jumps back quickly, just out of reach of the attack. Pylus stops his charge, staying low, ready to pounce.

Out of the corner of his eye, Pylus sees Joseph fall back, holding his stomach. Brock lets out a barbaric war cry and lands two heavy hits on the back of the kneeling assassin's head. The assassin falls to the ground, dropping the knife he was holding, now slick with blood. Brock grabs the man by the back of his collar and his waistband. With another war cry, he picks the assassin up over his head and slams him to the ground, breaking his neck. Pylus feels the snap from where he stands. Brock turns to make his way to Pylus but stumbles on the first step and falls to his knees.

Billy stands, wiping his eyes. His nose has already swollen immensely, but it's not bleeding. Definitely broken. Sting takes the opportunity and rushes Billy. Barely reacting in time, Billy blocks the heavy punch Sting throws at his head, but isn't able to block the knee that follows. He groans as the knee smashes into his stomach and again when Sting elbows the side of his face. Billy drops to the ground, moaning in pain. Before Billy hits the ground, Pylus reaches Sting and full-body slams him. Sting lifts into the air and hits the ground a couple of feet away. He quickly rolls over his shoulder and returns to his feet.

Pylus glances around to check on everyone. Billy lies on the ground in a tight ball. Ella kneels next to Joseph, holding her hands on his bleeding stomach. Brock is down on one knee with the other straight out behind him. His hand grips his straightened leg just above the knee, covered in blood.

"Looks like it's just you and me," Sting says with a sinister grin.

Pylus growls, "Not for long."

"Oh, come now," Sting says as if chiding a child, "Don't you want to know who I am?"

"Not really."

"Not very friendly, are you? Wouldn't you like to know about the time we first met?"

"I've never met you before," Pylus says as he circles between his group and Sting.

Sting's smile widens, "Your *wife* would disagree."

Pylus' heart stops beating. The skin on the back of his neck tingles uneasily, and his breathing catches in his throat. Sting notices and smiles even wider.

"Oh yes, Pylus," he whispers, "Or should I call you Slick? I remember you well. I was sent to your settlement to kill your friend Marshal. My employer at the time had a grudge against him and wanted to take over his little homestead. Unfortunately, that night his daughter was sick. I didn't know Marshal had left for the Shank Settlement the day before to get medicine. I snuck into the house and checked every room, but couldn't find him.

"However, I did find his daughter, and the person who was sitting with her that night was your beautiful wife. I thought I was hidden in the shadows, but your wife must have had a sixth sense because she noticed me. I couldn't leave now that she had seen my face, so I did what I had to do. Unfortunately, she was more prepared than I thought and attacked me with a knife, giving me this lovely reminder," he gestures to a scar running along his jaw, "Quite a fierce woman you had there. Not many people get the jump on me like that, but in the end, she didn't stand a chance.

"After I took care of her, I was going to kill Marshal's daughter as well, but I was rudely interrupted by none other than you. I jumped out of an open window and was gone before you got there."

Pylus' face pales as Sting recounts the awful night. He can see his wife lying on the ground. The knife she always carried lay beside her. He can hear his own voice crying his wife's name as he tries to bring her back. Until he remembers the little hole in the side of her neck, almost like. . .

"You poisoned her," Pylus whispers.

Sting rolls his head side to side, "Sort of. I stung her. You see, I was the world's first and only attempt at making an insect hybrid. After the procedure, the DNA barely took. I was considered the lowest of the lowbrids. Nothing really seemed different about me except this," he holds up the pinky on his right hand. Where the nail should be, there's only pink flesh. Suddenly, a black needle springs out in place of the missing nail. It's barely longer than the tip of the pinky and looks sharp. "My blood is laced with the most potent scorpion venom ever discovered. Rather useful for a professional assassin, wouldn't you say?"

Pylus' breath stays trapped in his chest. The man who took his wife from him is right here, and he can't bring himself to move. The memories of burying his wife and hearing Marshal's daughter tell him what she saw happen keep replaying in his mind over and over. The tears, the smells, the blood. Moments of agony ten times worse than seeing Edith's body, everything that came from that night holds Pylus captive.

"What a poetic ending," Sting continues, "You couldn't protect your wife then, and you can't protect sweet little Ella now."

Those words pierce through Pylus' mind haze. The memories of his wife are quickly replaced with memories of Ella. They fly through his mind one after another, ending with her terrified eyes watching him while she tries to help Joseph. Pylus snaps his eyes to Sting's. His breath returns as a deep, menacing growl. From where she sits, Ella can see the wolf has fully awakened inside him. He tightens his grip on his daggers and bares his teeth. The smile falls from Sting's face, replaced with a sneer.

With a primal roar, Pylus lunges, closing the distance between him and Sting easily. Sting jumps away from the attack and shoots in for his own. Pylus jumps and rolls over Sting's shoulder, landing behind him. He thrusts forward with his knife towards the small of the back. Sting spins quickly and blocks the attack with his left forearm. His right arm streaks forward to grab Pylus' throat, his stinger dripping venom. Pylus drops his weight to his left side, Sting's hand missing his throat by centimeters. Using his momentum, Pylus lashes out with his right leg in a savage back kick, connecting with Sting's knee. Sting falls with a cry but quickly rolls away and stands unsteadily on his good leg.

Pylus takes a moment to catch his breath as he slowly stands. Sting's confident smile has been replaced with a furious scowl, and he favors his right leg.

"I'm going to kill you slowly," Sting hisses.

Pylus snarls in response and then rushes the assassin. Sting waits until the last second, then jabs his right hand forward directly at Pylus' eyes, *exactly* how Pylus wants him to. At the perfect moment, Pylus changes his direction slightly. Sting's hand is now aiming just above his right shoulder. Pylus plants his left foot, twists his hips, and stabs the knife in his left hand through Sting's forearm. Sting screams and tries to pull his arm back, but Pylus holds tight to the weapon, keeping the arm closer to him. In one motion, he pushes with his left hand and swipes low with his right, causing Sting to step forward into his moving blade. The knife slices quickly and cleanly through Sting's clothes, leaving a deep cut across his ribs.

Sting drops his arm with the knife in it to block his injured side, pulling the weapon from Pylus's grip. No matter. Pylus, having used his momentum to move behind Sting, pivots to face his back. He smoothly switches his knife from his right hand to his left. Not giving Sting a chance to react, Pylus throws a quick kick to Sting's left knee, followed quickly by a back kick to his right knee. The assassin drops to his hands and knees, crying in pain.

Under normal fighting circumstances, Pylus can keep a level head about him. This, however, isn't a normal circumstance. Bloodlust has taken over. His vision is narrowed and red. The only thing in his sights is his wife's murderer, the man responsible for the pain his brothers now endure, and the one who put Ella through this Hell. He can smell the fear pouring off of Sting. His mind is closed to every thought except one. *Kill!* The wolf in him recognizes the thrill of the hunt and the moment before a finishing strike.

Pylus stands behind Sting, knife in hand, watching the man he has dreamed of ending for years, wither in pain. His anger slowly fades, replaced with cold indifference. Slowly, he reaches forward, grabbing Sting's head. He pulls it back until their eyes meet. Pylus takes one last look at the man he has spent his entire hybrid life preparing for. He relishes the terror in Sting's wild eyes. In one quick strike, he drives his knife into the base of Sting's throat. The assassin's eyes widen as he chokes on the blade. Slowly, his eyes roll back, and his breathing stops. Pylus pulls the

knife from the man's neck and allows the body to drop to the
ground.

23

"Are you sure you're going to be okay?" Brock looks at Pylus and Ella, eyes filled with concern. He kneels on the sidewalk next to Joseph, holding his brother down. A strip of fabric is tied around his leg, where the assassin caught him with a knife. Joseph lies where he fell as Billy stitches up the stab wound he got trying to disarm the assassin. It's a miracle Billy can see well enough to do the job. His nose has swollen to three times its normal size, and his eyes are already turning black.

"You're worried about us?" Ella asks, "You three are the ones who look like they need help."

"I've been worse," Joseph grunts from the ground, "And I think Billy actually looks better now."

"Just remember who's doing your medical treatment, brother," Billy says.

"We'll all be fine. Especially when we get back to our homestead," Brock says, "You two still have a long way to go, and you have no idea who hired Sting and his crew. For all we know, they could have sent more assassins to track you, like that Leifa lady."

"Not likely," Pylus says, cleaning his knife, "Sting didn't have any kind of communication device on him. Neither did his friend. Unless they have a vehicle somewhere, they don't have a way to relay any information to their employer. However, if they did have a vehicle, they would have caught us a long time ago. With how persistent Sting has been, I would assume he was the main gun for hire."

Brock sighs heavily through his nose, "I still worry."

Pylus sheaths his knife with a smile and crouches next to Brock, "That's just your older brother instincts coming out." He puts his arm around Brock's shoulders, giving him a squeeze.

"You always give them a reason to," Brock says.

Pylus shrugs, "What are little brothers for?" Joseph and Billy chuckle at their agreement.

"Don't worry, Brock," Joseph says, "With Ella by his side, I think he'll be fine. That girl has enough fight in her to keep up with old Slick."

Pylus smiles and looks at Ella. She smiles softly down at Joseph.

"Hey, Slick," Joseph says, grabbing Pylus' free hand, "Get her home safe. I'm sorry you couldn't protect Mya when you needed to, but you can protect Ella now."

A dark shadow falls over Pylus' face. He nods and gives Joseph's hand a tight squeeze. Brock mimics Pylus and places his arm around Pylus' waist. After wiping it on a rag, Billy places his hand on Pylus' shoulder. The brothers exchange looks, sharing in a silent conversation. Ella feels like she is witnessing something that should be private, but can't look away. Seeing this moment draws her attention to the hole in her heart. The one that should have been filled with siblings. Whether blood or bond, she wouldn't have cared. Her eyes fall on Pylus, and something starts to fill the hole.

After a moment, Pylus stands. He gives each of the brothers a final smile before grabbing the pack and turning to Ella. He steps past her, heading in the direction of the Boise settlement.

"I'll swing by and see you on our way back through," he calls over his shoulder.

Ella turns to follow, but is called back by Brock. "Take care of our little brother," he says, looking at her.

"I will," she says with a small smile.

"Don't do anything I wouldn't do!" she hears Joseph call as she catches up to Pylus.

"What won't you do?" Pylus calls back.

"Exactly!" comes the fading response.

Pylus chuckles and turns to face the horizon. He and Ella walk next to each other, feeling a weight off their backs. No more watching the shadows. No more checking over their shoulders. No more fear. Ella lets out a deep sigh. She looks at the clear blue sky and smiles. Just a couple of easy days of travel, and this will all be over.

Easy days, they are. The majority of the time, Ella spends the trip on Pylus's back. His athletic physique and animal speed help trim down the amount of time it takes to reach the Boise Settlement. By the end of the fourth day, the settlement can be seen in the distance. Pylus sets Ella down at the base of a foothill and begins pulling out the sleeping bag for her.

"I know where we are," Ella says.

"You do?" Pylus asks, genuinely surprised. Ella doesn't seem like the type to remember landmarks and geography.

Ella nods solemnly, "You see that big mansion on the hill up there?" She points to a luxurious building higher on the hill than any other house. It's obviously been built within the last decade or so. "That's Clive Blane's summer home. That's where we will be meeting my dad tomorrow."

Pylus studies her for a moment, "You nervous?"

Ella nods again, "I don't know why. I should be excited to see my dad again, but I feel like I'm not the same person after everything that's happened in the last few days. And I think he will be disappointed with what I want to do with my life."

"And what is that, exactly?" Pylus asks after a brief pause.

"I want to move away from everyone and everything. Live in a place like Brock and the others. I want simplicity."

Again, Ella surprises Pylus. It seems it's becoming a trend. After the Hell they had gone through the last few days, Pylus assumed Ella would kill to get back to her old life. She had talked about running away, but that was before the betrayal of Leifa and the fight with the assassins. Pylus assumed she would still want to live in a big settlement. Maybe not the Shank one, but at least one where she didn't have to rely on herself to provide her own crops. How would she live without makeup?

"I.... okay," Pylus says.

Ella smiles at his eloquent response, "I'm tired of being surrounded by people who are willing to stab whoever they can in the back. The politics of the business world are draining. I felt like every gala I had to attend took another two years off my life.

"Then, being out here, I've seen a new beauty in the world. There is a peace that comes from being away from everything. Out here, I've been able to forget about all the worries I used to have. I guess trying to survive does that to you. But aside from that, I've been happy. I've felt free. Now I have to step back into my life of boundaries and façades. Everything I wanted, the reasons I snuck out and rebelled, I've had out here. Especially these last couple of days."

She turns to look at the Blane mansion in the distance. Her face reveals strength, while her eyes struggle to hold back tears. Pylus studies her for a moment, seeing the fear she holds inside. It's like an animal that has lived its life in a cage being released for a short time into a vast wilderness, only to be forced back into the cramped confines of captivity.

Pylus stands and puts a hand on Ella's shoulder. Gently, he turns her towards him, "You know what I think? Your dad cares more about you than he does his business. If you tell him you want something else for your life, I believe he'll want you to be happy."

"You don't think he'll see it as losing his wife *and* his daughter?" One of the tears she has been holding back breaks free.

Pylus brushes it away with the back of his finger, then cups her cheek, "He won't be losing you. You weren't planning on living with him forever, were you? You're just growing up. Besides, your dad travels enough that no matter where you end up, he'll come visit."

Ella chews her lower lip, contemplating Pylus' words. "I guess you're right. I just always figured I'd leave after I got married."

"Well," Pylus says, prepping some wood for a fire, "Sometimes we grow up sooner than we expect."

"I guess you would know all about that," Ella says.

Pylus smiles sadly, "I guess I would."

The rest of the evening passes in silence. They prepare their dinner and eat, lost in thought. Ella casts glances at the mansion lights in the distance. Across the valley, other house lights shine in the darkness where the rest of the settlement sits. Clive Blane enjoys his solidarity but also likes to clearly flaunt his wealth. He ensures that nobody else in the settlement lives near him, but all can see his residence.

The Boise Settlement isn't large by any means, but it does house over 50,000 people. Ella remembers seeing the lights of the settlement from the Blane mansion's balconies a few years earlier. The separation of the classes is as distinct as black and white. In the Shank settlement, the rich and poor are separated by a couple of blocks. Many times, they mingle as they go about their daily lives. Here in the West, things work differently, and it makes her sick. The more she looks at the expansive darkness between the mansion and the settlement, the more hardened her resolve becomes.

"Tomorrow's going to be a new day," Pylus says, pulling Ella from her thoughts, "You never know what a new day will bring."

Ella looks at him resting with his back against a rock. He gazes across the void between them and the Blane mansion, twiddling the rings around his neck thoughtfully. The light from the flames illuminates something in his eyes. Almost like he's preparing himself, by the next evening, they'll be at the mansion waiting for her dad to show up and continue on with their lives. Whatever that entails.

"Pylus?" Ella asks, "Remember when I asked you to run away with me?"

"A couple of days ago? Yeah, I do."

"I'm going to tell my dad I want a simpler life," she says, staring into the fire, "Will you live it with me?"

Pylus looks at her. The events they've shared flit through his mind. Running for their lives, attending the galas and parties, pretending to be a couple, training, and finally, the first night she tried to sneak out. How much has changed since then? Ella has grown, maturing through trauma. He has changed, too. He's let himself care for someone again. After Ellie and George died, he felt the last place inside him reserved for those he let get close to him wither away. He didn't think he would let anyone become special to him again. Now here he is letting this girl know more about him than anyone ever has, and truthfully, it scares him. But he's never been one to let fear control him.

"Of course, I will," he says.

Ella smiles at him, then lies down, "Goodnight, Pylus. I'm glad you're here with me."

"Me too," Pylus says softly. He looks back at the mansion in the distance, "We made it," he whispers to himself.

247

24

Morning brings a feeling of anticipation. Pylus can't tell if it's a foreboding or a hope, but *something* is coming today. He and Ella had everything packed at sunrise, but couldn't find the motivation to begin the journey. They sit together, staring at the mansion. If they leave now, they will arrive a couple of hours before the other guests. No doubt, Ella's father will be there early as well, in hopes of her being there.

"You ready to go?" Ella asks.

"Are you?" Pylus counters.

Ella sighs, "No. But the longer I put it off, the worse it will get."

Pylus nods, but neither of them moves. The sun slowly rises into the sky, burning off the morning dew. A shiver runs down Ella's spine as the morning cold works its way out of her bones. Pylus rubs his hands together and leans forward with his elbows on his knees.

"Whatever happens today, I'll be there," he says.

"I know," Ella says. She takes a deep breath and stands as she exhales, "Here we go."

Pylus stands with her and shoulders the pack. They stand together for a moment, prepping themselves for what comes. Ella takes another deep breath and takes Pylus's hand in hers. He gives her hand a squeeze. She returns the sentiment, then takes the first step.

***

The large double doors of Blane Manor loom over Pylus and Ella as they climb the front steps. A posh front porch ornamented with potted plants wraps around the front of the manor. Several tall windows gleam in the sunlight. Lush red curtains are drawn across them, preventing anyone from looking in. Tonight, they will be thrown open wide for everyone to see the lavish party within.

Ella walks to the door and knocks loudly with the large metal knocker on the front. Several seconds pass with no hint of life. Just as Ella reaches to knock again, the lock slides and the door swings open to reveal a finely dressed doorman with a drab face and a bleak demeanor.

"Yes?" He asks without trying to hide his disgust.

Pylus hasn't looked in a mirror for a few days but he can imagine how they must appear. Dirty and matted like a pair of stray dogs searching for food.

Ella stands straight, putting on her best professional persona, "My name is Ella Rye. My father is Jefferson Rye. This is my bodyguard, Pylus Brek. We have been on the run from assassins for several days and are here to meet my father at tonight's gala. If you don't mind, we would like to talk with Mr. Blane and see about getting freshened up before tonight's events."

The doorman's eyes widen in recognition, "Oh! Miss Rye, I apologize! I did not recognize you. It has been a long time since you have been to our humble manor."

Humble? Pylus thinks.

Ella gives him a look that says she read his mind and had the same thought before turning back to the man at the door, "It is a pleasure to be back. Now, can you please show us to Mr. Blane?"

"Yes, yes of course!" The doorman says, stepping to the side with a nod of his head, "Please come in."

"Thank you." Ella steps past the man confidently. Pylus follows a step behind. The man meets his eyes as he passes. Pylus growls softly at him, making him stiffen. Pylus smiles to himself as he focuses on Ella. The doorman closes the front door, then hurries to lead the way to Mr. Blane.

The front door of the manor opens into a small foyer with a door to the right and one to the left, leading to coat closets. Straight ahead, a large archway allows entrance to a vast open ballroom. Windows cover three of the four walls from floor to ceiling. The ones around the top half of the room are stained glass and uncovered, unlike the lower ones. Sunlight shimmers through the multicolored glass, creating a kaleidoscope effect throughout the ballroom. On the opposite side of the room, a wide staircase rises to a set of double doors on the wall, which have no windows. Aside from those doors and the one through which the trio came, there are no other exits from the room that can be seen.

Pylus and Ella follow the doorman as he scurries through the sea of colored light to the other side of the ballroom. He climbs the stairs with quick, tapping steps. Ella follows close behind. Pylus hangs back to examine the ballroom from the stairs. Something seems off. Amidst the smells of cleaners and food being prepared for the night, there's a recognizable scent. Closing his eyes, he takes a deep breath. Ella's now well-known smell reaches him along with a dull aftershave that must belong to the doorman. He continues sifting through the smells. Obvious cleaners, a couple of less striking clean scents, food, fresh wood, and the overpowering smell of air fresheners spread throughout the manor, and there. Something. . . something almost familiar. . . but it seems muffled, almost like a car under a sheet. He thinks he knows it, but can't be sure.

"Pylus?" Ella's voice interrupts his concentration. He turns to see her standing at the top of the stairs, "You coming?"

He turns to scan the ballroom once more, "Yeah. Yeah, I'm coming."

Ella waits for him to reach the top of the stairs. She gives him a small smile and takes his hand. Together they walk down the long hall after the doorman.

The hallway stretches straight in front of them with two doors on each side. One door stands slightly ajar, revealing a sitting room of sorts with couches and plush chairs. The end of the hall comes to a T with a staircase going up in either direction. The doorman turns and briskly climbs the stairs on the right. As Pylus climbs after him, he catches a whiff of the same familiar smell mixed with another that he knows, but can't think of *where* he knows it from. The ordeals of the last couple of days have left his senses frazzled.

The stairs lead to a small room with two doors on the opposite side. A small coffee table and two couches sit between the trio and the doors.

"Please, wait here," the doorman says, gesturing to the couches. Without waiting for a response, he turns and walks through one of the doors after knocking twice.

Pylus leads Ella over to one of the couches and takes a seat. Ella sits close, keeping Pylus's hand tightly in hers.

"I don't like being here," she whispers, her eyes darting around the bare walls.

"Me either," Pylus says, "Want to make a run for it? We can hide outside and wait until we see your dad show up."

"Sounds good," she says.

Pylus stands just as a door opens and the doorman reappears. He looks at Pylus with a raised eyebrow but only says, "Mr. Blane will see you now."

Only now does Pylus realize he couldn't hear any voices from the room while the doorman was gone. *Must be soundproofed*, he thinks. He looks back at Ella, asking her what she wants with his eyes. She looks at the open door, then back to him. Her mouth forms a tight line, and she nods quickly. Pylus takes a deep breath and nods back.

The familiar smells Pylus has been smelling grow stronger as he steps into the room where Clive Blane sits, waiting behind a large desk. The man stands with his sickeningly debonair smile.

"Ella, Pylus, welcome to Blane Manor," Blane says, extending his arms to both sides. "You two look like you've had an eventful week and a half. I'm so happy to see you're both safe."

"Thank you, Mr. Blane," Ella says stiffly, "May I use a phone to call my father and let him know I'm here?"

"I actually just finished a call with him," Blane says, "He will be arriving here shortly. He has been showing up to all the galas early, hoping to find you there waiting. How ecstatic he will be to find you here. In the meantime, I can show you to a room where you can freshen up while you wait."

"How long did my father say he would be?" Ella asks.

"Within the hour. I'll have Oliver show you to a room where you can get cleaned up. I believe I also have some spare clothes here that I keep in case a guest needs a change. I'll have some brought to you."

"Alright, thank you," Ella says tightly.

As she turns to follow Oliver out of the office, Blane meets Pylus' eyes. His smile falters slightly, and a dark look flashes in his gaze. Pylus focuses his hearing. Blane's heart rate pounds quickly. The muscles in his face twitch as he tries to keep a straight face. He's furious, but why?

A tug on Pylus' hand pulls his attention. Ella stands holding onto him with a plea in her eyes. Pylus casts one last glance at Blane. The man reeks of anger, although he does a good job at keeping his face pleasant. With a nod, Pylus turns and follows Ella and Oliver back down the stairs and up the opposing flight.

The second flight of stairs leads to a hallway with several doors on one side and windows on the other. Oliver opens the first door and gestures for them to enter. Ella leads the way, still holding Pylus' hand.

"I will return shortly with clean clothes," Oliver says. He gives a curt nod, then closes the door, leaving Pylus and Ella alone in the unfamiliar room.

"You want to shower first?" Pylus asks, nodding towards the bathroom.

"Sure. Just don't leave the doorway," Ella says.

"Wouldn't dream of it."

She smiles as she walks into the bathroom and closes the door. Soon after, water starts running. Pylus takes a seat on the floor just outside the bathroom door. Oliver shows up a few minutes later with an elegant black dress for Ella and a suit for Pylus. After setting down the clothes, he turns and quickly leaves without a word.

Pylus takes the dress to the bathroom door and opens the door a crack, "Ella? I have a dress here for you."

"There's a hook on the back of the door you can hang it on," she calls to him, "but don't stick your head in. The shower is glass."

Carefully, Pylus reaches the dress around the door and hangs it on the hook. He makes sure to keep his head facing away from the crack in the door in case the shower is in view.

"Thank you," Ella calls when he closes the door.

Pylus returns to his post on the floor and closes his eyes. Aside from the shower running and Ella humming softly, the manor is quiet. Thoughts of the future occupy Pylus' mind. Once Mr. Rye arrives, what will happen? How will he take Ella's decision to leave the high life? And what about Ella asking Pylus to go with her? Is he ready to go back to that way of living? *Guess I'll figure it out as it comes*, he thinks, shutting down all his worries.

Ella finishes her shower and steps out in the black dress. Pylus stands with his mouth open. The dress isn't tight, but it fits her body well, accentuating her gentle curves. The front is lower than she likes as she keeps trying to pull it up. The sleeves barely sit on her shoulders and run all the way to her hands. Silver sequins swirl in matching patterns down her arms and her sides. Even with wet hair, she looks stunning in the dress.

Pylus's roaming eyes make their way up to her face, where they find her smirking with an eyebrow raised, "Enjoying yourself?" she teases.

Pylus simply stares for a moment longer before shutting his mouth and giving her a soft smile. "You look beautiful," he says.

Ella's smirk turns to a full-blown smile, making her look even more radiant. "Thank you," she says, her smile brightening her eyes. "It's all yours."

". . . What?" Pylus asks.

"The shower," she says, pointing, "It's all yours."

"Oh, right. Thanks." Pylus grabs his new suit and ducks into the bathroom. He leans against the door after he closes it. What just happened? Shaking his head, he steps into the shower and turns it on.

Ten minutes later, he stands in front of the mirror in a fresh suit, running his fingers over his head, trying to tame the mangy bush that has grown on top of it. Sighing in defeat, he leaves the bathroom. Ella looks at him from her spot on the couch.

"Need this?" She asks, holding up a brush.

"Think it will work?" Pylus asks.

She shrugs, "I mean, it is meant for hair, so...."

"This isn't hair," Pylus says, pointing at his head, "It's fur."

"Oh, well, in that case, only one way to find out," she gestures to the floor in front of her, "Sit."

Pylus raises his eyebrows, "Treating me like a dog now?"

Ella smiles mischievously, "Be a good boy and I'll get you a treat."

Pylus growls as he takes a seat. Ella runs her fingers through his fur, carefully detangling it. Once she has most of the snarls out, she runs the brush through it. Surprisingly, it only takes a couple of minutes before Pylus' fur looks semi-tamed.

"There. That looks good," Ella says, playing with his fur softly.

"Thanks," Pylus says, running his hand through it as Ella drops her hands to rest on his shoulders, "I don't think it's ever been this soft and smooth," he says with a chuckle.

"Sounds like something a guy would experience," Ella says.

Pylus drops his hands to his lap, playing with a callus on one of them. Ella absentmindedly runs her thumb up and down his neck. The touch is so soft that Pylus hardly realizes she is doing it.

"Do you trust Blane?" Ella asks.

"Not in the slightest," Pylus responds immediately, "I've been on high alert ever since we got here."

Ella nods, "Me too. What do you think is going on?"

"I don't know. But whatever it is, we just have to stay on our toes until we leave with your dad."

"You think Blane was telling the truth about him being here in an hour?"

Pylus thinks for a moment before nodding, "I'm not surprised your dad was going to the other events early in hopes we were there to meet him."

"Let's hope we can get through this quickly and quietly." She looks to the door as if expecting her dad to walk in at that moment. *Would that be more comforting or stressful for me?* She thinks.

A knock on the door startles them both. Pylus jumps to a crouch, instinctively reaching for his knives. He and Ella glance at each other, then back at the door. Slowly, Pylus stands and sheathes his weapons. He makes his way to the door as a second knock sounds. Opening it just a crack, he peeks out to see Oliver waiting impatiently.

"If the two of you are finished *freshening up*, Mr. Blane would like to speak with you," he says sourly.

"Alright, we are ready," Pylus says, opening the door and motioning for Ella.

She joins him at the door, taking his hand in hers as she walks through. Oliver has already begun the descent to the lower floor before they even reach the top of the stairs. Pylus can hear Ella's heartbeat speed up with every step they take. She keeps a strong face, but if her hand weren't being held by Pylus, it would be shaking. By the time they reach the lower floor and start the trek up the opposing stairway, Oliver has already reached the top and rounded the corner.

"He seems to be in more of a hurry than before," Pylus notes.

"I didn't think it was possible for him to walk any faster," Ella says, her voice quivering slightly.

Pylus looks at her as they near the top of the stairs. Her jaw is set, and her eyes are determined, but there is a slight dip at the corner of her mouth. She doesn't have the scent of fear. Her shaking would suggest nervousness, but that doesn't seem quite right either. Even after everything they had been through, Pylus still has trouble reading her at times. Maybe that's just because she's a woman. But still. One would think he would be familiar with how she displays her emotions at this point.

However elusive her current state of being is, Pylus knows that the adventure they have shared has taken its toll on her. She has changed from the sheltered little girl she once was. The woman standing next to him, holding his hand, has a coldness in her eyes. A determination to overcome, mixed with a self-doubt that she ever could. In this moment, determination is winning, but who knows what the next few minutes will bring out. As the familiar smell from earlier catches his attention again, he thinks the latter emotion might get the upper hand.

They reach the top of the stairs and turn the corner to find the door to the office open. Clive Blane leans against the front edge of his desk, talking to someone standing just inside the door. Oliver stands behind the desk with his hands clasped behind his back. Blane's eyes flick from the person he is addressing to Pylus and Ella as they near the door.

His slick, charming smile appears in an instant as he pushes off from his desk, "My, my, don't the two of you look like completely different people! Amazing what a nice shower and some fresh clothes can do, eh?"

Pylus glances to the side when they enter the door to see who Blane was talking to. Just inside the doorway stands a mountain of a man. Nearly seven feet tall and thick as an oak tree, the man watches them with eyes like a hawk. His hooked nose and slicked back, black hair give him the look of one as well. A really, really big hawk.

"I think you're all ready for this evening's activities," Blane continues, "I have to say young man you are truly something else," he gives Pylus a hefty pat on the shoulder with the compliment, "You surprised us all by jumping off a cliff, but then you went and exceeded all expectations by keeping our dear Ella safe for over a week in the wilderness. Who knows how many miles you traveled? And to top it off, being hunted by seven assassins the whole time!"

"What?" Pylus asks, the fur on the back of his neck bristling with a sense of danger.

"You made it all this way through unpopulated wilderness while being hunted by assassins," Blane repeats, "It's a miracle to say the least."

"You said *seven* assassins," Pylus says.

Blane tilts his head slightly, "Did I? Well, I can't be sure how many there were exactly. I didn't get a good look."

"No one else was on the balcony when the assassins attacked us," Pylus says, "so there was no way you could have gotten a good look. And there was too much chaos inside for anyone to care about what we were doing. Unless they were looking for us."

Blane watches Pylus, his smile slowly fading away. The rageful look in his eyes intensifying.

"Also," Pylus continues, his eyes narrowing, "You had already left several minutes before the attacks started. I saw you exit the party immediately after talking to Ella and I."

Blane stands still as a statue. His smile has vanished, his mouth now in a hard line. Hate and rage pulse from his eyes in deadly waves. Oliver's mouth hangs open, his eyes wide.

"You knew about the six server assassins, and you also knew about Leifa Ordonston. You knew she was sent after us," Pylus concludes, "Didn't you?"

"Well then," Blane says after a moment, his voice tight with barely controlled fury, "You continue to *exceed expectations*, Mr. Brek. I didn't peg you as highly perceptive."

"I wouldn't make a very good bodyguard if I weren't," Pylus says.

"Which is unfortunate for me," Blane says, "I see you have already come to the conclusion that I was the one to hire the assassins. You're correct. I also hired Ms. Ordonston as insurance to get you out of the picture. Obviously, I made some miscalculations."

"Why?" whispers a voice. Pylus glances at Ella. She stares wide-eyed at Blane, "What do you want?"

"In short, my dear?" Blane smiles wickedly, "You."

Ella's breath stops. "What?"

"It's simple," Blane explains, "The assassins kill your little *dog*, then kidnap you and bring you to me, where I give you this ultimatum. Agree to marry me, or I ruin your father."

Ella gasps and squeezes Pylus' arm. Pylus moves his eyes around the room, tracing the walls and shelves. While Blane had been talking, he had been listening not just to the words that were being spoken, but to everything else.

"You're lying," he says, letting his eyes fall back on Blane.

"How many times are you going to accuse me of that?" Blane snaps.

"Until you stop," Pylus retorts, "Everything you said was true except for the part about ruining Mr. Rye. Your heart rate changed when you said that. Also, as I listened to your heartbeat, I heard others. Eight to be exact. And unless my counting is off, there's only five of us in here."

The color of Blane's face slowly shifts from a furious red to a panicked white. Oliver's eyes begin to dart from the scene in front of him to the bookshelf to his left.

"Ever since we arrived here, I kept getting whiffs of familiar scents, but they were masked with some sort of scent concealer," Pylus continues, "I couldn't get a good enough smell to remember where I knew them from until you mentioned someone. Mr. Rye. What I'm smelling is his scent. He arrived here before us and has been here the whole time, listening from behind that bookshelf over there," Pylus nods to the corner Oliver keeps eyeing, "Isn't that right, Mr. Rye?"

Nobody moves for several tense seconds. The air itself seems to have frozen. Suddenly, the bookshelf Pylus indicated swings into the room. A figure appears in the opening and steps out to join the group.

"Well. . . that was unexpected," says Jefferson Rye.

25

"Dad?" Ella whispers so quietly that only Pylus can hear. Her hand tightens in his, and the shaking she had been containing takes over her body.

"I must say, Pylus," Mr. Rye says coldly, "I knew you were a good choice to protect my daughter, but never did I think you would do this good of a job. Unfortunately, now it is time for it to end."

"Why?" Pylus asks.

"Well, because I no longer need you, dear boy," Mr. Rye chuckles, "And you tend to get in the way."

"That's not what I'm asking," Pylus growls, "Why are you working with him?" He thrusts his chin at Blane.

"Ah, that. Where to begin?" Mr. Rye rubs his neck and squints at the ceiling, "You remember the big changes I wanted to make to my company that got some negative feedback from my board members?"

Pylus nods in response.

"I didn't get all the responses immediately. When I saw that the votes were shifting away from my favor, I knew I had to take action to ensure my favorable outcome. I told you Mr. Yen was the deciding vote for the proposal, but that wasn't entirely true. He was on the fence for a long while, but he was the second-to-last one to cast his vote. Clive was the last. He was initially going to vote against me, as his primary goal in life is to accumulate as much money as possible. However, after several one-on-one meetings, we came to an agreement to secure his vote in my favor. I knew he had an eye for Ella ever since she grew into a woman. To win his vote, I offered her to him. The only thing was, he had to make her disappear, or else we would have run the risk of her exposing everything.

"I knew Ella would never go along with it, so we devised the assassin plan. Every attempt to take Ella before you showed up, Pylus, was to make it seem as though someone was out to get me by using her. No one would be surprised; it's a common tactic among kidnappers seeking a major payday. I played the part of the concerned father by finding the best security I could for my little girl. Little did I know I got more than I bargained for."

Mr. Rye starts to pace behind Blane's desk, looking confident and almost proud of himself, "Things were going so smoothly. People were concerned but not panicked. They expected another abduction attempt, but not at a gala. The timing was perfect. The assassins would kill you and kidnap Ella. Everyone would panic and wait for the ransom note to come. However, there would never be one. Too late, we would all realize that I was never the target to begin with. It was always Ella.

"Distraught and angry, I would try desperately to find my beloved little girl. However, with limited resources and miles of uninhabited land, we would never be able to. No one would know that she had secretly been brought here to live the rest of her life," he stops pacing and stares at Ella, "as *Mrs.* Clive Blane."

Ella's face pales more than it already has. She stares at her father as if he is a monster, shedding the skin disguise of the man she thought she knew. Which probably wasn't too far off from the truth.

"I would have my way with the company," Mr. Rye continues, "and would forever be able to count on Clive to support me in any decision I make. And Clive would have the only thing he has wanted more than money in his entire life. Now I could have easily just gone ahead with the changes without the majority vote of the investors, but that would have been poor taste and would have lost me several of my most important assets. So, I needed to make the voting look authentic to keep everyone complacent."

Ella stares in horror at the man who can't possibly be her father. The way he talks about giving her away so heartlessly, as if she never meant anything to him, fills her stomach with bile. Her uncontrollable shaking has stopped. She stands motionless with her hand over her mouth. Silent tears stream down her face. If it weren't for her leaning against Pylus, she would probably fall over.

"And you're just willing to go along with this?" Pylus asks.

Rye and Blane exchange a confused look, "Are you talking to me?" Blane asks.

"Obviously not," Pylus sneers, "I told you I heard eight heartbeats. I'm talking to Brit and Phillips. I know they're still in that secret room. I recognized their scents shortly after Mr. Rye's."

As if waiting to be recognized, Brit steps out of the hidden room with his signature deep scowl. Phillips follows closely behind, eyes on the ground, shoulders slumped.

"Undying loyalty, eh, Brit?" Pylus asks.

"Money is the only thing I'm loyal to," Brit says.

Pylus' eyes flick to Phillips, "What about you? You getting enough money to go along with this sick scheme?"

Phillips responds by keeping his gaze on the ground.

"You all disgust me," Pylus spits.

"You don't get as far as we have with morals, kid," Blane says with an evil smile.

"Save your lecture on morality. I gave up everything for this company. Nothing is more important," Rye chimes in, stepping to the front of the desk, "Not even my wife."

Pylus's blood runs cold, and he feels Ella's heart literally skip a beat, "What do you mean?"

Rye looks to the ground as he speaks, "My beautiful Julia. She was the reason I strove so hard to be successful. She always told me I could be so much more than I thought I could. Little did she know I have monstrous dreams. I worked and slaved over my company until it was something amazing. And that was only the beginning. But as my company grew, so did the moral issues I had to face. I knew I would do anything to make my dream a reality. Julia, however, started to get in the way. She would try to talk me into taking the more righteous option, even if it meant holding my company back from its full potential. I didn't need that kind of dead weight in my life, so I removed it."

"NO!" Ella cries out, lunging at her father.

She slams into his chest, knocking him against the desk. Her fingers find their way to his face and begin to claw at it. Rye fights to hold her arms as Brit grabs her around the waist and throws her back at Pylus. He catches her and holds her back from attacking her father again. Brit helps Rye steady himself. Ella's attack did minor damage. Only a single scratch is visible under her father's eye.

"Insolent child," Rye mutters, "I should have just had you kidnapped on one of the nights you tried to sneak out. Would have made my life so much easier even if the story had been harder to believe."

Ella falls into Pylus' chest, sobbing, all the fight drained from her. Pylus looks at the men in the room. Blane and Brit focus on Rye, who delicately touches the small scratch under his eye. Oliver watches wide-eyed from his corner. Phillips looks at Pylus for the first time, revealing something in his eyes. Shame.

"Ella, listen to me," Pylus whispers quickly, "Make a run for it."

Ella stops sobbing when he speaks. She stays still for a moment, then slowly nods her head.

"Now!"

Pylus pivots backward, keeping Ella in front of him. Releasing his hold on her, he springs forward, latching onto the man standing guard by the door. He plants his feet on the man's hips and grips his shoulders tightly. Voices break out as Ella rushes out the door. The man Pylus hangs onto grabs Pylus' hips and throws him backward like a doll. Pylus rotates midair to land on his shoulder and roll to a crouch in front of Blane and Rye. Phillips watches with wide eyes, but Brit is gone. It won't be long before he catches up to Ella.

Pylus darts towards the door only to be met with the mountain man again. The massive man reaches to grab him with one hand. Pylus ducks to the side, throwing a quick punch to the man's liver. The man barely grunts at the impact of the strike and quickly swings his arm sideways in an attempt to clothesline Pylus. Barely ducking in time, Pylus jumps away to get a second opening. He reaches for his knives and crouches. Just as he is about to rush the man, something hits the back of his neck.

The world swirls around him. All his muscles lose their strength and ability to move. Sounds and smells blur together. He feels himself falling, then hitting something solid. No matter how hard he tries, he can't get his body to work. Darkness flits around the edges of his unfocused vision. A scream pierces the cotton in his ears. One of his arms starts to respond, and he pushes himself onto his elbow. He shakes his head to clear some of the clutter with little success. All of a sudden, his body begins to move. Someone has shifted him into a sitting position with his back against a hard surface. The mess of colors that he sees begins to take shape, forming blurry outlines.

One of the shapes moves close to him and says, "Good try, young man. But this ends tonight."

The shape moves away towards another larger shape. Pylus can now distinguish between people and objects. He assumes the one who just spoke to him was Blane, and the big one is the mountain. He can see something moving erratically just past Blane. A voice shouting his name comes from the same direction. Ella. He shakes his head again, this time getting some result. Ella fights against Brit just outside the room. Rye and Phillips stand with him. Blane is talking to the mountain with Oliver close behind him.

"Have fun," Blane says, patting the mountain on the shoulder, then walks out with Oliver.

The mountain closes the door behind them and cracks his neck as he turns around. By now, Pylus's vision has cleared, but his head feels like a lead balloon.

"I'm going to enjoy this," the mountain rumbles.

Using the desk for support, Pylus pulls himself to his feet, "Not as much as you think."

"We'll see," the behemoth sneers as he charges at Pylus, covering the distance between them in two steps.

Pylus slips to the side, parrying the mountain's outstretched arms. Unable to stop his momentum, the mountain slams into the desk, bracing his hands on the top to keep from falling over it. Pylus brings his hand down in a quick arc, stabbing a pen he had grabbed into the mountain's hand. The man screams and swings his arm sideways, sweeping Pylus off his feet. A large decorative urn on the edge of the room shatters as Pylus flies into it.

The mountain grips the pen sticking out of his hand and yanks it out. Blood drips from his wound onto the carpet, where he drops the improvised weapon. Pylus stands slowly, keeping his eyes on the man.

"Part gorilla?" Pylus asks.

The mountain cocks his head to the side, "How could you tell?"

"I knew you were a hybrid from the smell," Pylus says, shaking out the arm he had fallen on, "I figured it had to be gorilla from how far you threw me with one arm. Either that or bear. However, you don't have any other bearlike characteristics."

"Impressive," the mountain says with a smirk, "I guess you got a lot of experience identifying hybrids in Champion."

"Even more killing them," Pylus says.

"Not this one," the mountain says.

He rushes Pylus again. Pylus grabs a chunk of the destroyed urn and slings it at him. Barely dodging the projectile, the mountain swings a massive arm at Pylus in a deadly hammer fist. Pylus raises his own arm to block the strike. The force of the swing lifts Pylus off his feet and throws him for the third time. He twists in the air, dragging his claws lightly across the floor. As his momentum slows, he plants his hands and drops his feet to the ground. There's no way he can outmuscle this guy.

The mountain jumps in the air, both arms behind his head. Pylus rolls to the side as both fists slam into the floor where he was. Twisting quickly, he slashes across the mountain's tricep with his claws. The mountain roars and swings wildly with both arms. Pylus jumps sideways onto the desk. The mountain picks up the chair behind the desk and swings. Bending low, Pylus ducks back under the chair, then springs backwards, flipping off the desk. He lands as the chair comes hurtling at him, the wheel on the bottom grazing his cheek as it sails past.

Pylus reaches for his knives but only finds air. They must have been taken when Blane hit him, "Looks like I'm doing this the old-fashioned way."

26

Ella paces back and forth in the room that she had waited in earlier with Pylus. Blane had her locked in here after leaving Pylus in the study. She had already pounded on the door and yelled profanities at everyone involved. She hadn't expected it to do anything, but it did make her feel a little better.

Her pacing has less to do with her nerves and more with her search. She scours the room for some way to escape or, at the very least, a weapon. All the windows are solid glass panes that can't be opened. The only way in or out is through the door to the hallway. She's sure someone will be standing guard there. As far as weapons go, she has a vase holding some flowers, a small book about birds, and a plunger she found in the bathroom. She contemplates throwing something through the window and jumping out, but the fall would most likely be more hurtful than helpful.

She runs her hands through her hair, frustrated as questions crush her mind. How had her father been able to lie to her so easily? How could he be so heartless? How had she not seen this before? Did she really mean that little to him? Why would he hire Pylus instead of one of his cronies who's in on the plan? Is Pylus okay? Will he be able to get out of this one? If he does, will he be able to help her? Can she help herself?

The door to the hallway unlocks, interrupting her self-reflection. It opens to reveal her father, followed by Brit, Clive Blane, and Phillips, who stays in the doorway. Brit steps just to the side, probably to keep her from making another run for it.

"How are you, my dear?" her father asks, laying a hand on her shoulder.

She shrugs his hand away, stepping out of his reach, "What do you want?"

"We've come to make a deal with you," Blane says, taking a seat on the couch, "A deal for the life of your *mutt*." His characteristic debonair smile is gone, replaced with a thin line that bleeds impatience and irritation.

"So, he's alive?" Ella sighs with relief.

"For now," Blane says, "I told my man to subdue him but keep him alive. Our offer to you is simple. If you want him to live, then don't resist."

Ella looks from Blane to her father, then to Phillips and Brit. They all look at her expectantly, except Phillips, who keeps his eyes on the ground.

"So, what's the plan?" She asks, "We go downstairs and act like everything is normal during the party, then after everyone leaves, I stay here for the rest of my life?"

"Not exactly," her father answers, "We will make an appearance at the party, but we will say that you are exhausted from your journey and would like to rest. You and I will take our leave, at which point I will drive you to one of Clive's private mountain retreats. There you will wait for him to come join you. We will tell everyone that your "boyfriend" died valiantly trying to protect you from the assassins who were tailing you. It was only by his sacrifice that you were able to make it back to me alive.

"After the events of the gala, Clive is planning to move to the Shank Settlement to assist me in the transition of company policy. During that time, we will tell everyone that he has been most kind in helping you overcome your grief from losing Pylus and the trauma you faced these past few days. Over the course of a few weeks, you will start having feelings for him, and by the time he leaves, you will want nothing more than to be with him. You will return here and stay as his wife."

Ella looks at Blane with as much disgust and contempt as she can muster. Blane simply smiles at her, making her already burning rage explode. She grabs the flower vase and flings it at his stupid, arrogant face. He barely moves in time to keep his face from being smashed. The vase sails over the couch and crashes on the ground. Pieces of porcelain skid across the floor, shredding the flowers.

"I hate you!" She screams as her father grabs her to keep her from attacking Blane further.

Blane stands and straightens his suit, "Looks like you're not going to cooperate. You will go along with this plan one way or another. We were just giving you the option to save the hybrid," he turns to look at Brit, "Go tell Gib to finish off the mutt."

"No!" Ella yells, "Wait, please, wait! Don't kill him, please! Don't kill him!"

Brit hesitates as Blane turns to look at Ella, an evil look in his eye as he growls, "Then behave."

Ella stares at his heartless eyes. A lifetime with this monster? No. She just has to go along with him long enough for Pylus to get free and far away. After that, she can find a way to get out. Whatever that may be. But she can't let them kill Pylus. She can't.

"Fine," she spits, "I agree."

Blane smirks in triumph, "Good. No more shenanigans either. One more like this," he gestures to the shattered vase, "and your pet is dead." He turns to Brit and mutters something quietly, then turns back to Ella.

Her father lets go of her and rubs his hand over his eyes. Brit steps forward to guide her out of the room. Quietly, without anyone noticing, Phillips sneaks away.

***

Books lining the shelves of the study wobble as Pylus slams into the wall. He crumbles to the ground, breathing heavily. The mountain, Gib, lumbers his way across the room. He stops and towers over Pylus before reaching to yank him off the ground. Just before he can grab anything, Pylus twists his neck, sinking his teeth into Gib's hand. The same one he had stabbed earlier.

Gib screams and tries to yank his hand back. Pylus keeps his teeth clenched, letting Gib's yank pull him into the air. Releasing his bite, he plants his feet on Gib's hips and grasps his shoulder with his left hand. He shoots his right hand forward, sinking his claws into Gib's face. The big man instinctively pulls his head back, trying to get away from the pain, which gives Pylus the opening he needs. Putting all his strength into his right arm, Pylus pushes Gib's head back as far as he can, exposing the throat. Gib grabs the back of Pylus' shirt to pull him off, but it's too late. Pylus bares his fangs and sinks them into the vulnerable jugular. The man wobbles and chokes for a moment before falling backward. Pylus steps to the floor as his perch crumbles from beneath him. The floor shakes when Gib's massive body bounces off it. Then everything goes silent.

Pylus spits out the wad of flesh he had ripped from Gib's throat. The lump hits the floor with a sickening splat. Blood streaks cover the lower half of his face, slowly merging together. Crimson drops fall silently, forming a puddle on the carpet.

"The bigger they are, the harder they fall," he mutters, sitting on the ground.

His back screams in pain from slamming into the bookshelves. He should be running after Ella right now, but his legs can't seem to work. No matter how hard he tries, he can't get his body to respond right. The exertion from his fight, combined with the lingering effects of being knocked out, is taking its toll on him. Now that his adrenaline has worn off, he can feel all the pain. His eyes blur, then sharpen, then blur again. His nostrils burn every time he breathes in. Every smell mixes together, further throwing off his concentration.

Closing his eyes helps dampen the growing nausea caused by the conflicting senses. *I need to get to Ella*, he thinks while simultaneously thinking about how he might throw up. *I need to go.* Trying to stand proves futile as his legs shake and his arms feel like jelly. *She needs me.* Gritting his teeth, he tries to stand again, only to have his arms give out as he pushes himself up.

He lies on his back, eyes closed, praying to anything that can hear him. "Please," he says out loud, "Let me help her. After that, I don't care what happens to me. Please."

Hurried footsteps sound from outside the study. The door opens, and the footsteps hurry over to Pylus. Something slips under his head, lifting it slightly. A muffled voice speaks to him in an urgent tone, but no matter how hard he tries, he can't make out what it's saying. He cracks one eye open to see a blurred figure crouching over him. The shape moves, putting an object under his nose.

At first, nothing happens. *Is it a drink?* Pylus thinks, but then his nostrils start to tingle. One smell pierces through all the others, subtle at first but growing in strength until. . .

Coughing, nose burning, and eyes watering, Pylus shoots up, wiping his nose and eyes, trying to clear out the obtrusive aroma. He shakes his head and snorts until everything clears up. Within seconds, he can see the room clearly. Gib lies where he fell, his blood pooling on the floor. Books, papers, and furniture lay in disarray. Phillips crouches next to him, holding a small bottle.

"Phillips?" Pylus says.

"Come on we got to go," Phillips says, stashing the bottle in his pocket.

"What?" Pylus asks warily, "Go where?"

Phillips looks at him as if the answer should be obvious: "To save Ella."

"I thought you were on board with Rye's plan," Pylus says, keeping an eye on Phillips.

"I only pretended to go along with it until I could find a time to get Ella out of here," Phillips explains as he moves to the door, "But since you're here, I think you can do a better job than I can."

Unconvinced, Pylus stays where he is. Phillips looks back as he steps out of the room, halting when he notices Pylus hasn't moved. "What are you doing?" he asks.

"I don't trust you," Pylus says.

Phillips rolls his eyes and says, "If I didn't want to help you, why would I come back for you instead of just killing you where you lay?"

Good point, Pylus thinks. If Phillips had any kind of nefarious intent, it didn't make sense for him to help Pylus back to full function.

"What did you use to clear my head?" Pylus asks.

"Smelling salts," Phillips says, "Smelling blood makes me nauseous, so I keep a bottle of salts on me just in case."

"Interesting. I'm still not sure about you, though," Pylus admits. "What's your plan?"

"We don't have. . ." Phillips sighs impatiently and looks to the stairwell, "Alright, fine. Here's the quick version. Rodgers and I are planning on jumping Rye as he tries to leave with Ella. Blane and he have this elaborate plan to make it seem like Ella falls in love with Blane and goes to live with him. Tonight, Rye and Ella will make a brief appearance at the party, then excuse themselves, citing that Ella has been through a lot and needs her rest.

"While Rye is going about fraternizing with all the bigwigs, we will keep going about our duties like nothing is wrong. When an opportunity comes, Rodgers will distract Rye and Brit while I sneak Ella out. Rye and Brit think we're both on board with them, so nobody knows what Rodgers and I plan to do and won't suspect us of anything. Until it's too late."

"So, what do you want me to do?" Pylus asks.

"Stay hidden in case anything goes sideways. Once we have Ella out of the building, you take her and a vehicle and high-tail it out of here. Take her somewhere safe where no one will ever find her and give her the life she deserves," Phillips says.

"What will happen to you when Rye finds out you let Ella go?"

Phillips smiles mischievously, "Oh, I'll make it look like I put up a fight, but if Pylus Brek can take down that thing," he motions to Gib's body, "I'm obviously no match for him. Once everyone takes off on the wild goose chase to find you and Ella, Rodgers and I will slip away unnoticed and find our own lives to live."

Pylus stares at Phillips silently for several seconds. "Alright, I'm in," he says finally, "Let's go."

27

"Anything?" Phillips asks Rodgers who stands hidden at the top of the stairway, looking down.

"Rye and Ella passed by two minutes ago," Rodgers says, his voice surprisingly soft given his rough look, "Brit and Blane just passed."

Phillips nods and steps onto the first step, "Let's move."

He leads the way, quickly descending the stairs with Rodgers and Pylus close behind. They travel down and round the corner, coming face to face with Clive Blane. Phillips freezes, causing Rodgers to bump into him.

"What are you..." Blane's eyes settle on Pylus as he rounds the corner. Disbelief and rage fill his eyes as he realizes the betrayal. "Son of a... "

His curse gets cut off by Phillips' fist. Blane's head snaps back as Phillips hisses at Pylus to go. Together, he and Rodgers rush Blane, pinning him to the wall. Rodgers clamps his hand over Blane's mouth, stifling his attempt to cry out.

Pylus darts past the struggle, heading for the open doorway at the end of the hallway. Voices of gathering guests drift in from the ballroom, growing in volume the closer he gets. Suddenly, the light from the ballroom disappears as a figure steps into the doorway.

"You?!" Brit exclaims when he sees Pylus.

Instead of replying, Pylus drops his shoulder and slams into Brit's chest. Together they fall to the ground, landing in a heap. Brit grunts heavily, and his head smacks the ground. Pylus rolls forward over Brit's head, ending at the top of the stairs in a crouch. He quickly scans the growing crowd of arriving guests, searching for his prey. He sees them moving through the sea of people, halfway to the door, mingling with guests, but still moving with purpose. Rye keeps a hand on the small of Ella's back. An indiscernible form of control. Ella looks obviously uncomfortable. Most people probably think she's just worn out from the ordeal she's been through.

"RYE!" Pylus roars over the din of the crowd.

Amid the confused head turns, Pylus sees fear explode across Rye's face. Grabbing Ella gruffly by the arm, he directs his attention to the front door. Pylus growls as he launches himself into the air. He flies over the set of stairs and lands on the ballroom floor, rolling with the impact. Guests gasp and scatter away from him, creating an opening right to the fleeing figure of Jefferson Rye.

"Ella!" Pylus yells, sprinting towards her.

"Pylus!" she calls back, fighting her father to be able to face her bodyguard.

Two guards that Pylus recognizes but never learned the names of step out of the crowd, blocking Pylus's path to Ella. He growls without slowing. Before he can reach them, a third figure appears behind them. The new figure leaps into the air, wrapping its arms around the neck of one guard and its legs around the other. Pylus skids to a stop at the turn of events. Ming, the Chinese bodyguard to Mr. Yen, lies on the floor, the two guards wrapped tightly by his limbs, their faces already turning blue.

"GO!" Ming yells.

Pylus snaps out of his stupor, looking for Ella and Rye. The pathway that had opened remains so. Rye fights to keep his daughter moving forward as she struggles to break free from his grasp. Guests stare at the unfolding events, unsure of what to do. Arriving guests continue to flow in from the outdoors, impeding Rye's escape.

Pylus jumps over Ming and his victims, catching up to Rye. Wrapping him around the waist, he yanks him away from Ella. Rye stumbles away, falling into other guests. Wondering eyes dart from Pylus to Rye and back as the crowd backs further away from them.

"Pylus, let's get out of here," Ella says, grabbing his shoulder.

"You read my mind," he says, taking her hand.

They start towards the door when something slams into Pylus from behind. He falls to the ground, smashing his nose on the tile.

Whatever struck him falls to the ground next to him. Rolling to his side reveals his assailant. Brit crouches, fury ablaze in his eyes, one hand falling quickly. The fist strikes Pylus before he can move. His already impaired nose cracks from the impact. Blood splatters across the tile as tears fill his eyes. A roar of feral rage rips from his throat. He lunges at Brit only to be batted away, his watering eyes disabling his sight and depth perception.

Rye, having gotten back to his feet, grabs Ella around the waist again and drags her towards the door. Pylus dries his eyes, Brit looming over him, a beacon of doom, his fist already pulled back, ready to fall. Suddenly, an arm appears from behind Brit, wrapping his raised fist and yanking him away from Pylus. The force of the pull lifts the guard's feet off the ground, rolling them over his head, then bashes him onto the floor. In his place stands Phillips, clothes ruffled and askew, breathing heavily.

"Rodgers?" Pylus asks.

"He's fine, go!" Phillips responds, keeping his eyes on Brit.

Pylus leaps to his feet, looking desperately for Ella. He sees her being forced through the crowd by Rye. Arriving guests continue to occlude the small entrance, slowing Rye's escape and giving Pylus an opportunity.

Suddenly, screams erupt around the room, causing Pylus and Rye both to hesitate. Pylus looks behind him to see Phillips holding Brit's hand above his head. In Brit's hands, a sleek black object points at the ceiling. A deafening explosion of sound ricochets through the room, causing the screams to elevate in pitch and intensity. The intrigue that held guests back from leaving the scene erupts into full-fledged panic.

Terrified, onlookers rush the already congested entryway, colliding with confused arriving guests, resulting in a disconcerting mob trying to move in two separate directions. Neither group makes any progress. The more desperate, fleeing guests resort to more confrontational means of flight by shoving those who get into their way to the ground and trampling them. In the midst of all the madness, Rye tries to cling to his daughter.

Above the clamor of the competing forces, a voice bellows, "PYLUS BREK!"

Clive Blane stands atop the grand staircase, face bruised and clothes torn. His usually perfect hair hangs in his face, giving him a barbaric look. He raises a shaking finger pointing at Pylus, "I'M GOING TO KILL YOU, YOU SON OF A... "

A blur of motion catches Blane in the back, plummeting them down the stairs. The mesh of limbs rolls and bounces off stone and each other, ending in a heap on the ballroom floor.

"Rodgers!" Phillips screams, still struggling with Brit.

Slowly, the stocky bodyguard rises to his feet, using the banister as support. Blane remains motionless on the ground, a pool of blood forming around his paling face.

Pylus turns his attention back to Ella. She has broken free from her father, fighting through the crowd towards him. He rushes to the edge of the mob, reaching over heads and shoulders. Ella stretches out her hand, catching hold of his. Together, they force her between the few remaining barriers separating them. One last tug frees Ella from the throng. She falls forward, collapsing into Pylus' arms.

The joyful reunion is short-lived. Rye emerges from the dispersing crowd, eyes burning with the fires of Hell. He brandishes one of Pylus' knives in his hand with a white-knuckle grip. Pylus steps around Ella, putting himself between her and her father.

With a cry of fury, Rye charges, stabbing quickly at Pylus' abdomen. Pylus cats back, blocking the strike down and moving to the outside of Rye's knife hand. With his other hand, Rye reaches behind his back and pulls out the other knife.

The air stales around Pylus as Rye's hand moves. The chandelier light gleams off the blade, streaking across Pylus' eyes. The knife cuts straight through the air, but its target isn't Pylus. Ella's eyes widen as she realizes the knife's direction. Pylus' heart freezes, but his body reacts without thought. Rye's eyes, full of hatred, burn into his daughter.

The knife finds a home.

Ella screams.

Rye sucks in a breath.

Pylus stares into the eyes of the man holding the knife now embedded in his stomach.

28

Two knives. One protrudes from his abdomen. The other arching towards his chest in a deadly fall. The very weapons that had protected him and kept him alive on countless occasions would now be the death of him. A beautiful irony, one might call it, or a cruel one. But Pylus has no more need for protection. He is now the protector. This time, he will do what he couldn't before. Edith, his sister, his wife, Ellie, George, and Chip. He couldn't save them. But he can save Ella.

One hand grips the wrist that holds the knife protruding from his stomach, the other catches the falling blade before it can strike him as its counterpart had. He holds Rye's arms in place, letting the fear in his enemy grow. He can see it in the eyes and smell it in the sweat.

In one quick motion, he twists the wrist holding the upper knife while digging his claws into the soft flesh and tendons. Rye screams in pain, the knife he had been holding clatters to the ground, and the other stays in Pylus' stomach as he lets go of it and scampers back.

Two gunshots pierce the air, followed by a scream, then another gunshot. Pylus looks back to see Rodgers and Brit lying on the floor. Phillips holds his hands over Rodgers's chest, trying in vain to staunch the heavy flow of blood. Brit lies with part of his skull missing, eyes vast and empty.

From behind, metal clinks lightly on the tile floor. Pylus whips around, barely blocking Rye's arm as he stabs with the fallen knife. Rye cradles his injured arm to his chest, using his good one to attack over and over. Pylus can barely keep himself out of the attack range. The knife in his stomach limits his evasion ability and sends searing pain through his torso with every movement.

Ella steps back, keeping Pylus' retreat path clear as he struggles to stay out of Rye's reach. Rye moves with a ferocity that can only be fueled by insanity. The man she used to call dad is unrecognizable to her now.

With a fake stab and a quick flick, Rye catches Pylus' arm with the knife, dragging the blade along the underside of his forearm from the elbow to his wrist. Pylus cries out as he pulls his arm closer to his body. Distracted by the new wound, he trips over himself and clumsily falls to the floor.

Rye stands over him, shaking with rage. "Your days are over, mutt," he says in a voice that is not his own.

The crazed man swings the knife to deliver a final blow. Suddenly, a hand appears, catching the wrist and pulling it away. Phillips, hands stained with blood, wrestles with Rye for the knife. Dropping his hands to waist level, Rye throws his head forward, smashing it into Phillips's nose. Phillips yelps, releasing Rye's hands. Light flashes off the blade as it slices across Phillips's face. The man who had saved Pylus's life several times in the last few minutes screams a second time and falls to the floor, holding a hand over half his face.

Confident of his victory, Rye turns to face Pylus again. The hybrid lay on his side, trying to make his way to Brits' discarded gun. With a conceited snort, Rye casually walks to the gun and kicks it away just before Pylus can grab it. Crouching down, he lifts Pylus' beaten face with the tip of the knife.

Ella whimpers softly off to the side. She wills herself to move and fight as she did with Leifa, but her muscles won't respond. She can't let Pylus die, but can she really fight her own father? The uncertainty keeps her rooted to the spot where she stands, watching the horrifying events unfold.

"I'll be honest, Pylus, you exceeded my expectations several times over. You are much harder to kill than I anticipated. I mean, you just won't give up, will you?" Rye says, "But in the end you still die."

"I won't go alone," Pylus growls, revealing the knife that had been in his stomach, now in his hand.

Rye's eyes widen. Too late, he tries to slice Pylus's throat, but, already one step ahead, Pylus twists his shoulders and neck, moving out of the path of the swooping blade. Letting gravity work in his favor, Pylus falls to the floor, bringing his knife hand forward, directly into Jefferson Rye's throat. Rye's surprised gasp turns into strangled gurgling as blood fills his airway. He drops his weapon, falling back, weakly grabbing at the handle sticking out of his jugular. Seconds tick by, Rye's dying the only sound in the room, the hysterical crowd having found their way to the safety outside. Finally, everything stills as Rye's dying sounds fade to nothing.

Moments pass, and no one moves. Ella sits by Phillips, holding a ripped piece of cloth against his face. Phillips stares with his good eye at the line of bodies across the floor. Pylus stares at the ceiling, breathing hard, his wounded stomach and arm bleeding profusely.

"I did it," he whispers to himself.

The design of the ceiling swirls in his vision, giving the impression of ethereal beings looking down on him. He swears he can see faces. Chip and George look down with pride in their eyes. George gives him a quick wink, then they disappear. Ellie smiles her beautiful smile for him and blows a kiss. His sister appears with Edith. They wave to him, Edith looking like how he feels a mother should when her child accomplishes something great. His sister smirks at him like she has another secret for him to find out. Mya, his wife, forms slowly. She gives him her knowing grin, something she always did when she knew something he didn't. She blows a kiss to him, then turns away, beckoning him to follow. His eyes start to blur. The fading silhouette becomes a solid being calling his name.

"Pylus. Pylus! PYLUS!" the voice calls hysterically.

He opens his eyes, unsure of when they actually closed. The blurry figure hovers over him. Slowly, details come into focus, palpable features making their way into his realm of understanding. Strands of auburn hair hang down, caressing his face softly. Light, soft skin molds from an indiscernible blob to a detailed visage. Full, gloss-coated lips call his name over and over again. The nose and ears form their way out of the mesh of color. Lastly, beautiful, familiar, green eyes pierce through his mind fog.

Suddenly, surprise and recognition hit him harder than the floor had.

"Ella," he whispers.

"Oh, thank goodness," Ella gasps, cradling his head in her lap, "I thought you were gone."

"Not yet," he says with a weak smile, "Are you alright?"

She nods, biting her lip, "Just a little shaken is all."

"How is Phillips?"

"Still kicking," Phillips says, moving into view. Blood flows freely down his neck, but the makeshift bandage over his eye seems to be slowing the stream.

"Will your eye be okay?" Pylus asks.

Phillips shrugs, "Probably not. Good thing I got an extra."

Pylus tries to chuckle, but only gets a weak cough. Blood leaks out of the corner of his mouth and from his mashed nose.

"Ella," he says quietly.

"I'm here, Pylus," She says, stroking his cheek softly, "It's okay. Everything is going to be okay."

He takes her hand in his, holding it as tight as he can with his failing strength, "Now is your chance to live the life you want. The life we were talking about."

Ella nods but doesn't say anything. Tears stream down her face, dripping onto his. The warm water runs down his cheeks, leaving trails of heat across his skin; every other sensation fades into numbness.

"Don't hold onto today," Pylus continues, "Move on when you can. Let your life be happy."

"I will," Ellas sobs, "but you're going to make sure of that. You'll be there with me. You promised."

Pylus smiles softly, "I've already done everything I can."

"No!" Ella sobs, "No, Pylus. You're going to be okay. We're going to get you better. The life I want is a life with you! You promised to come with me!"

"I'm sorry," Pylus whispers, a single tear of his own running down his cheek to mix with Ella's, "that's one promise I can't keep."

"Pylus, please!" Ella begs through choking sobs, "Please don't leave me! I don't know what I'll do without you! I need you, Pylus. *I need you.*"

He slowly reaches to her face and brushes her cheek, wiping away tears, only to have them be replaced immediately by new ones, "I will never truly leave you. Take it from me, we don't ever lose the ones we love. They stay with us through their memories and in the lessons they taught us. I will forever be with you. I promise."

He drops his hand from her cheek, unable to hold it up any longer; it lands over the rings around his neck, "My love will always be with you," he whispers.

"Pylus," Ella whispers, nearly inaudibly. Her tears and sorrow taking away her ability to speak correctly.

The last thing Pylus sees is her. Beautiful, kind, incredibly annoying but endearing, Ella. The last thing he feels is an overwhelming sense of love for her and everything she is. Then the darkness creeps across his vision and pulls him into oblivion.

***

Weightlessness washes over him in waves of serenity. The pain he had felt scorching his body fades into the void that surrounds him. He floats alone, for the first time in a long time, feeling at peace. His body feels different somehow. Perhaps it's the sensation of floating in nothing. No. There's something different, yet familiar.

From above him, or in front of him, he can't tell the direction, a light appears. Its rays condescending lightly, almost lovingly, toward him, enveloping him in its warmth. The tendrils wrap around him, gently pulling him into their embrace. He glides into the light, feeling renewed and whole. People emerge from the brightness, smiling with their arms open. Their faces become clear as he crosses the celestial threshold. Ellie, Chip, George, Edith, a man and a woman he knows as his parents, even though he never met them, his sister, and his wife, Mya. One by one, they embrace him and let their love wash over him. As they do, he looks at them and realizes that they truly never really left him. They were always with him. His family.

Epilogue

My name used to be Ella Rye. Now it's just Ella. One year ago today, my father tried to sell me off for a business profit. My life was almost given away without my consent at my expense. I would have lived as a wife to a pernicious snake, little more than a slave or a trophy to be shown off to all his creepy snake friends.

But things didn't go the way my father planned. All thanks to him. The man who fought for me with everything he had, even though I didn't deserve it. He gave me a new perspective on worth. Until his last breath, he always tried to help me live a better life. He brought me true happiness and gave me the confidence I needed. He showed me life in a way I never could have imagined and helped me through the darkest parts of it so I could enjoy the beautiful ones. He showed me true unconditional love. In return, I gave him my heart.

Pylus Brek. The man who fought harder for me than anyone ever has. The only man I have ever loved. The man I never got to express my feelings to, and now I never will. A piece of my heart died the day he did.

After the events of Blane Manor, Phillips and I made our way to the small valley where Pylus had lived the days of his youth. We found Edith's boys and have been living with them for the past year.

It's been a quiet life in these mountains. Winter is harsh, but spring is beautiful. There's no end to the majestic artwork of nature in this valley. We work hard to provide for ourselves, and when the work is done, we spend time together as a family.

The moment we arrived, Edith's boys couldn't wait to introduce us to their families. All three are married with ten kids among the three couples. It's hard to distinguish which child belongs to which parent, as they all look similar and run freely between each house, spending the night wherever they feel like. Most of the time, it's outside when the weather is nice, and when it's not, they all plop down in the living room, piled around the fireplace.

There are others among this little home of ours. An older gentleman named Pete, a middle-aged couple, Ray and Jan, and three teenagers, Rib, Hal, and Fred, who found their way here from up north. Together we create our home.

Brock, Joseph, and Billy mourned with me when I told them about Pylus. The day we buried him, we sat around a fire telling stories of him and the things he accomplished in life. We reminisced on his humor and drive. The boys shared stories of Pylus' youth and the shenanigans he would get them into and out of. I talked about the days I spent with him reading in break rooms during the gala trips and our time in the safe house when we first met. Brock especially liked the story of when I tried to sneak out the first night I met Pylus. He shook his head and muttered, "Stubborn old boy". That night, we kept Pylus alive for one more night and then with us through our memories and the impact he had on our lives.

Today, I stand amidst a small gathering of buildings, looking at three headstones. One weathered and stained from years of seasons passing. The other two are crisper and more polished. Only mildly worn.

EDITH. BELOVED MOTHER TO ALL, reads the older headstone. Wilting flowers lay at the base, placed there weeks ago by the boys on Edith's birthday.

This time of year, wildflowers are all dormant in preparation for the cold winter months. Thanks to Joseph's wife, Jane, however, beautiful flowers are in bloom year-round in her greenhouse, keeping color in their lives. Today I hold a bouquet of these vibrant blossoms. Kneeling in the brown grass, I place them at the base of one of the newer headstones.

PYLUS (SLICK) BREK. ALWAYS IN OUR HEARTS. It reads. One year ago, today. It seems like it only just happened, and like it was an eternity ago at the same time. I finger the two rings that hang on a nail embedded in the headstone, remembering the times I watched Pylus play with them as they hung around his neck. I brush the dirt away from his name, picturing his face. I remember our first, tense encounters, back when I was conceited and irresponsible. It's a wonder he didn't throw me off the roof that first night.

I relive our walk through the woods the day before the first attack from Sting. The memory guides me to times when we shared a meal I had prepared and the fight training he had given me that saved my life more than once. I think about him sharing his books with me and convincing me to actually try reading. A small smile creeps across my lips, thinking of him sleeping on my floor the nights I was scared to be alone.

Tears fill my eyes as I think about the galas we attended with Pylus pretending to be my boyfriend. Even though it was a facade, I felt more comfortable with him in those moments than I ever had with anyone before. Even with his brooding attitude, Pylus had a way of putting me at ease. That stupidly annoying trait made it impossible for me to stay mad at him. Even before we jumped off that balcony, I had come to rely on him as my safe place. I could drop my guard with him.

Our travels through the wilderness flick through my mind quickly. Those aren't times I put effort into remembering. The high-speed slide show in my mind halts on the memory that I love most. We were sitting in the guest room at Blane Manor, and he smiled at me. No words were spoken; he just smiled. That smile told me everything would be okay because we were together.

The tears that I have been holding back burst through my emotional dam. They stream down my face, dropping into the flowers I brought. I cry. I cry for the first time since Pylus took his last breath. I cry as if I had just lost him again. I cry over the times we never got to have together. I cry because I have the life I wanted, but not with the person I wanted to share it with. I cry knowing that every good moment I spent with him could have been so much better. I cry for a future I will never get to experience. I cry until there's nothing left. I cry.

My breaths come in shaky intervals as my tears dry, my eyes having nothing left to offer. My breathing slows to normal as a hand rests on my shoulder. I don't turn to see who it is. I already know. Phillips takes a knee next to me, placing his own flower next to the ones I dropped while crying.

Phillips has been there with me in my grief. Rodgers had given his life to save Phillips and, indirectly, me. Unknown to most, Rodgers and Phillips were stepbrothers. Phillips told me they had been together since they were three years old. Losing his eye was nowhere near as painful as losing that constant in his life. The slash across his face healed, leaving behind a thin scar and a useless eye, but nothing has helped in healing the loss of his brother. These days, he wears an eyepatch to cover up the disfigured eye and a smile to cover his ruined soul.

"I can't believe it's been a year," he whispers, dropping his hand from my shoulder. He places a second flower on the third headstone. IVAN RODGERS. ALWAYS THERE WHEN NEEDED, it reads. A single tear rolls down Phillips' cheek.

"I know, at the same time I feel like it's been longer," I say.

"Funny how time does that."

I smile a little but don't say anything else.

"Before I forget," Phillips says, handing me an envelope, "Ming stopped by and dropped off a letter for you."

I take the envelope and open it. Mr. Yens' neat handwriting spreads across the page. After the fiasco at Blane Manor, I inherited all of my father's company shares. I promptly gave complete ownership to Mr. Yen. After my father had made the controversial changes to his company's affairs, Mr. Yen had suspected something deeper was going on. He had investigated the proceedings afterward and come across Phillips. Phillips, having been in on the whole scandal from the beginning, told him everything. Mr. Yen decided to keep an eye on my father and me during the gala trips and make a move to get me out when he could. Turns out, he didn't need to worry.

I read the letter quickly.

I fold the letter and slip it back into the envelope. Mr. Yen has good intentions, even if the letters he sends don't do much to help me feel better. He sends one a month, and I take the time to send a response, letting him know how life is in our simple part of the world.

"Do you think you've done it?" Phillips asks suddenly.

I look at him, confused, "Done what?"

"What he told you to do," he nods at Pylus' headstone, "Do you think you've let go of the past? Found the life you want?"

I look at the ground, then back at the headstones. Much of my time in the valley has been spent helping wherever I can, staying busy to keep my mind preoccupied with mundane tasks. Doing so prevents me from seeking answers I know I won't get. The first couple of months, I mourned. I hardly smiled, and when my jobs were done, I spent time by myself wandering through the mountains. Lately, however, I've found myself laughing and wanting to spend time with my new family. I play with the kids, talk with the adults, sing songs around the campfires, and read books we find in the old libraries. I enjoy life.

I hadn't noticed it until now, but the hollow feeling left from losing Pylus is slowly abating. The deceased piece of my strained heart had, at some point, unbeknownst to me, begun beating again. Nothing will ever replace Pylus, but the love I had for him is slowly being placed somewhere else. It's going to the laugh of a toddler, the hug of a teenager I've been helping, the smiles of those I've grown closer to. In this moment with Phillips, I now understand. All it took was a simple question to bring it to the light. Just because Pylus is gone doesn't mean my love has to go with him. I can let that love go somewhere else.

I think back to Pylus' dying words. He knew I needed to let him go to have the life I wanted. I glance at the letter from Mr. Yen and realize he told me the same thing. Maybe those letters had helped after all. I remember the peaceful smile on Pylus' face when he died. He was ready to move on. He accepted it. I guess it's time for me to do the same.

"Yeah," I say, my smile getting bigger, "I think I have. At least I've started to."

I glance at Phillips. He gives me a look that I can't identify. Some kind of knowing hides just behind his eye, like he has had a secret that he's been waiting for me to figure out on my own.

"So, what's the plan now?" He asks, the corner of his mouth turned up slightly.

I look at him and see something, "I don't know," I say, "Just see what life brings."

His smirk turns into a wide smile, "Sounds fun."